JENNIFER, the star. She could possess any man she wanted—except the one who set the fires raging in her heart.

☆

BRETT, her producer. She was a cinematic genius who made millions at the box office—and gambled with her life for an ex-con lover.

☆

SLOANE, her rescuer. A Hollywood "kept man," he would become a true friend to Jennifer. But would he ever know true love?

☆

LIZ, her agent. She was so successful, she had no time for love—until she met a superstud only money could buy.

☆

MATTHEW, Jennifer's first love. The doctor from her home town, he had broken her heart long ago. But still she wanted him—now and forever.

From the winner of
Affaire de Coeur's Silver Pen Award

LISA GREGORY

D0829125

"Fascinating ... Ms. Gregory proves that she is a writer of enormous talents and that any historical era has a memorable love story for her to tell."
                                    —*Rave Reviews* on *Before the Dawn*

Also by Lisa Gregory

Before the Dawn

Published by
WARNER BOOKS

ATTENTION: SCHOOLS AND CORPORATIONS

WARNER books are available at quantity discounts with bulk purchase for educational, business, or sales promotional use. For information, please write to: SPECIAL SALES DEPARTMENT, WARNER BOOKS, 666 FIFTH AVENUE, NEW YORK, N.Y. 10103.

ARE THERE WARNER BOOKS
YOU WANT BUT CANNOT FIND IN YOUR LOCAL STORES?

You can get any WARNER BOOKS title in print. Simply send title and retail price, plus 50c per order and 50c per copy to cover mailing and handling costs for each book desired. New York State and California residents add applicable sales tax. Enclose check or money order only, no cash please, to: WARNER BOOKS, P.O. BOX 690, NEW YORK, N.Y. 10019.

Solitaire

Lisa Gregory

WARNER BOOKS

A Warner Communications Company

WARNER BOOKS EDITION

Copyright © 1988 by Lisa Gregory
All rights reserved.

Warner Books, Inc.
666 Fifth Avenue
New York, N.Y. 10103

 A Warner Communications Company

Printed in the United States of America

First Printing: March, 1988

10 9 8 7 6 5 4 3 2 1

* *Prologue* *

The 747 nosed forward onto the runway. The plane was white, and the distinctive, stylized purple T of Trans Continental Airlines swooped up the side of its tail. Its body glistened with rain. A thundershower had just blown over, and another one was rolling up from the west. It was drizzling steadily, and the damp air, caged by the low-hanging clouds, stank of jet fuel.

As the airplane started down the runway a few people watched from the Trans Con terminal, mostly friends or relatives of the passengers and a few bored people waiting for their own flights. Not a big crowd.

The plane took off, tilting up into the air. Then, suddenly, the nose slammed back down as though hit by a giant fist. The airplane crashed nose-first into the ground and exploded into fire.

* * *

Three houses sat on a quiet cul-de-sac in Benedict Canyon, none of them visible from the road. The house in the middle was protected by a high, white brick wall and an electronic metal gate. The gate opened at the touch of a button, and a silver Rolls Royce eased onto the street. The gates closed behind the car as the Rolls continued down the street. The driver was of medium height, not a big man, but with a powerful chest and arms, and he was dark in a way that suggested a strain of Indian or Hispanic blood, or perhaps both. His attire went beyond casual: blue jeans that were almost white from washing and to the point of fraying at the knees, a blue workshirt in much the same condition hanging loose outside his jeans and scuffed leather boots. He didn't look like the owner of the car. He looked even less like a chauffeur.

But then the woman seated in the backseat of the car, two briefcases and a multitude of papers spread out around her, didn't much look like what she was either— one of the most successful producers in Hollywood. In a city in which appearance was the most important commodity, Brett Cameron paid little attention to hers. The clothes she wore were expensive, but they were bought in fast, impatient dashes through the stores on Rodeo Drive, and she wore them haphazardly, with more thought of comfort than style. Today she had on a pale blue T-shirt, a long, loose linen jacket, black Oscar de la Renta trousers, and blue Reeboks.

She wore no makeup except lipstick. There were times when she put on eyeshadow and mascara, but usually she forgot. Her hair was a warm reddish brown, shoulder-length and wildly curling, pushed back and fastened on either side with lacquered combs. Her face wasn't beautiful— narrow reddish brows, a wide mouth, an ordinary nose, gray eyes—but there was something intriguing in it, something almost naive yet also alive with intelligence and curiosity. At thirty-five she was the most powerful woman in Hollywood, with a string of colossal box office hits behind her.

Brett was engrossed with the papers in her lap. For years the hours she spent traveling from her home to her office in Burbank had provided her with her best work time. There were no phones ringing, no visitors waiting to see her, no hassles, just her work and the smooth running of the car and quiet presence of Joe Darcy in the front seat.

Darcy never spoke while he drove her to work. He watched the road and thought his own thoughts. The radio was on. He liked it for the soothing background noise. Brett never heard it. Almost nothing could break her concentration.

The song on the radio ended and a newscaster's voice came on, deep and serious. "This special bulletin just in: Airport officials have confirmed a crash at LAX Airport this morning involving Trans Continental Flight 145 to New York. Eyewitnesses report that shortly after take off the aircraft plunged to the ground and burst into flames. It is not known how many people were on board or whether there are any survivors. Trans Continental officials were unavailable for comment."

The reporter began to repeat his story. Joe glanced back at Brett. The story had gotten her attention. She was staring into the front seat. "Oh my God. How awful!"

There was a blankness to her eyes, and Joe knew that she was seeing the crash, constructing it in her mind, absorbing it as she absorbed everything, emotions, events, thoughts.

"Can you imagine?" she asked softly. "The people who'd just put their friends on the plane must have been standing there watching it. They would have seen it crash into the ground, and they'd know . . ." The title she carried was producer, but Brett was a creator. Imaginative, empathetic, creative, she never failed to respond to human drama. Joe was sure that now she was imagining herself watching the plane take off and crash, feeling the stunned horror, envisioning the terror inside the plane. And he knew that someday, somehow, that scene and those feelings *would show up in her work. It wasn't coldness; rather, just the opposite. Joe thought she felt too much, too readily. Her imagination allowed her to see what other people saw, feel what others felt, overloading her with life. And so she carried that overload to the screen, releasing it for others to witness it.*

The papers lay unheeded on her lap for the rest of the trip, and Brett stared out the window, seeing flames and tragedy.

Liz Chandler's office lay in a sparkling glass tower on Century Boulevard. It was on the top floor, and Liz's inner office had the corner, two walls of tinted glass looking out on the city. She liked the image of the location, but the truth was that she rarely looked at the view. She was too busy working. Her receptionist-secretary was the one who enjoyed the luxurious surroundings.

The peach carpet was sinfully thick underfoot, the furniture glossy and expensive. The walls were decorated with photographs of Liz's clients. There were shots of Liz with actors, directors and producers; publicity stills of the famous actors and actresses she represented; posters from their movies. Two television stars were up there, and a comedian-turned-actor with two hit movies in a row, a former football player who had made it bigger in the broadcasting booth than he had on the field, and the highest paid and most-hated villainess on daytime soaps. Dominating everything, Liz's first and biggest find, her favorite, her superstar: Jennifer Taylor.

There were advertising posters from Jennifer's movies, publicity photos from Drifter, candid shots, and blowups of magazine advertisements. In the center, above the couch, hung the color poster of her that had outsold all other posters across the country. It was a classic shot—wind whipping the luxuriant blond mane of hair and molding the *dress to her well-formed body, the vivid blue eyes leaping out at you, the delicate face that managed to be somehow shy and sexy all at once. And across the bottom, one simple word:* JENNIFER.

The outer office was empty, the receptionist away on her coffee break. The door to Liz's private office stood open, and she sat hunched over her desk, talking on the phone, a cigarette in her hand. She was thirty-eight and attractive. She wasn't a ravishing beauty, but she made the most of what she had. Her hair was short and smooth, a shiny blond cap, her face well made up, her clothes a crisp Calvin Klein suit. She was the picture of success—polished, expensive, powerful. Part of the image was natural, part she had worked very hard to present.

"I can't imagine how she'd have the time," Liz said, drawing on her cigarette, then exhaling, watching the smoke drift across her desk. "Ms. Taylor's schedule is so full. Perhaps you'd be interested in someone else." A faint smile touched her lips at the vehement protest on the other end. "I realize that, Mr. Marks. There's no one like Jennifer. But she is so booked up . . . Now would I do that to you?" The faint smile came and went again.

Liz cradled the phone against her ear and leaned back in the chair, listening to the man rattle on. Through her open door, she saw the receptionist, Carol, come in and toss her handbag on her desk. The girl walked straight across the outer room to Liz's door, a touch of excitement on her face. Liz raised her eyebrows and put her palm over the mouthpiece.

"There's been a plane crash at the airport," Carol said in a stage whisper and pointed questioningly toward the television set in the wall cabinet in Liz's office, next to the small bar.

"LAX?" Liz whispered back, motioning to her to turn it on.

"Yeah." Carol switched on the television.

Liz listened to Dave Marks with half her attention and turned the rest of it to the TV. A reporter stood at the *airport, talking about the crash. In the distance behind him was the awful hulk of the burned plane, black and broken.*

". . . of the manifest yet, so we're not sure of the exact number of people on board the plane, though early estimates have placed it at eight crew members and approximately 260 passengers. The exact cause of the crash of Trans Continental Flight 145 to New York is not known. There were several thunderstorms—"

"Trans Con!" Liz exclaimed, and the telephone receiver slid unnoticed from her hand. She stood up, her face white.

"What's the matter?" Carol turned to her, frightened by Liz's manner.

"Jennifer was flying to New York this morning. On Trans Con. Jesus! Jennifer Taylor's on that plane!"

* PART I *

* Chapter 1 *

The town of Sweet River lay on the edge of the Ozark Mountains, a wooded, hilly region, beautiful but poor. Poor town, poor region, poor state. But it had its social strata, like any other place, with one or two truly wealthy families at the top and the rest layered down from there. On the bottom rung of the social ladder were the Taylors.

The Taylors lived five miles out of town in a shack on Haskell's Ridge. Angie Taylor, a good, hard-working woman whom everyone had pitied, had died a couple of years back. Last summer Corey, the son, had been drafted. So now it was just old Mack Taylor out there with his girl, Jennifer.

Mack staggered along the dirt road that led to his house, stumbling frequently. It was bitterly cold, the middle of winter. Only a fool would be out at three in the morning—a fool or a drunk. Mack's blood was warm with alcohol, and he didn't notice that his toes were numb inside his thin shoes or that his cheeks stung. He was talking to himself, happily lost in a monologue of self-pity, regretting his dead wife and his unloving children, reviewing his pitiful lot in life and his own helplessness to change it.

He fell now and then and sometimes took a while to rise. Mack tended to forget that he should be walking and not sitting on the cold, hard earth. But then an idea or an image would pierce the beery fog in his brain and he would lurch to his feet and start again. From years of habit he managed to stick to the right path.

The shack was set amongst the trees, a two-room frame house set on concrete blocks, with more concrete blocks for steps. The roof was rusted corrugated tin, and it sagged across the porch where the supporting post had fallen away. The house had lost all its paint long ago. It wasn't much to see, day or night, though in the spring and summer flowering bushes and trees softened its harsh poverty—delicate white dogwood and vivid purplish red-buds, masses of white bridal wreath and bright yellow forsythia. Angie had planted jonquils and roses in beds across the front of the house, but those had died long ago.

Mack gave a sniff at the thought of Angie's flowers and sat down heavily on the bottom step. He was suddenly very tired, and the cold was creeping into him. He thought about sitting on the steps for a while, and his eyelids drifted closed. But he wasn't yet cold enough for that; he could still feel the chill, more and more each second. So he staggered to his feet and tried to climb the steps.

He didn't make it and crashed backwards. "Jenny!"

The bellow penetrated Jennifer's sleep, but she'd heard it so often in her life that it didn't rouse her. Mack crashed a shoe into the screen door, and that brought her bolt upright.

She had been dreaming about her father screaming at her and Corey and the two of them running for the back door, scurrying to safety while their mother blocked the old man's way. The dream was permeated with the old guilt at her cowardice. She shouldn't have left her mother to face her father alone, yet rarely could she come up with the courage to stay if she had the chance to run. Thank

God for Corey, who'd gotten big enough and tough enough to stop Mack. (He'd gotten tough before he got big; she would always remember him at age ten, facing off their father with nothing but a broom in his hands while Mack charged at them with his big, meaty fists.) And thank God that Mack tried to beat them only when he was drunk and therefore was much easier to evade.

"Jennifer Anne Taylor! Goddamn it, girl! Get out here and help me!"

Jennifer pulled the rough blankets and thin feather-filled top mattress higher around her shoulders, thinking bitterly that she ought to let him freeze. Then she sighed and flipped back the covers to hop out of bed. She wore a flannel nightgown and thick socks, but the cold was still shocking. The night air slipped in around the doors and windows and swept up between the wooden planks of the floor. No amount of taping newspapers across the windows or stuffing them between the cracks would keep it out.

She put on her car coat and wrapped it tightly around her as she ran to the front door. She pulled open the door, shivering against the blast of night air, and saw her father lying like a bug on its back beyond the steps. "Damn!" She'd thought he was on the porch, not clear out in the yard. She considered running back for her shoes, but decided the extra time in the cold wasn't worth it. She darted out the door and down the steps.

"What the hell took you so long?"

"I was asleep! It's the middle of the night." Jennifer grabbed Mack's arm and yanked. He floundered in the dirt, trying to find his footing.

She managed to get him upright. He looked sideways at her in the sly, nasty way she hated, and she hated him anew. "More likely some boy in your bed. Had to slip him out the back door 'fore you could let your daddy in."

Jennifer made a grimace of disgust. "You're drunk and filthy-minded, as usual. Come on, let's get you into the house."

"Don't think I don't know," he continued as she pushed

him up the stairs. He was twice her size, but she'd had a lot of practice. "I know about them boys that come round here, sniffing at your skirts. You're like a goddamn bitch in heat, that's what."

Jennifer kept her mouth clamped firmly shut. It never did any good to argue with him. Drunks knew everything. It only made her white with rage to get into an argument with him. Besides, he might swing at her; and, if he wasn't too far gone, he might connect. He hadn't hit her since Corey turned fourteen and knocked him cold for taking a belt to her, but Corey was gone now, with only the threat of his future wrath to keep the old man contained. She could feel that threat growing weaker daily; no point in testing it. Once he hit her, it would just get easier.

She aimed him for the sofa and let go. He crashed onto the couch, and Jennifer turned back to close the door. "Goddamn whore! Just like your mother."

Jennifer's hands closed into fists, and the blood rushed into her head. She wanted to scream, to tell him exactly what she thought of him. She hated herself for responding so easily, so predictably to his jabs, and she hated him for doing it to her. He knew, with his low cunning, that anything bad he said about their mother would always bring her and Corey to the boiling point. He wanted a fight; it was one of those drunks. Not a slobbering, sentimental drunk or a giggling, silly one. It was a mean, fighting drunk.

But this time he wouldn't get a rise out of her to give him an excuse to vent his bad feelings. She was going straight to bed and leaving him on the sofa. Usually he slept on it pulled out and made into a bed, but tonight she wasn't about to waste the energy. She walked past him without a word, heading for the tiny bedroom that Corey had decreed hers four years earlier.

"Fifteen years old," Mack ranted on, squinting up at Jennifer to judge the effect of his words. "Fifteen years old, and already you got 'em lined up outside your bedroom window. Every man in town panting for you. You ought to make 'em pay for it; at least we could live in style.''

She reached the sanctuary of her bedroom and closed the door, pulling the straight chair over and jamming it under the doorknob—just in case he took it into his head to continue his vilification up close. Hot tears rolled from her eyes, and she brushed them away angrily as she crawled into bed.

After years of listening to him, you'd think it wouldn't hurt so much anymore. He'd cursed like that at her mother and then at Jennifer when she started getting a woman's body. She ought to be immune to what he said by now, but Mack's words always cut her. To think that her own father thought that of her!

Or maybe what made it so hurtful was that he was only expressing what everyone else in town thought about her. Jennifer Taylor, poor white trash. Easy.

The tears gushed out and she shuddered, trying to stifle her sobs. She hadn't done anything to deserve the reputation. She was only fifteen, a sophomore in high school, and in truth she'd hardly even dated. But then, with girls like her, you didn't have to date them to get into bed with them, did you? She was considered trash, just because of her last name—and because of the way she looked.

Jennifer was beautiful. It was as if Nature, having given her the worst of life in so many other ways, had decided to shower her with physical blessings. Her hair was thick and golden blond, hanging in a straight, shiny fall down her back. Her eyes were large and a vivid blue, her face delicately heart-shaped, her skin soft, cheeks touched with natural color.

But she had something more than beauty—an unaffected sensuality that was beginning to flower into ripeness. It was there in the full shape of her mouth and the inviting texture of her skin and, most of all, in her prematurely voluptuous body. She had come into puberty early, and at fifteen she had the body of a woman. Her breasts were full and youthfully firm, her body curving smoothly downward

into a small waist and inviting hips. Her buttocks were taut
and rounded; her legs, though not long, were shapely. Just
to look at her made a man think of hot nights and tangled
sheets, the spicy scent of sex.

All of this was an accident of fate. Genes. Nothing to do
with her. Jennifer had never tried to look sexy—just the
opposite. She wore no makeup except the pale pink lipstick the other girls wore. Her dresses were the same
length as everyone else's—brushing the floor when they
knelt in home ec. class for a dress code check. She did
little to call attention to herself. Jennifer was naturally shy
and she didn't flirt. She hardly spoke to the other students.
She had dated only a couple of times. Boys her own age
were often scared by her astonishing good looks, and the
older men who had tried to pick her up at work hadn't
asked for dates. They had wanted only to drive down by
the river with her, and she knew what that meant. She
never went. She was grateful for the loose style of clothing
that was popular now, for it helped conceal the rich curves
of her body.

It seemed horribly unfair to her that people thought what
they did about her. She didn't doubt that the guys she'd
turned down had pretended she had put out for them. They
would have been embarrassed not to, because, after all,
"everybody knew" she would do it. It was obvious. Look
at her. And she was a Taylor.

Jennifer clenched her jaws tighter, fighting the hot,
angry tears. Everything was so awful. She hated the
people who talked about her, the men who looked at her
with sly, sideways glances. She hated her appearance. She
hated Mack. She hated her life and Sweet River and
everything about it.

But the hate was contained. Her emotions were always
contained—grief, rage, happiness. She clamped them down,
held them in check. Jennifer had learned long ago not to
let feelings show. Expressing them only got you a blow
from Mack or worse. He hated squalling. Besides, things
didn't hurt so much if you ignored them. You just shoved

them down and locked them away in some deep dark place inside.

She rarely cried. Instead she thought of stories. Movies she'd seen in the dark little theater downtown that was her refuge. Shows on the television set in the cafe. In her mind she became the characters, taking all the parts—weeping, screaming, laughing, daring. She saw herself saying the lines, knew how she would move and look. And everyone would applaud. Oh, how they would love her movies! She would go to Hollywood and she'd be famous. She'd be marvelous. Everyone would love her, and everyone in Sweet River would say, "Can you imagine? Jennifer Taylor. I always knew she was special."

And so, dreaming, she drifted to sleep again.

The shrill ringing of the alarm clock jerked Jennifer from her sleep. She slammed it off and lay for a moment longer, snuggled in the warmth of the blankets. She drifted, neither awake nor asleep, hazily dreaming. She smelled the delicious smoky odor of bacon frying and the sweet smell of pancakes, and a smile touched her lips. Mama was cooking her favorite . . .

Jennifer's eyes snapped open. There was no sizzle of fat meat, no clatter of pans. The smells were gone. She'd been dreaming. Mama had been dead for almost four years. She was no longer there, getting the house warm and breakfast on the stove before everyone else was up. But the dream had been so real! She'd almost heard Mama's voice calling her to get up. For a moment the aching emptiness was fresh in her chest.

She still missed Mama; Angie had been her friend and companion all her life. Jennifer had made few friends, even in school. She was shy, and Taylors weren't the kind of folks other people rushed to befriend. Living out of town as she did, Jenny never saw another child except Corey after school. But her mother had been there, had talked and laughed with her, listened to descriptions of school and the kids, believed in all Jennifer's dreams with her. Life had been so hard since Angie's death; and now, with Corey gone too, sometimes the cold loneliness threatened to overwhelm Jennifer.

She pushed back the memories and jumped out of bed, slipping into her loafers without touching the icy floor. The shoes were so cold they crackled. Her heavy car coat lay at the foot of the bed, and she wrapped it around her as she unhooked the chair from the door and scuttled into the living room to the low gas heater. She squatted down beside the heater and struck a match, holding it to the pilot light while she turned up the gas. It lit with a whoomp, and she adjusted the flame, crouching by the heater, absorbing its warmth. When one side grew hot, she turned to warm the other side, and finally she stood, steeling herself to run back to her cold room to dress.

When she was a child, she had dressed in the living room in front of the old wood-burning stove they'd had then. All of them had—holding their clothes beside the fire to warm, then ripping off their pajamas and jumping into the warmed clothes. But not since Mama died. Corey had given Jennifer the bedroom, facing down the old man until he agreed, and she dressed there.

She glanced contemptuously at Mack sprawled half-on, half-off the couch, snoring. Not that *he* would be likely to wake up. Still, she didn't want to dress in the same room with him. The idea gave her the willies.

Jennifer opened her coat, letting the heat warm her, then wrapped the coat around her again and darted for the bedroom. Her clothes were laid out on the chair, ready to be put on in a rush. She ripped off her nightgown, shivering, and pulled on her clothes—plain cotton underwear, knee-high socks, and a demure white blouse and blue plaid jumper. Her coat went back on top of it. She brushed her hair and teeth, put on a quick swipe of lipstick and grabbed her schoolbooks. She was ready to go. Breakfast at the cafe was part of her salary, and she always took advantage of it.

The sun was just coming up, and the frost on the grass sparkled like broken glass. It crunched softly underfoot. Even the dirt road seemed brittle this morning. Jennifer pulled up the wide knitted collar of her coat so that it covered her ears and chin. She loved the coat. Corey had given it to her two years ago, and it still fit well enough to wear, even if it was a little tight around the bust. It was the first brand-new coat she had ever owned. Only Corey could have guessed how much it would mean to her. He, too, had known the humiliation of entering school in a coat that some older kid would recognize as a hand-me-down that he had worn the year before.

Jennifer took the road at a much faster clip than her father had last night. The exercise warmed her; now only her bare knees stung with cold. She reached the meadow on the old Jackson place. No one lived there, though there was a broken-down barn beside the meadow. Mrs. White, in town, had inherited it, and her husband ran a few cattle on it. The cows were huddled beneath a tree close to the fence, waiting for Benny White to drop off their feed.

Jennifer paused for a moment. She loved this spot. In the spring Queen Anne's lace grew along the fence, and the grass in the meadow was long and vibrant green, dotted with wild daisies. Even in the winter it was beautiful, slipping gently away from the road, open at the end to a wide view of the rolling hills. Jennifer gazed at it for a moment, her breath pooling in mist before her face while a sense of peace settled into her bones. The meadow never failed to soothe her. It was the only thing in Nature she had ever known that called to her.

She turned away and hurried down the road to the bottom of the hill, where the dirt road ended at the asphalt highway. Mary Jim would be along soon to pick her up, and Jennifer always made sure that she was there early. She would be mortified for Mary Jim to have to wait for her when she was nice enough to pick Jennifer up on her way to work.

Jennifer was there five minutes before Mary Jim's old red Ford Falcon came into sight, and the cold seeped through her clothes. She hurried gratefully into the warm car. The Falcon always seemed to be just one step away from breaking down, but nobody could fault its heater.

"Hi, how you doing?" Mary Jim greeted her cheerfully. "Colder 'n a witch's tit out there."

Jennifer smiled. "Yeah. It's freezing."

Mary Jim put the car in gear and started forward. The radio was playing loudly, a country and western station, but Mary Jim chattered over it all the way into town. There was nobody, Jennifer thought, who could talk like Mary Jim. She was as thin as a knife blade, always moving, as though stillness was foreign to her. Mary Jim's hair was the dead black color peculiar to dyed hair, and she wore it shoulder length, with the top teased up high and sprayed into stiffness. Even this early in the morning she was fully made up, blue eyeshadow, rouge, and all. Her fingernails were long and bright pink; Mary Jim was very proud of her nails. She worked the first shift at the cafe with Jennifer's help during breakfast. The owner's wife, Jan, came in during lunch, and Mary Jim quit at two. After school every afternoon Jennifer returned to the cafe, and Jan left. Supper never drew the crowd that breakfast and lunch did, and one waitress was able to handle all the customers. Business was so slack, in fact, that Jennifer usually had enough free time to get her homework done, too.

Jennifer enjoyed her work. It wasn't hard compared to what she and her mother had done at home, and she had fun watching the people. She liked Mary Jim; the older woman had a blunt, sarcastic way of talking that lit a spark in Jennifer. She would have loved to have been able to banter with people the way Mary Jim did. In the afternoons, when Mary Jim wasn't there, Jennifer liked the peace and quiet. Frank kept a TV at the cafe, and as long as nobody needed service, Jennifer could watch it as much as she wanted. Of course, when the place closed at 8:30 every evening she had to walk all the way home, and the dark could be a little scary sometimes. But that was a minor problem. Desperate as the Taylors always were for money, she would have been grateful for any job, let alone the one she had.

The Byers' cafe was on the town square in Sweet River across from the tan stone courthouse. Mary Jim parked a block down, where the spaces weren't metered as they were in front of the restaurant, and they walked. The square was deserted. Mary Jim's was the only car on the street, and there wasn't a sign of a person or any of the usual town sounds; they could have been out in the country.

Mary Jim unlocked the door of the cafe and they went inside, Jennifer going to the bathroom in back to change into her uniform and Mary Jim stopping in the kitchen to chat with Preston, the cook. Preston always arrived early to make the biscuits and mix the pancakes, and he had had the heater on long enough to take the chill out of the air.

Jennifer changed into the clean white dress and red-checked apron that was her uniform and returned to the front room to gulp down her breakfast and help Mary Jim set the tables. They laid out silverware, paper napkins and coffee cups and filled the salt, pepper, sugar, and ketchup containers. At 6:30 Mary Jim unlocked the door and turned the "Closed" sign to "Open."

Two minutes later their first customer came in, a farmer dressed in jeans and a denim jacket, a felt cowboy hat on his white head.

"Hello, Mr. Wilson." Jennifer gave him a shy smile. She was careful about how she acted and what she said to customers because she was afraid of being thought bold and brassy.

Mary Jim, on the other hand, flirted with impunity. She flashed a grin at the older man and sauntered over, a hand cocked on her hip. "Why, say, Charley, what you up to this morning?"

He was up to the same thing he was up to every morning: a hot breakfast and a chat before he returned to his lonely farm work. His children were grown and his wife had died two years earlier. Jennifer suspected he came for the company as much as or more than the food. He was always their first customer.

After that people trickled in for the next hour, building up to the heaviest traffic from 7:30 to 8:00. These were the early risers, farmers and store people who opened early. Later those whose stores opened at 9:00 or 10:00, office workers, and the courthouse crowd would come in. They were nearly all men—usually Sue Stearns, who worked over at the department store, was the only woman who came in for breakfast.

Soon most of the tables were occupied, with one notable exception—the big round booth by the front window. It might as well have had a "Reserved" sign on it. Everyone knew that that was where Sam Ferris and his friends sat.

A little after 7:30 Sam Ferris strolled in. As he walked to his table, he nodded to several people, raising a hand or issuing a contained smile at a few. Everyone who caught his eye nodded back, and those close enough spoke. "Mr. Ferris." "Sam." "How you doing?"

Samuel T. Ferris owned Sweet River, Arkansas. Literally. Half the buildings around the square belonged to him; he leased to the local drugstore, the department store, the bank, the movie theater, and this very cafe. He owned and rented several houses, the largest farm in the county (which he leased to two chicken farmers and a cattle grower), and half the bank, which he shared with his cousin, Steven Richards. Several other businesses, including the feed store and the drive-in restaurant, sat on properties he had sold in the past at a healthy profit. He was an attorney, but he did little legal work, leaving the firm business to his partner and concentrating instead on his real estate holdings. He had obtained a law degree because of family tradition—the Ferris men had been lawyers for three generations back—but his heart lay in making money and building power.

He had been coming to the cafe for breakfast for years; it was a well-known fact that Johnette Ferris was no cook—and thank heavens they had a servant who cooked up the evening meal or Byers' Cafe would have seen even more of Ferris' business. In fact, they had been seeing more of it for the past few months. Sam had moved out of the house, and Johnette had filed for divorce.

There were rumors. Even Jennifer had heard them. Folks said there was another woman involved. Not that that was anything new with Sam Ferris, but this time it wasn't hushed-up. This time he wanted to marry her. People said she was the receptionist in the bank, but nobody knew for sure. He was never seen with any woman, not while the divorce was still up in the air.

Ferris sat down in the center of the booth and snapped open the plastic-backed menu to study as though he hadn't read it a thousand times before. Mary Jim hustled over to take his order. She had made it clear to Jennifer when Jennifer started work that the corner table in the morning was Mary Jim's, always and without question. Jennifer was happy to let her have it. Ferris and the men who sat with him were too powerful for her; they made her nervous. She was sure she would spill water on one of them or commit some other social sin. Worse, Ferris had a way of looking at women, as if sizing them up for his bed. Not that he was crude or anything, but he noticed. He approved. Everybody said he was a real ladies' man. But there was a coldness to his interest that made it worse than the hot glances or catcalls of younger, bolder acting men. Jennifer couldn't imagine love entering into his sexual transactions, or even a desire that was overwhelming in its heat. Sam Ferris was never anything but controlled.

Mary Jim didn't see it that way. She loved to flirt with him. He was a handsome man in his late forties, his dark brown hair brushed with silver at the temples. His body was trim and firm for his age; he'd been an athlete in his youth. The aura of power around him only heightened his sexual appeal.

While Mary Jim took Sam's order, Bill Huffner, another of the usual group, walked in. He owned the Ford dealership in town and he was everybody's friend. He smiled broadly at all the other customers and stopped to shake a few hands or slap somebody on the back several times before he took his seat. He was worse than a politician. Even Judge Holcomb, who came in a few minutes later, didn't glad-hand as much as Bill Huffner. Of course, the judge wasn't up for reelection for another year.

Those three were the regulars at the table, day in, day out. Sometimes Dr. Oliver joined them or Parke Bates, Ferris' law partner, and every once in a while Ed Daniels, who owned the department store, dropped in. But whoever sat there always possessed the same essential ingredient, the one key to the club: they were the men who were important in town. They were the wealthy, the educated, the influential. There was no membership list, no invitation to join; it was simply a matter of like gravitating to like. If you didn't belong with them, you'd never think of going to their table. The boundaries were loose; there was nothing laid out. People just *knew*.

This morning the three regulars were joined by Steven Richards, the bank president, and Johnny Schubert, the school superintendent. Later, after their food had arrived, Sheriff Wainwright showed up, and they all greeted him jovially.

"Well, hey, Boy," the judge said. "Pull up a chair and sit."

"Why, thank you, Judge. I've already eaten, but I'll have a cup of coffee with you."

Alvin T. Wainwright, known to his peers as Boy, wouldn't have been at the table two years earlier. But now the heavyset, shrewd-eyed man was sheriff, and that station qualified him for the table.

Wainwright glanced around the room. He knew everybody there, had known them all his life. He liked the feeling of being their protector. He was the man Edna Jackson called when Len was three hours late getting home; he found Len's pickup off the road in a ditch and Len bleeding from a scalp wound. He was the man who caught the three thirteen-year-olds trying to pry open a window at the drive-in during the middle of the night—one of them the Baptist preacher's son!—and took them down to the jail to give them a good scare while he called their parents to pick them up. And he was the man out setting up roadblocks with the highway patrol when the search was on for that bank robber from Fayetteville the year before.

He liked that. He had a place and an importance. Him, an old White Holler boy, who hadn't even known what his first name was until he was fifteen.

His eyes fell on Mack Taylor's daughter across the room. She was bending over to transfer dirty dishes from a table onto a large tray. Pretty thing. Nice legs and a tight little butt. Too ripe-looking for a girl her age, but she seemed like a good kid. Corey was all right, too. They got it from their mama's side, he guessed, because their father was sure a heller. Wainwright knew Mack well. He'd picked him up four or five times for being drunk and disorderly in town, and once or twice he'd stopped to give the old man a ride home when he found him staggering across the highway or sitting, dazed, in a ditch.

"Jailbait," Bill Huffner said, breaking the sheriff's thoughts.

Wainwright glanced at him. "What? Oh, the Taylor girl?"

Huffner grinned. "Sure. What else were you looking at?"

"What else does any man in this town look at?" Sam Ferris put in with a smile, and every man at the table turned his head in her direction. "But too young, gentlemen. *Toooo* young."

Boy Wainwright didn't doubt that Ferris had looked at

her plenty. Ferris had an eye for women, though he'd always been careful that there wasn't any scandal.

"One thing you can say about the Taylors," Wainwright commented, "they're a good-looking bunch."

The sheriff had a view out the front window from where he sat, so it was he who saw Ferris' son drive up and park a few minutes later. He smiled. He couldn't help but like Matt Ferris, even if the boy had been showered with blessings. He was a good kid, Boy's highest encomium. He had his father's brains and athletic abilities. He'd led the football team to the state championship in their division, and his grades were excellent. Nice looking, though his looks came more from Johnette than Sam, giving him a wide open face without the chiseled perfection of Sam's features. But more than those God-given attributes, Matt was kind. He liked people. He wasn't a troublemaker. The worst Wainwright had ever seen him do was break the speed limit—and the Lord knew, with that high-powered Mustang of his, it was a temptation no boy could resist.

"Your boy's here, Sam."

"Matthew?" Ferris twisted to look out the window. "Wonder what he's doing." He glanced at his watch. "School starts in ten minutes."

Matthew opened the door of the cafe and stepped in. His cheeks and ears were pink from the cold. His hands were stuck inside the pockets of his football jacket. He paused for a moment, and Sam quirked a finger at him. He came forward.

"Matt! How you doing?"

"Heard you signed with Alabama."

The older men greeted him with fondness, and he returned their greetings politely before he addressed his father. "I forgot to call you. I have to buy the tickets for the Football Banquet today."

Sam smiled and dug into his hip pocket for his wallet. He wasn't an expressive man, but anyone could see the pride in his eyes. Whatever anyone could fault Sam Ferris for, he loved that boy. Johnette had had a hard time with pregnancy, miscarrying twice, and after Matthew they hadn't had any more. Sam had doted on him as much as it was possible for a man like Sam to dote. He had worked with Matt on his athletic skills from the time he was five years old; he had reviewed his grades with pride. As far as Wainwright knew, Sam hadn't missed a game Matt played from the time he started in junior high. And now here Matt was, the perfect son, following in his old man's footsteps at Alabama. Sam had plans for the boy: The University of Alabama, then law school, then back home to Sweet River. He was the heir to the throne. Wainwright wondered if Matthew enjoyed that position as much as Sam enjoyed having him there.

"Can't miss that," Sam told his son with a smile, handing him a ten-dollar bill. "Is that enough?"

"Sure. Plenty. The tickets are only two-fifty apiece." Matthew hesitated. Sam waggled the bill impatiently, and Matthew took it.

"Guess you'll be getting a few awards at that banquet," Judge Holcomb put in. The judge was a master at stating the obvious.

Matthew grinned a little bashfully. "Probably."

"Try every damn one of them, Judge," Sam corrected. "Isn't that right, Son?"

"Well, not every one."

"No, they always give one or two for trying." It was clear what Sam Ferris thought of mere effort.

"Team spirit. You know." Matthew shrugged. He looked embarrassed. "Well, I gotta run, Dad. Thanks."

"Sure."

The boy nodded to the other men, saying his polite good-byes with the slight unease of youth. He turned and walked away, arriving at the door just as Jennifer Taylor was reaching to open it. He grabbed the handle and opened it for her, stepping back to let her pass before him.

Jennifer hadn't seen Matthew come in. She had been in the back changing into her school dress. But as soon as she stepped into the dining room, books tucked under her arm, she saw him. She knew Matt. Everyone knew everyone in a school the size of Sweet River's. But Matthew Ferris was the most noticeable. He was rich and handsome and the quarterback of the football team. He was perfect. He wasn't even arrogant. That he was just a touch uncomfortable with his ideal status made him human and appealing.

Last year when Jennifer moved up from eighth grade into the red brick high school on the hill, she had developed a crush on Matthew. So had half the girls in school. When she was a freshman her locker had been near the door of Matt's junior English class, and she had loitered outside her locker everyday before second period. She hadn't dared hope he would notice her; Jennifer wasn't foolish enough to believe that a boy like Matt Ferris would have any interest in a girl like her. He went steady with Shelly Daniels, this year's Homecoming Queen; and if he even knew who Jennifer was, she realized he probably thought of her only as a girl with a trashy reputation, the kind about whom one of his friends would make a low comment and then chuckle in that masculine, sexually aware way. She had heard that kind of laugh often as she walked down the hall.

No, she didn't expect Matthew's attention. All she wanted was to catch a glimpse of him and feel the familiar excitement gripping her stomach—to see how he looked and what he had on, to hear his voice—to fuel her dreams.

This year her locker was beside the home ec. room, and she never saw Matthew except at pep rallies or now or then in the halls. Without regular infusions the excitement in her had died out, but he was still the major hero of her daydreams.

To walk out and see him unexpectedly in the cafe made her heart skip into a double-time beat, and she felt suddenly warm and jittery. Trying to look at him without appearing to, Jennifer crossed the room. Matthew turned and came toward the door just as she did, and her stomach knotted. When he held the door open for her, she blushed and ducked her head. Her shyness embarrassed her even further. She forgot to thank him and didn't remember it until she was out the door and across the sidewalk, but it was too late then. What would he think of her? That she was mannerless, of course. A Taylor.

Anger at herself propelled her across the street, no longer so deserted, and she cut across the courthouse square, heading for the high school twelve blocks up Central. As she crossed the street on the other side of the square, out of the corner of her eye she saw Matt's dark green Mustang come around the courthouse and zip up to the stop sign. He stopped, the car idling with a low rumble, and opened the passenger door.

Leaning over to look out at her, he called, "Hey, you need a ride to school? It's awfully cold out."

Jennifer turned. Her insides were cold and quivering. Her feet wouldn't move. She could think of nothing to say. He was looking at her, waiting. He would think she was an idiot.

"Yes! Yes. Thank you." She walked over—God, what if she stumbled?—and slid into the low-slung vehicle. She closed the door and he took off, spitting gravel.

* *Chapter 2* *

Matthew drove a '67 fastback Mustang with a powerful engine. Jennifer had never ridden in a sports car before. It seemed too low to the ground, too small and enclosed. She was sitting inches from Matthew's right shoulder, with only the console between them. She cast a shy glance at him. His hair was thick and brown, with the slightest wave. His eyes were green, ringed with gold and darkened by thick lashes. She liked his face. She liked looking at him. He glanced over at her, and Jennifer looked quickly away.

The fact that she had averted her eyes amused Matthew. He hardly knew Jennifer Taylor, but he was aware of her reputation. He would have expected her to be boldly flirtatious, brazen. In fact, he almost hadn't stopped, not wanting to get into anything with her, however slight. But it was too cold, and he was too softhearted. Hoping that Shelly wouldn't hear of it, he had pulled over and offered her a ride.

Now, instead of the beckoning smile and the bold look, Jennifer was scrunched up against the door, avoiding his gaze. Could Jennifer Taylor be shy?

The thought intrigued him. Matthew reached over and turned down the volume on his tape deck, which was blasting out "Jumpin' Jack Flash." "You work at the cafe?" he asked.

Jennifer turned her head, surprised that he was actually talking to her. "Yes. In the mornings and after school." She dropped her eyes back down to the books on her lap. Looking at Matthew Ferris this close was too much for her.

"You like it?" he went on after Jennifer offered nothing further.

"Yes, very much. Mr. and Mrs. Byers are nice."

"Yeah." Again the silence stretched. Matthew glanced at her. He'd never noticed much about Jennifer before except her body. She had the kind of full breasts and tight ass that started a guy's blood pumping, and he hadn't bothered to go beyond that. But now he looked at her face, and he realized that she was beautiful. Her skin was baby soft, all pearl and pink. Her eyes were huge, blue, and dramatic in her delicate face.

Matthew turned his attention back to the road, feeling strangely stunned. He had known she was pretty. But how had he failed to notice the depth of her beauty? He sneaked another look at her, just to affirm it. She was lovely. Heat stirred in his abdomen. No wonder Randy always groaned when she walked by. Sweet Stuff, Randy called her. He wondered whether Randy had ever made it with her. They said half the guys in town had. Matthew looked at her again and found that hard to believe; there was something too shy and innocent about her face.

They turned into the high school parking lot and Matthew parked not far from the front door. As soon as he switched off the engine Jennifer hastened to open her door. It had been kind of him to give her a ride to school; she wasn't going to embarrass him by lingering and forcing him to walk into the school building at her side. "Thank you very much. I really appreciate the ride."

She was gone before he could reply. Matthew sat for a moment, watching her walk up the sidewalk to the front steps, her head down. Her legs moved like silk beneath the short dress. Again he felt that little prickle of heat.

But she was weird. She'd hopped out of the car so fast you'd think he had leprosy. It was hard to figure. Matthew knew he was popular, and the last thing he'd think of himself was that he was frightening. He watched Jennifer skirt a knot of boys on the front steps, sticking close to the opposite side. Maybe she was scared of all guys. Jennifer Taylor? That was crazy.

He picked up his books from the well behind his seat and left the car. Joe Bob Wilson and Randy Huffner were waiting for him on the front steps, hands stuck in their pockets, grinning. Matthew knew they had seen Jennifer Taylor get out of his car. The leering, taunting grin on Randy's face irritated him. He and Randy had been friends since childhood, but Randy could be a real pain in the ass, especially when it came to girls. It seemed sometimes like all Randy ever thought about was getting a girl, any girl, into the back seat of his car.

"Hey, Matthew," the two chorused in a singsong way.

"Saw you drive up with Sweet Stuff," Randy went on slyly. "Where'd you spend the night, Ferris?"

Matthew's hazel eyes turned hard. "Why don't you shut up, Randy? You don't know what you're talking about.

She was walking to school, and it was cold, and I gave her a ride. That's all."

"Okay, okay." Randy held up his hands placatingly. "Don't be so touchy. We were just teasing."

Matthew scowled. He could see the surprise in his two friends' eyes. The spurt of anger had startled even himself. Randy always teased him and everyone else, and it rarely got under Matthew's skin. "Sorry. I'm just in a bad mood." He'd been that way a lot the last few months. It was the trouble with his parents, he guessed. That colored everything. Shrugging the thought away, he climbed the steps with his friends.

Shelly was waiting for him at his locker, small, soft, and pretty—and so fiercely cold he could practically see the ice forming around her. Her brown eyes were as hard as rock. Matthew sighed inwardly and tried to ignore her mood.

"Hi." He opened his locker and began to pull out his books.

"Hi?" Shelly returned scathingly. "Is that all you have to say?"

She sounded like her mother. He'd heard Mrs. Daniels say exactly the same thing in exactly the same voice one Saturday when he'd brought Shelly back to her house later than her curfew.

He closed his locker carefully. He hated arguing. There was plenty of that at home. He and Shelly had been going steady for almost two years now, ever since they were sophomores. Everybody said they were a perfect match, and he guessed they were. Shelly was the prettiest girl in school, except Jennifer Taylor, and she wore the nicest clothes. She was a cheerleader and the Homecoming Queen. She was tempting; she could be fun. And if she was a little bitchy at times, it seemed like that was the way girls were supposed to be. But there were times when he'd nearly broken up with her because of her temper. He hated the arguments, and usually he either walked away or gave in, just to get out of the situation. It didn't look as if Shelly was going to let him gloss this one over.

"What would you like me to say?" He turned to her, his face hardening like hers.

"Jo Lynn saw you drive up. Jennifer Taylor came to school with you!"

"It was nothing. I saw her walking, and it's cold outside, so I gave her a ride."

"Nothing! Don't you realize how it looks? What everybody will say about me?"

He did, but it annoyed him. "Why should they say anything? You didn't do anything. Hell, *I* didn't do anything!"

"I thought you and I were going steady."

"That means I can't give someone a ride to school?" The anger that lately always seemed to be lurking in him below the surface was there again, ready, building. Matt knew Shelly wanted an apology. She wanted him to plead, just like she tried to make him beg when they necked in his car, teasing and refusing until he was ready to explode. She enjoyed the power over him. Well, God knew she was able to make him groan and swear and lie like mad then. But not today. Not about this.

"I'll be damned if I'll say I'm sorry for giving a girl a ride instead of making her walk all the way to school in the cold!" He turned and left Shelly standing at the locker, staring after him, open-mouthed.

The day didn't get much better. The guys continued to tease him about Jennifer, especially during basketball practice, and Shelly sulked. She pointedly did not sit with him and Keith and Randy at lunch, and between classes she avoided him. It irritated and embarrassed Matthew to have her fight with him publicly, and he disliked the feeling of anger bubbling in him all day. He was glad when school was over and he could escape to the gym, where he let out his feelings pounding a basketball down the court. He stayed thirty minutes after practice just to work off the excess adrenaline.

It was almost supper time when he left the school and drove home. He turned into the driveway of his house, a two-story red brick colonial that was the biggest house in Sweet River, and saw his father's car in the drive. His stomach tightened. Something was up. Dad hadn't been at the house since he moved out months ago.

Matthew hesitated, his hand hovering over the stick shift, about to put it into reverse. Then he sighed and cut off the engine. He might as well get it over with. If he didn't face it now, Sam would probably still be there when he got back.

Matthew walked into the house. His parents were waiting for him in the living room. Sam stood at the window, staring out, and Johnette sat on the edge of a chair, a short glass of amber liquid on the end table beside her. The knot in Matthew's stomach spread to his chest. This was serious. His mother had even put on makeup and a dress for the occasion.

Johnette Ferris picked up her drink and took a gulp. Matthew wondered how much she'd had today. Some days she was glassy-eyed by lunchtime; other days she held off until the cocktail hour. Both she and his father would be horrified if Matthew said she was a drunk, but that's what she was. Not poor or a slob, like old Mack Taylor, of course. But a drunk nevertheless. Money enabled her to hide it better.

She gave Matthew a tentative smile. "How was school?" She looked small and vulnerable sitting there; the contrast of his father's sleekness and power always made her seem worse. Matthew couldn't keep from going over to her as if to shield her.

Johnette wasn't older than his father, but she looked it. Genes and alcohol had combined to age her face, adding wrinkles and a looseness to her skin. The warm brown of her hair was dulled now and streaked with gray. She could have put color on it and given herself an extra five years, but she wouldn't go to the trouble. Johnette had never worked on her looks; she knew she couldn't match up to her husband and she hadn't tried. More than once Matthew had heard his mother laugh and say that at their wedding the groom had been better looking than the bride. Certainly it had been that way the rest of their lives.

She wasn't unattractive. Her bones were good, if a little too angular for a woman, and her hazel eyes were pretty, especially when she smiled. But she didn't have the perfection of features that Sam Ferris had, nor the compelling energy that made everyone notice him wherever he was.

"I got the tickets to the Football Banquet," Matthew told his father, more to stall than anything else. He had the feeling he wouldn't like what was coming.

"Fine. Just keep them." Sam paused. "Your mother and I want to talk to you."

"So I gathered."

Sam frowned at the touch of flippancy in his son's voice. If there was anything wrong with Matthew, it was a tendency not to take things seriously enough. Sam suspected he got it from his mother. "The divorce will be granted next week. No problem, of course; we've hammered out our agreement. But when it's done, your mother wants to move home to Georgia."

Matthew looked at his mother, surprised. She had never said anything about it. It hadn't even entered his head that she might leave Sweet River.

Johnette glanced up at Matt, wetting her lips nervously, and her eyes flitted away. She polished off her drink. Now that he thought about it, Matthew could understand why she wouldn't want to stay here. She would be an object of pity and faint scorn in this small town. She had been an outsider the whole time she'd lived here, and now, no longer married to a Ferris, she would be even more of one. If the rumors that Dad was going to marry his latest mistress were true, it would be humiliating for her to remain, living in close proximity to the new Mrs. Ferris.

His mother wasn't one for holding up her head and marching on.

Swift on the heels of that thought came another—what was he going to do?

His father rolled on smoothly. "Of course, that means you'll have to make a decision, Matt—either to go with your mother or to stay here with me. You're almost eighteen, old enough to choose where you want to live. I'll be moving back into the house as soon as the divorce is final."

Matthew looked at his father. Sam's face was calm and confident. There was no doubt in his mind what Matthew would decide to do. Pain curled through Matthew's chest, and his muscles tightened. He turned to Johnette. She sat with her head bowed, refusing to meet his eyes, and fiddled with the rim of her glass. Matthew could see that she was stiff with tension.

How could he let her go without him? She needed him. She had leaned on him since he was a kid. She hadn't been a wonderful mother. There were lots of times when she had embarrassed him in front of his friends by stumbling or slurring her words, lots of times she hadn't been there to watch him in a game (though his busy father always was). She was lousy at cooking and birthday parties and helping out at school like the other mothers. Johnette wasn't the kind you could depend on. That was Dad.

But she loved him. He'd never doubted that. She was always ready to give him a hug or a kiss or a laugh. She didn't require things of him. He didn't have to measure up to earn her love. He loved her. He ought to be with her.

But he couldn't leave Sweet River! How could he? It was his senior year. He was in basketball, and in spring he'd be running track. At a new school he wouldn't be eligible to play. Here he was known; he was important; he had friends and an established life. Sure, he would leave them when he went off to college next fall, but that was different. He'd be going on to something new and better. Moving to Georgia now just meant losing everything.

He looked at Sam. His father was waiting patiently, confidently. Matthew could envision Sam's disapproval if Matthew said he was going with his mother. Dad wouldn't understand, ever; he'd just think Matt was weak like Johnette.

He swiveled back to his mother, willing her to look at him. Why didn't she say something? Ask him to go with her. Tell him she needed him. Why did she leave it to Dad to do the talking, as she always had? Why the hell were they forcing him to make the decision? Why were they making him choose between them?

He wanted to cry. He wanted to explode.

"Mama . . ." he began tentatively, waiting for a response from her. Johnette stared down at her glass of scotch, clutched now in a death grip. "It's my senior year." There was a quiver in his voice that embarrassed him, and he cleared his throat. "All my friends—I—it's only three or four months." Why couldn't she wait that long? Just let him finish the year. Why couldn't she hang on for a few months? Face up to the town for a while for his sake?

Johnette looked up, and Matthew saw the defeat in her eyes. Defeat and something else . . . He realized that she had expected it. She had assumed that he wouldn't leave Sweet River. He saw the tension ooze out of her body and her hand ease around the glass. She was relieved. He knew she wanted him with her, but at the same time she was glad to have the pressure off.

"Oh, Mama." He didn't know what to say. *Hear how it hurts me. Please, see how I don't want to lose you.*

"It's okay. I understand." Johnette smiled at him wanly. "I know you'd like to stay with your friends. Senior year is important."

She rose and went to the mahogany buffet where the decanters of liquor stood. She poured herself another healthy dose of scotch with a spurt of soda.

"I can come to Georgia this summer as soon as school's over," Matthew went on, his voice a little pleading even though she hadn't asked for it. Why didn't she fight for him? Why did she always give in so gracefully? He wanted to shake her, yell at her, ask her if she just didn't love him.

"Yes. That will be nice." Johnette took a sip of her drink. "I'll go up to my room now, if you all don't mind. I'm sure Sarah has your supper ready. You're welcome to stay to eat, Sam."

"Thank you."

They watched her cross the hall and navigate the curl of stairs up to the second floor. She walked with the slow, cautious step of one accustomed to drinking and careful not to let the alcohol show. Sam rested his hand on Matt's shoulder, companionable and understanding. "Don't worry, Son. You handled it well. You let her down easy and that's all she really wanted. She knew you wouldn't go back to Georgia with her. It would be obvious to anyone."

Matt's fists knotted and he jammed them into his pockets. His father would never understand his pain, the way it tore him to tell his mother he wouldn't go with her. For Sam it was clear: Matthew stayed with the money, the car, and the house. The important things. "She's going to be all alone," Matthew said quietly.

"Your mother's never alone as long as she has a bottle of Chivas Regal."

Matthew wanted to hit him. For being right.

Sam sighed and shook his head. "Poor Jo. She let the drink get to her. She couldn't quite handle it. We love her, but she's weak."

His father had said that, or something like it, many times before, and it had never failed to irritate Matthew. Now it was like rubbing salt in a wound. Matthew jerked his shoulder out from under Sam's hand. "Damn you!"

"Matthew..." Sam gazed at him with faint puzzlement and exasperation and patience, a look he'd turned on his son often the last few months. "I know this is upsetting for you, but you have to face the facts."

"Oh, I faced the facts, all right!" Matthew lashed back, rigid with helpless anger. "My mother's an alcoholic and you made her that way! Sure it 'got to her'! Spending every night alone while you were out chasing skirts *got* to her. Living in the shadow of your perfect self *got* to her. You're a cold, selfish, unfeeling bastard! The only reason you give a damn about me is because your genes are in me. I'm part you. Unfortunately.''

Sam's face was tight, his dark eyes hard and bright like marbles. "That's unfair. Unfair and untrue. You know I love you. Who in the hell's always been there for you? Who watched you in elementary and junior high before there were any glory games? Who was there when you picked up your awards and when you talked to the college recruiters? Who the hell threw those balls to you every evening all summer long, every summer? It sure as hell wasn't your mother. She was upstairs in bed stewed to the gills!''

Matthew glared at him. His skin felt taut over his facial muscles, as if the roiling emotions inside were pressing against it, trying to burst out. What was so infuriating, so frustrating and goading, was that it was true. But it wasn't the emotional truth. "Maybe I didn't want to be out there throwing balls every evening all summer, every summer.''

Sam grimaced. "Yeah, and maybe you didn't want to make All-State or go to the championships, either. Maybe you aren't thrilled to know you'll be playing for Bear Bryant next year.'' He turned his head sharply away, and Matthew could see him gathering his control, his patience. It added another twist to the wound-up coil inside Matt. Why did his father always have to be so much in command of everything and everyone, including himself?

"Look.'' Sam swept his hands apart as if wiping something clean. "Let's forget it. I know you're under a lot of pressure. Why don't we run over to Fayetteville and grab something to eat? What do you say? A pizza, something different.''

"Why don't you take your girlfriend?''

For a moment they simply looked at each other, then Matthew turned and slammed out the front door.

He jumped into his car and peeled out of the driveway, the car bobbing on its suspension. He jerked out the Rolling Stones tape and jammed in Steppenwolf, turning it up until it blasted him out of the car.

Matthew roared out of town and into the network of narrow mountain roads, pushing his speed to the limit. He couldn't count the number of times it had ended this way, with him screaming at one parent or the other, then charging out of the house and driving like a maniac.

He hated his father. He hated them both. He wanted to drive a hundred miles an hour and smash into a tree.

He couldn't contain the anger. He couldn't let it out. All he could do was drive like a bat out of hell until it receded.

He came out on a dirt road and turned around and drove again. The tape went around twice, and he replaced it with the Doors. He slowed down to a normal speed and took the highway to Eureka Springs. He went halfway there before he turned around and started back.

He felt bone weary, yet still keyed up, and he thought about what he could do. He didn't want to return home. There was Shelly's house, of course. Sometimes he ran to her when he had to blow off steam. But he knew Shelly; she wouldn't want to listen to his griping, nor would she try to soothe him. She would want compliments and gossip. Besides, she wouldn't even let him inside the house until he apologized for this morning, and he wasn't about to do that, not in the mood he was in.

Maybe he'd simply go into town and drive around. Or he could drop by somebody's house—Keith's maybe. Randy, Joe Bob and Keith had been his friends for years, and he was as close to them, especially Keith, as he was to anybody. Even so, he'd never been able to confide in them about his parents' divorce. He could never talk to anyone about the things that hurt the most. Matthew's stomach rumbled and he realized that he was hungry. He hadn't eaten, and it was almost 7:30. Maybe he'd stop by the drive-in and get a hamburger. But he didn't want to have to talk to the kids that always hung around there. There was Byers' Cafe. It was more an adult place, while the kids went to the drive-in. It would be quieter, not many people this time of night. He thought of Jennifer. Yeah, he'd go to the cafe. He stepped on the gas. Suddenly he felt better.

Jennifer floated through the day. She heard a few whispers in class and she suspected they were about her getting out of Matthew Ferris' car that morning, but she ignored them. She was too happy, as if she had been filled up inside with fizz. Matthew Ferris had spoken to her. He'd given her a ride. He had been nice enough to talk to her. (She, of course, had responded like a lump, but Jennifer was too elated even to be hard on herself for that.)

It didn't mean anything; he was only being kind. Jennifer wasn't foolish enough to believe Matthew had any interest in her. But the fact that he'd been nice to her made her grin inside. She couldn't keep herself from daydreaming. She sat at her desk, head bent studiously over her books, and she thought about Matthew. She remembered every detail of his appearance from her brief, furtive glimpses of him. She recalled each word he said and the tone of his voice, the accent that was faintly different from everyone else's, tinged with a bit of his mother's Georgia drawl.

Scenes ran like a movie through her mind. She imagined meeting Matthew in the hall and his stopping to talk to her. She envisioned his words, his gestures, her responses. In her mind her clothes were straight out of *Seventeen*, the kind of clothes Shelly Daniels wore, and she talked without shyness, her voice lilting and flirtatious, her eyes sparkling. She was perfect, as she always was in her daydreams.

Jennifer loved to daydream. Most of her teachers thought her simply quiet or even sullen, depending on their view of her, but, in fact, most of the time she was in a completely different world. It was a talent she had perfected when she was very young, a way to draw within herself and hide, at least mentally, from her father's drunken rages or her hunger or the cold or the bleakness of their shack. Angie had told her stories when she was young, and Jennifer had then told them to herself whenever she wanted to escape, embellishing and changing them to suit herself. Whenever she could escape into the trees behind her house, she would act out the stories, taking all the roles from king down to serving girl. Dressed in ill-fitting hand-me-downs, living in a house without electricity or running water, she was in her mind the companion of royalty, nobility, of daring and beautiful people.

School, though it brought her embarrassment, also brought Jennifer a whole new world. She had learned to read, and she found that she could check out books from the library, and in them she had found even more fascinating people and stories. She had read every moment she could sneak away from her chores, careful not to let her father catch her at it. She had learned through bitter experience that the sight of her reading a book infuriated him, though she wasn't sure why, unless it was simply that he hated to see her enjoy herself. Mack classified reading as "giving herself airs," a phrase which he used to describe many things Jennifer did that he didn't like. Jennifer hid her books beneath her mattress, and she slipped out to her special spot in the fork of the old pecan tree to read.

She had read every book of fiction in the library. Then she had discovered movies. She had always been fascinated by the films shown in school, even if they dealt with geography, history, or science. When she was eleven Corey had taken her to the movie theater with some of the first money he earned, and she had sat spellbound through *The Birds*. She knew she had discovered the most wonderful thing on earth: stories that were acted out by people, just the way she acted out what she read in books. It seemed unbelievable that there were people who were lucky enough to spend their lives pretending to be characters in a story.

After that she went to the movies whenever she could scrape up the quarter, later fifty cents, admission. Sitting in the dark for two hours, watching a world unfold on the screen was like heaven to her, and it became even more precious after her mother died later that year. Movies and books gave her the companionship, the love, the friendship, that her mother once had provided. They were her escape and her protection from the world. When Jennifer wasn't reading or watching a movie, she spent her time daydreaming about them. She replayed the stories in her mind—out loud when she was alone—saying all the lines and imitating the gestures, tones, and expressions.

In the same way, she created a scenario of a romance with Matthew Ferris, playing it out behind her blank face through class after class. Even in last period home economics class, normally her favorite, she paid little attention to the dress on which she was working. Frequently she stayed in the home ec room for twenty or thirty minutes after school was out, for Mrs. Patterson let her use the sewing machines for the clothes she made herself outside of school. But today, ignoring the teacher's puzzled glance, Jennifer darted out of class with the other girls as soon as the bell rang.

She had nowhere to go; she didn't have to be at work until after four, but she couldn't stand to be cooped up inside the school a moment longer, pretending to be interested in her sewing when she had no patience for it. Cradling her books in her arms, she strolled to the cafe. The air was chilly, but the sun was shining, and the cold seemed crisp and cheerful this afternoon, tinged with the same happiness she had felt all day.

Jennifer took the longer way, passing by the movie theater. It was Wednesday, and the advertisements for the new movie beginning Friday were up. Jennifer paused to study them. *The Lion in Winter.* She'd seen previews for it for weeks now. She studied Katharine Hepburn in her medieval outfit, wishing it were Sunday already so she could see it. She had to work all day Saturday, but the cafe was closed on Sundays, and it was then that she always went to the matinee. Jennifer hated going on Friday or Saturday nights when dating couples were there and she felt conspicuously alone and freakish.

She smiled, anticipating the pleasure. Jennifer loved movies, all kinds, all qualities. She never missed one if she could help it, whether it was a spaghetti western, light comedy, or heavy drama. But when it was something like this, a special, wonderful movie with an actress like Katharine Hepburn who made a person glow inside just to see her—well, then Jennifer was as eager as a kid at Christmas, hardly able to wait until Sunday afternoon. She would sit through a movie like that twice and afterwards wish she could see it yet again.

When she arrived at the restaurant it was quiet. Only two old men sat at the counter, drinking coffee. Jan had already gone home and the owner, Frank, stood behind the counter. He raised a hand to her in greeting. "Hi, Jenny, how's it going?"

"Fine, thank you." Jennifer smiled at him and waved at Preston in the kitchen. She felt comfortable here. The people liked her and she belonged. It seemed more like home than anywhere else.

"Burger and fries?" Preston called out to her and she nodded. That was her standard supper. She rarely had lunch, eating a hearty breakfast before school and supper as soon as she got to work in the afternoon. It was another way to pinch pennies, something she was good at. Movies were her only extravagance. In every other area she scrimped. As much as she loved clothes, she rarely bought any. She made her own dresses, and her underclothes were cheap cotton. Someday, she told herself, when she was rich, she would splurge and buy only the softest, most luxurious satin and silk underthings. But for now plain cotton bras and panties would do. She bought her school supplies and a minimum of food and cleaning products for the house, and she paid for the gas that ran the refrigerator, stove, and heater Corey had bought.

She saved the rest of her money, along with what Corey sent her monthly. Her father often asked her for money, going from pleading to threatening and back; but she refused to give him any, knowing he'd use it to buy a bottle of sour mash. He had hunted through the house for her cache of money several times; she had seen the signs of his search. But she knew, smugly, that he'd never find her savings, for she stashed all her money away in the bank. She liked to think of it in there, slowly, steadily growing, waiting for her to finish high school. Then she'd take it all out and she'd be gone to California.

Jennifer changed into her uniform and sat down to her hamburger and french fries. Around five a few people came in, but supper was generally a slow time, and today was no exception. She was busy for less than an hour, and there was plenty of time for her to get her homework done and watch the little portable TV in the back. But tonight she had trouble keeping her mind on the shows.

A little after 7:30 the front door opened, and Jennifer looked up from her seat behind the counter. She stared, and her insides went cold, then hot. Matthew Ferris had walked in.

"Hi." He smiled at her and sat down at one of the booths.

Jennifer barely managed to get out a return greeting. What was he doing here at this hour? Teenagers went to the drive-in in the evening. If there had been another waitress there she would have tried to get her to wait on him, she felt so scared and eager all at the same time. But no one was there but Jennifer, and she had to make herself stand up and take him a menu.

"I didn't know if you worked here in the evenings, too."

She nodded.

Matthew glanced at the menu, and she started to move away, but his voice stopped her. "Wait, I know what I want. A bowl of chili; it's cold out there. And two orders of biscuits. A piece of apple pie. Is it good?"

"It's always good. That's Preston's specialty."

Jennifer put in his order and sat back down behind the counter. She tried not to watch him, but since the two of them were the only people in the cafe, it was hard not to.

He started talking to her across the room. "You going to the game Friday night?"

She shook her head. "I have to work."

"It doesn't start until eight. You could still see most of it."

Jennifer had never been to a basketball game. She thought of watching him play, and excitement stirred in her stomach. It was only thirty-five cents. "Maybe I will. I haven't been to one before."

"This year?"

"Ever."

"Ever?" Matthew looked at Jennifer as if she'd just landed from another planet. "You don't like sports?"

"I don't know. I've never gone to any games."

"Even football?"

Jennifer blushed. She felt like a freak. She'd never had a friend to go with, and games always seemed such a companionable thing, not something you went to alone. And they weren't in a dark place like a movie theater where you wouldn't be seen.

"Hey, I'm sorry." Matthew realized that he'd embarrassed her. "You don't have to like sports. Lots of people don't. I didn't mean to sound critical."

"It's okay. You weren't."

Now they sat looking at each other silently again. Behind her Preston rang the bell to let her know the order was ready, and she jumped up, relieved to have something to do. She took the dishes to Matthew's table and set them down in front of him carefully. It made her nervous to be so close to him. Her hand almost grazed his arm.

"Can I get you anything else?"

"Why don't you sit down and keep me company?" He gestured toward the seat across from him.

Jennifer glanced around the room. Nobody had ever

asked her that before.. "Well, I guess it's all right . . . until another customer comes in."

She sat down and clenched her hands in her lap; they were as cold as ice. She watched him eat. He glanced up. "Say, this is good. I was starving."

"I'm glad you like it." She felt like an idiot. She wet her lips. "I—I was surprised to see you here. Kids usually go down to the drive-in."

He shrugged. "Didn't feel like seeing a bunch of people tonight." He paused. "I had a fight with my dad."

"Oh. I'm sorry."

"My parents are getting divorced." He didn't look at her as he said it, but kept his eyes on his food.

"I know. I'm sorry."

He looked up at her. The reticence that had been in her eyes earlier was gone, and in its place were kindness and sorrow. He felt the anger and hurt begin to seep out of him. "That's the first time I told anybody. Crazy, huh? Everybody in town knows, but I'm scared to say it."

"It's not crazy."

Matt found himself telling her about the scene with his parents, the anger, pain and frustration tumbling out. If anyone had told him two days ago that he'd be telling his problems to Jennifer Taylor, he would have said they were crazy, but at the moment it seemed the most natural thing in the world. Her eyes were kind, her face sympathetic yet not pitying. As he talked, he could feel the band around his chest loosening, the jittering nerves relaxing, the sick anger draining out.

Jennifer listened, amazed that Matthew would actually reveal his thoughts and feelings to someone as unimportant as she. As she listened, she forgot to be nervous, her self-consciousness lost in her concern for him. Matthew Ferris had always seemed little short of a god to her, a walking perfection of looks, personality and abilities. She had never dreamed that he might feel torn or unhappy or frustrated. Yet here he was, real and troubled, and her heart went out to him. She wanted to comfort him, to reach out and hold him and make all the bad things disappear from his life. And the worshipful awe she had felt for him in the past changed subtly into something far more real and emotional.

Strangely, despite the apparent differences between them, sitting there in a vinyl booth at Byers' Cafe, they were linked. Matthew looked into her eyes and knew somehow that he was at home. Jennifer gazed back at him, thinking it was absurd and impossible, but sensing the same thing. Matthew curled his hand around hers and felt its incredible softness and delicacy against his palm. Excitement quivered in his chest, and his fingers tightened around hers.

"When do you get off work?" he asked. "I'll drive you home."

* *Chapter 3* *

For a moment Jennifer was too stunned to speak. She was very aware of his hand on hers, warm and callused from sports; she was afraid her hand might start to tremble. What did he want? He couldn't want to go out with her, not Matthew Ferris. It was impossible. Maybe he thought she was easy; maybe he was planning to take her down by the river and park instead of taking her home. Yet he had been so open and friendly. Surely the boy who had just poured out his troubles to her couldn't be scheming to seduce her. And no matter what, she could not pass up this chance to be with him.

"All right. Thank you." She hesitated. "It'll be a few minutes. You don't mind waiting?"

He shook his head.

"Well, I better get to it then. Excuse me."

She moved away, and his eyes followed her. Matthew felt good and peaceful, more at ease inside himself than he had in a long time. He couldn't believe he'd told her all that crap, but somehow it didn't really bother him. She had been so sweet and understanding that he couldn't feel embarrassed.

Jennifer gave the tables a final check, wiping at a spot or straightening the menus, napkins and condiments. She sensed that Matthew watched her, and it made her jumpy. What did he want? She could still feel his hand on hers.

Frank Byers came in, as he did every evening at closing time, to put up the receipts and lock up. Jennifer slipped into the bathroom and changed out of her uniform. She almost expected Matthew to disappear while she was in there, like one of her daydreams, but when she returned with her books and coat he was waiting for her by the cash register, chatting with Frank about the game Friday night. He smiled when he saw her and came over to take her books. Jennifer was breathless and scared. He was so close to her. She didn't know how to act.

But Matthew didn't appear to notice anything wrong. They walked out of the cafe, giving Frank a casual wave good-bye. Matthew opened the passenger door of his car for her. No one had ever opened a car door for her before, and Jennifer felt both awkward and pleased.

Matt started the car and turned to look at her questioningly. Jennifer stared back. "Where to?" he asked finally.

"What? Oh. I'm sorry." She blushed. "Go out the Nathanville highway. My road's just past the Anderson place."

He backed out and started down the street. Jennifer clenched her hands in her lap. In the dark, the car felt even smaller and more intimate than it had that morning.

Matthew talked as they drove and Jennifer answered him, but her mind wasn't on the conversation. It was on the cutoff to the river road that lay two miles before her house, and she went limp with relief when they passed it.

Matthew wasn't trying to take her down to the town's favorite necking spot.

His car rounded the curve past the Anderson house and Jennifer pointed. "The road's up there. Just turn off and stop. I'll walk the rest of the way."

"Don't be silly. I'll drive you."

"No!"

Matthew glanced at Jennifer, surprised by her abrupt tone. No doubt he would think her rude. But she couldn't let him see her house! And what if her father was there? She couldn't bear the humiliation. "Really, there's no need. The road's terrible; you'll hurt your car."

He chuckled. "It's used to it. You think there are any good roads around here?" He turned onto the dirt road leading up to her house.

Desperate, Jennifer put her hand on his arm. "No, please, Matthew. Really. Stop here."

He looked at her, puzzled, but put on the brakes. "Okay. But I don't understand . . ."

"I'd rather walk. I—I'd just rather walk." She withdrew her hand and looked down at the books in her lap. "Thank you for the ride."

"You're welcome." Matthew watched her. She was beautiful, even in the dim light of the car. Her eyes looked huge and dark, her skin unbelievably soft. The faint light settled on the lines of her cheekbones and jaw. He wanted to kiss her. He wanted to ask her out.

He knew what Randy would tell him: Kiss her. What Shelly didn't know wouldn't hurt her.

But it wasn't Shelly he was thinking of. It was Jennifer he didn't want to hurt. Maybe she was easy; everyone said so. Maybe if he reached for her, she would come into his arms eagerly. She might kiss him and let his hands explore her body. His mouth went dry at the thought. But even if she did, he couldn't do it. It would be taking her lightly, making her cheap to kiss her when they both knew he was going steady with someone else. He couldn't do that after she'd been so nice to him tonight. Besides, he didn't believe the rumors were true. Jennifer was too sweet, too pure.

Matthew made no move toward her, and when she said good-bye, he didn't even ask her to linger a little longer in the car with him. He just smiled and said good-bye and watched as she slipped out of the car and walked up the dark road. When he couldn't see her anymore, he turned and drove back home, alive and buoyant with strange new emotions. He went to bed, but couldn't sleep, just lay awake thinking about Jennifer and the kiss he hadn't asked from her.

Shelly and Matthew broke up the next morning. It was all over school inside of an hour. Jennifer heard Becky Yates and Jill Clements talking about it across the aisle from her in geometry, and her heart picked up its beat. She remembered Matthew's hand curling over hers last night at the table. But she couldn't let herself hope. It was too farfetched. However, she stopped by the table at the main entrance of the school to buy a ticket to Friday's basketball game with Nathanville.

She didn't see Matthew at school, but that night, a few minutes before 8:30, he walked into the cafe. Frank was already there, closing up, and he said jovially, "Well, hey, Matt, you're becoming a regular customer."

Matthew smiled. "I dropped by to give Jennifer a ride home." He glanced at Jennifer questioningly. She stared at him, wide-eyed, knotting her hands behind her back. Then she remembered how that gesture emphasized her breasts and quickly dropped her arms to her sides.

"Well, sure," Frank said. "Run on home, Jenny."

"Thank you. I—uh, I'll change."

Matthew Ferris was there to see her. He was taking her home.

The idea sank in on Jennifer as she dressed. Excitement swelled in her and she had trouble with her buttons and zipper. What was Matthew's interest in her? He hadn't tried anything yesterday. There'd been no groping, no attempt to kiss her, not even a suggestive look or word. Perhaps, being Matthew Ferris, he was just smoother than the other boys. But maybe . . . maybe he *liked* her.

She hardly spoke as he drove her home, and he seemed almost as shy. He turned onto her road. "Will you let me take you all the way to your house tonight?"

"This is fine. Right here."

Matthew stopped the car and looked at her, puzzled. "Why?"

Jennifer studied her hands in her lap. "Please. I just don't want you to."

"You ashamed of me?"

Her head snapped up. "Of course not!" Then she realized he was teasing and relaxed. "It's just . . . better."

"Your daddy the kind who carries a shotgun?"

She smiled faintly at the thought of her father protecting her honor. "No. He's just—a drunk." Her voice dropped bitterly.

Matthew brushed his fingertips across her hand. "I'm sorry." He shouldn't have teased her. He knew what Mack Taylor was like, and he should have realized that she was embarrassed to let anyone see him. Matthew, of all people, ought to know the humiliation of a drunken parent. And old Mack was ten times worse than Johnette Ferris ever thought of being.

Jennifer swallowed. She loved the feel of his fingers on hers. She wished his hand would stay forever, but she moved her hand away, wondering what he thought of her.

"Jennifer . . ."

"Yes?" She turned to him. He looked stiff and serious.

"I was wondering, will you go out with me after the game?"

"Go out with you?" she repeated blankly.

"Yeah. I could get you a ticket, and then when the game's over we could go by the drive-in and get a burger or something."

Jennifer felt as though Heaven had opened up in front of her, but she was too stunned and scared to take it. She swallowed. "I'd like to, very much."

Matthew relaxed into a grin. "Great. You can wait in the gym for me after the game—if you don't mind going to the game, that is."

She shook her head. "No. I don't mind. In fact, I bought a ticket today." She hesitated, and her gaze returned to her hands clenched together in her lap. "But, Matthew—I, well—I don't know what you expect." Her stomach twisted into a knot. She didn't know how to say it, was humiliated to have to talk about it. But she couldn't bear to have him paw her, to have him turn out to be just like all the others. "I'm not the way people say. I know you probably think I'm—easy, and all that. But I've never done anything with a boy. Honestly. And I don't want to go out if you think that I'm going to . . ." Her voice trailed off and she looked up at him.

Her eyes were huge and vulnerable, glimmering with tears. Matthew wanted to wrap her in his arms and protect her from the world. There was no question in his mind that she was telling the truth. She had been wronged by the rumors about her, and he knew a fierce hatred for the people who had imposed this on her. He brushed his knuckles across her cheek. "I don't expect anything except a date. We'll eat something and talk, and I'll probably bore you with a lot of stuff about the game. That's all."

Her smile was so radiant it took his breath away. "Then I'd love to go. I'd love to."

The game was the following night. Jennifer wished she could have made up a new dress for it, but there wasn't enough time. She searched her wardrobe Thursday night after she got home, hoping something new and beautiful would pop up, a miracle in her closet. But they were the same old dresses she'd worn many times before, not nearly good enough for Matthew. Finally she settled on a plainly styled dress in a luscious pink that brought out her delicate coloring.

She carried the dress to work with her Friday and left it hanging in the employee bathroom. When work was over Friday evening, she changed into it and walked back to the school gymnasium. She was late, even though Frank had kindly let her off half an hour early, for she had spent a great deal of time brushing her hair and putting on lipstick, bending and turning to try to see herself in the tiny mirror above the sink. When she arrived, the gym was filled with people, all making as much noise as possible. Jennifer wanted to shrink back inside herself. She didn't know where to sit. There were a few empty spots here and there, but she hated the idea of plopping down next to someone, intruding on them.

As she hesitated at the foot of the steps, Becky Yates came in behind her, carrying a paper tray of soft drinks. "Hi!" Becky shouted over the din. "Kind of crowded, isn't it?"

Jennifer nodded. She liked Becky. Though Jennifer certainly wasn't friends with Becky, who was part of the popular, "in" group to which Jennifer could never hope to attain entrance, Becky was always nice to her. She was a sweet girl with a friendly, unaffected nature.

"Did you just get here?" Becky went on.

"Yes. I'm a little late."

"It's hard to find a seat by this time. Why don't you sit with us?" She pointed to a row not far from the front.

Jennifer smiled. "Okay. Thank you."

She followed Becky up the metal steps to a bench where Jill Clements and two of Becky's other friends sat. They looked up at Becky, smiling, then their eyes turned curiously to Jennifer. Jennifer knew they wondered what she was doing there, and heat rose in her face. She hated putting herself in where she wasn't wanted. Becky sat down, handing out the drinks she had brought, and Jennifer sat next to her on the end of the bench.

Jennifer looked at the game for the first time. Matthew was running down the court, dribbling the ball, and to Jennifer's eyes he seemed nearly naked in the brief basketball uniform. His legs and arms were muscled and lightly covered with hair. Sweat darkened a triangle at the neck of his shirt and glistened on his shoulders and face. His muscles bunched and relaxed as he moved, pressing against his sleek skin. Looking at him, Jennifer's abdomen was suddenly bathed with heat.

She thought about him kissing her. Matthew raised the ball to shoot, his hands spread out on either side of the basketball, and she thought of him touching her hand, her arm, her back. She imagined his arms around her, pressing her against his chest, and everything inside her quivered.

Basketball was a fast-paced game, and Jennifer didn't understand it. Such a frenzy of waving arms, mad running, and tossing the ball around. But she loved watching Matthew. Her eyes followed him wherever he went, even during the times he was off the court. She enjoyed seeing him run and throw; his strength stirred her. She liked the play of his muscles, the quickness of his hands, the serious intensity of his expression. Everything about him was wonderful, from the way he leaped into the air, his hands arcing the ball to the basket, to the way he shoved his damp hair back from his face.

At halftime, as the teams desultorily warmed up again, Matthew glanced up into the stands several times as though looking for something. When his eyes fell on Jennifer, he grinned at her, then turned his attention back to the court. Joy surged up in Jennifer and she knew she must be glowing. She sensed Becky's thoughtful glance, but she refused to look at her, knowing how much her face must reveal of what she felt.

Sweet River was the better team—even Jennifer could tell that much—and they beat Nathanville soundly. When the game was over, the players ran off the court, and everyone around Jennifer stood up and began to move out of the building. Jennifer didn't know what to do; it felt strange to stay seated there when everyone else was leaving. She moved with the flow of the crowd down the steps to the wide doors in the lobby. There she hung back awkwardly, letting others pass her by. The crowd thinned out, and soon the building was empty except for a couple of men talking to the scorekeeper and a few girls by the court who were chatting with the cheerleaders as they packed up their megaphones and pompons.

Jennifer watched Shelly. She wondered what Shelly was thinking. What had happened between her and Matthew? She looked at Shelly's slim figure in the blue-and-white cheerleader uniform and thought that Matthew couldn't really be interested in herself. Shelly was so slender and fashionable, the model of a teenage girl.

The locker room door opened and Matthew came out. Several of the girls turned and spoke to him. Shelly studiously ignored him. He answered abstractedly as he looked around the gym. He spotted Jennifer standing at the doors, and he grinned and hurried toward her, oblivious of the several sets of interested eyes behind him on the court.

"Hi. For a minute I thought you'd gone. I'm glad you didn't." He was bursting with adrenalin from the game, and Jennifer looked luscious in that dress. He wanted to touch her, kiss her, put his arm around her, but he refrained, only putting his hand at her back to guide her out the door.

Jennifer smiled up at him. When he grinned at her, it was enough to melt her bones.

They went to Sammy's, the drive-in. There were several tables inside Sammy's, and Matthew chose to go in, saying it was too cold to sit outside. Jennifer wished they had stayed in the car. They were too visible for her comfort inside the restaurant. The place was full of kids, both inside and in cars, and she felt everyone's eyes on them as they walked into the building and sat down at a table. Jennifer knew their thoughts. First they were amazed to see Matthew with her. Then they decided that Matthew was taking her out so he could score with her later. They would speculate on whether Shelly knew about it, and what she would say when she found out, and whether Matthew was doing it just to make Shelly jealous. And at that thought, Jennifer herself wondered if that was true.

"You want something to eat?"

Jennifer shook her head. "No, a Coke is fine."

"You sure? I hope you don't mind watching me eat, then." He ordered a hamburger and fries. "I'm always starved after a game."

Jennifer smiled. She enjoyed watching him eat. She enjoyed watching him do anything. He began to talk about the game, too charged up and excited to be quiet. She hadn't seen him so animated before, so alight and full of energy. She listened and smiled, not understanding much of what he said, but happy simply to hear his voice and see the enthusiasm on his face.

Matthew knew he was babbling. He couldn't stop. She was so easy to talk to. She listened to him as though she hung on his words, as though she wanted to hear anything he could ever have to say. Her eyes were luminous, her face open and warm. Beautiful. There was a dimple in her right cheek when she smiled. Her mouth was full and incredibly sexy. He watched her sip her soft drink, her mouth pursing around the straw. He wondered if her lips felt as satiny as they looked. He thought about taking her lower lip between his teeth. He thought about sinking his tongue into the warm, wet cave of her mouth. Desire surged through him, and he talked more and faster to mask his thoughts.

He urged her to take one of his french fries, just to see her eat it. He watched her lips open. He glimpsed her tongue. Her sharp white teeth cut crisply through the golden fry. Matthew swallowed and looked down at the table, trying to remember what he had been saying. He wished that he didn't like her so much, that he didn't enjoy talking to her. He wished he could just take her out on a deserted road and make a pass at her.

He looked up. She was watching him, her face open and

trusting, lovely. "Let's go," he said, and was surprised to hear how normal his voice sounded.

After they left the drive-in, Matthew drove aimlessly around the town and out into the hills, not caring where they went, only wanting not to have to take Jennifer home yet. Finally he pulled off on the dirt road that led to Jennifer's house and stopped. It was almost twelve o'clock.

"I've really been running off at the mouth, haven't I?" he asked ruefully. "I'm surprised you didn't tell me to shut up."

"I enjoyed it. I like listening to you."

"I like talking to you. You probably noticed. You're real easy to talk to. There are things I can't tell my parents or other kids. Everybody thinks I'm so good. You know? A lot of the time I feel like such a sham. I get full of anger and bitterness. I feel wild inside. Do you know what I mean?"

Jennifer nodded. Corey was wild like that sometimes, despite his essential goodness. Only with Corey, the wildness showed.

"Really?" Matthew smiled a little. "Most people, if I told them that, would laugh and say I was crazy." He looked at Jennifer. He wanted to kiss her so much it hurt. And he couldn't. Not yet. He took her hand in one of his. It was soft and fragile. He smoothed his thumb over the back of her hand.

Jennifer watched his thumb. It was setting up a tingling all through her. She remembered his hands on the basketball, sure and strong and large. With a naive amazement, she realized that she wanted to feel his hands on her body. She wanted to taste his mouth. She had never felt desire before, but now it began to shimmer in her.

Matthew's voice broke into her thoughts. "I'd like to take you out tomorrow night. We could go to the movie." He looked up at her. "Would you like to?"

Again she was amazed, but she managed to answer, "Yes. I would."

"Will you be at work?"

"No. Frank closes at six on Saturday."

"Then I'll pick you up at your house."

"I'll meet you here."

There was a mixture of puzzlement and frustration in his eyes, but he only nodded. "Okay."

"I better go in now. I have to get up early tomorrow."

"Good night." He released her hand slowly. He made no move to kiss her.

"Good night. Thank you. I had a wonderful time."

"Me too." Matthew watched her leave the car and walk away, the sweet ache of desire deep in his gut.

Jennifer hardly felt the dirt beneath her feet as she walked to the house. She thought she might have been able to fly home. She didn't notice the cold, and when she reached the house, her eyes flickered over her father's recumbent, snoring form on the couch without resentment. Nothing could bother her at the moment. She was in love.

The next day at lunch Jennifer took part of her week's pay and instead of stashing it in the bank went to Daniels' Department Store and splurged on a blue knit dress that turned her eyes a vibrant blue and was shorter than what was allowed at school. It was the prettiest thing she owned and far too expensive, the first dress she had ever bought ready-made. But she wanted to look pretty for Matthew, to be worthy of him.

And when Matthew got out of the car to greet her at their meeting place that evening, the look on his face made the expense worthwhile. They went to the movie theater downtown and Matthew held her hand throughout the long movie. For once, Jennifer wasn't wholly wrapped up in the drama on the screen; her attention was too fragmented by his arm beside her and the feel of his rough palm against hers. Afterwards they had a Coke inside his car at the drive-in and talked until the place closed. He took her back to the turn-off to her house, and again they talked, turning the car's heater on now and then to thaw their feet. When at last Jennifer started to get out of the car, Matthew leaned across and kissed her softly, briefly, on the lips. For an instant his breath fluttered against her skin, and she smelled the dark masculine fragrance of his aftershave. She wished he would linger, but he pulled back.

"Next Friday?" he asked, and she nodded. It seemed like an eternity.

Jennifer didn't see Matthew at all on Sunday, and without her job or school to occupy her time, it was a desperately dull and lonely day. She read a letter from Corey that she had received yesterday but had been too busy getting ready for her date to read. It was brief; Corey wasn't much of a letter-writer. He was still at Fort Hood, with no assignment yet to Vietnam, but he didn't expect that situation to last long. He hated the scrubby, broken Texas countryside where he was, but at least it was warmer there than in Sweet River. He had gone with a couple of buddies over to Austin last weekend and prowled around the University of Texas campus. Everybody there seemed to be either hippies or frat rats, he wrote, and though he had seen a few girls "almost as pretty as you," none of them were inclined to have anything to do with a skinhead from Fort Hood. He hoped she was doing okay and that Mack was behaving.

Jennifer's chest ached, thinking of Corey, and she wished he were home again. She wondered what he'd think about her dating Matthew Ferris. Knowing Corey, he'd probably consider it only her due.

Her father woke up with a hangover late in the morning and shuffled over to the refrigerator to take out a beer. He felt better after a couple of swallows and sat down at the kitchen table. "Hey! How about fixing a little lunch for your old man?"

Jennifer made a couple of bologna sandwiches. She resented doing anything for him, but it was easier than arguing. Mack watched her, his eyes narrowed. "I heard last night you were seeing the Ferris boy."

Jennifer's stomach tightened. "I went out with him."

"Two nights in a row, what I heard." He grinned, and for an instant there was a resemblance to Corey in the crinkle of the skin around his blue eyes and the twist of his mouth. She hated seeing anything of Corey in that coarse man. "Sounds like you're moving up in the world."

Jennifer shrugged. "It's no big deal. He's just a nice boy."

"A nice boy whose daddy owns half the county. I went to school with Sam Ferris. Proud son of a bitch. I bet he's none too pleased to have his boy seeing you."

"Mr. Ferris has other things to think about. I doubt he considers his son's dates important." She set his sandwich down on the table in front of him and started toward her room to avoid any more conversation on the subject.

Mack chuckled. "Not that Sam wasn't always interested in a little piece of tail. Like father like son, they say."

"He's not like that!" She whirled and glared at her father. "Matthew likes me. He enjoys my company."

Mack's smile spread. "Sure. That's what any eighteen-year-old boy wants with you. He's not thinking about getting his hand up your skirts. Probably just wants to talk."

"Why do you always have to make everything dirty?" She hated him for talking this way about Matthew. She hated him even more for bringing alive the doubts deep inside herself. *What else could someone like Matthew want with her?*

Matthew's father picked him up after church on Sunday. It was Sam's custom the past few months to take Matthew to Fayetteville or Springdale for Sunday dinner. On the way over they usually rehashed the previous week's game, then moved on to the subjects of school or Sam's business projects or Matthew's future. Therefore, it was a surprise to Matthew when, shortly after he got in the car, without even mentioning the Nathanville game, Sam said, "I understand you broke up with Ed Daniels' daughter."

"Yeah." Matthew glanced at his father warily.

"Martha Springer told me today at church that you were out with Jennifer Taylor last night."

Matthew rolled his eyes. "Doesn't anybody in this town have anything better to do than gossip?"

"Not much." Sam smiled faintly. He paused. "Pretty, that Taylor girl."

"Yes, she is." Beautiful, in fact, and Matthew wished he were with her right now, instead of getting grilled by his father.

"You interested in her?"

"I guess."

"Not very communicative today, are you?"

"I don't know what you want. You want me to tell you the details of my love life?"

"Hardly." Sam's dark eyes were amused. No doubt his own love life was far more entertaining, Matthew thought sourly. "Just wondered why you were dating her, that's all. I would have thought you could get whatever you want from her without taking her out."

Matthew's mouth tightened. "She's not like that. You're like everybody else, condemning her without knowing a thing about her."

Ferris shrugged. "She's a Taylor. Hard to imagine her being pure as the driven snow."

"The Taylors aren't all bad. Mom once told me Jennifer's mother was a nice lady. And Corey's okay."

"Hard worker," Sam agreed, lighting a cigarette. "But wild."

"Maybe. But that doesn't mean anything about Jennifer. She's only a sophomore, you know."

Sam blew out his smoke on a laugh. "Age and experience aren't necessarily the same thing, Son. She looks like a grown woman."

Anger surged in Matthew. "She's a *girl*. And she's not

trashy. It's all rumors—just because she's beautiful and because her father's a lousy drunk!"

Sam cut a sideways glance at his son. Bright red spots of fury stained Matthew's cheekbones. "I don't have anything against your chasing Jennifer Taylor," Sam said mildly. "If I were your age I'd probably pant after her, too. Hell, I could probably pant after her right now if I didn't have more sense. I'm just saying that with a girl like her you better make sure you're not the one who winds up getting caught."

"She's not like that! Damn it, why won't you listen to what I'm saying?"

"I'm listening. But what I'm hearing sounds like a naïve kid talking. Take her, Matt. Screw her all you want. Just don't get a youthful hormonal drive confused with something else."

"Like love."

"Yeah. You don't love girls like Jennifer Taylor."

"Hell, Daddy. You don't love anybody."

Ferris shot Matthew the icy black look that had always tied Matthew's stomach into knots, and neither of them spoke the rest of the way into Springdale.

* *Chapter 4* *

Jennifer was surprised Monday morning when she left work to find Matthew waiting for her outside in his car. She burst into a grin, unaware of how dazzlingly it lit up her face. Matthew jumped out to open the door for her.

"Hi," Jennifer said shyly. "I didn't expect to see you here."

"I dropped by to take you to school. No point in walking, is there?"

"No." She quickly folded herself into the car.

They didn't say much on the way to school. They just kept glancing at each other and grinning, feeling slightly idiotic and perfectly wonderful. Matthew walked with her into the school building and to her locker. Jennifer felt sure there wasn't a pair of eyes in the whole area that didn't follow them, and it embarrassed her a little, but not enough to dampen the glow within her.

Every morning the rest of the week, Matthew was outside the cafe, waiting to take her to school, and every evening he came in to drive her home. They met after the basketball game Friday, the last of the season, and Saturday he took her to another movie. Jennifer went through the week in a haze of astonishment and excitement, unable to concentrate on either school or her work. All she could think of was Matthew Ferris.

Saturday night, after the movie and a prolonged drink at the drive-in, Matthew drove to the spot where she always left him. He stopped the car and they talked, their fingers intertwined, his thumb stroking her palm and the soft inner flesh of her wrist. Once he raised her hand to his mouth and kissed it. Jennifer glanced at him, her stomach tightening in a strange combination of desire and fear. Every night when he brought her home he had kissed her, his kisses growing in length and intensity, until finally the pressure of his mouth moved her lips apart. Last night his tongue had crept into her mouth, startling her. She hadn't known what to do. Surely she wasn't supposed to allow that. It felt strange—yet it felt nice at the same time. Well, not nice, exactly, but exciting. Stirring.

She wondered if he would do it again. She wished he would. Yet she didn't want to have to face the situation. What did he think of her? She wanted to please him, to give him anything he desired. But she couldn't bear it if she did anything that made him think she was cheap like everyone said.

He kissed her. His lips were warm and soft as they moved on hers, urging her mouth open. He ran his tongue over her lips, and she clenched her hand. It was all so new. So hard to know how to react. His tongue slipped inside her mouth, and heat gushed through her. Jennifer thought about his hands on her body and knew she wanted to feel them. His arms went around her, pulling her to him. Her breasts were flattened against his chest; his arms were tight and strong around her, squeezing her until she was breathless— only she wasn't sure that was what made her breathless.

Matthew changed the slant of their mouths to kiss her even more deeply. She could hear the harsh quickness of his breath, feel its hot gust against her skin, and it excited her. She clung to him, her arms tight around his neck. Her fingers couldn't resist inching upward to brush his hair. He made a funny groaning noise and ground his lips against her so hard she could feel the sharpness of his teeth. And that excited her, too.

She hadn't realized. She had never expected this, that there would be something inside herself that made her want to do it. Made her breasts tingle to feel his touch. Made her want to arch up into him and kiss him back, as she was doing now, her tongue tangling with his.

Matthew's hands clenched painfully in her hair, but Jennifer hardly noticed. He broke away and buried his face in her hair, his breath shuddering and uneven. "Oh, Jenny. Jenny." He nuzzled her ear, and fresh shivers darted through her. "You're so beautiful."

His lips teased her earlobe, his breath caressing her. His tongue slipped into her ear. Then, very gently, he nibbled at the soft lobe, and Jennifer felt her insides melting, oozing away. "Matthew . . ."

He kissed her ear and neck and face with wild, hungry, brief kisses as if he wanted to love her everywhere at once. Jennifer leaned back, soft and warm, loving the feel of his mouth. His hand slid down from her shoulder to her breast, cupping the soft mound, and she stiffened, the haze of pleasure receding. Surely this was something a nice girl wouldn't allow. "Matthew, no."

He froze when she tightened up, then dropped his hand and turned away from her, gulping in breaths. He crossed his arms on the steering wheel and leaned his head against them. He didn't speak. It scared Jennifer. *He was angry.* She knew it. The last thing in the world she wanted was to make him mad. Yet she couldn't let him think . . .

"I'm not easy, Matt."

His head snapped up and he looked at her. "I never thought that, Jen, I swear. You're so beautiful, and I . . . I want you so badly. I can't help it."

His words did nothing to ease the quivering, clashing emotions in her. "I don't want you to think I'm cheap, that's all. My whole life, everybody's thought I was trash. I've heard the snickers, the whispers. But I'm not like what they say. I couldn't bear it if you thought that of me."

"Oh, Jen, I don't. I don't. I could never think anything bad of you. I don't want to—" He stopped, unable to deny that what he really wanted right now was to make love to her. That was all he thought about anymore. Her breasts. Her legs. Her mouth. Being sheathed in her. Jeez! All he had to do was think about her and he would turn hard as a rock. He wanted to have her, all right.

Yet he didn't expect her to let him. It was insane. Anything less than lovemaking would only make him hungrier. But the wild animal force in him wasn't controlled by reason. It just wanted and went after what it wanted until it was stopped. Insane. But that was the way things were. You necked until you were ready to explode, always trying for a little more. No reason, just unbridled energy and lust. Only Jennifer didn't seem to understand the rules. She thought his passion was somehow an indictment of her.

"Baby, I want you. I can't help myself. But that doesn't mean I think anything bad about you. I couldn't. I love you!"

Jennifer stared at him in astonishment. Matthew was almost as surprised as she. He hadn't really thought about it. But he knew it was true. He had never felt this way about a person before in his life. He could hardly get through the hours until he could see her again. He wanted to kiss her, touch her, talk to her, simply be with her.

"I'm crazy in love with you," he said again softly, and his eyes searched Jennifer's face, looking for her feelings. He pulled off his senior ring and silently extended it to her in his open palm. Jennifer looked down at it, and her mouth crumpled. Tears began to trickle down her cheeks. She reached out a hand that trembled slightly and closed her fingers around the large ring.

"Oh, Matt. I love you, too." It was she that moved across the console this time, flinging her arms around him and holding on for dear life. "I love you so much!"

Matthew and Jennifer were inseparable. He walked her to class. He picked her up on Sunday afternoon and spent the rest of the day with her. He took to coming to the cafe an hour before she got off, when the crowd was light, and talking to her whenever there wasn't a customer. Jennifer had not been in the habit of eating lunch at school, but now she sat with Matthew for those precious thirty minutes everyday, munching at a bag of chips and dreamily watching him.

All the time they were together, they were in a world of their own, where they didn't need anyone or anything else. Matthew no longer sat with Randy, Joe Bob, and Keith at lunch, preferring to have Jennifer to himself, and he rarely saw his friends any other time, either, except at track practice after school. He didn't ask any of them to double date. When he and Jennifer went to the drive-in, they sat alone in their car or at a table inside. Matthew was selfish, possessive of her.

And he was protective. There was no telling what

Randy Huffner might say that would hurt Jennifer's feelings. Randy had made a couple of remarks to Matthew that Matt had almost punched him for, but Randy had backed down at the sudden fierceness in Matthew's face. Matthew knew his friends didn't understand his relationship with Jennifer. They didn't approve. They figured you didn't date a girl like Jennifer, and he knew there was no way he could change their opinion. It created an awkwardness, a strain whenever he was with them, and he felt more comfortable without them around.

He didn't need anyone but Jennifer. Johnette left for Georgia, and it tugged at his heart, but there wasn't the pain he would have felt earlier because Jennifer was with him. She was his comfort, his surcease from pain, his kind and understanding friend. His glory and passion. He loved her as he'd never dreamed he could love anyone.

Warmed by his love, Jennifer came alive. She glowed as if lit from within, and people who before had thought her sexy or pretty now looked at her with astonishment and realized she was breathtakingly beautiful.

All her life, it seemed, she had been hungry for love, and now she had it in full measure. In return, the love stored up inside her came pouring out on Matthew. He was her world, her first thought in the morning and last at night. Everything she did was with him in mind. No longer did she dream of going to Hollywood and becoming a movie star; all she dreamed of was marrying Matthew someday. No longer did every extra cent go into savings. Now her salary and tips every week were spent on jewelry, shoes, and material for the dresses that she sewed in the home economics room after school. Money wasn't important anymore, and neither was the future. The only things that mattered were Matthew and looking good for him.

They drifted through March and into April, gloriously lost in each other. The weather warmed, and trees sprouted pale green buds. The little sarvis tree bloomed first, followed by the redbuds and dogwoods. The tiny white flowers of the spirea bushes spilled over fences and drooped heavily in front of houses, accented by the harsh gold forsythia. Wild plum trees blossomed among the heavy pines and tall oaks and elms. Jonquils, then tulips, bloomed in neat rows in front of the Ferris house. The ripening beauty of the spring seemed inseparable from their love, an extension of their own inner joy. The world was colorful and beautiful and alive, a perfect backdrop for the high drama of their lives.

Matthew knew he would never forget the warm spring nights spent sitting in his car, windows open to the sweet scent of honeysuckle growing wild along the fence on Jennifer's road. Each night when he brought Jennifer home they would park just past the turnoff from the highway, enclosed in velvet darkness, listening to the familiar, soothing night sounds—the whir of insects and the croak of frogs, the distant bark of a dog. They would talk and hold hands. Sometimes Matthew's hand would drift across her hair. Sometimes he would pull her across the console into his lap, and they would snuggle up together, dreaming, talking, laughing, cocooned from the world.

He would kiss her. And she would feel the flush of heat through his body. Matthew was always hungry for her, his kisses hot and desperate. He wanted to touch her, undress her, feel her body beneath his. There were times when he thought Jennifer would yield to him if he pressed her to, for her tongue twined around his just as ardently and her skin was as hot to the touch. She moaned when he slipped his hand beneath her blouse to touch her breasts, and her nipples were tight and hard beneath her thin brassiere. She twisted as he caressed her, squeezing her thighs together to ease the ache between them. Jennifer wanted him. Yet she always pulled back at some point and asked him to stop. If he had ignored her and just gone on or if he had kept asking her, he thought she loved him too much to deny him long.

But it was for that very reason that he stopped as soon as she asked. Jennifer would give in for love and then she would hate herself for doing it. She would doubt him—and herself. She would wonder if the things they had said about her were true, after all. Matthew would not think her easy because she let him love her, but she would. And she would fear that he thought so, too. He had seen how much her reputation hurt her, and he hated everyone for doing that to her. He couldn't do anything that might increase that hurt.

So Matthew let Jennifer take the lead, never asking more of her than she was willing to give, even though at times he thought he would explode from the effort of holding back. Someday, he told himself, she would come to trust him enough, to believe in his love enough to make love with him. Until then, he'd have to clamp down on the raw passion surging through him.

It was a wry irony to think of all the times he'd argued and begged and tried to tempt Shelly into going all the way with him. Yet now, when his passion was so hot that it made what he had felt for Shelly seem laughable, he wouldn't even try to pass the boundaries Jennifer set up. Because he loved her.

If the time they spent together in the bucket seats of his Mustang were sweet torture to Matthew, they were equally so to Jennifer. She had never dreamed that she could feel such a rush of desire, that she could want so much for their loving to continue to its natural end. Just looking at Matthew stirred her—seeing the taut cords of his arm as he opened a door for her or watching his hand spread out on the table between them at the cafe or looking at the curve of his lower lip. Once he glanced up at her as they were sitting at the drive-in, sipping their drinks, and suddenly his eyes went dark and the skin around his mouth tightened. Jennifer knew that he was thinking about touching her, and desire flamed through her. When he kissed her, when his hands roamed her body, she quivered all through, and she wanted him to make love to her. She ached to feel him.

Fear held her back, fear that she was the slut everyone thought her, fear that Matthew would despise her for it, fear that she would lose him. The one thing in the world

Jennifer knew she could not bear was losing Matthew. So when he kissed her, she pulled away eventually and whispered a shaky, "No."

Time hardly moved, each day part of a seemingly endless stream of contentment. Yet, conversely, at the same time it rushed, one moment March and the next, April, and then suddenly May and time for graduation and the prom and summer. It seemed to Matthew that suddenly he looked up and saw that it was the end of the school year. Three months of summer lay ahead of him—three months before he went off to college.

He didn't want to go.

All his life he'd planned to go to Alabama. He and his father had talked about it ever since he could remember. Everytime they'd practiced throwing and catching the football in the front yard, his dad had called him the future quarterback of the University of Alabama. His father had talked about his own career with 'Bama, and Matthew had wanted to be just like him. Only back when Sam was there, the "Bear" hadn't been the coach, but now he was, and that made it perfect—if perfection could be improved. The Crimson Tide. Matthew had heard it all his life. He'd wanted it all his life. And now he hated the thought of going there.

He wouldn't have believed it. None of his friends would believe it. His father least of all. If he didn't go, his father's disappointment in him would be boundless. Matthew would let everyone down. He had signed a letter of intent. It was tradition. Duty. Responsibility. It was what he had always wanted.

Against all that was one lone girl. How could he leave Jennifer? How could he bear to not see her next year except at the Christmas holidays? He was supposed to visit his mother in Georgia this summer. He had told her he would, but he knew now that he would cut down the visit

drastically. He didn't want to be without Jen that long.
How much less could he stand to be away from her for a
whole school year? He couldn't think of anything more
bleak. He felt suspended between two impossibilities.

The night of the Junior-Senior Prom, Matthew picked
Jennifer up at her house, the first time he'd ever managed
to talk her into letting him do so. He had flatly refused to
let her walk in her prom gown down the dusty road to their
usual meeting place, and finally Jennifer had agreed.

When Matthew saw her house, he understood some of
the reasons why Jennifer had never wanted him to go
there. When Mack Taylor opened the front door to him, he
understood the rest.

He had seen Mack over the years, but he'd never given
Mack's staggering form more than a haphazard glance.
Now he looked at him close up, seeing the stubble on his
chin, the broken capillaries aflame across his nose and
cheeks, the sagging gut in a dirty white undershirt. It was
grotesque to think that this was Jennifer's father and to see
traces of resemblance to her in the color of Mack's eyes
and the structure of his face before it went to seed.

Matthew nodded to him, unsure how to act in the face
of Mack's hostile, wavering gaze. "Mr. Taylor." He spoke
with the politeness drilled into him over the years. "I'm
here to take Jennifer to the prom."

The older man mumbled something and shot him a
knowing glance that left Matthew slightly confused. Mack
moved aside, shoving the screen door open to admit
Matthew. He grinned slyly. "Come in. Come in. Tain't
often we get a visit from a Ferris."

Matthew stepped inside and stood awkwardly, very aware
of the worn furniture around him and the bare plank floor
beneath his feet. Jennifer dressed nicely and always looked
so proper and neat that even though he had known the
Taylors were poor, he hadn't guessed the real extent of
their poverty. He was ashamed of himself for not realizing
it. It was obvious, if he had stopped to think about it. Old
Mack couldn't hold down a job longer than two days

running, and what little he did earn he no doubt spent on booze. Corey was gone. Jennifer's money from her part-time job was about all they had. He thought about the fact that Jennifer never ate lunch, except maybe a bag of chips or cheese crackers from the snack bar. He hadn't thought much about that, either, marking it down to her wanting to watch her weight, like girls seemed to do all the time. But now he wondered if it wasn't lack of money that made her decision, not concern about her figure, and he told himself he'd find a way to get lunch into her everyday without wounding her pride.

Mack made his way to the couch and sat down on it heavily. There was a bottle beside the couch, and he picked it up and took a swig. He grimaced, swallowing, and extended the bottle to Matthew. Matthew shook his head. "No, thanks."

"Too good to drink with me?" Mack asked, his eyes mocking and mean. "I always heard you were a perfect boy."

Matthew said nothing. He was realizing that it was difficult to talk to Jennifer's father. He wished Jennifer would hurry.

"Perfect except when it comes to one thing, though." Mack lolled back against the couch, grinning. "You got quite an itch when it comes to the girl, don't you?" His eyes flickered toward the door on the other side of the room, and his smile turned even more leering. "Speaking of the devil. Maybe I should say she-devil."

Matthew turned in the direction Mack was looking and stared. Jennifer stood in the doorway leading to the next room. She wore a long dress made out of shiny blue satin, belted under her breasts. Her hair was done up, with a tendril on either side of her face twisted into a fragile curl, and it made her look suddenly as much woman as girl. She knocked the wind out of him.

"Hello, Matthew."

"Jennifer." He guessed his heart was in his eyes, because the old man cackled.

"Gotta hand it to you, Sis. You got this one hooked but good."

Jennifer shot her father a glance of withering dislike and walked across the room to Matthew. A flush rose in her cheeks at her father's behavior, and she wished—not for the first time—that she hadn't let Matthew talk her into picking her up at the house.

"Why'd you keep him hidden so long?" Mack went on, his watery eyes gleaming with malice. "What do you do, give it to him in the back seat of his car? Or do you sneak him in through the window at night when I'm asleep?"

Jennifer's face paled, and she looked so sick and hurt that Matthew wanted to kill Mack for doing it to her. He started toward the couch, his fists clenching, but Jennifer grabbed his arm. "No. Matthew, please, let's go."

Jennifer thought she could have watched her father drop down dead right then and not felt a single regret. Mack wanted his kids as ruined as himself; he wanted to believe they already were.

He had spoiled the evening that she had dreamed about for so long, that she had worked and planned so hard to make perfect. She had spent so much money on her dress that she felt guilty, and even more time sewing it. It was to have been the most wonderful dress for the most wonderful night of her life. And already Mack had trampled all over her happiness. She was sick with humiliation. What must Matthew think of her father? Of her?

Jennifer rushed out the door and down the steps to the yard, Matthew right behind her. "I'm so sorry," she said in a low voice, not daring to even look at Matthew.

Matthew put his arm around her, stopping her, and pulled her close. "I love you."

"Oh, Matt!"

"Shh. Don't cry; you'll ruin your mascara, and we can't have that. You're going to be the most gorgeous girl at the prom."

"I shouldn't have let you come here."

"I insisted. Besides, I'm tough. I can take it. What did

you think—that you could put up with him all your life and I couldn't stick it out for five minutes?"

"You shouldn't have had to."

"I'd like to shoot him for what he said." How could a father insult his own daughter that way? Particularly one as sweet and lovely as Jennifer! It seemed the height of perversity. "It makes me ill to think of you having to put up with him all these years." He curled his fingers under Jennifer's chin and tilted her face up to look into her eyes. "Does he ever hurt you?"

"He threatens a lot." It was hard to get out the words. She felt humiliated before him. "He hasn't hit me in years. Corey told him he'd kill him if he did. And Corey would, I think."

Matthew's arm tightened around her so hard she could scarcely breathe. "But Corey's gone. If he ever hurts you, come to me. I won't let him touch you. Promise you'll come to me."

Jennifer looked up at him, the tight sickness receding from her face. The sight of her father hadn't turned him away from her. "I promise. Oh, Matthew, I love you so much."

He thought about going to Tuscaloosa next fall and leaving Jennifer alone with that twisted old drunk, nobody to protect her, and he knew he couldn't go. Mack Taylor had shown him his decision tonight.

He hugged Jennifer again, hard. "Come on, now, let's go to the dance. This is going to be the best night of our lives."

The familiar old gymnasium was a magic place that night, crisscrossed with twisted streamers of crepe paper, glittery stars dangling from the steel beams above. There were tables of refreshments at one end of the gym and a raised platform at the other where a band from Fayetteville played. There were a few tables and chairs near the refreshment area and a photographer taking pictures of couples on a bench beneath a plastic arbor.

Jennifer had never been to a dance before, and the place

looked beautiful to her. Matthew had seen it this way many times before, but tonight with Jennifer it seemed special. They danced to the music in the dimly lit half of the gym, and the slow tunes were the best of all.

The dance went on until one, but the couples began to drift away after midnight, most of them going to their favorite spots down by the river. Jennifer and Matthew drove home slowly, silent and dreamy in the moonless night. He took the road to her house and drove on past the house, stopping a mile or so beyond it where the road ended at a barbed wire fence.

"That's part of Fred Johnson's land," Jennifer commented, nodding toward the fence.

It wasn't really, Matthew knew. It was his father's land that lay adjacent to the Johnson place which his father had leased to Fred for over fifteen years. Most people assumed it was Fred's, he had worked it so long, but Sam had shown Matthew all the pieces of land around that belonged to Sam and would someday belong to Matthew. He was the heir to the kingdom. Matthew knew that eventually he would have to take over, but the idea had always made him feel restless and confined. He wanted to go someplace else, see something else, not just settle down in his niche in Sweet River.

But, looking over at Jennifer, that didn't seem such a terrible thing now. She eased his thirst for a taste of the world—for anything. Matthew traced the line of her cheekbone with his forefinger and slid it down to her lips.

Jennifer smiled, loving the faint roughness of his skin against her lips, the trace of salt. She kissed his finger.

He smoothed back her hair. "Jennifer, I've been thinking about something."

She glanced at him, alarms going off in her. Her mind leaped to at least ten horrible possibilities. "What?"

"I'm not going to Alabama in the fall."

It was so far removed from anything she'd expected that it took a moment for her to absorb what he had said. "What?"

"I don't want to go. I don't want the scholarship. I'll go to the university here instead."

"Fayetteville?"

"Yeah."

"But why?"

He gave her a funny look and smiled. "Why do you think? Because of you, silly."

"Me!"

"Yeah. I don't want to leave you. Do you realize how far Tuscaloosa is from here? I'd never see you except at Christmas and in the summer."

Jennifer's knees began to tremble. The past few weeks she had been depressed everytime she thought about Matthew leaving in the fall, certain that she would lose him to the sophisticated beauties at the university. She had never imagined . . . "But what about football?"

"They've got a hell of a program at the University. They tried to recruit me, too. I would have to sit out a year because I signed with Alabama, but I'm sure Arkansas would take me my sophomore year. Arkansas will probably win the conference this year. Hell, they could be number one in the country. There's nothing sacred about 'Bama."

"But your father wants you to go there."

"My father doesn't own me."

Jennifer smiled. "Then you're one of the few things in this town he doesn't."

"I don't want to leave you, Jen. I can't. If I go to school in Fayetteville I could come home every weekend to see you. I could make sure you're all right." *I could hold you and kiss you and feel the excitement rip through me.*

"Oh, Matthew . . ." She didn't know what to say. Matthew's father would be furious, and it swelled her heart to think that he would face Sam's fury for her. "I just don't want you to regret it."

"I won't. Not ever."

"But you did want to go to Alabama. You must have."

"Maybe." He shrugged. "Sometimes I'm not sure how much I wanted to go for me and how much of it was for Dad. Because it was what he expected." He smiled at her. "It doesn't even come close to being as important as you. I love you more than anything in the world. I want to marry you."

"Marry me!" Jennifer's mouth dropped.

"Sure. Is that such a big surprise? When you finish school, I mean—that is, if I can wait two years."

"Matthew..." Jennifer took his hand between both of hers and raised it to her lips. She looked at him, her eyes soft and swimming with tears; it turned him to butter inside. "Oh, Matthew."

"Jennifer! What's the matter? Why are you crying? If you don't want to commit yourself that far in the future—"

"Oh, no! No. It's not that. I'd marry you in a second or in ten years or whenever you wanted. It's just—you make me so happy. I don't deserve you. But I love you. I'll marry you anytime, anywhere. I love you."

Matthew told his father about his decision the next day after church. Matthew had never seen his father at such a loss before. For a long moment Sam simply stared at him, and when he spoke, his voice was slightly unsteady. "What?"

"I said I'm not going to Alabama this fall."

Sam was quick to recover from the shock. His face hardened and he frowned. "Is this your idea of a joke? Because if it is..."

"No. It's not a joke. I don't want to go to Alabama to school." Matthew managed to keep his voice level and his hands still. He knew from experience that his father would seize on any sign of weakness or emotion.

"You've signed a letter of intent. You can't back out now."

"People have done it before."

"People who don't mind going back on their word."

"People who aren't afraid to admit they've made a mistake. I want to stay here and go to the university."

"We considered the University of Arkansas before and rejected it, if you'll remember." Sam's voice was patient, the anger held in check.

"You mean *you* rejected it."

"Are you implying that you didn't make the choice?"

"No. I chose Alabama, but it was always the school you wanted me to choose. You had a hundred arguments against the others, but none against 'Bama."

"Of course I preferred my alma mater, but you can't say I wasn't fair. I kept an open mind. I listened to what Royal and Broyles and all the others had to say. You and I went over all their good and bad points later. Right?"

"Yes."

"And you agreed that, everything considered, Alabama was the one. The chance to learn from Coach Bryant."

"That's right. It's true. But I changed my mind! Look, Arkansas has one of the best football programs in the country."

"Of course, but academically—"

"Academically? You aren't worried about academics. If you were, you'd want me to go to Tulane or Rice or someplace like that."

"It's the totality of the program."

"It's the fact that you went there youself!"

"This is pointless." Sam's voice was clipped and cold. "None of these things are the issue here, are they? The reason you want to go to Arkansas next year has nothing to do with the school or with football or with me. It's because of that girl."

"Her name is Jennifer Taylor. And yes, she's why I want to stay. I love her."

Sam sighed. After their initial conversation about the Taylor girl's unsuitability, Sam had kept his mouth shut on the subject. He knew that nothing would keep a teenage romance alive faster than parental opposition. He also knew that reason held little sway when a boy's blood was running hot. So he had kept quiet, assuming that eventually it would run its course. Matthew would tire of the girl; he was bound to once he'd had her.

But it hadn't worked out that way. Maybe the little piece was more clever than Sam had thought; maybe she was stringing Matt along, holding him off until he agreed to marry her. The thought chilled Sam. "Damn it, Matt! I won't let you throw away your entire college career on a slut from Haskell's Ridge."

Matthew's face flamed with color, and he jumped out of his chair. "Don't say that about her! I won't let anyone talk about Jennifer that way, including you!"

"I can't believe you're this naive."

"It has nothing to do with naivete. You don't know a goddamn thing about Jennifer except the rumors you've heard. They're all lies."

"Don't tell me you're the only kid in town who hasn't gotten into her pants."

Matthew's eyes flamed, and for an astonished moment Sam thought his son was actually going to hit him. Finally Matthew said through clenched teeth, "I can't talk to you."

He spun on his heel and stalked across the room to the door.

"Matthew!" The years of authority in Sam's voice stopped him at the door. Matthew turned, his face closed. "If you don't go to Alabama you won't be getting any money from me."

"You think Arkansas won't give me a scholarship? I don't need your money, Dad." Matt paused. "I'm surprised. You used to be more subtle about forcing your will on people."

Sam watched him leave. His hands curled into fists on the arms of his chair. Fury and frustration ate at him. He'd be damned if he'd let that little girl ruin his son's life! First Matthew refused to go to Alabama; next he would decide he wanted to marry her—or she would make the decision for him by getting pregnant. Sam could see Matt in two years, barely twenty and tied to a girl whose lack of grace and class would blaze glaringly as she grew older. She would keep him bound to her with children. It would be a mistake that would haunt Matthew the rest of his life.

There was no way Sam would let that girl get her hook into Matthew. He had protected his only son all his life. And now he would protect him from himself.

He sat for a moment, frowning out the window. Then a small, tight smile touched his lips and he rose and went to the telephone. He flicked open the small directory, found a number, and dialed it. A teenaged boy answered at the other end. "Huffner residence."

"Randy?"

"Yes?"

"This is Sam Ferris. I'd like to talk to you this afternoon. It's about Matthew."

* *Chapter 5* *

"What does he want to see us for?" Keith Oliver complained, folding his long, skinny frame into the backseat of Randy's car. Joe Bob got in the front.

"How should I know? Mr. Ferris just said it was about Matthew and to bring one or two guys I could trust."

"Trust?" Keith repeated. "That sounds weird."

Randy shrugged and pulled out of the driveway and into the street. Joe Bob turned on the radio without saying a word. He had little curiosity and was content, as always, to follow along in the others' wake.

"Why would a grown-up want to talk to us about his

son?'' Keith went on reasonably, leaning forward and resting his arms on the back of the front seat.

''He probably wants us to talk Matt out of his obsession with Jennifer Taylor.''

Keith snorted. ''Sure. Those two are so close you'd have to separate them surgically. Hell, we hardly even see Matt anymore.''

For a moment hurt glimmered in his eyes. Once Keith had considered himself Matthew's best friend. He had been the first one Matt called when he wanted to go somewhere or talk to someone. Most of the time, Randy or Joe Bob would join them. The four of them had been good friends since grade school, even before, really. Keith couldn't remember a time when he hadn't known Matthew Ferris, when he hadn't been Matt's friend.

Then Jennifer Taylor had come along and wrapped Matt around her little finger. It had been different when Matt was going with Shelly. Hell, they all dated; Keith went steady himself. But Matt and Shelly had gone out on double dates with Keith and Mary Ann. They had all sat together at the movies or hung around each other's cars at the drive-in. And the four of them had done stuff together, just the guys, gone hunting or driven over to Fayetteville and gotten drunk or just sat around listening to records and talking about football and girls.

Keith guessed Matt still would say he was their friend. But the old companionship was gone. Matthew spent all his time with Jennifer, and it seemed like the only time Keith saw him was during track practice after school. It was crazy. Matt was like a different person. He was eaten up with Jennifer Taylor. Keith wouldn't have admitted it, none of the guys would have, but he was jealous of Jennifer. She had taken Matt out of their lives.

Sure, Randy and Joe Bob were still there, but it wasn't the same, anymore than the football team or the basketball team would have been the same without Matthew. He was special, the greatest guy in school. Joe Bob was nice, but he could be a real clunk; he didn't catch a lot of Keith's jokes or understand what Keith said almost before he said it, like Matt did. Randy was fun, but he got on Keith's nerves after a while. He was too abrasive, too full of himself. Keith knew that he himself was too quiet, too lazy. It was Matt who sparked them, who made them fit together. Without him, nothing was as much fun.

Keith settled back in his seat, feeling faintly depressed. He really didn't want to see Matt's father. He had never liked Sam Ferris much, and he didn't want to talk about Matthew with him. He wished he had told Randy he wouldn't go. But no one turned down a request from Sam Ferris.

Randy stopped in front of the Ferris house and the boys slid out. Keith felt strange. It had been over two weeks since he'd been here, and then Matthew hadn't been at home. Before Jennifer it seemed like he'd spent half his time here.

Sam Ferris answered the door and took them into his darkly panelled study. Keith settled gingerly into a heavy leather chair. The room intimidated him. He could see it had the same effect on Joe Bob, though Randy got a cockier look on his face. Sam offered them soft drinks, but they refused. Keith tugged at the knees of his blue jeans, a quick, nervous gesture. Sam's eyes flickered toward him and a smile touched his lips.

"No need to be so jumpy, Keith. This isn't an inquisition."

"No, sir."

Sam sat down on the edge of his desk, one foot braced against the floor. Authoritative but casual. Part friend, part grown-up. He figured it was the best way to handle them. He looked at Randy. Randy was the key. Keith was soft, softer than Matt, and Joe Bob Wilson was only a follower. But Randy had brains and wiliness and a hard shell. Without Matt in the group, Randy was the power figure.

"No doubt you're curious about why I wanted to see you."

"A little."

"Well, as I said, it's about Matthew. I'm worried about

him." He had to get through the barrier between adult and teenager to the natural alignment of class among them. There was no point talking about Jennifer Taylor's unsuitability or family tradition or the dangers of marrying young. He went straight to the point most likely to touch them. "Matt told me tonight that he's planning to give up his football career."

"What!" They couldn't have been more startled or horrified if he had said Matthew intended to commit suicide. Slow-moving Joe Bob was so upset he even jumped to his feet, then glanced around, embarrassed, and sat back down.

"He's decided not to go to Alabama. You know what that means. Since he signed a letter of intent with Alabama, he's ineligible to play anywhere next year. After he sits out a year nobody will be as hot to get him. After all, when he's backed out once, any coach is bound to distrust him."

"But why? Where's he going?" Keith asked. "What is he going to do?"

"Why?" Sam repeated, his voice filled with scorn. "Because he wants to stay close to Sweet River."

"He wants to stick around Jennifer." Randy's face was grim, his wide mouth pinched in at the corners. "Damn!" He glanced quickly at Sam. "Excuse me, sir."

Sam gave a little grunt of amusement. "Don't apologize. That's precisely how I feel."

"I can't believe it." Joe Bob shook his head. "Matt's always wanted to go to Alabama. He was so happy when they offered him a scholarship."

"Of course he was," Keith put in bitterly. "That was before he started dating Jennifer."

Sam watched the anger and resentment in them build. "I have tried not to say anything. I want Matt to make his own decisions, even if sometimes they're mistakes. But this one . . ." He shook his head.

"He's crazy. Out of his head about her," Randy responded flatly. "He wouldn't listen to you or anybody."

"Matthew thinks she's some sort of angel. He told me tonight that it's only rumors about her, that she hasn't—"

"Oh, sure!" Randy rolled his eyes. "Sure she hasn't slept around. And I'm Joe Namath."

"I don't think Matthew would believe it unless he was given proof of it," Sam told him.

"How could you prove it?"

"I imagine he'd believe someone who had actually slept with her."

"We might find someone willing to admit it," Keith said doubtfully, "but I don't think Matt would believe him."

Randy's eyes met Sam's, and they changed subtly. Sam knew he understood. "He might if he knew the guy," Randy said. "If the guy was his friend."

Keith glanced over at Randy. "Are you talking about you?"

Randy rose slowly. "Yeah. I guess I am."

Hope and excitement stirred in Keith. "But he'll be furious. He'll hate you."

"Nah. Not for long. In a few months Matt will be grateful to me for getting him out of the situation. Look, he's just temporarily gone off his head about her. Once he realizes what she is, he'll get over it. He'll go back to normal. He won't stay mad. You know Matt. He never stays mad long."

"I think you ought to do it," Joe Bob agreed. "It's the only way you'll get her hooks out of him." Joe Bob's attitude surprised Keith; he hadn't realized how much Joe Bob resented Jennifer's intrusion into Matt's life. Perhaps he disliked it as much as Keith; Matt had always helped Joe Bob more and had more patience with him than the others. Maybe he felt equally deserted by Matt.

Curiously, Joe Bob's anger heightened Keith's own. Jennifer was ruining Matt. She didn't love him. She couldn't, or she wouldn't keep him here instead of letting him play football. "Maybe you ought to."

"We all ought to."

"Huh?" Joe Bob blinked in surprise.

"Are you crazy?" Keith cried. "I can't tell Matt I've gone to bed with her. I've never even been near her."

"So what? Neither have I. Improvise. You always make A's on your short stories."

Keith stared. "You're going to lie to him?"

"Come on, Oliver. Quit acting like the Tooth Fairy, for Christ's sake. So what if I haven't actually slept with her? She's done it with lots of guys. The important thing is that Matt realizes it instead of fooling himself."

Keith swung around to look at Sam. Sam gazed blandly back at him. "You don't mind if he lies to Matthew?" Keith asked incredulously.

"I'll tell you frankly, Keith. That girl is trying to ruin my son. How long do you think it will be before she persuades him to marry her? And how long after that before Matt realizes what he's done, what he's given up? I don't want my boy to have to live with regrets and misery the rest of his life. Do you? Do you think it really matters if the truth is fudged a little for Matt's sake?"

Keith gnawed at his lower lip. Randy made him sound like a prig, and now Matt's father was acting like he didn't care enough about Matthew.

"You're just a coward," Randy sneered.

"That's not true!"

"Sure it is. You're afraid Matt'll sock you. Hell, Joe Bob and I won't let him hurt you. Joe Bob's not afraid, are you, Joey? You'll tell Matt, just like me."

"Yeah. I'll tell him."

Randy turned back to Keith, his expression smugly questioning.

"I can't lie to him, Randy." Keith felt low, like he really was a coward. But he couldn't lie to Matthew! He hesitated. "But I'll go with you when you tell him."

"Okay. Just be sure you don't mess it up."

"I won't. I won't say anything."

* * *

Jennifer was sitting on her front porch waiting for him when Matthew drove up. He was late because he'd driven around for a while after talking with his father, trying to rid himself of his anger before he saw Jennifer.

Jennifer didn't care that he was late. She was never angry or even irritated at Matthew. She couldn't imagine it. Besides, today her world was too sparkling to be dimmed by anything. Matt loved her and wanted to stay with her.

They drove out to the lake and took one of the dirt roads that wound back into the trees, coming out on a cove where there were no other people. Matthew spread out an old blanket on the ground near the shore, and they sat watching the undulating water. Matthew peeled off his shirt. Jennifer had made sandwiches, and they ate them with the chips and drinks they'd picked up at the bait and tackle shop at the entrance to the lake.

It was still too cool to swim, but the sun on them was warm enough to bring a faint sheen of perspiration to Matthew's forehead and along his shoulders. Jennifer lay back on the blanket and watched him. She never tired of looking at Matthew. His body was lean, despite the muscles put there by sports, youthfully long and spare and narrow-hipped. She loved the bony outcropping of his shoulders, the dip created by his collarbone, the curve of muscles in his arm and across his back. He was already beginning to tan in the way she never did, his skin golden and without freckles, satin stretched over the thrust of muscle and bone. His hair was getting shaggy and she was sure it would get more so throughout the summer. It was becoming sunstreaked, too, from being outdoors, dark blond strands mingling with the brown.

Jennifer reached out and smoothed a strand of hair into place behind Matthew's ear. She would have liked to sink her hands into his hair and comb through it, just as she would have liked to trace the patterns of hair on his chest and feel its texture against her skin, but she was too shy to do such things, too uncertain of what he would think of her.

Matthew turned and smiled at her. He eased down beside her, propping himself up on his elbow so he could look at her. She was so beautiful it made him hurt. His thumb traced her eyebrows and cheekbones. The heat in his loins was instantaneous and familiar and no less intense for its familiarity. He loved it, and he dreaded it for the conflict it always brought.

"Can you get off work Thursday morning?" he asked, delaying the physical contact he knew was coming, enjoying the anticipation.

Jennifer nodded. The way Matthew looked at her stirred her. Her mouth opened slightly. It seemed easier to breathe that way. "Why?"

"It's your birthday, that's why." He smiled indulgently. "You think I'd forget?" He already had her present tucked away in the top drawer of his dresser, a ring with an iridescent opal set in gold lacework. Delicate, elusive, gleaming with a cool fire, it had reminded him of Jennifer the instant he saw it in the jewelry store in Fayetteville. It was the most expensive thing he'd ever bought with his own money—and not worth nearly enough for her.

"I wanted to take you out to dinner someplace special Thursday. Springdale or Fayetteville. Would you like that?" His fingers cupped her face gently, his thumb skimming over her lips. Her mouth was soft and seductive. He thought of how it looked after they'd been kissing, wide and moist and almost bruised. Desire clenched in his gut.

"Yes. I'd like that." Jennifer gazed into his eyes. She knew what he was doing, playing with them, teasing them, and it was as frustrating and pleasurable for her as it was for him. She wanted to move her body, to touch him, and she knew that either one would stop the leisurely, torturous anticipation. But she didn't move. She liked too much the darkness in his eyes and the heaviness of his mouth.

His hand moved downward over her neck. Jennifer's eyes fluttered closed. There were times, like now, when she wanted to lie back and open herself to him. Her breasts ached for his touch. She wanted to feel his fingers on them without even the material of her bra between. His hand slid over her breast and paused, fingers spreading out to cover it.

Jennifer's breath was shallow. Matthew felt its rise and fall beneath his palm. He looked at her breasts, his hand big and possessing over one, the other nipple puckering visibly beneath the cloth of her blouse. His hand tightened on her. It was nothing compared to what he wanted to do. He thought about taking her nipple into his mouth, blouse and all. He thought about her breasts without the concealing clothes and he wondered, as he always wondered, how her breasts would look—how they were shaped, how white they were, how large the circles of her nipples, what color.

He began to unbutton her blouse, his fingers trembling. He felt huge and clumsy and so eager he might burst. Jennifer made no protest, only covered her eyes with her arm. He moved apart the sides of her blouse, exposing her chest and stomach. A white cotton bra broke the stretch of naked skin, cupping the fullness of her breasts. Matthew's hand slid under her back and up to the catch of her brassiere. He unfastened it and pushed her brassiere down. He forgot how to breathe.

Her breasts were full and firm and tilted up slightly at the tips. The dark rose nipples were puckered and pointing. Tentatively, almost reverently, Matthew brushed his fingertips across one nipple and felt its tightening response. His fingers spread out over her breast. It was incredibly soft. His hand was dark against her milk-white skin. Blood pounded in his head. He could hear his own breath rasping through his throat.

He bent and kissed the top of her breast, then the nipple. Nothing had ever felt so good. Nothing had ever excited him as much. "You're beautiful."

His breath was hot against her skin. Jennifer didn't dare open her eyes. She loved the touch of his hand and mouth.

Her breast seemed to swell, to reach toward him. She loved him so much. She wanted him so much.

Matthew's lips grazed her breast and settled on her nipple. His mouth was hot and gentle. His tongue slid over the taut bud and Jennifer made a noise deep in her throat. Suddenly his mouth wasn't gentle anymore.

He moved onto her, settling into her soft body, and Jennifer reached out for him. His skin was slick with sweat beneath her fingertips. His mouth went to her other breast, his hand cupped around the quivering flesh. He slid upward, dragging his body over hers, and she felt the swollen hardness of him, knew his desire. He said her name; it was a groan in his mouth. She felt his breath against her lips. She opened her eyes. His eyes were hazy and dark, the pupils huge.

"I love you."

He kissed her mouth. His tongue went deep. He wanted to be inside her. He wanted to fill her everywhere. He wanted to bury himself in her until they were part of each other. Matthew's arms went around her and he rolled over onto his back, pulling Jennifer on top of him and wrapping his legs around her.

They rolled across the blanket, lost in a delirium of desire, unable to get close enough, to have enough of each other. Matthew's mouth was desperate, his hands frantic. His fingers dug into her buttocks, pushing her into him, and he ground his hips against her pelvis. His mouth trailed along her neck and onto the hard plane of her chest, to her breasts. He lost himself in them, feasting on their sweetness, their softness. His hand went down to the juncture of her legs. She closed them around him, squeezing his hand tightly against her.

Matthew moved his hand, feeling the hardness of bone and exquisite softness. He thought he might die if he didn't have her. His hand left the sweet prison of her legs and popped open the snap of her jean shorts. The zipper rasped down and his hand went inside and beneath her cotton panties. There was the soft prickle of hair and heat and moisture. His desire was so intense he couldn't think. Every nerve in his body sizzled.

"Matthew!" Jennifer's voice was small and uncertain. She tightened all over.

He wanted to scream. He wanted to rip the shorts from her, to shove her legs apart and force her to take him. For a moment he thought he might not be able to stop.

But he did. He rolled from her and lay utterly still for a moment, the blanket beneath him clenched in his hands. Jennifer sat up dazedly, straightening and refastening her clothing.

"Matthew." She reached out a tentative hand to him, and he flinched at her touch. Tears filled her eyes. "I'm sorry. I shouldn't have let it go on so long. It's just . . . that I liked it so much."

He let out a groan. "Oh, God, Jen. So did I."

She wavered, stung with guilt. She hated herself for causing him pain. "Matthew, if you want, I—it's okay."

Matthew glanced at her sharply. His face was so taut and sharp it looked as if it had been carved with a knife. He doubted that Jennifer knew how very much he wanted to take her up on her offer, but he didn't want their first time to be with doubts in Jen's mind. He wanted her to trust him, to believe in him and want him as much as he wanted her. He didn't want her to think that he expected her to pay him for the words of love and marriage he'd spoken to her last night. It wouldn't be right if she came to him only out of guilt or gratitude, not because she desired him too much to do anything else. He had to refuse her—but, damn, it was hard! Matthew let out a funny little half breath and shook his head. "No. I'm okay. Just give me a minute."

He paused, then took her hand in his. "I want you to know something. I want to make love to you, and I hope that someday we will. That you'll feel okay with it. And when we do, I'll feel just the same about you; I'll love you just as much. I believe you, you know. I know you've never been with another guy. My wanting you is never, *never* anything to do with thinking you're cheap.''

Jennifer smiled tremulously and swallowed. She couldn't speak.

"I love you." He smiled and kissed her on the forehead. "Maybe we better go back. It's starting to get dark.''

Matthew returned to his house before 8:00. Finals started tomorrow and, though as a senior with good grades Matthew was exempt, Jennifer needed to study. He felt a little at loose ends coming home this early, and he was glad to see Randy Huffner's car in the drive. Randy would take his mind off the lonely evening. He hadn't spent much time with any of the guys since he'd started going with Jennifer. The four of them—him, Randy, Keith, and Joe Bob—had been buddies since grade school. He no longer felt the need to hang around with them as he once had. He guessed that was part of growing up, part of really falling in love. Still, they were part of him in a way that would never change, their friendship woven into the framework of his past.

Matthew pulled up behind Randy's car. His friends were sitting inside it with three of the doors open. Randy was turned sideways, smoking a cigarette, his feet stuck out onto the driveway. Matthew walked up, giving the car a slap. "Hey, guys. What are you doing? Come on in.''

They followed him as he went into the house through the garage. Their first stop was the kitchen; it always had been. Matthew opened the refrigerator and pulled out a bottle of Coke. He levered the top off with an opener, turning toward the others inquiringly. "What do you want to drink?''

"Nothing," Randy replied, and the other two shook their heads. Keith looked strange; he was staring out into the rest of the house, not looking at Matthew.

"Hey, what gives?" Matthew started to laugh, but it faltered. "Is something the matter?"

Randy cracked his knuckles. "Yeah. Yeah, something's the matter. We've been waiting for you. We came over a while ago, and your old man was here. He told us—he told us you were quitting football."

All three looked at Matthew as if he'd betrayed them. "No, now, wait—"

"You *are* going to Alabama, after all?" Keith asked, suddenly hopeful that it had somehow been a mistake.

"No. I'm not."

"You're staying here. For her." Randy's voice sneered on the last two words and Matthew straightened, his mouth suddenly tight.

"Yeah. I'm staying here for Jennifer. What does that have to do with you?" Matthew's gaze swept them, hard and remote—as if they were strangers, Keith thought.

"For Christ's sake, Matt, when are you going to wake up?" Randy exclaimed. "She's slept with everybody in town."

There was an instant of taut silence. Matthew's eyes flamed with fury. "Get out! Jesus! I thought you were my friend!"

"I am!" Randy retorted, a red flush of anger rising in his face. "That's why I never told you before. But I have to tell you now. I can't let you throw yourself away because you think you love a whore. She slept with me."

Matthew hit him before any of them could move, or even think. His fist crashed into Randy's face and knocked him backward. Randy stumbled and fell to the floor, blood trickling from his mouth. Joe Bob and Keith grabbed Matthew, hanging onto him with all their strength. Randy stared up at him, stunned.

"Goddamn you, you're lying!" Matthew shouted, lunging against the other two boys' hold. "You've always been a bragging, lying son of a bitch."

"I'm not!"

"I'm going to kill you. Damn it! Let go of me!" Matthew pushed Keith aside, tearing his arm loose.

Matthew was so strange, so different that it frightened Keith. He had never before seen the fury that contorted Matthew's face. He hadn't intended to say anything, but now, with Matt struggling with Joe Bob, fighting to get loose and hit Randy again, he couldn't be passive. He couldn't let Matthew rip the fabric of their friendship so completely.

"No! Wait!" Keith cried. "Matt, it's true. It's true! I had her, too!"

Matthew went suddenly still, and his face drained of all color. He turned his head slowly, carefully, to look at Keith. "What?"

"I've been with her down by the river." Keith colored and looked away. "I slept with Jennifer."

Matthew turned to Joe Bob. "You, too?"

Joe Bob nodded his head. He released his hold on Matt. It wasn't necessary anymore. The fight was gone from him. Matthew backed up a step. He looked around the kitchen as if he'd never seen it before.

At first he felt only shock, the stunned bewilderment of one caught in a collision between his love and his life. But then the realization began to sink in on him. They said Jennifer had slept with them, all three of them. Randy alone he wouldn't have believed. But Keith. And Joe Bob. All three of them. They'd been his best friends since he could remember. He knew them in a way that only those who have grown up together could. They wouldn't lie to him; they could never hurt him like this. They had to be telling the truth. He knew it, just as he knew them.

A searing pain sliced through the numbness deep into his gut. Jennifer had slept with them—and how many others? She had lied to him. She'd tricked him.

"She wanted to catch you, man," Randy said, cementing his position. He wiped at the blood on his lip and chin. Fury and embarrassment bubbled in him, and he directed it the only place he could—Jennifer Taylor. "She wanted to

be your girlfriend, not just a lay. So she held out on you.''
He saw by the expression in Matt's eyes that he was right.
''That's the only way she could keep you on the string.
Otherwise you'd have spent a couple of evenings in the
backseat of a car with her and then you'd have been
through. She had to tease you to keep you in line, and she
couldn't hold out on you if you knew she'd given it to
every other guy in town. So she lied.''

''Shut up, Randy.'' Keith jerked Randy to his feet. He
felt sick inside. Matthew was so white and rigid he looked
like he might crack right down the middle. Keith wished
he hadn't said anything. But there was no way he could
take it back now. Matthew would hate them forever.

Matthew backed up a step. Jennifer had lied to him right
from the start. *She'd manipulated him. Every step of the
way.*

''Matthew...'' Keith began tentatively.

Matthew glanced at him and Keith almost shivered.
There was something cold and dead in Matt's eyes. He
walked away from them and out the garage door, leaving
them standing in his kitchen. The three boys looked at
each other, then discovered that they really didn't want to
meet each others' eyes. ''Let's go home.''

Matthew got in his car and drove. He turned the tape
deck up as loud as it would go, blasting out Steppenwolf.
Now, following the pain, came anger, twisting through
him, mushrooming. He thought of how much he loved
Jennifer, of all the things he'd said to her, and how she
must have laughed to herself when she heard how well
she'd fooled him. What an idiot he'd been! He thought of
the times he had wanted her. This afternoon he had
thought he would die he'd been so hot for her. His blood
was still thrumming in his veins. But he had held back out
of respect. What a joke!

The anger built into fury, pushing aside the pain. That
would come back later to gnaw at his gut, but for now
there was only rage and hate. He wanted to smash something. He drove a hundred miles an hour around the

curving mountain roads and twenty minutes later was across the county line. He hadn't had any plan to go there, but he realized that was just what he wanted to do. There was a liquor store in the little town across the line, and a guy down the road a bit would buy liquor for him for a few extra bucks. He had the man buy him a fifth of Wild Turkey.

Matthew unscrewed the cap and took a gulp. He didn't drink often, and the straight swallow burned his throat and made his eyes water. But the second time it wasn't so bad. The third shot tasted real nice.

He turned back toward Sweet River, drinking and thinking about Jennifer. The alcohol stoked his rage, keeping it white-hot. How sweet she had always acted, how innocent, until sometimes he felt like an animal for desiring her so. And all the time . . .

Matthew turned off the highway onto the road to Jennifer's house. He jolted to a stop in front of her house, barely missing the pear tree, and tumbled out of the car. He climbed the steps. His bottle slipped from his hand and shattered on the cement steps. He pounded his fist against the door, and after a moment Jennifer answered it.

"Matthew?" She looked sweet and slightly puzzled and as beautiful as ever. It surprised him; somehow he'd thought that seeing her with the eyes of truth he wouldn't still want her. Still love her. The hurt came back in full measure, squeezing and twisting through the anger.

"Damn you!"

Jennifer stiffened. "You've been drinking." She felt as if her insides had dropped to the floor.

"Yeah. Real wicked, aren't I?"

"Matthew, what's the matter?" She took a hesitant step toward him and stopped at the fury on his face.

"I found out, that's what's the matter! Randy and Joe Bob and Keith came over tonight. They told me the truth."

Jennifer stared. "What truth? What are you talking about?"

"About you. The truth about you. That you put out for

them, like you did for every other goddamned guy in the county."

The blood left her face. For a moment Jennifer thought she would faint. "Matthew..." Her voice was tiny and lost. "What are you saying? It's not true. You know it's not true."

"Don't pull the innocent act on me again, sweetheart. It won't work. I'm not that dumb."

"They're lying!" Desperation seized her. She felt as if she were struggling, flailing around while someone slowly cut off her air. "Matthew, listen to me. Whatever they told you, they were lying."

"Why would they lie? Tell me that. They've got no reason. They're my *friends*. You're the one who's lying, who's been lying from the first!"

"Oh, yeah." Jennifer's mouth twisted. When it got down to it, he was like all the others. Her words dripped with years of accumulated bitterness. "You've known them all your life. They're your own kind, so they couldn't lie. It has to be me, right? I'm the one from the wrong side of the tracks, so naturally I'm the liar!"

"I believed you." Matthew shook his head, giving a little chuckle that had nothing to do with humor. "I thought you were so damn pure, but you're just what everybody said you were."

"And I believed you when you said you loved me!" Jennifer retorted heatedly. She felt betrayed and helpless and angry. He wouldn't believe her, she knew. Not if his friends told him that she had lied to him. She should have known that it couldn't last. There was no way a girl from Haskell's Ridge could be loved by Matthew Ferris. "You didn't really love me or you wouldn't take their word over mine. You just wanted to get me into the sack."

"Apparently I'm the only guy in town who hasn't managed that."

"I see." Jennifer looked at him with a remote coolness, as if he were a stranger, and somehow it tore his heart afresh. "That's why you're upset. You feel left out, like the only kid at the party who didn't get any candy. Poor Matthew.''

His nostrils flared. "You bitch!" Matthew had never known such rage. He wanted to explode, to hit her and curse her.

Jennifer swallowed her tears. She knew how to hide her emotions, and she would be damned if she'd let him see her cry over him. She reached up to the chain that held Matthew's class ring around her neck, but her fingers trembled so that she couldn't unfasten it. She broke the delicate chain and held out the ring to him.

Matthew looked at her hand as if she held a snake. "No." He backed up a step. "I don't want it." It was too much for him; he couldn't touch the ring that had lain against her skin for three months, warm with her body heat. It had joined them, and he couldn't bear the reminder. "I just don't want to see you again."

Jennifer turned paler at his words, but she didn't flinch or say anything. Matthew turned and slammed out of the door. She hurled the ring after him, and it crashed against the door and fell, bouncing across the floor. She dropped to her hands and knees and searched for it. When she found it, she curled her fingers around it so tightly that the metal bit into her palm. She began to cry, holding the ring and rocking back and forth.

Jennifer failed her final the next day and barely passed the others. She was numbed and battered by her grief, wrapped in misery, and the only thing that kept her going to school was her pride. Everyone looked at her with sly sidelong glances, eager to see her pain and embarrassment. But she refused to give them the satisfaction. If there was one thing she had learned from her mother, it was never to let the others see the pain or fear she felt. Grimly she stuck it out through final exams. And she stayed at the cafe despite the fact that she had to see Sam Ferris at his favorite table every morning. He never glanced in her direction, but just seeing him was like a fresh cut of the knife.

She didn't see Matthew. She waited, one minute bitterly sure that he had never loved her, the next crazily hopeful that he would come tell her he was sorry. He didn't.

Jennifer crept into graduation at the school gym and stood back by the door, in the hopes of seeing Matthew, but he wasn't there. His name was called and his diploma put aside. Two weeks later Mary Jim mentioned that she'd heard Matthew had gone to Georgia for the summer to visit his mother.

Her last hope died. It was really and truly over. Matthew was out of her life. The night she realized that, Jennifer lay in bed and cried for two hours. The door to her bedroom opened, startling her, and Mack came in. He walked over to the bed and stood looking down at her. Jennifer wondered dully what he wanted. She was too miserable to be scared.

He patted her hand, astonishing her. "Life's hell, ain't it?"

Jennifer curled her hand around his, squeezing a little bit of comfort from him. "Yes, Daddy. It is, for a fact."

"People love to have somebody to look down on." He grinned derisively. "I've made them happy that way most of my life." He stood for another moment, awkwardly holding her hand, then shuffled back out the door.

Jennifer hadn't thought that Mack had even noticed her misery, let alone cared. Most of the time he seemed intent on making her unhappy. Not for the first time, she wondered how he really felt about her. She wondered how she felt about him. That, she guessed, was something that would never be answered.

She sat up in bed and wiped her eyes, pulling her knees up and wrapping her arms around them. The summer stretched out bleakly before her. Her whole life stretched out bleakly before her. She could see nothing except more of the same—going to school and working at the cafe, alone, an object of contempt. Daddy was right. People liked to look down on others, and they weren't about to let her climb out of her place in life at Sweet River.

She thought of the plan she'd had to go to California before Matthew came into her life, the money she'd saved. Los Angeles. Hollywood! For the first time since Matthew had left her there was a flame of life inside her. She could act; she knew she could. And in the movies her beauty would be an advantage, not a hindrance. Nobody knew her there; she could build a new life for herself, a new identity. She would get over Matthew. She would be someone. People would love her.

What was the point of waiting until she graduated from high school? She was sixteen now and already looked like a woman. Having a high school diploma wouldn't get her a thing in the movies.

Jennifer jumped out of bed and rushed to her closet. She pulled her grandfather's cardboard suitcase from the back of the closet and began to pack.

The next morning she turned in her notice at Byers' Cafe and walked straight to the bank, where she closed out her account. She caught the 11:07 Greyhound to Fayetteville and Tulsa. And Los Angeles.

Los Angeles, June 20, 1987, 8:15 A.M.

Liz Chandler stood in front of the television set, staring at it, willing information from it. The reporter talked about wind shear and thunderstorms. "I don't give a damn about that! Why doesn't he say who was on it?"

She didn't realize that she was trembling all over. Her face was the color of flour. "Goddamn it! Why did Jennifer have to go to New York today!"

Liz turned toward her receptionist, who was watching her, transfixed. It was almost as much of a shock to Carol to see her boss this shaken as it was to hear that Jennifer might be dead. Jennifer Taylor! No, it couldn't be possible. She was the best, the most beautiful, the nicest—Carol had been almost overcome with excitement and awe the first time Jennifer walked into the office. She had been beautiful, just as she was on the screen, yet she had been so real and nice, like anyone else, and that had only increased Carol's admiration for her. She couldn't be dead. She couldn't!

She must have blurted out the thought because Liz responded to it. "No. Surely not." Liz glanced down at her desk as though she had never seen it before and wasn't quite sure what it was. She straightened a stack of papers. "Karen!"

"Of course." Carol grasped at the idea as if Liz had come up with a reason Jennifer couldn't be on that plane. "Sure. Karen will know what flight she's on. Maybe it wasn't even today."

"Yeah. Maybe." But Liz had had dinner with Jennifer just the night before and she was sure Jennifer had said she was leaving today. She was also certain it was an early morning Trans Con flight. Still, she hoped.

Liz picked up the receiver she had let drop earlier and depressed the button to get a dial tone She pushed the single digit for Jennifer's home office. It rang twice, and the cool, efficient voice of Jennifer's personal secretary came on the line. "Karen Olechsy."

"Karen. Liz. Where's Jennifer?"

"In the air, I guess. She left early this morning, before I got here. She's flying to New York today."

"Oh, Jesus." Liz' voice broke, and tears began to seep from her eyes. "Oh, God."

"Liz!" Karen's usually calm voice scaled upward. "What's wrong? Are you crying?"

"A plane crashed. A Trans Con."

There was stunned silence on the other end. Karen Olechsy, sitting in Jennifer's spacious office, felt as if someone had punched her in the solar plexus. She shoved aside the stack of mail on her desk and reached for Jennifer's appointment book. Her fingers shook as she opened it and turned the pages. She couldn't find the right page. Damn it! What was today? "Liz. What's the date?"

"Uh, twentieth."

She flipped through several more pages and found the twentieth. "It says 7:35, TCA Flight 145."

Liz went icy cold. "That's the one," she said, barely a whisper coming out. "That's the one that crashed. Jennifer was on it."

PART II

* *Chapter 6* *

Los Angeles, March, 1971

Liz Chandler was Jack Schiff's secretary, receptionist, and bookkeeper, and anyone who knew anything about the business knew that Liz was the one who really ran the office. Jack was a mediocre talent agent at best, and over the past few years he'd taken to drinking more and earlier in the day until nowadays it wasn't unusual to find Jack slurring his words and stumbling by lunchtime. He was on the edge of financial ruin when Liz began working for him.

She was an average-looking girl from the Midwest—Ohio or Illinois, someplace so Middle American that Californians considered it almost foreign. She was twenty-four, and she knew how to make her looks appear better than they were, always neat and trim and as fashionable as possible on the money Schiff paid her, but never obtrusive. Crisp, that was the best way to describe Liz. Crisp and competent. She loved the movie business, and she loved California, and she swore she'd rather die in an earthquake than go back to the snow and the boredom.

She had walked into Jack's office four years earlier, a few months after she, her husband, and their year-old daughter had moved to Los Angeles. This was her second job in LA. The first one had been boring, and it hadn't taken her long to discover that she wanted to work in "the business."

Jack's office was perfect for her. She soon had it in order and running smoothly, and she turned to learning the business. Jack wasn't the best person from whom to learn; but Liz was clever and she caught on quickly, both to what Jack did right and what he did wrong. She began making suggestions and taking over more and more of the detail work herself. Along the way she lost the husband, who had returned to the Midwest, but the job filled up the empty spaces of her life. Although she dated now and then, the men weren't significant in her life. Mostly there was the agency and her daughter, Kelly, and that was enough for Liz.

Or almost enough.

Schiff was an obstacle. He messed up some of her best efforts with his drunkenness and incompetence. Unfortunately, Liz could exercise only so much behind-the-scenes control, and when Jack acted on his own he fouled up. She would have been better off without him as a figurehead, but setting up her own office would require capital and a certain leap of faith that Liz, at twenty-four and with a daughter in kindergarten to raise by herself, was not ready for.

So she stayed with Schiff and struggled to keep him afloat while she added to her list of friends and favors owed her in the industry.

She was seated at the front desk, a telephone receiver propped between her shoulder and ear, talking to an irritated client while she slit open the morning mail, when a young blond woman walked into Schiff's office. Liz glanced at the appointment book and cupped her hand over the mouthpiece. "Jennifer Taylor?"

"Yes. I have an appointment at eleven."

Liz pointed a pencil toward a love seat. "Be with you in a minute." She returned to the phone conversation, but her hands were still now. Her attention was on the girl across the room.

Jennifer Taylor was pretty. But pretty was all over the place in Los Angeles. Excellent figure, though she didn't show it off to advantage. Good skin. Thick hair, nice color, though the shoulder-length cut was not as attractive as it could be. The makeup wasn't bad, but all in all Liz had the impression that she didn't make enough of herself. There was a shyness, almost an awkwardness that was out of place in Hollywood. Still . . . there was something about her that caught Liz's attention, a fragility, almost sweetness to her face that aroused an instinctive sympathy and liking.

Liz finished calming down the client on the phone, then rang Jack in the inner office. "Miss Taylor's here to see you."

"Who?"

"Eleven o'clock appointment."

"Oh. Is she a client?"

"No. Not yet, anyway."

"What do you think of her? Pretty?"

"Yes, quite."

"I'll be out in a second."

Liz smiled at the girl. "Mr. Schiff will be here in a moment. Can I get you anything? A cup of coffee?"

She smiled at Liz, and Liz went dead still. She thought about Jennifer smiling like that on screen. It could turn people to butter. "No, thank you," Jennifer said. "That's very kind of you." There was the faintest trace of a Southern accent in her voice, more a softening than anything else.

Liz got herself a cup of coffee. It gave her an opportunity to walk past Jennifer. The girl interested her. Up close, Liz realized, Jennifer was truly lovely. She had a beautiful, creamy complexion that couldn't be faked. The odds were it would glow on screen.

"Where are you from?" Liz asked, settling herself on the front edge of her desk, coffee in hand.

"Arkansas."

"Not much accent."

Jennifer smiled again. "I've lived out here for two years, and I've been taking a diction class."

"It's worked."

The inner door opened and Jack came out. He was a short man in his fifties, not heavy, but with the fleshy look of a drinker. Not bad looking in his day, Liz suspected, but he had gone to seed. He saw Jennifer and fixed a smile on his face. "Miss Tyler? Please come in."

"Taylor," Jennifer corrected softly, rising to follow him. "Jennifer Taylor."

He stood aside and let her pass through, then closed the door behind them. Jennifer glanced around the office. She had been in hundreds like it since she came to LA. She handed Jack her portfolio, and he thumbed through it. She knew it wasn't particularly impressive. She had spent a lot of money on the glossies, and they were good, but she had almost no experience. In the two years she'd been here, she had had only a few jobs as an extra, and she hadn't even been able to get an agent.

When she arrived in Los Angeles that summer two years earlier, it had taken her months simply to get over the culture shock. It was a different world from Sweet River, so huge and busy and alive. She had never seen so many different kinds of people or heard anyone speaking in a foreign tongue. The vegetation was tropical and vibrant, palm trees and brightly colored flowers. The traffic was terrifying. People dressed wildly. They were flamboyant and expressive. Jennifer had never seen a real hippie before, except in the news programs on TV, but they were all over the Strip—spaced-out, sitting and standing around, talking lazily, singing on the street corners, zonked in doorways, even begging for money. They had lots and lots of hair, straight or frizzled, beards, mustaches, braids. They wore bizarre color combinations or washed-out jeans, boots and sandals, leather, T-shirts, long skirts, tattered jeans. They painted their faces. Faded, dirty, vivid. The scene was like an explosion in her face.

Then there was the war. There was only one: Viet Nam. She had seen things about it in the news, of course, and that's where Corey would be sent. For that reason it had frightened her. But in Sweet River the only discussion about the war was how all the protesters' heads ought to be busted and the problem would be solved. There wasn't any argument over it at home, and its place in their lives was not large. It wasn't as important as the price of chickens or who was sneaking around with whose wife, except for the brief spate of interest when Mrs. Tarrent's grandson was killed there three years ago.

But out here, the war seemed to be the major topic on everyone's tongue. Oh, there were other causes that were taken up with fervor: black rights, women's lib, the environment. But the central one, the lynch pin of all of them was the peace movement. They protested about it, talked about, argued about it. Wherever she went, it was there.

Drugs were everywhere, too—marijuana, speed, acid. Magic mushrooms, blue devils, yellowjackets. Sunshine. Bennies, barbs, buttons.

It had taken Jennifer six months just to get over the shock. In a strange way, her sorrow over Matthew had helped her through it. If she hadn't been desperate to stay away from Sweet River and the memory of him, she probably would have turned and run straight home. Instead, she had stuck it out, thinking that anything was better than seeing reminders of him everyday. The pain had helped. Only bits and pieces of the shock of LA had been able to seep in around the edges of her anguish. Her misery had been like a wall around her.

She had found a cheap studio apartment in Inglewood and had worked two jobs, a small natural foods restaurant during the day and a hamburger place in the evening. She was too busy to think too much, either about Matthew or

Los Angeles. She didn't look for a job in the movies. She just tried to adjust, and she saved her money.

Gradually she did begin to adjust. The things she saw around her began to seem less strange and appalling. She looked at the people. She walked past stores and studied the items in the windows. She read; she went to movies; she listened. And after several months of careful saving, she began to spend. It hadn't taken long to learn that a car was a necessity in Los Angeles, and that was where her first money went. She bought an old beat-up red Datsun, took a driving course and got her license. She changed her hairstyle, had it cut off to the shoulders and curled it a little. She studied makeup, buying and applying it until she got it right. She bought new clothes that fit in California. Then came the diction lessons to get rid of the hick accent. More money to a good photographer for glossies for her portfolio.

Then, almost a year after she had arrived in LA, she had pulled together all her courage and gone to her first interview with an agent. There had been hundreds of them since. Jennifer had been to casting offices, agents, production offices, auditions. None of it had brought about anything except a few days' work as an extra, a walk-on part at a suburban dinner theater, and countless invitations to sleep with the interviewer.

Strange, back home she was an outcast because everybody thought she slept around. Out here she couldn't get anywhere because she didn't.

Jennifer could see that it was going to be the same today. Something in Schiff's eyes tipped her off; she had seen it many times before. He barely gave her portfolio a glance. He was interested in her body. He showed her to a chair in front of the desk and settled down in one beside her instead of sitting behind his desk. Jennifer sat rigidly upright, her hands folded in her lap. She could smell whiskey on him.

"Any experience?" he asked, edging the chair a little closer.

Jennifer told him about the extra jobs and the walk-on part.

"How about training?"

Sweet River High hadn't even had a speech or drama class. "I went to a weekend workshop at UCLA."

Schiff made an airy wave of his hand. "It's not worth much, anyway. What matters is talent. Natural talent." He stroked his forefinger lightly down her arm. The hair on the back of Jennifer's neck stood up. She pulled her arm away.

"Mr. Schiff, do you think you'd be interested in representing me?" This was a no-win situation if she'd ever seen one, and the quicker she got out of it the better.

"Maybe." He pursed his mouth consideringly. "You're a beautiful girl, Jennifer."

"Thank you."

"We could discuss it over lunch." He leaned closer to her. The smell of alcohol was overpowering. "I'll get Liz to bring something in for us, and we'll have a friendly little lunch." His hand was on her arm again.

Jennifer stood up. She could imagine what a friendly little lunch they'd have here. Lunch on the couch. "I'm sorry, but I have an appointment at noon. I can't stay."

He stood up, too. "I'm sure we could work something out."

"I don't think so."

Schiff rocked back on his heels, his head tilted to one side, considering her. "You're an awfully unfriendly young girl."

"Mr. Schiff, please. All I'm interested in is acting." Her eyes flickered involuntarily toward the small couch against the far wall. "Nothing else."

Why did everything turn out this way? It seemed that unless she was talking to a woman or a gay all anyone cared about was getting her in the sack—and one time even a woman had propositioned her, shocking Jennifer all the way down to her backwoods toes. Her body had to be the payoff just to get in the door. She had never been willing to pay the price, and as a result she was always getting left on the outside.

"Too bad." Schiff shrugged and moved away. She was a pretty thing, but looks were a dime a dozen out here, and most of the girls were more willing than this one. "Thank you for coming in, Miss . . . uh . . ."

"Taylor." Tears of anger started in her eyes. She would have liked to punch the agent right in his flabby gut. Instead, she turned and walked out the door.

Why did she put up with the humiliation? Often she vowed that this was the last time, that she couldn't stand anymore rejection and failure. Each interview made her doubt herself more. No matter how hard she tried, she always came up wanting. Yet, even though each interview plunged her into a depression, before long she'd be back out there, knocking on another door. She couldn't explain why, even to herself. She just knew that she had to keep going. Her hopes were the only thing she had in life.

The receptionist looked up and smiled at Jennifer as she came out. Jennifer blinked back her tears and managed a halfhearted smile in return. "Thank you."

Liz saw the tears glimmering in Jennifer's eyes and they tugged at her heart. After four years in LA that was unusual. "I'm sorry."

Jennifer shook her head. "I should be used to it."

"Does anyone ever get used to it?"

"I don't know."

Impulsively Liz stood up. "Listen, I was about to go to lunch. Want to come with me? My treat."

Jennifer stared. "What? Why?"

"Don't look so suspicious. Just my good deed for the day." Liz grabbed her purse and moved around the desk. "Come on. It'll pick you up, I promise."

They went to a Mexican food place down the street. Mexican food was another thing Jennifer had never experienced before California. She loved it now. The small restaurant was bright red and yellow inside and the background noise made it possible to speak almost privately.

They sat down at a flaming red table and ordered tacos, and Liz had a large, vividly green margarita. She asked to see Jennifer's portfolio, and Jennifer handed it over.

It was much what Liz expected—no experience—but she was impressed by the quality of the photos. At least the girl had had the sense not to scrimp on them. She passed the portfolio back. "Nice pictures. Not enough experience, though."

"I know." Jennifer gave her apologetic smile.

"How long have you been in LA?"

"Almost two years."

"Can you act?"

Jennifer laughed. "Yes. At least I think so. I feel like I can act. I mean, I feel it inside. It sounds crazy, I guess, but I read the parts aloud in my room. Act them out, you know."

"It's not crazy. Half the people in this town probably do that. But have you ever done it in public?"

"No. Except for one walk-on part."

Liz sipped at her drink. She wasn't sure why she was doing this, but there was something about this girl that intrigued her, something in her face; a strange combination of purity, beauty and sensuality, and just a hint of sadness lurking in the big blue eyes. Liz had been aware of the number of men's heads that had turned to look at Jennifer when they walked into the restaurant. She didn't know what it was; there was nothing overtly sexy about Jennifer as there was with so many Hollywood starlets. But she had a definite allure, a subtle blend of innocence and sex.

Liz could see possibilities. A little change in Jennifer's makeup, a different hairstyle, better clothes. Liz knew how to make the most of what Jennifer had. The question was whether it would be worth the trouble. Could she act? Would she have that special quality onscreen that made people shell out their money to look at her for two hours? Was she tough enough to make it? She appeared too delicate, too introverted and awkward. But there were actors like that who came out of their shell in front of the camera. And there were fragile-looking women who were tougher than army sergeants when it came to getting what they wanted.

Liz lit a cigarette and blew the smoke upward. "I know a guy who's casting an amateur production of *Bus Stop.* No money, but at least it would give you some experience. You interested?"

The stunned amazement in Jennifer's eyes amused her even as it aroused her pity. The girl obviously wasn't used to having anything given to her.

"Yes. Yes, of course I'm interested. I'd love it."

"Good." Liz pulled a notepad and pen from her purse and jotted down an address. "Here's the address of the theater. It's tonight at 7:30. The director's name is Kevin Walters."

Jennifer took the small piece of paper and smiled that beautiful, sunny smile that had intrigued Liz earlier. "Thank you. You're a very kind person."

"Probably not as kind as you think."

Their food arrived and they dug in. It was delicious, but it was obvious that Jennifer's mind wasn't on the food. Liz knew the look. Jennifer was already into the play inside her head, focusing on that strange world inside herself which actors seemed to have, a world of hope and fantasy. Actors were a weird bunch; Liz doubted she would ever understand them. When Jennifer had come out of Jack's office she'd been in the depths of despair, but with just the possibility of a nonpaying role, her eyes sparkled and she was filled with hope again.

After lunch, Liz returned to the office and Jennifer hurried off to buy a copy of *Bus Stop* at Bennett's on Hollywood Boulevard. She drove home and ran up the stairs to her one-room apartment. It was sparsely furnished; Jennifer did not waste money on furniture. Nor did she always consider food essential. Most of the money she spent went for clothes, gas, and repairs to her old car. The rest she saved for acting lessons and the days when she would have to quit her job or work only part-time because of an acting opportunity.

Jennifer had spent a lot of nights in the dreary little apartment, lonely, scared, and sad. She had cried herself to sleep over Matthew Ferris more times than she cared to remember. She still carried the hurt around like an inner bruise, and sometimes the memory of Matthew would wash over her and the tears would come again.

But not today. There was nothing in her mind now but the play as she curled up on the bed and began to read.

Jennifer called in sick to her evening job and drove to the tiny theater in an old building downtown where the audition was to be held. Jennifer didn't think it could hold an audience of more than a hundred and fifty. She arrived twenty minutes early, having allowed plenty of time to find it, and cooled her heels outside with a few other young people until a man in jeans and a dark green T-shirt arrived to unlock the door. Jennifer wasn't sure whether he was the janitor or the director.

It turned out that he was the director. He told them his name was Kevin Walters and handed out small index cards on which they were to write their names, telephone numbers and theater credits. Jennifer finished quickly and her tension mushroomed as she watched the others scratching away for long minutes after she finished. She glanced around and folded her hands in her lap; they were icy. So was her stomach.

She looked up to find the director watching her. He was in his late twenties, with curling brown hair and reddish brown eyes, not bad looking. She wondered how good a friend he was to Liz. She hoped it was good enough that he wouldn't be looking for a bed partner more than an actress. But she couldn't quite see him with the crisp, no-nonsense Liz.

He held out his hand, and she realized that he wanted

her card. Coloring a little, she handed it to him. He continued to look at her. It occurred to Jennifer that perhaps he was staring because she was all wrong. Another furtive glance around the group told her that everyone else was wearing jeans. She was the only woman there in a dress. She wished she had worn more casual clothes, but she was used to dressing up for job interviews.

When the director had collected the cards, he sent the prospective actors into the wings and called them onstage two at a time, paired boy-girl, to do a scene. He sat out in the theater to watch.

Jennifer waited while two pairs did their scenes. She thought she might be sick to her stomach. That would make a really nice impression on him.

Jennifer's name was called along with that of a slender, dark young man not much taller than she. He slouched out onto the stage beside her, looking like he couldn't care less about anything. Jennifer's nerves were screaming and her insides were cold and weak. This was only her fifth audition, and she was so scared she was afraid she wouldn't be able to speak. Then the boy began to read his opening lines. Jennifer faced him and moved into the role, drawing her hands onto her hips and putting indignation on her face. She answered him and her nerves fled as they had every other time she had read for a part. She felt suddenly, marvelously in control, powerful in her ability.

They read to the end of the scene and when they stopped, Jennifer stepped back, leaving the part. Her heart was racing and she was alive with excitement and elation. She was sure she had done it beautifully; she wanted to laugh and shout with sheer joy. She glanced out at the director to judge his reaction. She couldn't see his face well, but it looked perfectly bland to her. He called out a new set of names in a voice devoid of interest. Jennifer followed her partner off the stage.

Twenty minutes later Kevin Walters called her name again, as well as those of four others. "You five stay. The rest of you can go home. Thank you."

It took Jennifer a moment to realize what had happened. She had made the first cut! Elation soared in her.

The next time the director paired her with a lanky blond young man; her first partner had been cut. They read a different scene, and with this partner her reading went even better. He was into the role as much as she, and his naturalness increased hers. Then Walters had her read the part of a young waitress in the cafe with the oldest man there. The others read the same two scenes, then the director came back to Jennifer and a new partner for what Jennifer thought was her part's best scene in the play. When she finished her heart was pumping adrenalin through her like a freight train. She had felt so good in the reading. So right!

Jennifer moved back to allow another couple to play the scene and looked out at the director. Sitting next to him was Liz Chandler.

Liz hadn't planned to come. She had considered and then rejected the idea, reminding herself that if Jennifer Taylor was good enough to get a part she would be able to see her later in rehearsals. But after supper one of her daughter's friends in their apartment complex had begged for Kelly to come over, and Liz had suddenly had a free evening before her. Without really thinking about it, Liz had jumped into her old Volkswagen Bug and driven to the theater where Kevin was auditioning.

She had arrived after the first round of tryouts was over. There were only five people left onstage, and Liz felt a spurt of pride to see that Jennifer was one of them. She slipped into the seat beside Kevin and he glanced at her, surprised. "You didn't say you were coming," he whispered.

"Spur of the moment." They turned their attention back to the stage.

Kevin called out Jennifer's name and that of one of the young men. They began to read. Liz went perfectly still.

Jennifer was good. Damn! She was more than good! Gone were the shy tilt of her head, the awkward stance, the repressed movements. She was someone else—the brash, naive, hungry Cherie of the play.

Kevin glanced at Liz in the amused manner of one springing a pleasant surprise, and she knew that he thought Jennifer was good, too. How could he not think so?

They sat through another couple of readings. The other girls paled in comparison to Jennifer. Kevin paired Jennifer with a different man for another scene. Afterward he had the others read the same scene, then said, "That's all for this evening. Thank you for coming. I'll be getting in touch about callbacks in the next few days. Thank you."

The actors trailed out of the theater. Liz saw Jennifer cast a curious glance her way, and Liz raised her hand in a wave as Jennifer walked up the far aisle and out of the theater. When the actors were gone, Kevin turned to Liz, propping up his feet diagonally on the row of seats in front of them. "You sure have an eye, Liz. I'll say that for you."

Liz grinned. "She was good, wasn't she? Does she have the role?"

Kevin sighed. "I don't know. I'm holding auditions for two more nights. Someone else might turn up, but so far she's the best talent. Her voice isn't strong, but that's not a big drawback with a theater this small. No training. It's glaring in the way she moves. She needs some help in the nuances and in her interpretation. But I'll tell you what, she's got a lot of raw talent."

"You can supply the rest. You can teach her how to move onstage and how to speak. You're a good director. You'd be giving her something invaluable, and in return you'd get a great performance."

"You don't have to sell her to me." He smiled. "What's your motive in this? You get ten percent of her nothing? I've been wondering about it ever since you called me this afternoon. What's the deal? She one of Schiff's clients?"

Liz shook her head. "Are you kidding? Jack can't see

past a whiskey glass.'' She shrugged. ''I don't know what my interest is. There's just something about her—I think she'd have real screen presence. She's beautiful, but more than that she has a certain appeal. When I look at her I want to like her. That could come across powerfully on film.''

''You have good instincts, Liz. So what are you going to do about it?''

''Do?''

''Yeah. Are you going to persuade Jack to take her? Or will you take her on yourself?''

''I can't.''

''Why not?''

''It's too much of a risk. There's Kelly to think of.''

''I think you're ready. You could do it. This girl could be your chance.''

''You really think so?''

''How many times will somebody waltz into Jack's office who has real star potential?''

''She's the first I've seen.''

''Right. You want to start off your career with a beautiful girl who can act and who has something or you want to hang around Jack Schiff's office for a few more years putting together a little money and cementing relationships with a few mediocre actors?''

Liz gazed at him steadily. ''You're serious, aren't you?''

''Damn straight. Aren't you?''

''Maybe I am.''

They went out for a drink and talked. Kevin asked her back to his apartment, but she turned him down gently. Whatever interest she had had in him had faded long ago, and tonight she just wanted to be alone and think. It didn't seem to hurt him, and she had the impression that his offer had been more polite than real.

Liz drove home and picked up Kelly at her friend's house. Kelly was lively, singing and jumping around, going off into strings of giggles. Liz's nerves were frazzled by the time she got the child into her nightgown and into bed. Liz kissed Kelly good night and went back to the living room. She flopped down on the couch and pulled out a cigarette.

She wasn't made for motherhood, she thought. Thank God she and Chuck had had just one child. Kelly was a great kid compared to a lot she'd seen, and Liz loved her. She couldn't imagine what she would do if something happened to her. But motherhood was not her forte.

Nor had marriage been something she was particularly good at. She had to admit that the majority of what went wrong with their marriage had been more her fault than Chuck's. He had wanted a loving wife and mother. That was all, not a demanding request, she supposed. He hadn't objected to her working; in fact, he had been happy to have the extra money. But he had wanted her focus to be on him and Kelly, not on her job and the outside world. And Liz hadn't been able to do that for him. The world was too interesting, the movie industry too exciting.

She had made her choice way back when Chuck returned to Indiana. She wanted a career more than anything else. Work was her thing. She loved the business of agenting— the hustle, the pace, the salesmanship, the excitement.

But if she loved it so much, Liz thought now as she sat on her couch and smoked, then why did she stay in the dead end job of Jack Schiff's secretary, receptionist and general dogsbody? Sure, it was nice to have Jack as a front so that she didn't have to take the risk and responsibility, but Jack limited her, too. She couldn't prove herself, do what she knew she was capable of doing. The job gave her security, but surely she couldn't be content with that.

Liz stubbed out her cigarette and rose. She wandered aimlessly through the apartment, thinking. She stopped at the bedroom door and gazed at Kelly's sleeping form. Kelly was always her excuse. She couldn't risk financial disaster when she was responsible for a five-year-old girl.

But Kelly would never have anything better unless Liz made the move. As it was, they were barely getting by. A secretary's pay wouldn't improve, and Kelly would get more expensive. Liz didn't want to continue this way. She had never planned to. Ever since she started working for Jack Schiff she had intended to have her own agency someday. She meant to be the best and give Kelly all the things she couldn't now. She had just been waiting for the right time, learning the business and trying to put by a little money.

But Kevin was right. The opportunity was now. If her instincts about Jennifer Taylor were on target, she could be big. Liz might never get another chance to make a star out of an unknown. The only thing holding her back was the fear of risking it all, of failing.

Liz grimaced. Damn it! She wasn't about to start running her life by her fears. She strode into the kitchen, looked up a number and dialed quickly. A soft, tentative voice answered on the other end.

"Jennifer?"

"Yes?"

"This is Liz Chandler. I've been thinking for some time now of leaving Jack Schiff and starting my own talent agency. You're very good, Jennifer, and I think I could help you."

For a moment Jennifer was too stunned to say anything. "You mean you want to represent me?"

"Yes. Would you want me to?"

Liz was young, and she was only a secretary to an agent. There was no assurance that she could do the job. But Jennifer liked and trusted Liz instinctively—and Liz was the only person who had ever wanted to represent her.

"Yes," Jennifer responded, excitement rising in her. "Yes, I'd like that very much."

Two days later Kevin called and told Jennifer she had the lead role in his production. When she hung up the phone she danced around the apartment, giggling and hugging herself with joy. It offered her no money and would probably be seen by very few people, but Jennifer was as excited as if she'd won a role in a movie.

She had to quit her evening job in order to rehearse, but she had no qualms about doing so. She plunged into rehearsals with all her energy. She listened to Kevin's every instruction and followed it to the letter. She memorized her lines and practiced every minute she wasn't at work or rehearsal.

Kevin was amazed. He had taken a risk casting her in the lead when she had no experience. What if she couldn't memorize? What if she couldn't take instruction? What if she froze? What if she was irresponsible? Maybe auditions were her best performance. But the more he worked with her, the more glad he was that he had chosen Jennifer. She was the most apt pupil he had ever worked with, a quick study, sharp and eager to learn. After two weeks she had memorized all her lines. She was never late or missed a rehearsal—in fact, she was usually there early, asking him questions and soaking up knowledge. She didn't pout or argue. She simply listened to him gravely, then did exactly what he told her. Kevin found himself eagerly going to rehearsal each night, filled with the excitement of finding raw talent to mold.

Jennifer hadn't felt so alive and happy since Matthew had stormed out of her life two years ago. She didn't go to bed until twelve, then rose at six the next morning to go to her daytime job. By the time she tumbled into bed she was exhausted and drained, both physically and emotionally.

But she loved it. She felt so fulfilled, so sure. Even in Matthew's arms she had been haunted by fears of losing him and by her sense of her own unworthiness. But here, at last, she had found praise, success and joy. Days went by without her thinking of Matthew or feeling even a twinge of the old, familiar pain of his leaving. She was too busy, too happy, too wrapped up in her craft. She had found a place where she belonged.

Sometimes she thought that Kevin might be a part of that belonging. There were moments when she glanced at him to find him watching her, and she sensed that he might feel more for her than what a director normally felt for his lead actress. She wondered if she might not be able to feel something more for him, too. He was very nice, and he had helped her tremendously. She was grateful to him. She admired him. She loved listening to him. But something held her back. She didn't encourage him, didn't smile or look at him in the way of a woman who was interested. She stuck to the play and he didn't make a move.

Jennifer was glad. The play was enough.

Liz was a dynamo, Jennifer discovered. She gave her boss two-weeks notice and found a tiny, cheap office perfect for her needs. She borrowed enough money from her parents to live the first few months. Jennifer found out later that she'd also sold her wedding and engagement rings. When Jennifer remonstrated about that, she simply shrugged and said in her flat, dry way, "Sweetheart, there's no sentimental attachment there."

It made sense, of course, but Matthew Ferris' senior ring was still hidden in one of Jennifer's drawers at home, and she wouldn't have sold it even if she were starving.

Liz was gratified that several of Jack's better clients followed her when she left. She got one of them, a male dancer, an audition for a backup spot in a singer's Las Vegas nightclub show and landed a spot in a laundry detergent commercial for another. The terror of falling flat on her face began to recede. She could do the job.

Jennifer was Liz's pet project, the one on which she spent the most time, energy and skill. At first there were no tangible rewards, but she was certain that she was building something.

First she took Jennifer to the best hairstylist she knew. Jennifer almost fainted at the price, but when she saw the result, a full, fluffy cut streaked with silvery blond, she had to admit that Liz was right. She looked a little older, sexier, more sophisticated. Out of the ordinary. They went shopping and Liz insisted that, despite the cost, she buy two dresses that looked dazzling on her.

"You have to spend money to make it, remember?"

"Yes, but—" Jennifer looked doubtfully at the pink linen dress.

"You can wear rags the rest of the time if you want. But for auditions and interviews, you have to look your best. This dress is perfect. It's the right color and it shows off your figure without being blatant. It makes you look like you know what you're doing. Like you're successful. Half of this business is bluffing. If you dress well, you must be doing well. If you're doing well, somebody else must want you. And if other people want you, you must be good. Impressions are all-important."

"All right, you win. But if I stick with you much longer I'm not going to have any money left."

"Maybe not. But you'll have a career."

Jennifer sighed and bought the dress.

They left the store on Wilshire and drove through Beverly Hills toward Hollywood. Liz loved driving through this area, with its wide, tree-lined streets and large houses, its elegant hotels and exclusive stores. Sometimes she came out with Kelly on the weekend and simply drove around Beverly Hills and Bel Air. Kelly loved the houses, too, though she was disappointed that she couldn't get out and tumble on the rolling green lawns or go inside the houses.

Jennifer glanced out the window. She liked Beverly Hills and had promised herself that one day she would live there, but she didn't have the love, the hunger for the place that Liz did. Jennifer's hunger was for the screen, for acting, for love and fame and praise. To her Beverly Hills was only a symbol of those things.

"Jennifer," Liz said in her most serious voice. "I want you to take lessons."

"Acting lessons? Sure." She knew Liz was right; she needed training. But where would she find the money? Her reserves were perilously low, and she knew she would need the money to live if Liz began to get her jobs. Acting jobs were always sporadic and low-paying at first. They demanded so many days that you couldn't keep a steady job, yet they didn't provide a continuous source of income.

"I want you to study with Annice Loehrmann."

"Annice Loehrmann!" Jennifer stared at Liz. "You're crazy! She's the best coach in the city. Probably in the whole country! She'd never take me. And she's expensive. I could never pay that kind of money."

"She gives scholarships to students she thinks are good enough."

"Liz . . . come on. I'd sweat getting in there, let alone winning a scholarship."

"Don't sell yourself short. Kevin's told me how good you are and how well you learn. You can get in. Hell, you'll never know if you don't try. What are you planning to do for the rest of your life? Sit around being scared that you might not be good enough for this part or that? That's not exactly the kind of career I have planned for you."

"Of course not."

"Then don't do it now. Keep reminding yourself how good you are. You can get a scholarship. Your only problem will be money. Annice Loehrmann's very demanding. Two-hour sessions every day and lots of practice time. When you're putting on a production it's practically full-time. I don't think you'll be able to swing more than a part-time job."

Jennifer sighed. She didn't need much to live on. She had never had much, and she'd always been a scrimper and a saver. Maybe with a part-time job . . . and maybe she could find a roommate to help share expenses. Somehow she would find a way. It was too wonderful an opportunity to pass up—provided, of course, that she could get in.

She felt the familiar thrill of mingled fear and excitement. She looked at Liz, her eyes beginning to shine. "Do you really think I could win a scholarship?"

Liz grinned. "You can do anything."

* Chapter 7 *

Liz arranged an audition for Jennifer at the Loehrmann School two Saturdays later. Miss Loehrmann never auditioned students except on Saturdays. Sunday was her day of rest, and she spent the weekdays entirely on her students.

There were at least ten other young men and women there when Jennifer arrived, and another ten or fifteen came in after she did. They sat in uncomfortable straight-backed wooden chairs in the hall. Some smoked incessantly. Others read and reread their audition parts, lips moving as they rehearsed the lines for the hundredth time. Still others rolled, unrolled, and rerolled their playbooks time and again. A few, like Jennifer, sat as still as statues on their chairs, icy hands folded together in their laps and the blankness of terror on their faces. All of them sweated.

Jennifer had never been so scared in her life. It made her fear the night of auditions for *Bus Stop* seem laughable in comparison. Even when Mack had been in a drunken rage, hitting and screaming and chasing her around the house she hadn't known this kind of stomach-clenching fright. At least then she had known she had a chance to escape. Here she couldn't even leave; she had to force herself to face what was so scary.

Annice Loehrmann had a reputation as the best acting teacher in Los Angeles. Anyone who went to her school came out a far better actor. Her acting course offered no assurance of success in Hollywood, but it gave one an edge with directors. They knew that if you'd been to Annice's classes, you had a certain level of skill and professionalism.

Annice Loehrmann also had a reputation as the toughest

coach around. She never approached a play lightly. There were those who said she had no sense of humor. She required all of her students to approach their work in the same way. Her tongue could be razor sharp, her remarks scathing. She had reduced more than one arrogant young actor to a mass of jelly with a few well-chosen comments on his work, and it was said that no one escaped her school without being brought to tears at least once. Jennifer dreaded to think what the woman would say if an auditioning actor read poorly.

Jennifer filled out a large index card with the usual information as well as a scholarship form. A young man with longish hair and horn-rim glasses collected the cards and disappeared with them behind a double door. Later he returned and called one person into the room. Fifteen minutes later he called in the next person. The first person to audition never came out. Neither did any of the others who went in. Jennifer envisioned some monstrous machine in which all the rejects were tossed, to be chewed up and never seen again.

At last Jennifer's name was called. She rose and walked past the bookish-looking young man into a medium-sized room, empty except for a folding table with two plastic molded chairs behind it. The man who had called her name took a seat at the table. The other chair was already occupied by a thin woman with graying hair cut in a Dutch-boy bob. The woman's skin was deeply tanned and leathery, and her pale green eyes were startling against her dark face. She wore tan slacks, a long red tunic blouse and scuffed, broken-down loafers. She studied Jennifer as she smoked a cigarette. Her hands were square and broad, and her fingers stubby, the nails cut short. She put out her cigarette and immediately reached for the pack and lighter on the table before her.

"I'm Annice Loehrmann. This is my assistant, Glenn Farrell. Now then, Miss Taylor, what do you propose to perform for us today?"

Jennifer tried to hide her shock. She had assumed the woman must be Miss Loehrmann's secretary and that Annice herself had left the room. She had expected the best acting coach in Los Angeles to be a sleek, sophisticated woman, someone who *looked* like a glamourous actress, not a plain, squat woman with a cigarette-roughened voice.

"I—uh, my comedy reading is from *Auntie Mame* and the dramatic reading from *The Glass Menagerie*." She had chosen two young parts, following Liz's advice to stay somewhere close to her own age and looks. ("They too often choose the meatiest part they can think of, without any regard to their own age or range, and it just emphasizes their lack of skill, rather than covering it up," Liz had warned her.)

"Glenn will cue you," Annice said, and Jennifer handed him the marked playbooks, open to the pages she planned to use.

Jennifer's stomach was in knots. Glenn read his line, and Jennifer went into the character of Patrick's snobby young girlfriend. Her stomach relaxed and the familiar adrenalin surged up as she began to talk.

Annice Loehrmann chain-smoked throughout the two scenes, and when Jennifer ended, she sat looking at her thoughtfully. "I understand you want a scholarship."

"Yes, ma'am."

"Come back tonight at 7:00. I'm having callbacks for the ones I'm considering for scholarships."

Did that mean she was accepted to the school? Jennifer's legs went so suddenly rubbery she was afraid she might fall. "Yes, ma'am." She was too frightened of Annice's reputation to question her.

"And don't bother to prepare anything. We'll do sight-readings."

"Yes, ma'am."

"Glenn will put your name on the list. I have five openings in the school next section. Unless I see an extraordinary amount of quality in the next hour or so, you will be one of them. However, I have only two scholarships. Will you be able to attend if you don't have a scholarship?"

"I don't know how," Jennifer answered honestly. "But if you're accepting me—" Her face hardened. "I'll find a way."

The faintest trace of a smile flickered across the other woman's lips. "Well, come tonight at 7:00 and we shall see."

Jennifer was not as terrified by the auditions that evening. There were six other people there, two men and four women, and they read the same pieces, two dramatic and one comedy. Jennifer had the sinking sensation that they all read more professionally than she, and she went home with her buoyant mood of the afternoon slightly deflated.

Annice's assistant phoned her the next day to say that Miss Loehrmann had accepted her into the school. His tone of voice implied that it was a far greater privilege than she deserved. "The next six-week session begins two weeks from Monday. I have you scheduled for the four o'clock class. I presume that is all right with you."

"Of course." Jennifer had the feeling that it wouldn't have mattered what her reply had been.

"Miss Loehrmann awarded only two scholarships, as you know, and she was unable to give you one at this time." Jennifer's heart sank. Where would she get the money? "However, there will be another scholarship opening up at the next six-week session, and Miss Loehrmann has allotted it to you."

Jennifer burst out laughing. "Oh, thank you. Thank you!" She had to find tuition money only for six weeks! It would take the rest of the money she had saved up and a great deal of her salary each week, but surely she could swing it. And she would be studying under the great Annice Loehrmann!

Jennifer floated through the rest of the week. The world had never seemed sunnier. Matthew Ferris hardly crossed her mind. Liz suggested that they move in together to help reduce both their expenses, and they found a small, two-bedroom apartment in Glendale that would suit. Liz had been leery about such closeness with a client, but it didn't take her long to be glad she had decided to make the offer. It eased her own financial situation and it was nice to have someone to help with the chores. Jennifer was quiet and easy to live with, and she got along very well with Kelly. Jennifer seemed to love kids, and she talked and played with Kelly with more ease than Liz usually did.

Jennifer was even happier with the arrangement. She had never had a friend before, and now she discovered how nice it was to have someone to talk to and do things with. Liz and Kelly were almost like a family—a nice family, the kind a person was supposed to have.

The play's first performance was the Friday before Jennifer started her lessons. She was gripped by intense stage fright just before it began, and she was certain that she would freeze and be unable to deliver a single line. But when her cue came and she stepped onto the stage, the familiar rush of power and excitement came. Her performance was flawless, and when the cast took their final bows, the applause for her was twice that for the other players.

Kevin popped a bottle of champagne for the cast and crew after the audience had left, and they toasted their success. Hours later, when they had hashed and rehashed the evening as much as they could, they left the warehouse. Kevin invited Jennifer to his apartment for a celebratory drink and she accepted. She was too excited to go home yet.

He opened another bottle of champagne, and Jennifer took a glass, not wanting to say that she didn't like the taste of alcohol. Or perhaps it was the memories she didn't like. She rarely drank even wine. She sipped her drink a couple of times, then set it down on the coffee table. Kevin settled down on the couch beside her.

"You were terrific tonight," he told her. "You amazed even me." The excitement of an actual performance had put a keen edge on her performance. Some actors were like that, more brilliant under pressure. Kevin had also seen ones who did wonderfully at rehearsals but lost it when they had an audience.

Jennifer grinned. Her skin glowed and her cheeks were alive with color. She had been more than pretty when Kevin met her, but in the past few weeks since Liz had taken hold of her she had blossomed into an extraordinary beauty. He wanted her. He had wanted her for a long time now, but it was his policy not to sleep with a cast member. And Jennifer had never given him any encouragement. There was always something a little remote about her, an unconscious wall.

But the play was as good as over now. No need now to worry about losing his objectivity or putting pressure on her. She was beautiful. And he would lose her when the play was done. She would go on to study under Annice Loehrmann. From there she might go anywhere. Jennifer had more talent than anyone he'd ever directed. It stung to admit it, but she had potential he wasn't nearly good enough to tap. She was one of the special ones, the rare ones. He knew, sadly, that she would leave him far behind.

Kevin trailed a finger down her cheek. With the stage makeup removed it was smooth and creamy. He leaned toward her, and Jennifer watched him, wide-eyed, not moving a muscle. His mouth brushed hers. He put his hands on her arms and pulled her to him. He kissed her again, more deeply.

Jennifer tried. She liked Kevin. Maybe he could make her finally forget Matthew. She opened her mouth to him. Her arms went around his neck. She closed her eyes.

She felt nothing except a faint repugnance at the feel of his wet tongue in her mouth. Kevin pulled back. His eyes were glittering and the ridges of his cheekbones were stained with red. It was obvious that he wasn't suffering from the same lack of enthusiasm.

"God, you're beautiful." His hand skimmed her hair. He bent toward her again.

Jennifer moved back sharply. "No." She slipped off the couch and rose to her feet. "I'm sorry. It's nothing to do with you. I—well, there's somebody I haven't gotten over, I guess. I'm sorry."

"It's okay."

She knew it wasn't. But what could she say? "I better be going."

Kevin protested, but Jennifer felt too awkward to stay. She picked up her purse and drove home, angry with herself for being such an idiot. A nice guy like Kevin, she would think she could feel something. When Matthew had kissed her she had lit up inside. But she couldn't even work up a spark for somebody who really liked her, who accepted her as she was, without doubts or condemnations. Why did it have to be that way? It had been almost two years. She had thought she had gotten over Matthew. But if so, why was she unable to feel any desire for Kevin? She wondered if her capacity for passion had died when Matthew left her, ground to dust under the heavy heel of his distrust and rage. Or was it that her body could respond only to Matthew Ferris? Either way, the future looked bleak.

The bleakness was still written on her face when she got home. Liz was waiting for her, eager to discuss the evening. She had been to the play and had stopped by afterwards to congratulate Jennifer, but she had had to rush home to relieve the babysitter and hadn't stayed for the party.

"Jenny!" Liz jumped to her feet, astonished, when she saw Jennifer's gloomy face. "What's the matter? What happened?"

Jennifer shook her head. "Nothing."

"You don't look like nothing's the matter."

Jennifer sighed. "Well, nothing that I can do anything about."

Liz pulled her over to a chair. "So tell me what this nothing is."

Jennifer sighed. She might as well tell her. When Liz

set her mind on something there was no stopping her. "Kevin kissed me tonight and I didn't feel anything."

"That's no crime. Did he try to put a guilt trip on you?"

"No. He was very nice about it. But it was my fault." She glanced at her friend, and suddenly she wanted to tell her about Matthew. She had never talked to anyone about it, but now it came out in a rush, the whole story of her life in Sweet River, her father's drinking and temper, her mother's death, her love for Matthew, and his final, cruel rejection of her. She cried, sometimes breaking off when tears clogged her voice so she couldn't speak. By the time she finished, Liz's own eyes were awash with tears.

"That son of a bitch."

Jennifer smiled faintly. She felt better having finally talked about it, lighter and freer. "Sometimes I wonder what Matthew's doing. I've even bought newspapers during football season to read the stories about Alabama's games. But I never find his name."

"If we're lucky, maybe he fell off a cliff."

"Lots of times that's what I wished." Jennifer shrugged. "But I can't blame him, really. He'd known his friends all his life. There wasn't any reason for them to lie; I don't know why they did. If I were Matthew I probably would have believed them."

"No, you wouldn't. You're too nice and fair."

"Maybe. I don't know." Jennifer's eyes were suddenly hard and dark with a passion Liz had never seen in her before. "When it came to Matthew, if he'd been seeing some other girl—I don't know that I'd have been nice and fair at all."

Emotion shimmered on her face. Liz studied her. She had often wondered where Jennifer got the depth of emotion she pulled up for her acting when she seemed such a calm, quiet girl. Now she could see it. The emotions were there, deep inside and tamped down so hard they couldn't escape until she opened the crack with her acting and let the volcano inside boil up. For the first time Liz had glimpsed the volcano. She didn't think she would like to have to live with that inside her.

Liz reached over and patted her hand. "Well, I'll tell you one thing: We are going to make you the biggest star in this country. And Matthew Ferris is going to look at you up there on that screen and curse the day he let you go."

The doorbell rang early the next morning. Jennifer heard it, but she pulled the pillow over her head and went back to sleep. Moments later there was an insistent tapping at her bedroom door. It was impossible to sleep through that. She took the pillow off and sat up, disgruntled. "What?"

Liz stuck her head inside the door. She smiled, amusement dancing in her eyes. "There's a good-looking young man out here to see you. Better get up. I don't think you want to miss this."

Matthew! A sudden, crazy hope filled her. Jennifer thrust it back down. It couldn't possibly be Matthew. It was probably one of the guys from the play. But then why was Liz grinning like that, as if she knew something special? Curiosity impelled Jennifer to jump out of bed and slip into jeans and a T-shirt. She ran a brush through her hair and went into the living room.

A young man stood beside the couch, his hands in his pockets. He wore Dingo boots and jeans and a Led Zeppelin T-shirt with a dark green Army fatigue jacket open over it. His hair was dark blond, heavily streaked with silvery gold from the sun, and his eyes were a dark, vivid blue. He was as familiar to Jennifer as her own face, yet curiously strange as well. For a moment Jennifer couldn't move, then she flung herself forward. "Corey!"

"Hiya, kid." Her brother grinned and opened his arms. Jennifer wrapped her arms around his waist, and for a long moment they clung together.

Liz smiled benignly on them. She had heard Jennifer talk about Corey often enough to know how special he was to her. Jennifer would love having him here, and it seemed a particularly opportune time, considering the unhappiness Jennifer had expressed last night. Liz motioned to Kelly to turn off the TV, which was blaring out Kelly's favorite Saturday morning cartoons, and follow her into the kitchen.

"I can't believe you're here." Jennifer laughed, leaning back to look up into her brother's face. They had corresponded with each other ever since he left Sweet River, although the last few weeks she had been so busy she hadn't been very good with her letters. "You look super."

"Not as super as you." He held her off to admire her. "You've grown up so much I hardly recognized you."

"Oh, Corey..."

"It's true. You don't look like a kid from Sweet River, Arkansas, anymore. You're definitely a California girl now."

"Don't be silly. I hardly even have a tan."

"You hardly even have an accent, either." When Corey grinned, his teeth white against his tan, you could see the charm Mack Taylor was reputed to have had before it dissolved in liquor and age. "What's happened to you, girl?"

"I took diction lessons. I wrote you about that. Now stop teasing me and tell me what you're doing here." She took his hands and pulled him to the couch to sit. "I thought you were working on an oil rig in Texas."

"I was. I've been in West Texas since I got out of the army last fall. But I decided I'd had enough. I'm going back to Sweet River."

"I hate to tell you, but you're going the wrong way."

"All right." He gave her hair a playful yank. "I wanted to see you first, and I figured, hell, out there past Odessa I was halfway to California anyway. So I came to LA."

Jennifer squeezed his hands. "I'm so glad you did. How long are you going to stay? You won't leave right away, promise. You can stay here. You can sleep out here on the couch. Can't he, Liz?"

"Sure." Liz carried a tray of coffee and cups into the living room and set it down on the coffee table.

He smiled. "Yeah. I'll stay a while. You can show me the sights."

"Sure. Oh! You can come to the play tonight! Did I write you that I was in a play?"

His eyes twinkled with amusement. "A few times."

She made a face at him. "We started our run last night. You have to see it."

Liz had never seen Jennifer so animated. She was beautiful, even in a plain T-shirt and without makeup. If that essence could be captured on film, Jennifer would be number one at the box office.

The three of them sat and sipped their coffee while Jennifer chattered excitedly about the play, her career and Annice Loehrmann's acting school. Later Jennifer suggested breakfast.

Corey laughed. "Hell, girl, I had bacon and eggs almost four hours ago." So he took her out to lunch at the Hamburger Hamlet on Sunset and they talked some more, lingering over their food.

Jennifer couldn't get enough of looking at him. He was the same, yet different. His hair hadn't grown out completely from its military cut, and she missed the silky shagginess. He looked bigger; the lean teenage musculature had filled out and matured. He was twenty-one now, two and a half years older than the last time she'd seen him. But the difference was more than any of those things. His eyes had aged, and there was something in the faint lines around his mouth—something tougher, older, more removed. It made her sad. Yet it made her love him all the more fiercely.

Afterwards she drove him around Beverly Hills and Hollywood, and that evening he went to the play. When it was over they drove up Mulholland Drive to look at the lights of the city. Corey glanced at the couples necking in the cars around them and grinned.

"Not so different from Sweet River, huh? Except it's the river there."

"Yeah. I guess."

They were silent for a moment, looking out at the view. "How come you left Sweet River so early?" Corey asked with seeming casualness. "I never figured you'd drop out of high school."

Jennifer's stomach tightened. She didn't want to tell Corey about Matthew. He was returning to Sweet River, and it wouldn't help him to get crosswise with the Ferrises. Knowing Corey, he'd probably go after Matthew with his fists if he thought Matthew had wronged his sister. Jennifer shrugged. "I got tired of it, that's all."

"Daddy giving you trouble?"

Of course that was the conclusion he'd jumped to. "No more than usual. He hadn't hit me or anything. I just—oh, you know. I hated the town, and I hated people thinking I was trash. It didn't make much sense to keep hanging around there when I knew this was what I wanted to do."

Corey didn't think she was telling him the truth, at least not all of it. But he understood. She was like him. They kept things inside themselves. He respected her privacy. Besides, whatever had happened, it was long over and done with. Jennifer had a new life out here.

"You were good tonight. I was amazed—my little sister up there on that stage dazzling everybody."

Jennifer smiled at him. "You might be a little prejudiced."

"Maybe. But I heard the people sitting around me, and they were impressed. You've got talent."

"Thank you."

"It'll take money, though, won't it? I mean, this acting school and all, even with the scholarship. Liz said you wouldn't be able to keep up a steady job."

"Probably not. But I'll make it. I could get a job in a nightclub serving drinks. That would be late hours and wouldn't interfere with my classes or rehearsing. I bet—"

"No." His voice was firm. "I won't let you do that. You're not going to have a bunch of drunks harassing you."

"I can take care of myself. Honest."

"I have a better idea. I made nice money on that oil rig, and I saved some while I was in the army. I have eight thousand dollars saved up. I want you to have it."

"Oh, Corey, you're the best." Jennifer leaned over and hugged him. "But I can't take your money. You must have had some reason for saving all that money, something you planned to do with it."

"It can wait. I was going to buy a baler—get up a crew and hire out baling hay around Sweet River, like that crew I worked on in the summers. I figured it would be a lot more profitable if I owned the baler instead of working for Dennis Bangston."

"Then that's exactly what you ought to do. I won't take your hard-earned money away. You buy that baler and make tons of money."

He grinned. "I doubt I'd make that much. Besides, I can work for Bangston another couple of summers and get a job at the processing plant in Springdale in the winter. In a year I'll probably have enough for the down payment."

"But Corey—"

"Look. I want you to have it. I can't think of anything better to invest in than you. You're going to be the best damned actress ever, and when you get rich and famous you can pay me back."

Jennifer wavered. The money would help her. She could concentrate on her career without worrying about starving. It was the answer to her problems. If she paid it back, if it was just a loan . . . "Well, maybe, on two conditions."

"What?"

"One, I'll pay you back, with interest."

"Okay. What else?"

"Second, I don't need that much money. I'll pick up part-time jobs here and there without much trouble. So I'll split the money with you. Four thousand each. Then you could put down a down payment on the baler, couldn't you?"

He smiled. "Yeah. I could do that. Okay, it's a deal. We'll split it."

Corey stayed another week, and though Jennifer started her classes on Monday and had her job as well, they managed to spend time together. Jennifer showed him the city, and they visited the beach and Disneyland, taking Kelly along with them. Every night they sat up late talking, hashing over everything under the sun except Corey's time in Viet Nam. He turned the subject aside every time Jennifer brought it up, and because she knew him so well, she understood. There were some things that were better left alone.

Jennifer was sad to see him drive away the next Sunday. The first few days of lessons had been hard and frightening. It had been overwhelming to realize how little she knew and how much there was to learn. It had helped having Corey there each evening when she got home from class. He had always been her strength, her protector.

For a moment, walking with him to his car, she wanted to go with him. Whatever Sweet River was, at least she knew it. Suddenly Los Angeles seemed as foreign and scary as when she had first arrived. She didn't belong here. She would never be able to make it. She thought of Matthew. He'd be home from college in a few more weeks.

Jennifer's eyes welled with tears as she hugged Corey good-bye. He got into his pickup and started the engine. The truck rolled out of the parking lot, and he waved out the window to her before he turned onto the street. Tears rolled down Jennifer's face, and she waved long after Corey could see her. She wanted to run after him and beg him to take her, too, but she didn't. It wasn't the first or the last time she had been lonely and afraid. She would stick it out.

Jennifer threw herself into her lessons with Annice. For the next few months she ate, drank, and slept acting. The school was hard, both physically and emotionally. Annice

Loehrmann never let up, and she never allowed any of her pupils to do so, either. The ultimate sin in her eyes was to be content with one's performance.

Annice pressed her students to the utmost, but her methods were tailored to the individual. With some she prodded and poked; others she led. She used tricks; she thundered; she coaxed. Jennifer saw her demolish an arrogant young actor with her acid tongue, but she never felt the lash of it herself. Instead, Annice asked Jennifer for all she had, and when Jennifer gave it, she asked for more. Jennifer would always struggle to give what anyone asked of her, and with her uncanny understanding, Annice realized that. Harsh criticism would wither Jennifer, but an appeal to her courage and determination pulled extra effort from her.

Jennifer worked constantly. She went to school, and in the evenings she worked in an outdoor theater production in Claremont. In what little spare time she had, Jennifer studied, both alone and with other students. She went over and over her parts, trying out different movements, gestures, tones, and inflections. As Liz had predicted, Jennifer soon had to cut her waitressing job back to part-time, and in six months she dropped it altogether. There was no time for anything but learning the theater. It consumed her life.

With every passing day Jennifer grew in ability and confidence. She no longer assumed that everyone did a better job than she. Nor was she eaten up with terror before a performance, though she still felt the sharp bite of anxiety that was essential to keep her at her best.

Liz got Jennifer a weekend job at a car show, where she dressed in a slinky dress and breathed raptures about a Japanese automobile. A couple of months later she had a small bit in a national television ad, then a larger part in a local ad. Liz also found her a minor part in an experimental film. It paid only scale and had very limited distribution, but at least it gave Jennifer some experience in front of the camera.

Jennifer went to audition after audition, but they always

seemed to be looking for someone older or with more experience or plainer or sexier or dark-haired or shorter or taller. In the fall, though, she was one of the women called back after an audition and asked to do a screen test for a small role in a TV movie that was a pilot for a series. A few days later Liz called her to tell her she'd been offered the role.

Jennifer was ecstatic. It wasn't a major role, just the blond bombshell secretary of the private detective hero, but at least the girl had several lines. And it was a real, honest-to-God two-hour movie! It was the biggest break of her career so far, and Jennifer skipped the next six-week session at school to be in the film. Annice was not pleased at her action, but she was too used to the realities of acting to make a fuss about it. What struggling actor would turn down a paying role to study his craft more completely?

Jennifer did well in the part, managing to hint at humor and intelligence behind the vapid sexpot exterior. Ted Mahler, the director's assistant, took her under his wing, giving her hints on dealing with the show's star and the director, filling her in on television terms she didn't know and instructing her how to play to the camera.

At the end of the filming one day Ted asked her to grab a hamburger with him, and they ate supper and talked. Ted seemed to know all the gossip about everyone in Hollywood, and some of his stories were so wild that Jennifer suspected he made them up. But he was pleasant to talk to, and she didn't object when he suggested that they stop by his apartment for a chat after the meal.

Nor did it surprise her when he made a pass at her at his place. It had certainly happened to her before, and at least she liked Ted. It would be nice if she felt something for him. After all, more than two years had passed since Matthew, and it seemed about time that she got over him. She wanted to like Ted's kiss, to feel heat stir in her as it always had with Matthew. She didn't want to feel dead the rest of her life!

But there was no answering surge of passion in her when he kissed her. Jennifer continued to try as he kissed her again and again. His hand drifted down to her breast. Jennifer jumped to her feet. "I'm sorry. I can't."

He scowled. "What the hell's the matter with you? Why did you encourage me if you didn't intend to do anything?"

"I didn't mean to encourage you. I'm sorry. It's—well, I thought I might feel something, but I don't."

"Great. What does that mean, that you're frigid or something?"

Jennifer swallowed. Was that what it meant? Was there something wrong with her? "I don't think so. I'm just— not interested."

His scowl deepened.

"I'm sorry." Jennifer felt stricken that she had hurt his feelings. "I better go now. Good-bye."

Ted didn't urge her to stay, and the next day on the set he didn't speak to her unless it was necessary. Jennifer knew she had hurt his ego. She found men difficult to deal with. She looked like the sort of woman who knew how to flirt and twitch her tail and get a man to do anything she wanted, but in truth she didn't know how to handle men.

They finished filming and Jennifer returned to school. The movie was aired a few months later. Jennifer, Liz and Kelly watched it together. Jennifer stared at her image, entranced and a little embarrassed and wishing she could somehow hold onto it, make it go more slowly. It was astounding. Glorious. She would have watched it twenty more times if she could have.

Corey called to congratulate her, vowing that she would put Sweet River on the map. Liz broke out a bottle of champagne and they stayed up late, drinking it and talking, dreaming magnificent plans for the future. They finally wound down and went to bed. Just before Jennifer drifted off to sleep, the thought of Matthew insidiously wormed its way into her mind. She wondered if he had seen the show and what he had thought. What he had felt.

*   *   *

A few months later, Jennifer heard that one of the networks had picked up the pilot and planned to make a series of it, and she was hopeful that she would be cast in the secretary role in the series, as well. But she never heard from the producer. She didn't know that the director had suggested her for the role again, but his AD had told him Jennifer was no longer in LA, so they cast another girl in the part.

Jennifer's year at the Loehrmann school ended, and as much as she had loved it, she didn't take another session. She had studied enough for the moment, she thought; now she wanted experience. Even Annice agreed with her. She continued the round of auditions, which Liz was indefatigable at finding for her.

Liz's business was improving. She had a good comedian for whom she had booked several stands at various clubs in LA and San Francisco. One of her clients had landed a good part in a TV movie, and another had received a lucrative commercial contract. Liz worked hard for them, always keeping in touch with casting agents, directors and producers, staying abreast of the industry news, talking, inquiring, selling her clients at every opportunity. But the one on whom she worked the hardest was Jennifer. Jennifer was her star, and no matter how slow Jennifer's career might seem at the moment, Liz knew it was only a matter of time until she came into her own.

Jennifer's break finally came the following summer, after she had turned nineteen years old. Liz heard about a minor, one-time role on a popular situation comedy, "Around the Corner," that sounded right for Jennifer, and she sent her to audition.

Jennifer got the part of the neighbor's dippy daughter who was visiting from LA. The show was a witty, acerbic comedy, and the cast and crew were excellent. Jennifer was thrilled simply to be able to work with them. The female lead was an established star whom Jennifer had watched on the television set in Byers' Cafe back in Sweet River. Her knees shook when she met the woman, and

Jennifer could only nod and gulp in response to her pleasant greeting. She blew her first line, but after that she calmed down, and everyone involved was so professional that it was easy to act with them. To make it even better, the part was a joy to play.

A month later, JAK Productions, the producers of "Around the Corner," told Liz that they had decided to do two more shows in which the neighbor's daughter appeared, and they wanted Jennifer back. When the shows aired, the audience response to Jennifer and the character was so positive that the next season the producer wrote her into the series as a regular.

The part wasn't large, and Jennifer wasn't on every week. But at least she was consistently in front of a camera; at least she was actually appearing on TV! She wasn't paid much by the standards of the stars of the show, but to Jennifer it was a lot, more than she had seen at one time in her whole life. At first she was afraid to spend it. She lived as frugally as she always had. Except for paying back Corey, she stashed away most of her salary in a savings account, afraid that the good times wouldn't last and she would need something to fall back on.

Liz laughed and shook her head when Jennifer explained why she didn't spend any of her salary frivolously. "Listen, kid, don't worry. This is just the beginning. The only place you're going is up."

It seemed as though Liz was right. Jennifer's part was enlarged. Though "Around the Corner" was a respected, first-class series, it had been on for several years now. Its ratings had begun to slip, and the writers had had trouble coming up with new plots for the same characters. But Angela, Jennifer's character, breathed new life into the series. She gave the writers something different to deal with. And the audience loved her. Jennifer played her part to perfection, but more than that she was appealing, no matter how silly she might seem. People liked Angela; there was something sweet and vulnerable about Jennifer's rendition of the character that created sympathy in the viewers.

JAK Productions renewed Jennifer's contract for the next season, and this time Liz had some bargaining power. She knew as well as the producer that "Around the Corners'" ratings had picked up that season and the reason for that increase was Jennifer Taylor. She got Jennifer more money and a better position on the credits, as well as a guarantee that at least three episodes that year would be focused on her.

Liz had no trouble getting Jennifer publicity now, and she went after it with a vengeance. Newspapers and fan magazines interviewed Jennifer. Liz sent her on arranged dates to nightclubs, restaurants and parties, and there was always a photographer or a gossip columnist there to record that she was there. Jennifer hated doing it; she hardly knew the men and usually was bored by them. But it got her name and pictures in the magazines.

She began to spend her money a little. She moved out of Liz's apartment and into a place of her own. She bought a new car, furniture for the apartment and pretty clothes, spending her money almost surreptitiously, with a secret, guilty joy, like an alcoholic sneaking a drink.

The next season, JAK Productions made a spin-off from "Around the Corner." They named it "Angela," and it revolved around Jennifer's character. In the first episode Angela moved back to LA and got an apartment in an old house with various oddball tenants. She was hired at a magazine as a secretary, and in her ditzy, naive-shrewd way, she came up with such successful ideas that she made her dim-witted boss look good and became the power behind the throne.

The show was funny. The writers were good. And Jennifer shone in the part. The viewers loved it. "Angela" shot to the top of the ratings, pulling in a twenty-four share. Almost overnight, it seemed, Jennifer Taylor became a household word. Her fan mail skyrocketed. She couldn't believe the number of fan letters that poured into the studio. Suddenly everyone knew her—or pretended to. Everywhere she went people asked her for her autograph. The attention embarrassed her, but she loved the adoration, the praise, the love flowing from her audience to her. She had always been hungry for love, and now, even though it was remote and sometimes a little peculiar, she had it in abundance.

Jennifer could hardly believe it was true. She was twenty-one years old and the star of her own TV show. Her dreams had materialized.

Los Angeles, June 20, 1987, 8:40 a.m.

Brett Cameron left her office, a small building that looked like a Victorian house, on the Royal Studios' lot. She walked across the asphalt parking lot past two sound stages to one of the post-production buildings. A receptionist glanced up as she entered and smiled. "Hello, Miss Cameron."

"Hello, Ann." She always remembered their names. It was something she'd learned from her grandfather long ago—along with nearly everything else. She nodded toward the TV set Ann had been watching when she came in. "Looking at the plane crash?"

"Yeah. It was horrible. They've been showing pictures of the wreckage. They don't know how many survivors yet."

"Were there any?"

"Yeah. A few. They showed the ambulances taking them off."

A balding man opened a door down the hall and stuck his head out. "Brett. There you are."

"Hi, Ken."

"We were about to start. Want to watch?"

"Sure." She followed Ken Rosen into a darkened room and up several steps onto the platform. Plush seats lined the wall. Directly in front of the seats and a step down was a long console filled with lights and switches. A man sat before the console, controlling the "mixing," or sound editing of the film. On the opposite wall was a large screen where Drifter was running in black and white. Ken's AD and the production manager were already sitting in the plush seats. They rose to shake Brett's hand.

She waved them back into their seats, whispering greetings, and sat down with Ken to watch. Jennifer Taylor's face filled the screen. Brett watched her with a familiar admiration. This was Jen's toughest role yet, the one most removed from her image, but she had done it well. The play of emotions across her face was perfect, natural, not too much. Her usually luxuriant hair was skinned back and tied at her neck, and she wore almost no makeup. She looked tired and careworn, but still there was that essential beauty that nothing could hide, the hint of vulnerability that made one care about her.

Ken asked a question, and in front of her Burt, the mixer, stopped and went back a few frames. "Here, Mr. Rosen?"

"Yeah. That's fine." They watched the film replay. "Let's cut Melinda's line there. It intrudes."

"Sure thing."

The door into the hallway opened softly, and the receptionist slipped in. Brett glanced at the door. Ann came to the railing. She looked tentative and something worse— shocked or scared.

"Miss Cameron?"

Brett left her seat and went to crouch by the railing. Ann knew Brett hated to be disturbed when she was viewing a film, so it must be something important. Up close, Ann looked worse than Brett had thought. "What is it?"

"Miss Cameron," she began again. "I'm sorry. But I thought you'd want to know. That wreck—"

"The plane crash?"

"Yeah. They think Jennifer Taylor was on it."

"Jennifer Taylor!" They had been speaking in whispers, but now Brett's voice rang out, and everyone turned to look. Brett stood up. "Are you sure?"

Ken Rosen came to Brett's side. "What's the matter?"

"Ann says Jennifer was on the plane that crashed."

A chorus of exclamations rose around the room. "They said they didn't know for sure," Ann hastened to add. "Trans Con hasn't given them a manifest, whatever that is, but the reporter said they'd learned Miss Taylor had purchased a ticket on that flight."

Ken's AD had risen and now sat down heavily. The production manager began to curse. Brett hurried down the steps and out to the reception area, with Ken at her heels, *and the rest of the men in the room followed. On the TV, a well-groomed reporter stood at the airport explaining to the station's anchor team back at the news set that Trans Continental Airlines had not yet released a list of the passengers on board the doomed aircraft. "Even the number is not certain, but Trans Con has given us an estimate— and this is only an estimate, remember—of 246 passengers and eight crew members."*

"What about the number of survivors?" the anchor asked with smooth concern.

"Again, we aren't sure. The survivors have been rushed to several area hospitals, many of them badly burned. Because of the dispersal to several hospitals, it will be some time before we have an accurate number."

"John, has there been any official word on whether Jennifer Taylor was actually on board the flight?"

"No. It is known only that a ticket was purchased on Flight 145 in her name, and that fact has been confirmed by her personal secretary. The airline refuses to comment regarding Miss Taylor's presence. There is a possibility that she was on board the plane, as well as a possibility that she was among the few survivors."

Brett turned away from the set. She and Ken looked at each other, white with shock. Ken had spent the past few months directing Jennifer in Drifter. *It was the third film Brett had done with her.*

Ken put his arm around Brett. "Are you okay?"

Brett shook her head. "I don't think so."

"You want me to call Darcy? You want him to take you home?"

"Yes. Call Joe."

Brett sat down on the long padded bench by the door, hardly aware of the buzz of excited, horrified voices around her. Jennifer! Dead? She couldn't take it in. Jennifer had been so happy during this film, so vibrant and alive it had been doubly hard to tone down her beauty. She had been happier than Brett had ever seen her, and Brett had known Jennifer for—what, seven, eight years? Yes, it must have been that long. Their first film together had been Refuge, and that had been in 1978.

Brett leaned her head back against the wall. She wished Joe would come get her. Funny, she'd found Joe that same year, too. She thought about Refuge and that little town in New Mexico. And Jennifer.

PART III

Chapter 8 *

Brett Cameron bent over the papers on the desk before her. She was an angular woman, a little on the thin side, dressed in worn blue jeans and a soft, bright pink sweater, with blue Nikes on her feet. She wore large horn-rim glasses, as she usually did for reading. A pen and a pencil were stuck into the curling mass of her unruly red-brown hair.

She had a few minutes until Liz Chandler's appointment at 10:00, and Brett didn't believe in wasting time. It was the only way she managed to get everything done. She was one of the busiest and most successful independent producers in Hollywood. Straight out of college she had directed a sleeper that had achieved a good deal of success. She had gone on to direct and produce two more solid box office hits, and at the age of twenty-six she had established herself as one of the new wunderkinder of the film industry.

It seemed only fitting, considering her background. Brett Cameron came from Hollywood royalty. Her mother, Cheryl, was the only child of Kingsley Gerard, the head of

Royal Studios, and his first wife, Mona. Cheryl was pretty, fun to be with, thoroughly spoiled, and rather neurotic. She and Brett's father, a British actor of little note named Bramwell Cameron, divorced when Brett was a year old. It was the first of five marriages for Cheryl.

After her divorce, Cheryl devoted herself to having fun, and as a result, Brett spent most of the first few years of her life with her grandfather and his second wife, Lora. Lora had been a thirties film star at Royal. She was the love of Gerard's life, but she had been unable to bear children, and they had always regretted their childlessness. They adored Brett. She was more child than grandchild to them. Gerard took her with him to the studio to show her off, and little Brett was often seen sitting quietly to one side in production meetings or coloring at a low coffee table in King's large office. She listened to Kingsley discuss movies with the leading directors of the day and heard raging arguments when they disagreed. She knew costume designers, cameramen, makeup artists, grips, and leading actors by name. Susan Hayward blew her a kiss when she saw her, and Clark Gable chucked her under the chin and winked at her. One day when Kingsley's secretary lost track of Brett and ran frantically around the huge studio lot looking for her, she found the little girl sitting outside a sound stage with Montgomery Clift, gravely discussing a scene he had just shot.

From the time Brett could speak her grandfather talked movies with her. At a time when other children were out playing, she could be found sitting in a screening room, looking at dailies or film classics. When she was at home with Lora, legendary stars of the screen often dropped by to visit, and Brett heard tales of the glory of movies in the thirties.

When Brett played, it was usually by herself. She had no siblings, and no "neighborhood children" dropped in when one lived on an estate several acres in size. Now and then Lora would realize how little time Brett spent with other children and would arrange for some director or producer's child to come play with her. And, of course, Brett went to the elaborate birthday parties the film people gave for their sons and daughters, always striving to put on a more fantastic show than the last one, hiring clowns, animal acts, jugglers, even renting a carousel.

But most of the time Brett was alone. She roamed the grounds of Whitecliffe, the Gerards' large estate. She climbed over the man-made hillock, to watch the man-made waterfall spill over the carefully arranged rocks to the man-made pool below. She explored the wilder back reaches of the place, where brush and trees and vines tangled, taking Lora's spaniel with her. At those times she was a frontiersman. At other times she played in the huge, echoing ballroom of the house, and then she was a princess.

Wherever she was, she lived in a world in her head. She created daring adventures and sweeping romances, stories such as she had seen at the studio with Kingsley or in the theater room at home. Brett was not content to make up imaginary friends. She created whole kingdoms and peopled them with kings and queens, prime ministers, wicked dukes, court jesters, and armies. There were castles and towns, dances and parties and brave rescues.

When Brett turned six, her life became less lonely. Cheryl married Ken Rosen, a well-known director, and Brett had a new family. Ken and Cheryl took her to live with them at their Beverly Hills home, and Brett came back to Whitecliffe only to visit. Two years later, Cheryl and Ken had a daughter, whom they named Rosemary. Brett was enchanted by the baby and eagerly took care of her whenever she got the chance. Taking care of her was something Brett got to do more and more as the years passed and their mother's marriage worsened.

Those years when Cheryl was married to Ken were the most stable in Brett's life. Brett adored Ken. He was part of the world of the movies, just as her grandfather was. He was a calm man, one who always appeared to have everything under control even when there was chaos all around. Brett had the same sort of calm, almost remote way of viewing the world around her. They often sat together, quietly reading, or with Ken answering Brett's seemingly endless questions. Brett regarded Ken as her father, not the man who had actually sired her whom she couldn't even remember.

Unfortunately, the marriage fell apart by the time Brett became a teenager. Brett was heartbroken to lose Ken, and she visited him on the weekends with Rosemary. Cheryl returned to life in the fast lane, this time choosing the French Riviera, and Brett returned to Whitecliffe, taking young Rosemary with her.

Brett attended Westlake, a conservative girls' school in Bel Air, an expensive place but not flashy like Beverly Hills High. She was a quiet student, never acting up, but never excelling, either. Her grades were mediocre except in English. Brett had little interest in school. Her life centered around one thing: the movies. She had been certain of it all her life. She would make movies and someday she would run Royal Studios. While the other girls at school were dating and giggling over boys, Brett was writing movie scripts and reading everything about the industry.

After high school, she went to the film school at UCLA, where she finally was allowed to study something that had meaning for her. She wrote and directed a film for a project in one of her senior classes, and it was this that she turned into her first movie. An independent producer produced it, and Royal Studios distributed it. Even her grandfather hadn't envisioned how well the film would do. Brett attended the first night of its LA run—it wasn't big enough to have a premiere—with Ken Rosen on one arm and Kingsley Gerard on the other. It was the proudest night of Brett's life, and she was only sorry that Lora had not been there to share it. She had died the year before.

Brett knew that the only way to really control a movie was to produce it as well as direct it, so she raised the money for her next picture and produced it herself. Even without well-known actors, it had been a tremendous success. Her third movie had become one of the biggest money-makers of all time.

Brett understood movies; she knew them inside and out. More than that, she had a sense of what the public wanted to see, what would touch them, what would make them laugh or cry. And she understood Hollywood. She knew the ins and outs, the methods and habits, the backstabbings, feuds and politics. She wasn't burdened with the fears and insecurities that plagued most people there. Brett had always been indisputably at the top, not because of what she had done or how she looked or other things that one could lose, but simply because of her name. That fact gave her an innate confidence that few who had worked their way up could match, an inner assurance that allowed her to go her own way without jitters and pretensions.

She planned to produce independently for a few years to gain experience, then quit and take over the helm of Royal Studios when Kingsley retired. She named her production company Dragowynd, after the dragon queen of the stories Ken had made up for her when she was a child. The company's office was in a small stucco building off Hollywood Boulevard. The location was perfect for her, despite the general decline of most of the area. This was Brett's Hollywood, the Emerald City of her childhood, with Kingsley Gerard as the Wizard. Only three blocks away were the old Royal Studios and not much farther was the Brown Derby, where her grandmother had often taken Brett to lunch, sitting at "her" table. Brett had ridden in the Christmas parade down Hollywood Boulevard with her grandparents, fake snow blowing down upon them from huge studio fans atop the buildings. It was at Paramount Studios in Hollywood that Ken had directed his Oscar winner, and it was in a nightclub on Sunset Strip where her mother had met Ken and fallen in love with him.

Of course, her mother was now on her fifth marriage, and Royal Studios was located in Burbank. But Brett's memories and dreams were still in Hollywood.

Brett laid the paper she had been studying aside and

dictated a quick memo into her dictating machine. She
picked up another file, but just then her secretary opened
the door and stuck her head inside. "Liz Chandler's here,
Brett."

Brett set the file back down and went out to greet Liz.
She didn't believe in keeping a visitor sitting in the outer
office, cooling her heels, in order to make herself look
important. She didn't have the time or the inclination for
such Hollywood games.

"Hello, Liz."

"Brett. It's nice to see you." Liz stood and stepped
forward to shake Brett's hand. She was dressed in an
expensive blue suit, and her hair and face were kept
carefully in shape at Elizabeth Arden. As Jennifer's fortune had risen, so had Liz's.

"Angela" was in its third season now, and Jennifer was
so popular that Liz had been able to renegotiate her
contract for a healthy sum. But her success wasn't due just
to having a commission on larger sums for Jennifer. The
number of her clients had risen dramatically. Liz took only
the people she thought were good, and she never tried to
push a client into a role that he didn't fit. She had gained
credibility with producers, directors and casting agents,
and several of her clients were doing very well.

Brett and Liz went into Brett's office. It was a large
room, but so crammed full of stacks of paper, boxes, file
cabinets, and chairs that it seemed cramped. No decorator
had been at work here. The furniture was utilitarian, and
the only adornments were a few old movie posters hung in
frames on the walls.

"Would you like some coffee?" Brett asked, plopping
down behind her desk. She twisted back her unruly hair as
she talked and fastened it with a large tortoiseshell clip.

"That's fine." Liz sat down in the chair on the other
side of Brett's desk. They chatted for a few minutes while
the secretary brought their coffee. Brett took a phone call,
and when she hung up, she turned back to Liz. Liz knew it

was time to talk business. "I understand you're casting for *Refuge*."

Brett nodded. *Refuge* was her newest project, in pre-production now. "Yeah. I've signed Richard Farley for the lead."

"But you don't have a girl yet."

"No. Why? Do you have somebody for me?" Brett had been impressed with what she had seen and heard about Liz. Liz had done well by herself and her clients in the few years she had been in business. Brett had used one of her actors in a minor role in her third movie, and he had been good. Perhaps more important to Brett, when she had called Liz last year looking for a certain type, Liz had straightforwardly admitted that she had no one who could fit the bill, instead of wasting Brett's time sending over people who were wrong in the hopes that she would get lucky. If Liz said she had someone for the role, it aroused Brett's interest.

"I certainly do," Liz responded, her eyes lighting up. "Jennifer Taylor."

Brett looked at her blankly. "Angela?"

"Yes."

"But Liz, maybe you heard wrong. I'm not looking for a dumb blond. I want a fragile, almost ethereal woman."

"What's more fragile and ethereal than a blond?"

"The hair color's okay. It's the chest."

"So what if she's well built? You don't have to empha-size it like they do on the show. Look at Jennifer's face." Liz whipped out a black-and-white glossy from her brief-case and slid it across the desk to Brett. "It's delicate."

Brett studied the picture. She had never paid much attention to Jennifer Taylor because her interests didn't lie in television. But Liz was right, the triangular face was delicate, and her enormous eyes emphasized the delicacy. Still . . . "But Liz, she's a TV personality. You know they rarely translate well to the big screen."

"I know. But some do. And Jennifer's one who will; I'm certain of it. I've always thought she belonged on the screen. She has a certain quality, a real presence. And she can act. I tell you, Brett, this woman's got more potential than anybody around.''

Brett looked doubtful.

"Just give her a chance. A test. You, of all people, wouldn't prejudge someone. I'm sure you've heard plenty of that yourself: 'she's too young'; 'it isn't talent, it's her name.' You proved them wrong. So can Jennifer.''

Brett smiled wryly. "You certainly know which buttons to push.''

"I'm not pushing buttons, just speaking the truth. I tell you what.'' Again Liz delved into her case, and this time emerged with a can of film. "Here's one episode of her show that I think comes closest to showing her potential. Will you at least look at it?''

"Yeah. I'll look at it.'' Brett motioned toward an empty space on her desk.

"You'll consider a screen test?''

"If I like what I see on this film.''

"Fair enough.'' Liz knew when to stop pushing. She picked up her briefcase and said good-bye.

Brett returned to her work. But the can on the edge of the desk tantalized her. Something onscreen was always more appealing to her than paperwork. She reached over and buzzed her secretary. "Midge? Get hold of Lewis for me. I have some film I want to see.''

A half hour later, Brett sat in the small projection room down the hall, watching an episode of "Angela.'' It was amusing, but Brett didn't smile. She wasn't watching it for enjoyment. She leaned forward, elbows on her knees, hands clasped together and her chin propped on them. She watched Jennifer Taylor with a concentration that excluded everything else.

Good figure, but Liz was right. The clothes she wore on the show were designed to emphasize her bosom. In the right clothes, her figure wouldn't cause a dissonance with the story. She had a great comedic touch, a mobile face that expressed everything she thought without overdoing it. This show also had a touching moment with a small girl, and in it the overt silly sexiness receded, and real emotions shone through.

It wasn't a long segment. Brett had it rewound and looked at it again. It was hard to tell from such a short part. Yet what she saw had been done well. Brett ran it past three more times. There was something about Jennifer's face—a softness, a hint of vulnerability—that took the hardness from her character and made it appealing. You had to like her. She had a tenderness, a glow that might look good on the big screen. But Brett couldn't tell from this little piece.

She picked up the phone on the small table beside her chair. "Get Liz Chandler's office for me. Tell her I want to set up the screen test for Jennifer."

Jennifer's Mercedes turned into the gates of Royal Studios. Her hands were clenched around the wheel, and in her head she was reciting the lines she'd learned from the script Liz had given her. She was more nervous about this test than she had been in five years. The guard checked his list, found her name, and smilingly directed her to the correct building.

Jennifer parked and walked to the sound stage. Her stomach was cold with dread. The chance of acting in a Brett Cameron production was the biggest opportunity she had ever had. She had been successful in "Angela." She drove an expensive car, had a beautiful house in Beverly Hills, and owned so many clothes it was sinful. But she wanted more than a lot of money and a successful television series. She wanted to try new things, test her skills, prove to herself and the world what she could do. She wanted to explore and expand, to create. She wanted to star in the movies; that had been her lifelong dream. Nothing could have given her a better opportunity at those things than a Brett Cameron movie.

When Liz had come to her dressing room on the set of "Angela" yesterday and told her that Brett wanted to test her, she had been ecstatic. Now she was terrified.

But even terror couldn't eliminate the tickle of excitement along her nerves. Jennifer stepped inside the sound stage. She was surprised to find Brett Cameron herself on the set. Brett turned at her approach and smiled. "Miss Taylor."

"Jennifer, please."

"Jennifer. I'm Brett Cameron." Brett's eyes moved over her assessingly. Jennifer was used to the impersonal, judging look.

"Yes, I know. I'm a little surprised to see you here."

"I like to direct my own screen tests if I have the time. It gives me a sense of how it will be to work with the actor." She paused. "Are you ready to begin?" Jennifer nodded. "Good. Then Cindy will take you over to a dressing room and we'll start as soon as you return."

Cindy whisked Jennifer off to a portable dressing room, where makeup was applied, hair restyled, and a simple cotton dress substituted for her own. There was little of Angela's flash left. As she walked back to the set, Jennifer began the process of withdrawing, settling herself into the character. By the time she reached Brett, she was the vague, uncertain, wistfully lovely young woman who was the heroine of *Refuge*. Even Brett was a little surprised by the transformation.

"Do you know the story?" she asked Jennifer.

Jennifer nodded. The movie was about a loser who got the Mob angry with him. He fled to the mountains, and along the way he ran into a girl, beautiful but generally regarded as being somewhere between stupid and crazy. The girl helped him escape the men after him, and in the process both of them proved themselves.

"Good. Let's start the test."

There were actually three tests, one with the man who would play the girl's father and two with a stand-in for the male star. Each test required several takes, and as they worked, Brett's excitement grew. Jennifer took direction well. She was smooth, competent and professional. More than that, she could act! Now if only she came across well on the screen . . .

Jennifer knew she was in command of the role and her fear left. She settled down to enjoy the experience. Brett Cameron was wonderful to work with, an actor's director who discussed and explained and pulled the best from her. She could capture in a few words the essence of what emotion or attitude she wanted. But she left it to the actor to create in his own way what she had suggested. By the time the shooting was over, Jennifer was both drained and elated.

She glanced over at Brett. It was impossible to tell what she thought of Jennifer's performance. Her face was impassive, almost remote. Brett said a pleasant good-bye to Jennifer, then went off to talk to her crew.

Brett could hardly wait to get the film developed so she could see it. She wished Richard hadn't been so adamant about not shooting tests with the hopefuls. She would have liked to see the two of them together, just to make sure they worked. She returned to her office and muddled through some work until finally Midge came in to tell her that the tests were ready and waiting in her projection room. Brett hurried down to the room to watch. She sat hunched forward in her chair, every muscle in her body tense. Jennifer's face came on the screen, soft and beautiful. First there was a close-up, then a full-length shot. Brett straightened. She watched six of the best takes, a small smile touching her mouth. Jennifer had it—that elusive quality of screen presence that her grandfather summed up as "the camera loves her." The camera loved Jennifer Taylor, and Brett knew, with a bubbling excitement, that she had her female lead. More than that, she had a star.

After the screen test Jennifer left the lot and drove aimlessly around Los Angeles. She didn't know what to do with herself. She didn't want to go home and sit around waiting for a call—who knew when she might hear anything about the test? But she couldn't think of anyplace to go.

She dropped by Liz's house and spent an hour or two playing a board game with Kelly while Liz spent most of her time on the phone. She and Liz talked in between the phone calls. She told Liz about the test. Finally she left, still restless, and drove home. She roamed through her house, knowing she should work on the "Angela" script she was shooting the next week, but she was too jittery to make herself do it.

She wished there was someone to talk to, to help take her mind off the test. A friend. A lover. She had had very few of the former and none of the latter.

Usually the lack of a man didn't bother her much. She was, after all, young, only twenty-four; there was still plenty of time for love to enter her life. The series kept her busy, and during the break each year she had done a TV movie. She had little time for anything.

But today . . . today she was very aware that something was missing in her life. Would she never again feel as she had when she had loved Matthew? She wanted the same kind of excitement she had had with him, the same closeness.

Liz called later, her voice bouncing. "You got the part! Brett wants you for *Refuge*."

Jennifer laughed and babbled right along with Liz, but even as she did so, deep inside she knew regret that there was no one there to share it with her.

* *Chapter 9* *

Brett detoured past her grandfather's house on her way home. He more than anyone she knew would understand the kind of excitement she felt about Jennifer Taylor's screen test. She took the test film with her.

A guard sat in a sentry box beside the gate to Whitecliffe. When he saw Brett's car, he came out, smiling, to open the gate. He had been the guard there since Brett could remember. He must be sixty years old—not much protection, really, but Kingsley would never fire him. Too much of the old days were gone; her grandfather kept whatever he could.

"Miss Cameron." The old man smiled broadly. "How are you today?"

"Just fine, Arnie. How about you?"

He nodded. "Can't complain."

"Is my grandfather in?"

"Oh, yes, ma'am. He'll be happy to see you."

Brett waved and drove through the open gates. The road curved around trees and flowering shrubs and finally emerged at the wide, green front lawn, treeless to provide the best view of the house. It was a monstrosity of a house. No one could afford to buy such a thing today except a rock star or an Arab oil sheik. It sprawled haphazardly across a small rise at the end of the drive, a jumble of different levels, balconies and angled roofs. It was built of off-white stucco with a red-tiled roof, and scarlet bougainvillea cascaded down one expanse of wall. A large tower sat at one corner, out of place and dominating the scene. It was too much for the eye, supremely ostentatious—and beautiful to Brett.

She stopped her car in the circular driveway in front of the house and stepped out. By the time she reached the front door it opened, and a smiling servant greeted her. "Hello, Miss Cameron."

"Phyllis."

"Mr. Gerard is in his study. Would you like me to tell him you're here?"

"No. I'll just run up and surprise him." Brett moved across the entryway, laid with faded tiles transported from a Mexican hacienda, past the large, tinkling fountain and up the dark, hand-carved stairway (shipped in pieces from a castle in Spain).

Kingsley's study was on the second floor. Its door was closed, and Brett eased it open. Kingsley was stretched out on the couch beneath a full-length oil portrait of Lora Michaels. Brett gazed at her grandfather. When she caught him napping like this, she could see his age. His hair, though thick, was pure white now, and the hands folded across his chest were mottled, his knuckles knotted. Without the animation that was usually there his face looked wrinkled and slack, and though his arms and shoulders were still powerful, his formerly stocky body seemed to have shrunk.

Sadness pierced Brett. She wondered if she should move back into the house. King must be terribly lonely in this huge old place by himself now that Lora was dead. King's eyes flew open, and he fixed her with his sharp, dark gaze, and the age fell away from him. "Brett!" He rose, smiling, and the quickness with which he moved belied his seventy-five years. "How are you, darling?"

"All right." Gerard put his arms around her and squeezed. There was still strength in him, too.

"How's your sister?"

"I think Rosemary is okay." Brett was never sure. As long as she heard nothing from her, she hoped things were going smoothly. Rosemary always seemed to be in some kind of trouble. A few months ago she had dropped out of college and as far as Brett could tell was doing nothing except living off the trust fund Lora had bequeathed her. Rosemary always had one problem after another with men or school—even the police once—and it usually fell on Brett to help her out of them.

"What time is it?" Gerard glanced at his watch. "I must be getting old, falling asleep like that every time I get in a horizontal position. Will you stay for dinner?"

"Sure. But first I want to show you something." She held out the can of film. King's eyes brightened with interest.

"What's this?"

"A test. I think you'll be impressed."

"Then let's take a look."

They went downstairs to the small theater, and Kingsley buzzed for his valet, who also ran his film. They settled down side by side on the plush chairs, and Leo ran Jennifer Taylor's test. Brett looked less at it than at her grandfather's reaction. At first he leaned back in his chair. As the film ran, he brought his forefinger to his lips and rubbed them thoughtfully. Then he leaned forward, propping his elbows on his knees. He glanced at Brett, his eyebrows going up, then back at the screen. When the clip was over, he turned to Brett.

"Who is she? I've seen her before."

"On television. She has a show named 'Angela'."

"Yeah. Sure. TV, huh?"

"Yes, but her agent convinced me to test her for *Refuge*."

"Let's run it again."

Gerard's concentration was no less intense the second time. When the film stopped, he flicked the lights on and looked at Brett. "You've got something there. You know that?"

"I told you you'd like it."

"You going to put her in the movie?"

"I've already called her agent with an offer."

Kingsley nodded and took a cigar from an inside pocket. "She reminds me faintly of your grandmother. There's something of Lora's quality in her, that special thing that pulls you."

"'The camera loves her.'"

He smiled. "Yeah. It does. And she's prettier than Elly, even." He was the only person Brett had ever heard call her grandmother by her real name rather than her screen name, Lora. "Not quite as sexy, by you don't need it in this movie."

"She toned it down a lot for the test." Brett paused. "So. Do you approve?"

"Hell, yes! If we still had the contract system, I'd snap her up in a second. That girl will make both Dragowynd and Royal a bundle. Now they'll say you're a starmaker as well as bankable."

He put his arm around Brett's shoulders and they left the theater room, laughing and talking. Dinner was served to them in the small dining room, and they remained there talking over their coffee long after the meal was through. Despite the vast difference in their ages they were kindred spirits. They could discuss movies for hours at a time and never grow tired. There was no aspect of the business that didn't interest them, no actor, director, or film that didn't merit their discussion. Their knowledge of movies and the people connected with them was enormous, and they were as likely to argue over a 1950's horror flick as a present-day, big-budget film.

King told a funny story about a William Wyler film Lora had been in, and Brett told him about her trip to New Mexico the next week to look at locations for *Refuge* that her location manager and art director had chosen. Later, as King lit his second after-dinner cigar, his lined face turned serious.

"How long will you be in New Mexico?"

"A couple of weeks. Frank's done the preliminary work, but I want to go over all the possibilities he found. Why?"

"You won't be here for the press conference, then."

"What press conference?"

"The one I'm holding." He stood up and began to pace the room, one hand thrust into his pocket. "We've been in negotiations for two months now, and we finally agreed on the deal yesterday." Brett looked at him, waiting, and he went on. "I'm selling the studio."

She looked as blank as if he'd spoken in Portuguese. "What?"

"Royal's being bought by a conglomerate. Krill-May."

"Krill-May? They make laundry detergent!"

"Hell, they make everything. They own a clothes com-

pany, a chain of department stores, a publishing company—
you name it.''

Brett went weak inside. He must be joking. ''I don't
believe you.''

''It's the truth.''

''You're selling Royal?'' She pushed back her chair and
rose. Her hands were trembling. ''You can't!''

''Why not?''

Because it's mine! she wanted to scream. Because in her
heart she had run Royal Studios since she was a child. It
was her goal, her destiny, her future. ''Granddad—I can't
believe you'd sell it. To some stranger!'' Her eyes were
pleading, and she looked vulnerable in a way King had
never seen before. He started toward her, but she backed
away. ''What's going on? What happened?''

''Sweetheart, I'm seventy-five years old. It's gotten to
be too much for me to run. I lost interest in it when Elly
died. Hell, you know I'm just chairman of the board now;
it's being run by my executives. If I don't run it, I don't
want to own it. Besides, it hasn't been the same since we
went public in the sixties. Shareholders to report to, the
board. There's no autonomy. Krill-May wanted it, and
they offered a good price. It seemed the time to sell.''

''But what about—'' Brett glanced around a little vaguely. ''I thought I'd take over from you. I thought when you
retired, I'd come in. It was what I always wanted.'' Her
voice caught, even though she struggled to suppress it. ''I
thought that's what you wanted, too.''

''It was! Of course it was. Is that what's bothering you?
You think I didn't want you to take over? I used to dream
of it.''

''Then why—''

''It didn't work out that way. You went into directing,
then producing. You have your own company. You didn't
belong at Royal.''

''Don't belong!''

''Not that you aren't good enough. You're one of the
best, Brett. We both know that.''

"You think that because I started my own company I didn't want to be at Royal? I did that for experience—on my own so I'd know I wasn't being treated specially because I was your granddaughter. So I could prove I was really capable of running Royal. But I love the studio!" Tears started in her eyes and Brett blinked them back fiercely. "Is it because I'm a woman? You don't want to entrust your studio to a mere female?"

Gerard's eyebrows rushed together in a frown that had once made famous stars and powerful directors quake. "That's not it and you know it," he thundered. "Hell, I've trained you to run that place since you were a girl. But I've looked at your movies. I've seen what you can do. You don't belong in a studio executive's office. Things are different nowadays. Used to be, we cared about the movies. We knew them inside and out. I alone was responsible for all my pictures, both flops and successes. Now a studio executive's a businessman. He could be in a hundred other businesses just as easily. They don't work their way up through the ranks. They come from Harvard Business School. Jesus, they don't even call them movies; they call them 'the product.' And all they're concerned about is reporting to the board. Getting a raise or getting fired. It's the independent producer now who's the real movie man, the one who loves and understands the movies. He's the only autonomous one left. That's what you are, and it's where you belong."

Brett stared at him, not speaking. Royal Studios was what she had built her life on. It was what she and her grandfather had planned for years. Now it seemed that he had changed his mind. He didn't want her. Whatever reasons he gave, she felt as if a chasm had opened up at her feet. King had betrayed her.

Kingsley frowned. He saw Brett's stunned dismay, the hurt that blazed across her face, and he felt confused and guilty. He hadn't expected her to take it this way. In fact, he had thought she'd be relieved to be rid of the future burden of the studio.

"Sweetheart, you're a creative person. Sure, you're a business person too; you understand profit and loss. How else could you have made your company so successful when all around us directors and producers are shooting up and down like rockets? But you don't belong in an office pushing a pencil, filing reports, dealing with only numbers. You should be making pictures. The studio would be a burden to you. An albatross. If I gave you Royal, you would sacrifice yourself for it. And I won't allow that."

"It wouldn't be a sacrifice. I love the studio." It was all Brett could do to keep the tears from coming. She refused to cry in front of her grandfather; she never had.

"So do I. You think it didn't kill me to sell it? But it's best all around."

"Sure." Brett turned away. It was over. He'd said he had agreed to the deal. Nothing could change it now. But she wondered if she would ever get over the hurt and betrayal. All her life she had loved Royal Studios. And now it was gone. She pushed her hair back from her face and looked around vaguely for her purse. "Well, I guess I better be going."

"Brett—" Kingsley didn't know what to say. He had never dreamed she would take it like this. He must have presented it badly. Suddenly he felt very old and tired. He wished Lora had been here. She would have handled it better.

Brett shook her head. "It's okay. I'll be in New Mexico next week, so it'll be a while before I see you." She picked up her purse and keys and gave him a peck on the cheek. "Bye. Talk to you when I get back."

Brett drove home and packed her bags. She wasn't scheduled to fly to New Mexico until Tuesday, and then she had planned to rent a car. But tonight she wanted to drive. The road and the dark sky beckoned her. She felt lonely and lost, and she yearned to run. She wanted to feel the steering wheel beneath her hand and watch the road zip by endlessly under her tires. There was an ache in her that could be matched by the vastness of the West and the loneliness of a highway at night.

She packed a suitcase and stowed it in the trunk of the Mercedes and took off. She could put off what she had scheduled for Monday and go to look at the possible locations now. Going to New Mexico would give purpose to her need to drive.

She took the San Bernardino Freeway east and drove through most of the night. It was a relief to reach the desert, with its dark emptiness and bright, faraway stars. It always seemed to clear her mind. Her grandparents had owned a weekend house in Palm Springs and she had loved visiting there. The desert brought things into focus.

The movies had been her whole life, and Royal Studios had been the embodiment of the movie industry. She had never considered doing anything except eventually taking over Royal Studios and running it. Now what was she to do? She reminded herself reasonably that it was her grandfather's studio to do with as he wanted; he had no obligation to give it to her. Perhaps he really had acted in what he thought were her best interests, believing that her creativity would be crushed in the life of a studio executive. But such thoughts didn't help. Whatever Kingsley's intentions, she felt as though the heart had been torn out of her.

She stopped finally at a motel in Arizona, exhausted, and slept. Early the next afternoon, after a greasy hamburger in the cafe next door, she set out again. She drove into the mountains of southern New Mexico, exploring the first area Frank had noted. She spent Sunday night in Ruidoso and early Monday morning she called her office to let them know where she was. By then the immediacy of the hurt was beginning to wear off, and she felt a little foolish at her impulsive action. But that was the advantage of running her own company; she could do what she wanted.

Brett answered her secretary's questions and gave her all the instructions she could think of to keep things running in her absence. She spent the afternoon driving and walking through the mountains, taking notes on the small hand-held recorder she always carried with her. At least the work took her mind off Kingsley's sale.

The next day she went east out of the mountains toward the flat, barren oil and cattle country known as Little Texas. She stopped in a small town for lunch and ate a bowl of chili that set her stomach on fire. She got into her car to leave, but a small shop of Indian jewelry caught her eye and she stepped back out of the Mercedes and went inside. Brett wandered among the turquoise and silver jewelry, Navajo rugs and serapes, business forgotten for the moment, until a laconic voice near the front of the store inquired, "That fancy car yours, lady?"

"What?" She looked up.

"If so, somebody's stealing it."

"What!" Brett hurried to the front window just in time to see her sleek green Mercedes turn the corner and disappear. She clapped her hand to her purse and remembered, with vivid clarity, the sight of her keys dangling in the ignition. She had jumped out of the car and left the keys in it! "Damn!"

"You want me to call the sheriff?"

"Oh, hell! Yes, please." Brett felt like slamming her fist through a wall. How could she have been so stupid? Just because this was the middle of nowhere didn't mean she could go around leaving her keys in the car. Now she was stuck in this hole-in-a-wall town for God knew how long, filling out forms and waiting for her office to hire a limo in El Paso or Albuquerque to pick her up. It would take hours. She might even be trapped there for the night. Worst of all, her briefcase was in the car! Her notes, her tape recorder, the papers she planned to work on in the long, boring evenings in motel rooms. She could take losing the car much more easily than losing her briefcase.

The man behind the cash register called the sheriff and gave him a description of the car. Soon a young deputy arrived and drove her over to the county jail. The jail was an old white stone building with iron bars on the windows. It gave Brett the creeps just to enter it. Inside there was a cramped, dark waiting area floored in old linoleum where Brett sat in a straight-backed wooden chair and waited for the sheriff to interview her. A young woman in a short dress sat behind a desk across the room and sneaked glances at Brett. Brett looked down at her boots, long skirt, and silk blouse and felt distinctly out of place.

Finally the sheriff emerged from his private office and escorted her inside. He was a muscular man in his fifties, and he looked tough, as if years of hardness had scoured his soul. Brett felt a twinge of guilt for having her car stolen when she looked at him. She was glad she wasn't the culprit. She related what had happened and gave the description of her car again. He looked disapproving when she couldn't remember her license number. The longer she sat with him, the more Brett disliked the man. He had a heavy, avuncular attitude, condescending toward her city female foolishness in losing her car. She expected him at any moment to call her little lady and pat her on the hand.

Brett was glad when he released her to the secretary outside, who typed up the information and had Brett sign the forms in triplicate. When she finished, Brett sat down again, not quite sure what to do. Should she wait there or call her office and tell them to send a driver for her?

In LA she would have given up already on recovering the Mercedes; it would have been stripped, repainted and sporting new license plates by now. But in a little town like this a Mercedes would stick out like a sore thumb, and where could one run except along the straight, flat highways? Plus, the store owner had spotted it being stolen immediately. Surely there was a good chance of catching the thief.

Another thirty minutes crept by. Brett decided to return to the cafe and wait there over a cup of coffee. Anything was better than sitting in the narrow, depressing room. But just as she stood up to leave, the inner office opened and the sheriff stepped out. "Miss Cameron?"

"Yes?"

"They found your car."

"What! Oh, thank God!" A grin burst across her face, giving her a lively prettiness.

"All in one piece, too. They should be bringing it and the suspect in any minute now; Darrell just called in to say they were on their way. You can identify the suspect, and we'll be all set. 'Course you'll have to come back here to testify when his case comes up."

"I understand." Brett sat back down, relieved.

Minutes later the outer door opened and a burly man in a Highway Patrol uniform entered. Behind him came a sheriff's deputy and a man whose hands were pulled behind his back and locked in handcuffs. The man was young, probably not more than a couple of years older than Brett herself. He was dressed in boots, worn jeans and a black T-shirt, and his muscled arms were darkly tanned. His head was down, thick black hair shielding his face, and the deputy beside him gripped his arm tightly.

Brett rose, a faint touch of fear nipping at her stomach. The situation was entirely foreign to her, and it made her uneasy. The sheriff came out of the office behind her, his boots clumping noisily on the floor. "Well, Darrell, what you got?"

"That breed you saw hanging around town yesterday. Says his name's Joe Darcy."

"I suspected it was him," the sheriff said triumphantly. "Didn't I tell you to get out of town, boy? What's the matter, you can't hear too good? Look at me when I talk to you!"

The man looked up then, tossing his head back and facing them defiantly. It was all Brett could do not to gasp. The man's lower lip was split and swollen, and dried blood crusted his upper lip. His cheekbones were purpling with bruises, and one eye was puffed and bruised, swollen shut.

The eye that wasn't shut glared at her, then swept beyond her to the sheriff.

If there was one thing Brett was adept at, it was recognizing human emotions, and beneath the defiance and the anger she saw fear in the man's dark eye. It was obvious that the lawmen had beaten him up. And, considering the antagonism that crackled in the air between the thief and the sheriff, she was certain that he would probably suffer the same fate here in the jail. Brett's stomach quivered sickly.

"Miss Cameron, is this the man that took your car?" the sheriff asked, his tone indicating the question was merely a formality.

Surprising even herself, Brett replied, "No, it's not."

Joe Darcy looked at her, his face impassive, but she could see the instant alertness in the way he stood, poised for a fight, but uncertain whom to fight. The deputy gaped at her. "But we found him driving your car!"

"Of course. He's my driver. My chauffeur."

"Now, Miss Cameron—" the sheriff began in a bullying tone.

Brett fixed him with a cold glance. She was used to being in charge, and she had watched Kingsley Gerard move over opposition like a steamroller all her life. She had the innate assurance of one who commanded, and she used it full force now. "Please release Mr. Darcy. Obviously there's been some mistake."

"I'd say so," Sheriff Metzger replied with heavy irony. "You report your car stolen, and now you say the guy we caught in it is your chauffeur?" His gaze flickered contemptuously toward Darcy. "He doesn't look like any chauffeur I've ever seen."

"He is also my bodyguard. Besides, I don't see how his manner of dress is any concern of yours."

"You know, I'm beginning to get real suspicious about this whole thing. How do I know you two aren't in this together some way?"

"Stealing my own car?" Brett's mouth curved in faint

amusement. She whipped open her purse and pulled out the documents of her life—driver's license, credit cards, car registration—and showed them to the sheriff. "Why don't you call California and check?"

"I think I will." He gave a terse order to the deputy and the other man disappeared into the sheriff's office.

"While you're at it, you might want to call my office to see if I'm really who I say I am." Brett tossed him one of her cards. "Or perhaps my grandfather, Kingsley Gerard. He's the chairman of the board of Royal Studios." She pulled out another card. "Or Mr. Piña in the New Mexico tourism office; he's been working with me on filming my next movie in New Mexico. I'm sure he'd be more than happy to vouch for me."

It appeared he was. When Sheriff Metzger called Piña on the receptionist's phone, Piña's agitated voice on the other end was so loud that Brett could hear it from where she stood. He was no doubt terrified that a lucrative movie deal was going down the tubes right in front of him. After the sheriff hung up the phone on Piña, the deputy emerged from the sheriff's office. "The car belongs to her, all right."

The sheriff turned to Brett, his eyes suspicious and filled with frustration. "It doesn't sound right."

"It was all just a silly mistake. I didn't actually see my car being stolen; the man at the cash register told me it was being stolen. When I looked it was already gone. Obviously my driver simply had to go somewhere."

"Why didn't you mention any driver before now?"

Brett shrugged. "In the excitement it slipped my mind. I never thought about it being Joe. I thought he was in the restaurant."

Metzger set his jaw. Brett crossed her arms and took a step toward him. "Sheriff, I'm asking you to release my driver now. I've told you that he didn't steal the car. I'm certainly not pressing charges against him. If you don't allow both of us to leave immediately, I'll come back with

an attorney and file suit against you and the county for
false arrest—and assault.''

The sheriff gave a short, angry nod at his deputy.
Frowning, the deputy stepped behind Darcy and unfastened
the handcuffs. Darcy looked at the sheriff, then at Brett,
his expression unchanging and guarded.

''Thank you, Sheriff.'' Brett gave him a brisk nod and
held out her hand. ''My keys.''

The highway patrolman hesitated and glanced at the
sheriff, then handed them over to her. Brett strode to the
door and opened it. She turned, quiet command in her
voice. ''Joe.''

He followed her, walking stiffly. Brett wondered if his
body was as bruised as his face. She walked to her car and
went to the driver's side. Joe Darcy hesitated on the
sidewalk. ''Don't worry, Joe,'' Brett said in a clear voice.
''I'll drive. You just get in.''

He said nothing, but he opened the passenger side of the
front seat and slid inside. Brett saw him wince as he sat
down. Quickly she started the car and pulled away from
the courthouse. Her only thought was to get out of town
and the county as fast as she could.

They left the little town behind. Jasper. Hopefully she'd
never see it again. Brett's hands and legs began to tremble
with the aftermath of adrenalin. She glanced over at the
man on the seat beside her. He leaned against the door, his
eyes shut, his bruises dark and ugly in the sunlight. Brett's
stomach knotted all over again. What in the world was she
doing?

She must have lost her mind. Here she was jumping into
the car with the man who had just stolen it and driving off
into the deserted countryside. He was a thief and no
telling what else, and she was putting herself in his hands!
In the sheriff's office she had noticed only how bruised and
mishandled he'd been, and the fear that lurked behind his
defiance. But now she noticed how large and supple his
hands were, how well-muscled his back and arms. She
wondered what had possessed her to act as she had.

And yet . . . Brett stole another glance at him. He didn't look dangerous, only hurt, and she couldn't have left him there, knowing what would happen to him. She had acted out of instinct, and usually her instincts served her well.

Brett curled her fingers tightly around the steering wheel. She was committed now. She would take him to the next county and put him in the hospital. She ought to be safe until then. He didn't look to be in any condition to harm her right now. In fact, he soon appeared to be asleep.

Brett was careful not to exceed the speed limit—she had no desire to tangle with the law again today. As she drove, she kept thinking about the scene in the sheriff's office, weaving it into *Refuge*. It was perfect for the movie and the character, and no matter what was going on, Brett's mind was never very far from a film.

When she reached Roswell and had to stop for the first time for a traffic light, her passenger woke up. He glanced around, confused, then his eye settled on her. Carefully he straightened up. He moved more stiffly than before, and his blackened eye looked even worse. Over the years Brett had seen lots of men made up to look like this, but she had never seen the real thing. It didn't look as bad as the makeup, but somehow it was more frightening. Brett turned her eyes back to the road, trying not to stare. Her heartbeat picked up, and her palms were sweaty on the wheel.

"Who are you?" His voice was low and a little hoarse. It was the first time she'd heard him speak.

"My name's Brett Cameron."

"Why'd you do that back there?"

"They had beaten you up. And they were going to do it again, weren't they?"

"I imagine."

"I couldn't let them. I mean, well, I just couldn't."

He studied her without speaking. He seemed to be waiting, and she sensed that he expected an ulterior motive to reveal itself.

"We're in Roswell now," Brett told him. "I'll take you to the hospital and—"

"No! I don't want to go to the hospital. I don't need to." Brett shot him an eloquent glance.

He shook his head. "I'll be okay. It's happened before."

"You need to have a doctor look at you. You could have a broken rib, and a broken rib could pierce your lung."

"I'll be okay," he repeated stubbornly.

Brett set her jaw. She was used to dealing with difficult people. She swung the car into the first filling station she saw and stopped. She turned off the engine and pocketed the key. "I'll be back in a second. Don't go anywhere."

Joe watched her go into the women's restroom. He couldn't figure her out. Why had she done that for him? What could she have to gain? He knew he should get out and start walking. He didn't like depending on people. But he felt too lousy, so he waited.

Brett was soon back with a couple of wet, wadded paper towels in her hand. She came around to his side of the car and opened the door. Leaning in, she took Joe's chin firmly in one hand and dabbed at the bloody streaks on his face with the wet towel. It hurt, but he didn't move, didn't speak. Joe Darcy had never been taken care of in his life, and he didn't know what to do. It was curiously pleasant, despite the pain. When she finished cleaning his face and the cut below his eye, Brett tossed the bloodied towels into the trash and went around to the trunk of her car. She returned with a small first-aid kit and applied antiseptic to the cuts. Joe drew in his breath sharply at the pain, but said nothing.

Brett closed the kit and stepped back, shoving one hand into her hair as she studied his face. It didn't seem as though she had helped him much. But what else could she do? Suddenly she smiled: "I know. Ice—that would take down the swelling. And there's one of those machines right there."

Before he could say anything she hurried over to the metal ice machine, put in some coins and pulled out a large bag of ice. She returned to the trunk and rummaged around in it for a while. When she reappeared at his side, she had piled a couple of handfuls of ice inside a satiny garment and tied it. Her slip, he thought. He felt strange taking it.

"Hold this to your eye. It'll help the swelling. Here, put a piece in your mouth. Maybe it'll help."

He obeyed her, wondering more than ever which one of them was crazy. Brett shut his door and got back in the car.

"Why are you doing this?" Joe asked.

Brett glanced at him, frowning. "I'm not sure. But I hate for people to be in pain, and since you're too stubborn to go to the hospital, I did what I could. Besides," she grinned, lighting up her face, and she looked beautiful to him, "I guess I'm just bossy." She started the car and pulled out onto the highway. "You want to eat? There's a Dairy Queen."

He nodded. She went into the restaurant and returned with two sacks. She handed him a large hamburger, fries and a chocolate shake. Again, he wondered what she was up to, but he was too hungry to think about it, just as he was too hungry to worry about the pain of chewing. It had been two days since he'd eaten a decent meal.

Brett watched him out of the corner of her eye. She had suspected that it had been a while since he'd eaten. She knew a pang of pity. It was her nature to empathize, to feel what others felt. It was part of what made her a good storyteller, even though sometimes it hurt. She felt Joe's hunger just as she'd felt his pain that morning, and she wished somehow that she could help him. Yet even as she hurt for him, her cool moviemaker's eye was filing away the scene in her mind. It seemed almost fate that she kept seeing things in him that reminded her of her protagonist in *Refuge*.

"Why did you steal my car?"

Her tone carried no anger or resentment, only curiosity. Joe had never met anyone like her before. He shrugged, then grimaced at the pain the unthinking gesture cost. "Just stupid, I guess. The sheriff told me to get out of town. I knew what was coming if I didn't; I know his type. I was stranded, broke. Then I saw your car. I figured somebody with a Mercedes could afford to lose it; you'd have insurance." He looked at her, and for an instant warmth gleamed in his uninjured eye. "And it was so damn beautiful." His hand touched the leather seat in an unconscious caress.

His answer surprised Brett; she hadn't expected a hunger for beauty to be part of his motivation. "It's also awfully easy to spot out here."

She thought he smiled, though with his swollen lip it was hard to tell. "Yeah. That's the stupid part. When I saw you go into that store I thought, a fancy lady like that, she'll be in there an hour, at least. I could have been halfway to El Paso in an hour; there are more Mercedes in Texas. But you must have seen me drive off."

"The man at the cash register did." She paused. "Can I ask you a question?"

This time she was sure it was a smile. "You're asking permission now?"

"Why did they beat you up? Did they have something against you?"

His face was smooth, impassive. "I'm the kind of guy that doesn't know my place. I smarted off to them, so they taught me a lesson. I've been taught a hell of a lot of lessons to still be as dumb as I am."

"What's your place? How do they know you belong there?"

He shot her a doubting glance. "Are you serious?"

"Yes."

"I guess my place is on the bottom. I'm half Anglo, one-quarter Mexican and one-quarter Indian, which I guess makes me all mongrel. And I'm an ex-con." Brett opened her mouth and he forestalled her. "Don't ask me how they knew. They just did. Cops always do. They can smell it."

His tone was joking, but Brett could sense a lifetime of

defeat and pain behind his words. He was a loser, like Jack in *Refuge*, yet she sensed in him the same sort of potential, crushed down by the years of losing. "I'm driving to Hobbs," she said. "If you'd like, you can hitch a ride."

He simply looked at her for a moment. Finally he said, "Yeah. I'd like it." Brett started the car and barely heard the words that followed in a low voice. "Thank you."

* *Chapter 10* *

Joe fell asleep again and didn't wake up until the car stopped. He sat up gingerly and looked around. They were in a small town, and Brett was outside walking around, looking at things and talking into a tiny tape recorder. He wondered what in the hell she was doing. What *was* she, anyway? A pretty California girl in a sea-green Mercedes, driving around New Mexico, saving thieves—it didn't make sense.

Brett walked along the main street, down a couple of side streets, and back to the car. As she approached, she saw that the hood of her car was open and Darcy was standing beside it, leaning over into the engine. She came up beside him and he glanced up at her.

"Your engine was idling rough, so I checked it. No problem. I stuck a plug wire back in; that'll take care of it."

Brett started the engine. He was right. The vibration was gone. Joe slammed the hood shut and got in beside her.

"Thank you."

He looked at her, surprised. "It wasn't anything."

"More than I could have done."

She started the car. As she drove, she asked him questions—about his life, where he grew up, his family, what he did for a living, New Mexico, Texas. Joe had never heard so many questions at one time. He didn't like questions, but he found himself answering her. She asked them with such a charming air of good will and innocence that it was impossible to resent it.

She drove to a ranch house, and there she went off in a Jeep with a middle-aged man. Brett suggested that Joe wait for her in the house, but he stayed in the car. He didn't feel comfortable in houses that looked that nice. Brett returned at dusk, looking tired and hot, and they left the ranch.

Joe looked at her. "Can I ask you a question now?"

"Sure."

"What in the hell are you doing?"

She laughed, a happy, almost childlike laugh. "I'm looking at location shots for my next movie."

"Your what?"

"My movie. I produce and direct movies."

"You're a producer?"

"Yes."

"You don't look old enough."

Brett shrugged. "Nevertheless, that's what I do. My location manager drove all over New Mexico looking for suitable spots, and now I'm checking out the ones he thought best. We need mountains, a cabin, a small Western town, and a ranch."

Brett shot Joe a sideways glance, then said a little tentatively, "You know, it would be a lot easier to look at everything if someone else were driving. It also would be nice to have someone along who could fix the car if something happened to it. I thought you might be interested in the job. I'll be here a couple of weeks. I'd pay you fifty a day plus expenses."

He stared. "You want me to work for you?"

"Yes, if you feel well enough to drive. Provided, of course, that you don't run off with my car."

Laughter shook him and he hugged his chest against the pain it brought. "Lady, you are strange."

Brett raised an eyebrow. "I realize that. But will you take the job?"

"Yeah. I'll take the job. Your car's safe from me."

Brett checked them into the nicest motel in Hobbs, then took him to a steak place to eat. The prices seemed enormous to him, and he felt out of place and grubby. He and Brett were the only ones not dressed up, and he knew everyone was staring at his marked, swollen face. But the situation seemed to bother Brett not at all.

She was accustomed to people looking at her. She had lived with publicity all her life; the first time she remembered someone staring was when she was three or four years old and out with her grandmother. Nor did it make her uneasy to sit with someone who wasn't dressed right or who looked odd. Eating in a commissary with people dressed in all manner of costumes or covered with fake scars and monster makeup inured one to oddity.

Joe didn't understand her unflappability, but it impressed him. Her generosity impressed him even more. He'd never eaten a steak so thick and succulent or slept in a place as nice as the motel room she'd given him.

Even more amazingly, the next morning Brett drove to a bank and got an envelope full of bills which she handed to Joe, saying, "Here's your salary in advance. You'll need some clothes, since yours got left behind."

He had looked at the money, stunned. Fourteen fifty-dollar-bills. Seven hundred dollars. She'd given it to him before he'd done a lick of work for her. Why, he could just walk off and leave her, money in hand. Stupid, he thought at first, then realized that she meant to give him that opportunity. If he wanted to take off, she was slipping him some money. And if he stayed, she was giving him a chance. He took the money out of the envelope and stuck it in his billfold. There wasn't a chance in hell of him running.

For the next week Joe drove Brett around New Mexico. He took his job seriously. He couldn't remember anyone ever trusting him as Brett had trusted him, and he wanted to give her back full measure. More than full measure. He drove carefully, never exceeding the speed limit, and he kept the car in mint condition. Every evening after supper he washed away the dust of the New Mexico roads and vacuumed out the floors and seats, then went to his motel room and mapped out the next day's route. Every morning he got up early to check the engine and correct anything that was awry, no matter how minor.

When Brett complained about the record keeping, he offered to take over the task for her. Brett looked as if he'd given her a million dollars and promptly handed over the notebook and envelope of receipts. The next day she handed him a wad of money and asked if he would take care of paying their expenses as well, since he was keeping the records. It stunned him. Joe stared at the money she had given him. "Lady, you are too damn trusting. I'm surprised you've got a cent left."

Brett gazed calmly back at him and replied, "If you were going to steal from me, you would have already taken the car and the money I paid you the other day and split. Wouldn't you?"

"Yeah."

"But you didn't."

"Somebody else might."

"I wouldn't have given the job to somebody else, let alone the money."

Joe folded up the money and stuck it in his pocket without saying anything else. He kept meticulous records of every cent he spent.

Through Brett he saw a world he'd never known. Though they weren't faced with much elegance driving around the countryside, what they ate and where they stayed seemed like luxury to him. In Santa Fe they stayed at a hotel that was so old and elegant he felt ill-at-ease even being in the lobby, and they dined in restaurants where the tables were laid with a variety of forks, spoons and knives the uses of which he couldn't even guess. Brett had coffee and a chat with a couple of expatriate Texans at their pueblo-style house, which was large enough for a motel, and Joe waited for her in the kitchen, drinking iced tea and thinking that he could have put the entire house where he grew up in that one room.

Brett decided to visit several of Santa Fe's excellent art galleries, and Joe followed along, expecting to be dead bored. But the strong, vivid paintings took his breath away. For the first time in his life something spoke to his soul. He bought a pack of plain white paper and several charcoal pencils and began trying to draw during the long stretches of time that he sat waiting for Brett.

But if Brett opened up a whole new world for him, Joe also introduced Brett to a life she didn't know. The morning that she gave him his salary in advance, he went to a budget store to shop, and Brett roamed the store, fascinated. A few days later, when their small supply of clothes were all dirty, Joe introduced her to a laundromat. Though Brett traveled a lot, she was used to staying in hotels where one's laundry was whisked away and taken care of. On location there was always a worker who handled such things. Even in college she had had her clothes laundered.

Brett watched with interest as Joe loaded the machine, bought a tiny box of soap from the dispenser and poured it in, then stuck a quarter and a dime into the washing machine to start it. Joe glanced at her. "You've never done this, have you?" Brett shook her head. "Lady, where have you lived all your life?"

She grinned. "Beverly Hills and Bel Air."

Common, ordinary things interested her. She even insisted one day that he take her into a broken-down bar by the side of the highway, despite his vehement protests. He hadn't wanted her to see it or be in it, and the whole time they

were inside, he stood inches away from her and glared
fiercely at the other occupants of the room. Another time
she had him stop so that she could take pictures of a cheap
motel. She took pictures of everything wherever they
went.

And she asked questions.

At first Joe had been dismayed at the number of her
questions and had tried to find a pattern in them, a reason.
One minute she asked him about Texas, where he had
grown up, and five minutes later she turned to him and
said, "What do you think about Jennifer Taylor?"

"What? Jennifer Taylor? Why?"

"You've seen her, haven't you?"

"Yeah. I watched her show a few times."

"What do you think about her?"

His face moved in the way he had of smiling without
really smiling. "She's sexy."

"So are a lot of women."

"Not like her."

"What's special about her?"

He frowned, concentrating. "She's beautiful. You want
to take her to bed." He paused. "But she makes you want
to just hold her, too. You know? You want to help her,
protect her."

Brett smiled. "Good. I think she has that vulnerable
quality, too."

And that was all she said about the subject. There was
no figuring her. After a while he gave up. If there was a
reason to what she wanted to know, only Brett knew it. He
relaxed and quit trying to guess what she wanted him to
say. Instead, he simply answered what he thought or didn't
answer the questions at all, as he chose. Brett wasn't
offended when he didn't answer. Nor did she require him
to make conversation. Except when she was asking questions, Brett was rather quiet. There were often long silences between them, yet both of them were comfortable.

Joe had never met anyone like Brett. She treated him
differently from the way people always had, with regard

for him as a person. There was no trace of contempt in her voice or eyes, and neither his past nor his mixed blood seemed to bother her. She took him at face value. It now mattered to Joe that his face value be good. He hated the thought of seeing disappointment in Brett's eyes. If she had asked him for anything he would have gotten it for her, no matter what it took. She had moved into his life like a goddess, changing everything, and he felt for her a primitive, unquestioning loyalty.

As for Brett, she liked having Joe around—a little to her surprise. It was nice to be freed from the demands of driving, to be able to simply look and think. It was equally as nice to be taken care of, as he had begun to do with the bills and travel records. She appreciated his silence. The last time she had looked at locations, Frank, the location manager, had accompanied her. He was good, but he was talkative, and the week they had spent together had almost driven her crazy. With Joe it was different. When he spoke he usually said something worth saying—interesting, informative, sometimes even amusing.

She asked him questions about his life, hoping for insight into the character in *Refuge* who resembled him, and she was surprised to find out how well his mind worked. He was sharp and perceptive, and though he knew nothing about the movie business, he had an eye for detail and color.

His opinions were honest and to the point, and he spoke from the viewpoint of the real world, not Hollywood. She asked his opinion more and more often and bounced her ideas off him. She had started out pitying him, but before long she wound up liking and respecting him. It made her a little blue to realize that in a few days she would return to California and not see him again.

Brett called her office every day. Midge always had a million questions for her, as well as countless messages that she had been assured "couldn't wait."

But one day, only two days before she planned to return to California, Midge had no list of questions when Brett called. Instead she said in a relieved voice, "Brett! Thank God!"

"What's up?"

"It's your sister."

"Rosemary?" What was she up to now?

"Yes. Mr. Gerard's been trying to get you, and the hospital, too."

"The hospital!" Brett straightened, anxiety rushing through her. "What happened?"

"I don't know. Mr. Gerard said your sister was in the hospital. He left his number there."

"Give it to me." Brett jotted down the number, then hung up to dial her grandfather.

The telephone rang once before it was answered in a familiar Southern drawl by Kingsley's secretary.

"Dorothy? This is Brett."

"Brett! Honey. We were waiting for you to call."

"Is Granddad there? What happened to Rosemary?"

"It looks like she'll pull through now. King's gone home, but he left me here to answer your call. Rosemary took a bunch of pills and they had to pump out her stomach. But the doctor says she'll make it."

"Oh, God." Brett closed her eyes, thinking of her baby sister lying in the hospital. "Suicide?"

"God knows, honey. It could have been an accident. You know."

"Yeah." Brett sighed. "I'm sorry I wasn't there."

"Couldn't be helped. King took care of it."

Yes, but Rosemary would have needed her. Brett had always looked after her. "I'll be there as soon as I can."

"Okay. I'll tell King you called."

Brett hung up the phone and went outside. What was Joe's room number? Her mind was a blank. She started to go back in and call the front desk for it, but then she saw him standing by the car, waiting for her to come down for supper.

"Joe?"

He looked up and saw Brett's white face. Something

was wrong. He took the steps two at a time. "Brett? Are you okay?"

"Oh, Joe." Her voice came out in a quivery sigh. "I—I have to leave."

Without hesitation he took her arm and led her toward the car, asking only, "Where do you want to go?"

"I have to get back to Los Angeles. My sister's in the hospital."

"Okay." He settled her in the car. "I'll run up and get our bags and check us out of the motel."

She nodded and leaned her head back against the seat. Thank God Joe didn't ask questions. He just did what was necessary. He returned after a few minutes, throwing their bags into the backseat and sliding in under the wheel. "Sorry I took so long. I called the airports."

"Good. Thank you. When can I get a plane?"

"You can't."

"What?"

"The last flight to LA out of Albuquerque left thirty minutes ago."

"Oh, no!"

"It's okay. I'll drive you. If we go straight through the night you'll make it earlier than you would waiting for a plane tomorrow morning."

"But what about you? You can't drive all night!"

"I've done it before." He backed out of the parking lot and turned onto the highway. "You just rest, okay?"

That was easier said than done. All she could think about was Rosemary. Why had she done it? "She took a bunch of pills," she said suddenly and wondered why she was telling Joe.

"Your sister?"

"Yeah. They don't know if it was an accident or suicide." Tears filled Brett's eyes. She thought of Rosemary lying in the hospital, tubes and needles stuck in her. "I feel so guilty."

His hand curled around hers on the seat between them. "It's not your fault."

His gesture surprised Brett, but it was comforting to have his hand on hers, and she didn't pull away.

"I've looked after her ever since she was a baby. She depends on me. When Mother divorced Ken, it was harder on Rosemary than it was on me. She was younger, and he was her father, not just a stepfather. Going to live with my grandparents was tough on her, too; she didn't know King and Lora as well as I did. When our grandmother died, Rosemary was only fifteen, so she went to live with Mother. That was the worst thing. She was at an impressionable age, and life with Mother is so . . . unstable."

"But you lived through the same things, and look how you turned out."

She gave him a brief smile. "Yeah. Well, it's not always easy being related to a whiz kid, either. Besides, it was different for me. I was much closer to King and Lora. I was even closer to Rosemary's own father than she was. We all loved the same thing: the movie business. Rosemary's like Mother. She isn't interested in movies, so she felt excluded." Brett sighed. "She needs so much affection and understanding, and I'm never there for her. I'm busy, and lots of times I'm impatient with her. I deal with temperamental people all day long, and when Rosemary comes crying to me in the midst of some emotional turmoil it just seems too much."

"You give her what you can. Nobody can ask for more than that."

"Thank you."

"Why don't you lean your seat back and get some rest?"

Brett didn't think she could sleep, but she did as he said. To her surprise, she began to doze. She awakened hours later. It was dark outside and Joe was pulling into the parking lot of a fast-food restaurant. Brett realized that she was hungry; they hadn't gotten around to supper earlier.

"Where are we?" she asked, sitting up and combing her hands through her hair.

"Arizona. We're making good time."

They went inside, stretching out their stiffness, and ate a quick meal. Then Brett drove for a while so that Joe could catch a brief nap. She was over the first shock and in control again. Joe took the wheel again, and Brett slept. When she woke up they were close to Palm Springs. She yawned and stretched. Her mouth tasted terrible, and she was stiff from sleeping in the odd position.

She looked at Joe. The dawn light was harsh on his face, exposing the lines of sleeplessness and exhaustion and highlighting the faded bruises around his eye. A day's growth of beard further roughened his face. He looked mean and tough, and it was strange how reassuring it was to see him. She was coming to depend on him.

They had another meal on the run and drove the rest of the way to LA. Brett directed Joe to Cedars-Sinai Hospital. He walked with her to Rosemary's room, then went to the waiting room down the hall.

Brett stepped into Rosemary's room. Her sister's eyes were closed. She looked young and fragile with her curling hair spread out on the pillow around her, eyelashes shadowing her pale cheeks. Rosemary opened her eyes when Brett entered and she began to cry, holding out her arms to Brett like a child. Brett went to her and held her.

"Oh, Brett. It hurts," Rosemary whispered. "My throat's so sore and my stomach hurts."

"I know, sweetheart." Brett patted her back. "I know. But it'll go away." She drew back to look at Rosemary.

"Don't look at me that way." Rosemary flopped back on her pillow, her mouth pulling into pettish lines.

"What way?"

"Like you're wondering whether I tried to kill myself."

"How can I help but wonder that? Rosemary, what happened? Why did you do it?"

"I just took a few pills too many. No big thing."

"Do you take a lot of pills? Often?"

"Are you going to preach at me?"

Brett wanted to. She couldn't count the number of

careers—not to mention lives—that she'd seen go down the tubes because of drugs. Still, she knew how well a heavy, moralistic tone would go over with her sister. Rosemary wouldn't listen; she would simply get defiant. "Sweetheart, I care about you, about what happens to you. You must know that."

"Yeah, I know. It's more than I can say for my mother and father." Her eyes glittered with wetness, and the sight tore at Brett's heart.

"Ro, that's not so. They care."

"I don't see either of them around here, do you? No. Only Granddad and you, as always."

"That's not fair. Mother's in Europe, and Ken's shooting a film in Mexico. They had to contact him by radio, and it'll take hours of driving before he can reach even a provincial airport. They'll be here."

"Dad's job comes first. It always has. And Mother— well, Mother comes first with her."

How could she make Rosemary see? Ro didn't have the understanding, the love for the industry that Brett did. She was unable to cope with the fact that her father poured everything into his movies. Nor could Brett make her realize what a burden she had put on Ken with this overdose—tearing him away from location so that the company wasted at least three days of shooting, with all the actors and technicians bored and griping and the money burning up. Brett sighed. No doubt Rosemary blamed her, too, for not being in town.

Brett clasped her sister's hand and sat down on the edge of the bed. "Well, I'm here, and they will be soon, too. What you need to do is just rest and not think about it."

Rosemary closed her eyes and, holding Brett's hand, drifted into sleep. Brett was sleepy, too, but she had too much to do to nap. She phoned King to find out the time of her mother's arrival. Next she called her office and spent a good hour on business. After that she found Rosemary's doctor and discussed her condition with him.

She fell asleep finally, sitting straight up in the chair,

and was awakened some time later by the sound of the door creaking open. It was Joe, a white paper sack in his hand. She smelled the delicious aroma of a hamburger and french fries. He set the bag beside her. "Thought you might be hungry," he whispered.

"I am. Thank you."

"I'll be in the waiting room, whenever you're ready to leave."

Brett polished off the hamburger. Rosemary woke up, and Brett spent the next hour trying to make her comfortable and cheery. Their mother arrived shortly after two, her usually well-groomed face ravaged by the long hours of nonstop traveling. Cheryl went to Rosemary and hugged her. Rosemary clung to her, tears leaking from her eyes. When Cheryl turned to Brett to greet her, Brett saw the strain and fear that Ro's boundless needs always aroused in her mother. Brett gave her an extra squeeze for encouragement. She and her mother had never been as close as Cheryl and Rosemary had been, but theirs was a more comfortable relationship.

Brett seized the opportunity to excuse herself. She desperately wanted to bathe, change clothes, and lie down in her own bed for a few hours. She went in search of Joe. He was lying down on the couch in the waiting room, eyes closed. His eyes popped open as soon as she stepped into the room, and he was instantly alert.

They went downstairs and took the side door to avoid the reporters waiting in front. Anything to do with King Gerard or Brett Cameron was news in this city. But they ran into a reporter who had taken a chance that they would try to slip out this way.

He hurried up to them, pad and pen in hand. "Miss Cameron, what's the condition of your sister?"

"She's doing well now, thank you." Brett continued walking, and Joe stepped around her to place himself between her and the reporter.

"Is it true that she tried to commit suicide?"

Brett's eyes flashed. "No. It's not."

"There are rumors that your sister has been taking drugs. Is that true, Miss Cameron?"

Brett shook her head. "Please. That's all I have to say."

"What about the sale of Royal Studios to Krill-May? Were you surprised by your grandfather's decision? Weren't you expecting to be the heir to Royal Studios?"

Brett clenched her jaw. Why did he have to bring that into it? No doubt he was hoping to catch her in a weak moment. She shook her head again, turning her face away from him.

Joe stopped abruptly, and his hand around Brett's arm brought her to a halt, too. The reporter pulled up short, surprised. "Didn't you hear the lady?" Joe asked, his voice clipped, his face as hard and cold as stone. His eyes shot into the other man, a killing look that made Brett shiver. "She doesn't want to talk to you."

The reporter stepped back. Brett didn't think she had ever seen one so effectively silenced with a look. Joe took her arm, and they walked to the car. The reporter didn't follow.

Brett directed Joe to her apartment building and leaned her head back, watching the city move past. She would call Midge and have her bring her some cash to pay Joe.

Joe walked her to her apartment from the car. She got him a beer from the refrigerator and he drank it, standing at the bank of windows and looking out at the view.

"Thank you for driving me out here."

Joe shrugged.

"I guess you'll want to go home now."

Again he shrugged. Brett hesitated. "Joe, I—have you ever thought of living in LA?"

"No, I never thought about it."

"Would you consider it? What I mean is, it would be nice to have a driver full-time. It'd give me some extra time to work going to the office in the mornings. And I hate the hassle of traffic." She grinned. "And you sure can take care of reporters."

"You want me to work for you all the time?"

"Yes."

"Yeah. I'll stay." It was that simple with Joe.

* *Chapter 11* *

Jennifer finished filming *Angela*. Her contact with the show was up and she had refused to sign another one, so when they shot the last day for the season, she was very aware that it was the last episode she would ever shoot. It was the last episode for the show, as well. The network had considered bringing in a new actress to play Angela but had decided it wouldn't work; and without the title character there wasn't enough to carry a show. On the last day of shooting there were tears and hugs and good wishes. There were also a few cold, tight smiles and unfriendly glances from those who resented what her leaving would do to their jobs. It hurt Jennifer to leave; she had worked closely with the people for four years and they seemed almost family. It hurt even more to see the resentment in some.

But the touch of sadness was soon lost in the excitement of filming *Refuge*. It was challenging and scary and exhausting. Jennifer had never worked so hard in her life, but even though she came home each day weary in mind, body, and soul, she loved making the movie. Brett Cameron was a wonderful director. She asked for the best from each actor and managed to pull things from them that even they didn't know they had. Jennifer had never felt as stretched, but she had never been as fulfilled and invigorated, either.

Brett asked for nothing from her people that she wasn't

willing to give herself. Every morning at 5:30, when
Jennifer arrived on the set for wardrobe and makeup, Brett
was already there, discussing her plans for the day with
her technicians and assistants. Brett was brisk, capable,
and practical, and she was prepared for whatever foul-ups
or delays might occur. Jennifer had never heard of a filming
that ran as smoothly and quickly. Brett was creative, but
she also had a healthy dose of producer in her soul, and
she was constantly aware of the profit margin. She
prided herself on bringing her movies in on time and on
budget.

Wherever Brett went, a dark, muscular man was never
far away from her. He sat or stood at the edge of the set,
and though he doodled on a pad most of the time, his eyes
kept watch on Brett. His hair was shaggy, his clothes just
short of scruffy, and there was a look to his face that made
no one want to mess with him. His name was Joe Darcy,
and he was Brett's driver—and, from the looks of it, her
bodyguard as well. There were lots of rumors about him,
everything from his having been in prison for murder to
his being Brett's lover.

But Jennifer didn't believe the gossip about him and
Brett. Joe never touched Brett, nor she him, and there was
no suggestion of intimacy between them when they walked
together or stood talking. Brett never spoke of Darcy
except as a trusted employee, a friend perhaps, but not a
lover.

Jennifer loved making *Refuge* so much that she was
depressed when it was over. It wouldn't have been so bad
had she had something to do, but for the first time in her
life she was idle. Liz insisted that she wait until exactly the
right part came along. Her next movie, Liz said, would be
what established her as a star. Too many actors made the
mistake of rushing into a mediocre film after a hit because
they were offered good money or were scared they would
be forgotten. As a consequence they often slowed down or
even ruined their careers. Liz was determined not to let
that happen to Jennifer. While they waited for the perfect

script, Jennifer's publicist worked at keeping her name before the public. It meant a lot of arranged dates and interviews about *Refuge* and working with Brett Cameron. Jennifer didn't mind the interviews, but the dates only added to her depression.

Her blues lifted miraculously one day when she picked up a script entitled *Lady Money*, mailed to her by one of the lesser known producers in Hollywood. It was a marvelously funny story, with crisp, humorous dialogue, and Jennifer liked it instantly. When she showed it to Liz, she agreed. Within three weeks Jennifer signed to do the movie.

By the time she finished shooting *Lady Money*, *Refuge* was out, and Jennifer spent several weeks promoting the movie, appearing on talk shows and going to premieres across the country. The movie was an enormous hit, number one at the box office for fourteen weeks running, and the top-grossing film of the year. Jennifer had been famous for years and hadn't been wanting for offers of parts, but she was overwhelmed by the response to *Refuge*. She couldn't go anywhere without being surrounded by people wanting her autograph. And all the moviemakers in town suddenly wanted her for their movies.

She chose *All the Runners* for her next movie because its director was known as one of Hollywood's leading geniuses and because the part she was offered, though not the lead, was a plum. It was another departure from type for her, a role packed with emotion and sadness. She played a beautiful prostitute, a drug addict who hated her life but hadn't the courage to leave it.

The movie was a disaster from the word go. The director, carried away by his accolades, followed his creative vision to the exclusion of all else. He described in detail exactly how actors should play their roles, leaving no room for the actors' own interpretations. Scenes were shot over and over. They spent two months on location. The script was changed almost daily. Waste abounded, and they ran way over schedule and over budget. It was the opposite of working for Brett Cameron, and it made her appreciate Brett all the more. Though Jennifer's part was a good one and she played it well, Jennifer was grateful when the filming was finally over.

She had made three feature films in two years, plus numerous promotional appearances for her films, and Jennifer was exhausted. *Lady Money* was out, and it was a smash, too. Jennifer was bombarded with offers at salaries that astonished her. Everywhere she turned people pulled at her, wanting something from her—charity work, interviews, favors, invitations, commercials, films, television. It seemed as if half of Hollywood claimed her as their friend. Perversely, that only made her feel lonelier. She had few real friends. Most people just wanted something from her, and the only people she really trusted were Liz, Brett, with whom she had grown close while filming *Refuge*, and Karen, her personal secretary.

She was lonely and tired. And for the first time since she'd moved to LA Jennifer wanted to go home. She thought of Sweet River with longing, remembering the quiet, the space, the open air. She wanted to see Corey. She wanted peace.

Jennifer flew to Little Rock, and Corey met her at the airport. He was dressed in jeans, workshirt and a heavy denim jacket. His hair wasn't as long as it had been when they were teenagers, and the blond color was darker, though still sun-streaked. His blue eyes were bright in his tanned face; he was obviously a man who worked outside. He looked handsome, unpretentious and belovedly familiar. Jennifer flung her arms around him and hugged him tightly. He smelled good, clean and outdoorsy and masculine, and she knew an urge to bury her head in his chest and rest there forever.

Corey pulled back to look at her. She was lovely, at 26 really coming into the full maturity of her beauty. And she was sophisticated—dressed in designer clothes, well made up, every hair in place. She looked exotic in this location, foreign. Yet the lines of her face, her vivid eyes, the rich color of her hair, all of those were still Jennifer, his baby sister. He loved her; he was closer to her than anyone. But he felt a twinge of strangeness being with her, an awkwardness at being in the presence of someone so obviously a film star.

He covered up the awkwardness with a grin. "You're gorgeous, kid. What's the matter with those guys out there? How come one of them hasn't snapped you up?"

Jennifer shrugged. "Are you kidding? I hardly even have time to date."

He looped an arm around her shoulder and walked with her to the baggage claim area. Many of the people around them turned and stared at Jennifer. Six were bold enough to come up and ask if she was really Jennifer Taylor. Smiling her now-famous smile, Jennifer signed the tickets and notepaper, even napkins, that were held out to her. Corey watched the knot of people grow as others were emboldened by the first ones' success and decided that he had better get his sister out of the terminal before they were swamped. Taking her arm, he firmly led her away. Jennifer smiled with regret, waving to the crowd as she walked away.

"Whew! I never realized what being around you was like," Corey commented as he hurried her across the parking lot, "or I would have taken you straight to the car. It didn't seem that bad the times I visited you."

"Maybe they're more used to fame in LA. Besides, in LA I know where I can go and not get harassed. But it's gotten worse the past couple of years, with *Refuge* and *Lady Money*."

"We went to see *Lady Money* in Fayetteville a couple of weeks ago. Damn, you're good. You know that?"

"I hope so."

"I still can't believe, looking up at the screen, that that's my baby sister."

He settled Jennifer in the car and drove around to the

terminal. Corey went inside and returned minutes later with her luggage, and they left the airport. He had planned to take her out to a nice restaurant in Little Rock for lunch, but now he realized that there would probably be the same sort of scene that there had been in the airport, so he picked up hamburgers at a fast-food place and they ate them as they drove northwest to Sweet River.

Jennifer looked out the window at the familiar scenery. The car began to climb into the hills. It was winter, and the trees were bare, but the pines were green. She could almost smell them. They passed through Nathanville. Only thirty miles from home. Home—it was odd, but Sweet River didn't feel like home anymore. The countryside looked the same; she could remember it so well. Yet she felt like a stranger.

They approached the turnoff to their old house. "You want to stop and see Mack?" Corey asked.

Jennifer hand's clenched together. "No. Not yet, anyway. I—need to adjust a little."

"Sure." He passed by the turnoff.

"How is Daddy?"

Corey shrugged. "Mean as ever. I don't see him much. But he's comfortable, if that's what you mean. I had a good house built for him with the money you sent, all the appliances. Mary Dawson goes out twice a week to clean and fix him a meal. He gets the money you send every month. Drinks it all away, of course."

Jennifer sighed and Corey patted her hand.

"Don't worry about it. You've done as much for Mack as you could do. Money won't turn him sober."

"I know."

Corey drove through the town. It was as she remembered it. The drive-in had changed names, and newer cars were parked around it, different kids in different clothes, but it was the same place. Some of the storefronts on Main Street had been painted. A few stores were empty or had different names, but Daniels' Department store was still there and Gannett's Drugstore, Byers' Cafe. The courthouse. The Grand Theater, sporting advertisements for a Bruce Lee movie.

It made Jennifer feel strangely aching and empty. For the first time in a long while she thought of Matthew. She could almost see him lounging against his car outside the cafe, almost feel his hand around hers as they strolled along the sidewalk to the Grand. Memories pierced her. She was sorry she had come.

Corey turned onto Central and went up the hill past the high school and on out of town. About five miles out in the country he pulled to a stop in front of a modest yellow frame house. White shutters adorned the windows. A white wooden swing sat on the porch. A huge oak tree arched over the front of the house, shading the porch, and rosebushes grew in front of the foundation.

"Oh, Corey, how pretty!" Jennifer exclaimed softly, leaning forward to look at the house.

"Yeah. Isn't it?" It wasn't much compared to what Jennifer was used to now, of course, but Corey knew she remembered where they had both come from. She understood how beautiful its quiet homeyness was to him. "It's because of Becky."

Jennifer looked at him. She knew he didn't mean his wife had bought the house or painted it or fixed it up. "Then you're still happy?"

He smiled, his eyes content. "Yeah. I'm still happy."

The front door opened and a dark-haired young woman came out, two children on her heels. She was pretty and fresh-faced, with bright color along her cheeks and light brown, almond-shaped eyes. She hurried down the steps to greet them, smiling. "Hi! It's so nice to see you! I'm sorry I couldn't come to the airport with Corey, but I had to pick up the kids at school."

"It's fine." Jennifer smiled at her sister-in-law. She liked Becky. She had always been nice to Jennifer; Jennifer still remembered that Becky had asked Jennifer to sit with her at the first basketball game Jennifer had gone to. She made Corey happy. Jennifer loved her for that.

Becky turned to her husband, and Corey bent to kiss her. "Hi, sweetheart."

Becky's face glowed. Corey's eyes were soft and loving on her face. Jennifer felt a sweet, piercing pain in her chest. She might have wealth and success, but it wasn't worth a tenth of what Corey and Becky had in their sweet love for each other.

The children hung back behind their mother, shyly looking at Jennifer. Jennifer smiled at them, a lump growing in her throat. How much bigger they were since she'd seen them in Los Angeles the year before!

Jennifer squatted down, holding out her arms. "Come on, now, don't you remember me? Can't you give your aunt a hug?"

They came forward then, grinning, a little hesitant, and stepped into the circle of her arms. Jennifer held them to her, drinking in the sweet smell of children. She kissed Melissa's cheek, then Andrew's. "Oh, it's been so long." She sat back on her heels. "You know what? I bet if we went inside we'd find something in my bag for you two."

"Presents?" Their faces lit up and Jennifer chuckled.

"Yes, presents."

They went into the house. It was small and neat. One wall of the living room was dark rock, with a huge fireplace and a wide ledge running on either side of it. "Corey made that wall," Becky told her proudly.

"You built it?" Jennifer looked at Corey, impressed. "Why, it's beautiful."

"He's so good about things like that," Becky went on. "He did all the painting, and he laid the cement for the patio, too."

Looking around, Jennifer could see how much effort both of them had put into it—wallpaper, creamy paints, waxed hardwood floors with brightly covered throw rugs, curtains that no doubt Becky had sewn herself. It wasn't an expensive house, but it was a lovely home, filled with caring. Tears sparkled in Jennifer's eyes. She had never had that: the warmth and sharing, the love between a man and woman that was the foundation of their lives, the joy of children. She guessed she never would.

"It's lovely," she said, her throat tight. "You've put a lot into it."

"Thank you. Here, let me show you your room."

Becky led the way, Corey carrying Jennifer's bags and the children dancing along behind. The room Becky showed her was small but charming, obviously decorated for a little girl. Sprigs of flowers covered the comforter on the bed, and the pattern was repeated on the dainty curtains. A toy box sat in one corner, piled high with dolls and stuffed toys. There was a little white dresser and a child-sized chair and a set of shelves containing books and toys. Across the top lay a row of lovely collector dolls that Jennifer had given Melissa through the years.

"This is my room," Melissa told her proudly.

"It's very nice. I hope you don't mind my sleeping here."

Melissa shook her head. "No. I get to sleep in Andrew's room, and then I'm not scared at night."

Andrew shot her a scornful look. "I'm not ever scared."

Jennifer looked suitably impressed. "I'm sure you're not."

She opened her suitcase and gave the children their toys. They ran into the family room to play with them, and the adults followed more slowly. Corey left the house to feed the cattle. Becky turned to Jennifer and smiled a little shyly. "I better get supper started. Is roast okay with you?"

"Fine." Jennifer followed Becky into the kitchen. "Let me help you."

"Oh, no!" Becky looked horrified. She couldn't imagine anyone in a Bill Blass dress cooking. She couldn't see those manicured, delicately tinted long nails dipping into dishwater. "You'd ruin your dress and all. You don't really cook, do you?" Every time they'd visited Jennifer in Los Angeles her housekeeper had done the cooking.

"I've been known to in a pinch." Jennifer smiled. "I'll change my dress."

She returned ten minutes later in designer jeans and a cashmere sweater. Becky wondered if Jennifer considered the outfit her "grubbies." The clothes had probably cost more than what Becky made in a month at her part-time job.

Frankly, Becky was a bit uncomfortable around her sister-in-law. It was one thing to visit Jennifer in California, but quite another to have her here in Becky's own little house, amidst the furniture they'd bought on time from the store on the square. Becky loved her little house and had always been proud of it, but she couldn't help remembering how grand Jennifer's house in Beverly Hills was. What would Jennifer think of their three little bedrooms and their self-built rock wall? Standing there in Becky's kitchen, Jennifer, so obviously wealthy and glamourous, looked completely out of place, like a being from another planet.

Becky thought of her own face, bare of all cosmetics and her thick hair, cut every few months in Nora's Beauty Shop. She wanted to hide her work-roughened hands with their short, unpolished nails behind her back. There was little of the shy, young Jennifer that Becky had known in this poised, well-groomed, gorgeous woman. Becky didn't know what to say to her or how to act.

"Shall I peel the potatoes?" Jennifer picked up the peeler from the counter.

"Uh, sure." Becky stepped aside to give Jennifer the sink, where the potatoes sat.

Jennifer picked up a potato and began to peel it efficiently. It was obvious Jennifer knew what she was doing. She didn't seem quite so out of place now. Becky prepared the meat, and as they worked, Becky began to relax. After all, Jennifer had been complimentary about the house. There had been nothing in her voice to hint that she was used to much more. She didn't act all that differently from anyone else. Becky remembered the times they had visited Jennifer in California. She had always been very nice to her. She genuinely loved the kids and Corey. Perhaps there was nothing to worry about except in her own mind.

Jennifer looked out the window above the sink while she worked. She saw Corey's pickup truck turn into the long dirt driveway that circled behind the house. "Here comes Corey."

The truck rattled to a stop in front of the barn, and Corey jumped out and went into the barn. Jennifer smiled, watching him. "He seems very happy. I'm glad." She glanced at Becky, and to Becky's astonishment it occurred to her that Jennifer still was a little shy. "I think you're the one to thank for that."

Becky smiled. "Oh, no. It's Corey who's made *me* happy. He's so good to me and the kids. Sometimes I think I'm the luckiest woman alive. Corey's the best."

"You won't hear any argument from me."

"You know, when I was first dating him, people told me how wild he was—that he lived too fast, drank too much, got into fights. But he was always gentle and sweet to me." Becky's eyes glowed with love. "My mother told me he was worthless. But he's worked hard and saved every penny he could. He has a good-sized farm now and he works some more land that he rents from Sam Ferris. He owns two houses in town that he fixed up and rents out. He's really made a success of himself. I'm so proud of him."

Jennifer saw the love shining in Becky's eyes, and again the sweet-sad pain shot through her. She reached out and squeezed Becky's hand. "He did it for you and the kids. He loves you very much."

Becky smiled. "I know. But not any more than I love him."

Later Corey came in, and they sat and talked while the roast finished cooking. They ate supper, then the children cleared the table and Becky put the dishes in the washer while Jennifer gave the kids their bath and got them ready for bed. When Melissa and Andrew were clean and dressed in their pajamas, they snuggled up in their bunk beds while Jennifer read them a story. They begged for another when she finished, and Jennifer easily gave in. She kissed them good night. They were so sweet and beautiful it clutched at her heart.

She turned off the light and slipped out the door. Corey and Becky were sitting in the den. They didn't hear Jennifer enter, and she stood for a moment, watching them. They were cuddled up on the couch, Corey watching TV and Becky reading a magazine. His arm was around her shoulders, his cheek rested against her hair.

Jennifer's eyes filled with tears. This, she thought, was what was missing in her life. No matter how much success she had attained, no matter how fulfilling her acting was or how much of her time it consumed, no matter how gratifying the response of her fans, there was an emptiness to her life. She was missing something at the core, an essential element that others had. Love. Home. Family. That was what kept a person going, what made a person strong.

She had never been in love except with Matthew. Sometimes she wondered if she was capable of it. After all, she had been so young when she had loved Matthew. It couldn't have been anything more than a teenage crush. Surely what a fifteen-year-old felt for a boy wasn't the enduring love she wanted, the kind Corey and Becky had. Since Matthew there hadn't been even one man for whom she felt anything other than mild affection. No one had heated her blood as Matthew had. Sometimes she thought that her heartbreak over Matthew had killed something inside her, destroyed her ability to feel love or passion.

Would she always feel this way? It seemed a bleak future. She was twenty-six and at the top of her profession. She had more money than she could have dreamed of when she was growing up. People admired her, adored her. She was a star. She had gotten what she'd always wanted. But now she found she wanted more.

She wanted what her sister-in-law had.

* * *

Jennifer didn't stay long in Sweet River. As much as she liked seeing Corey and his children, the visit didn't lift her spirits as she had hoped. If anything it made her feel more blue. She visited her father, but he was as boozy and caustic as ever, making snide comments about her fine clothes and "fancy airs." Jennifer hadn't really expected Mack to be any different from the way he had always been, but seeing him left her depressed. Everyone else in town treated her with a sort of awestruck reserve.

She made a nostalgic visit to Byers' Cafe. Jan Byers was at the cash register and Mary Jim was waiting on a table when Jennifer walked into the restaurant. They both glanced up with faint interest and froze when they saw Jennifer. Every head in the place turned to look at her. Jaws dropped. Jennifer was used to being stared at, but here, among people she had known when she was young, she was embarrassed by it. Dr. Oliver was there and Jim Mason, who ran the feed store; Mrs. Carlyle and her sister, Maureen Fitzhugh, both powerhouses in the Baptist Church; a couple of farmers. All of them were older than she and respected members of the community, the kind who had looked down on Jennifer all her life, but now they gazed at her as if they couldn't believe they were in the same room with a star.

Jennifer offered a tentative smile. "Hi, Jan. Mary Jim."

"Jennifer Taylor. I can't believe it." Jan came out from behind the cash register, nervously wiping her hands on her apron. "Please sit down." She gestured toward the corner booth by the window.

She had certainly risen in the world, Jennifer thought. Jan was offering her Sam Ferris' table.

"Would you like something? A cup of coffee? Mary Jim, get uh, Miss Taylor a cup of coffee."

"Miss Taylor?" Jennifer repeated in amusement. "You used to call me Jenny."

"I know, but, gee, you look so grand and beautiful and all. It doesn't seem right to call you Jenny."

Hardly anyone called her Jenny anymore. It struck her that it was rather sad to have no one close enough to nickname her.

"Call me Jennifer, then."

Mary Jim brought a cup of coffee and set it down in front of Jennifer. Mary Jim's hair was still as black, her makeup as colorful, though there were ten more years of lines in her face and she'd put on a little weight. "I can't believe you're actually here," she said excitedly. "I've seen every one of your movies, and your TV series, too. It's so wild—I mean, somebody I used to work with!"

They stood back from her, as if afraid to get too close. Jan's eyes flickered over Jennifer's clothes and face and hair. Jennifer felt absurdly out of place. Mrs. Carlyle came over and asked her to autograph a napkin for her granddaughter. Mary Jim and Jan made stilted conversation with her. Jennifer was relieved when she finished her coffee and was able to escape without seeming rude.

It was the same everywhere she went. A few bold people asked her for her autograph. The others simply stared. Jennifer would have thought that she would be glad that the people who had always looked down on her were now in awe of her. But, strangely, it only made her uncomfortable and a little sad. She was a foreigner in her own hometown. From the top of her perfectly styled and colored head to the bottom of her Helene Arpels-clad feet, Jennifer didn't belong there.

But worse than the attitude of the townspeople were the memories of Matthew. She had thought those feelings were long dead, and it was alarming to discover how swiftly they rushed back in on her. Everywhere she looked there was another reminder of him and the brief time when she had been so happy, so much in love. She hadn't thought of Matthew in a long time, but now she remembered the way his mouth quirked up when he smiled, his green-brown eyes flecked with gold, his large hands, the palms roughened by sports. She remembered how his hands had felt on her skin—cupping her face, stroking her arm, sliding over her breast. She wondered if he still lived in Sweet River, if she might run into him one day on the street. The thought made her stomach knot with nervousness and a crazy sense of anticipation.

One morning, trying to sound casual, Jennifer asked Becky, "What's Matthew Ferris doing these days?"

Becky shot her a sidelong glance. She remembered Matthew's romance with Jennifer. It had been the talk of the school for months. She remembered, too, its abrupt ending. Nobody had ever found out exactly what happened, but suddenly Matthew was gone and Jennifer looked as if her world had caved in. Then, just as suddenly, Jennifer had left town, too.

"He lives in Dallas now. He's a doctor, did you know?"

"A doctor! No, I didn't know. I'm surprised. I would have thought he'd be an attorney."

Becky shrugged. "I imagine that's what Sam Ferris wanted him to be. But instead he became a doctor. I guess he's about through with his residency now."

"What kind of doctor is he?"

"I'm not sure. I think Mama told me he was a cardiologist."

Jennifer looked at her hands. "Is he married?"

"I think so. I don't know much about him. He hardly ever comes back to Sweet River."

"Why not?"

Becky shrugged. "I don't know. But I haven't seen him in town in, oh, probably three or four years."

Jennifer wondered why Matthew avoided Sweet River. Did it bring up painful memories for him, as it did for her? She wondered what his wife looked like. Did he love her? She wondered if Matthew ever thought of her. And if he did, what did he remember—the beautiful, happy days when they had been so much in love or the pain of the ending? She wondered if he still hated her and if he'd ever learned the truth. If it would even matter to him anymore.

* * *

It was a relief to leave Sweet River behind and fly into Los Angeles. The trip hadn't done much to refresh Jennifer. She felt more at ease here in LA, where she wasn't a misfit and where there were no sad memories.

A limo picked her up at the airport and brought her home. Her house was dark and quiet; Karen and the housekeeper had already left for the day. Jennifer wandered through the house, turning on all the lights and trying to reorient herself. She warmed up the casserole her housekeeper had left for her and ate a little, then unpacked and dialed Liz's number.

Liz was still at her office, just as Jennifer had expected, and she greeted Jennifer with a cry of joy. "Thank God you're back! I have the most wonderful news."

"What?"

"Brett's got a movie for you. And what a movie!"

"Really?" Jennifer's interest was piqued. Everything Brett did was quality, and it was fun working with her.

"Yeah. It's a romance, a fantasy and an adventure. You'll love it. The female lead is a really strong character."

"You have the script?"

"Right here on my desk. You want me to drop it by on my way home?"

"You know I do."

Thirty minutes later Jennifer had the screenplay in hand. She sat down to read and didn't stop until she finished it. Liz was right. It was pure romance and adventure, with a beautiful, strong heroine and an equally strong hero, the kind who clashed and struggled throughout the movie and came together at last in a fiery love scene. It was by turns sad, funny and suspenseful, and Jennifer loved it.

She glanced at the clock and was surprised to see how late it was. She phoned Liz anyway. "I want it," she said without preamble, and Liz laughed.

"I'm glad. 'Cause you've got it. Brett wants you for this part. She'll meet our price."

"Who's playing Ryker?"

"I don't know. She has a guy she likes for it, somebody that's only been in a couple of minor parts. Brett wants to test him with you before she hires him to see if you have the right chemistry."

"Sure."

"Brett says he's perfect for the part."

"Then he must really be something."

He was.

Jennifer met him a week later when she went to the studio for his test. He was standing talking to Brett, his back to Jennifer, when she walked in. He wore jeans and a scoop-necked T-shirt, and the clothes emphasized his athletic build, long-waisted and narrow-hipped with a wide chest and shoulders. His arms were corded with muscles but lean.

Jennifer came to a dead stop. Matthew! But of course it wasn't. It couldn't be. He was simply built like Matthew, with the same slender strength. He turned and she saw that he didn't look like Matthew, really. His coloring was different, coal black hair and gray eyes, and he was more handsome than Matt. Still . . . there was something about his face—the curve of cheek and jaw, the way he held his head—that reminded her of Matthew. Something stirred deep inside Jennifer.

Brett introduced them. His name was Scott Ingram. He was nervous and obviously a little awed by testing with Jennifer Taylor, and it touched her. She was especially helpful as they ran through the scene for practice, just smiling encouragingly when he flubbed a line. The second time he was more at ease, and when they shot it, the two of them worked together well. They rehearsed and shot another scene, this one a flaming argument. When they finished, Jennifer looked over at Brett. Though Brett's face revealed little, Jennifer knew her well enough now to know that she was pleased. The next day Liz told her that Scott Ingram had been chosen for the role.

They started filming three months later. It was a strenuous movie. Jennifer had never worked as hard physically on a film. She and Scott were forever chasing or escaping from someone, and it seemed as if they ran all the time. When they weren't running they were riding horses or climbing out of windows or scaling walls. Much of it was shot on location in Spain, substituting for the Arabian desert and various Mediterranean countries. The weather was hot, dusty and airless. The cast and crew were put up in a hotel in a small village miles from any city. The food was limited, and there was no entertainment except what they made themselves.

Yet, despite the physical hardships, it was the most satisfying film Jennifer had worked on. Everyone involved was a true professional and made it all go as smoothly as it could under the conditions. Brett, as always, was magical in coaxing her vision out of the cast and crew. And Jennifer and Scott were marvelous together. They had a chemistry, a rapport. Moreso than in any other film, Jennifer stepped into the character she played and lived it.

Most of her scenes were with Scott. Off the set they spent just as much time together. They were never bored. Jennifer couldn't remember when she had been this happy, this excited, this eager to meet each day. With some amazement she realized that she was falling in love with Scott.

He didn't push, unlike all the other men she had dated since she came to Hollywood. He was her friend first, and he was content to let the physical side of their relationship develop as slowly as Jennifer wanted it. Because he didn't push, Jennifer gradually relaxed and opened up to him. They became lovers. And if there weren't all the sparks she had felt with Matthew, it didn't bother her. She was crazily in love, and that mattered far more than a mere physical sensation. She was mature enough now to realize that; with Matthew she hadn't been.

Four days after the cast returned from Spain, Scott and Jennifer got married.

* *Chapter 12* *

The love that had bloomed in the secluded atmosphere of location shooting in Spain fell apart in the real world of Los Angeles. At first Jennifer put it down to the normal adjustments of marriage. After all, she had lived by herself for years, doing exactly as she pleased when. Any marriage involved working out differences. Jennifer was accustomed to coming home from a day's filming and winding down, then retiring early. Scott wanted to go out. He accepted almost every invitation Jennifer received to parties, and on the nights when there were no parties, he wanted to go out for drinks or dinner or dancing.

Jennifer found Scott's style of living exhausting, and it was desperately hard to awaken at five in the morning to drive to the studio after staying up until one or two o'clock drinking, dancing and talking. But, struggling to adjust to the compromises of marriage, she tried. Despite her dislike of parties, crowds and the hoopla of publicity, Jennifer went out. She smiled for the photographers who snapped their picture as they emerged from restaurants and nightclubs. She signed autographs for the fans who invariably popped up. She chatted at parties, enduring the flattery of opportunists and the meaningless social patter. She told herself she would grow to like it. She told herself they would work it out.

She soon realized that she was the only one "working it out." There was no compromising on Scott's part; they were doing exactly what he wanted. When she pointed out to him that she hated such things and suggested that they go out only two or three times a week, he looked at her with a pained expression and said, "But baby, I need the publicity! Sure, it's okay for you; you're established. I still have to make my career."

Jennifer felt guilty. She remembered the arranged dates she had gone on at the beginning of her career, the endless, awful times of sticking herself out in front of the public. Scott was right. A budding career required publicity, and it was selfish of her to deny it to Scott simply because she no longer had to do it. So she swallowed her distaste and went out again.

They finished shooting and the movie went into post-production. The only thing Jennifer had to do was the looping, or dubbing in of her voice, in certain scenes. She was able to rest during the day, which made the nights less tiring and gave her time alone at home with Scott. That, she was sure, would ease the quivers of doubt and disappointment she had experienced lately.

Instead it got worse. Scott was different. Or maybe the difference was inside herself. She and Scott seemed to have nothing to talk about anymore. The spark, the rush were gone. Frantically Jennifer scrambled to recapture it. Their love couldn't simply have vanished in a couple of months!

Yet somehow it had. Slowly, sadly, Jennifer realized what had happened. She hadn't fallen in love with Scott Ingram at all. Before the movie, she had been desperate to be in love. Then Scott had come along, playing her lover in a movie, and she, caught up in her role and wanting so much to be in love herself, had practically willed herself to fall for him. But when the movie was over, the roles gone, the feeling had died. What they had was so shallow it couldn't stand up to reality. It was no wonder that they had nothing to talk about; looking back on it, Jennifer realized that all they had ever talked about was the movie. It had been the movie and their imaginations that had provided the spark.

Still, Jennifer tried to make the pieces fit, to make them love each other, after all. She couldn't fail at love again! All her life she had wanted love more than anything else, yet it seemed to be the one thing that always eluded her.

She tried to talk to Scott, but more and more often it degenerated into a fight, with angry accusations and blame flying through the air between them. Seeking release, Jennifer flung herself into another movie. She chose the best of the immediate offers she had. It wasn't a great script, but it would do. Almost anything would do as long as it took her mind off her increasingly terrible marriage. She spent her days immersed in her work and her evenings alone. She had stopped going out with Scott to the parties he craved, despite his bitter assertion that she was trying to ruin his career by doing so. But her refusal to go didn't stop him from going. They rarely saw each other. It seemed as if the only time they met was in bed.

And that wasn't any good, either. Jennifer had lost whatever enjoyment she had had in his lovemaking. She hardly felt herself a participant; she just went through the motions because he wanted her to. Because she couldn't bring herself to admit that it had all been a mistake.

Finally, in January, Jennifer gave up. She knew they would have to get a divorce. She couldn't live like that anymore. She felt desperately tired all the time and her stomach was frequently queasy, both manifestations, she thought, of her inner stress. But the Academy Award nominations came out and she was up for Best Supporting Actress for *All the Runners*. Though the picture itself had bombed at the theaters, critics had given her performance glowing reviews. Scott was delighted with the idea of going to the award ceremony and sitting beside a nominee. Jennifer knew he was thinking again of publicity. She couldn't deny him the opportunity; it would be too cruel. Besides, she didn't know if she had the nerve to face the occasion without someone sitting beside her. She put off the confrontation with Scott and hung on until after the awards ceremony.

Jennifer was nauseated throughout the presentations. She felt no disappointment when she lost; she was too busy trying to keep her stomach in its place.

The next day she informed Scott that she wanted a divorce. He stared at her, stunned. "Damn! *You're* divorcing *me*?" He swung away, slamming his fist into his thigh, barking out a short laugh of disbelief. "You're divorcing me?"

"That's what I said." Jennifer felt sick and wrung out. "Surely it can't be a big surprise to you. It hasn't worked from the very first."

"Because of you!" he accused, swinging back to face her. "I did my best."

His fury surprised Jennifer. She hadn't expected this. She sat down in a chair, too tired to deal with his anger.

"If you weren't so goddamned limp in bed," he went on fiercely, "maybe we could have had something. But a man might as well make love to a wet rag as to you! Some sex symbol! I always heard really beautiful women were like you, so wrapped up in themselves they couldn't feel anything for a man."

To Jennifer's humiliation, tears started in her eyes. "That's not true."

"No? Christ, you were a goddamn virgin when we met! And the way you've been since, I should have left you that way."

Tears coursed down her face. Again he reminded her of Matthew, as he had the day she met him. But a furious Matthew, reviling her before he stormed out of her life forever. Both of them despised her for her sexuality. For Matthew, she hadn't been good enough morally; for her husband, she hadn't been good enough in bed.

"Get out!" she shrieked, hating him. Hating herself.

"I'd love to!" Scott strode to the closet and yanked out a suitcase. He flung it onto the bed and began stuffing clothes into it. "Nothing could make me happier." He went into the bathroom and returned with his shaving kit and shoved it into the suitcase. He zipped the case closed, picked it up and started from the room.

He paused in the doorway and turned to look at her. "You expect guys to fall at your feet, don't you?" His voice was cold and bitter. "You're so beautiful you think you don't have to do anything. It's a gift simply to let a man touch you. Well, let me tell you something—I was never that hot for you. You know why I married you? For the publicity. Anybody Jennifer Taylor marries gets a lot of press, and when that guy's also the love interest in her new movie, it's really news. I married you for the people you could introduce me to, the contacts I could make."

"Scott . . ." Jennifer stared at him, his words piercing her heart. He had never loved her! He had used her. She felt small and dirty and humiliated.

"Surprised? You didn't know how good an actor I really am."

He left. Jennifer heard his feet on the tiles of the hallway and the slamming of the front door. She brought her knees up, curling her arms around them and tightening herself into a little ball, and she cried.

"He's a son of a bitch," Liz said flatly, pouring a drink for Jennifer and one for herself. She came out from behind the bar and handed Jennifer her drink.

Jennifer looked like hell, Liz thought. She had missed two days on the set, something she had never done before, and tonight she had called Liz and asked her to come over, her voice weak and teary. When Liz arrived, Jennifer had poured out the whole story to her. It pained Liz to see her this way. If anybody deserved to be happy it was Jennifer. But she didn't seem to have the knack for it.

Jennifer looked at the scotch and soda Liz set down before her as if it were a snake. She turned her head away. If she drank it she'd throw up.

"Brett told me when you got married that she didn't trust him. She thought Scott was out for what you could give him."

"How did she know? Was it that obvious?"

"Not to me. I thought he loved you. I was happy for you. But Brett's more knowledgeable—or cynical—however you want to look at it. She grew up in the business."

"Why didn't she warn me?"

Liz cast her a glance of disbelief. "Have you ever tried to tell someone in love that the guy she loves is a jerk? It's wasted effort. All you get is one less friend."

"Yeah. I guess."

Seeing Jennifer so pale and worn tore at Liz's heart. Quickly she went over to the couch and sat down beside her friend. "Listen, don't get down about this. You're better off without him. Hell, it's been obvious to me how unhappy you were the past few months. Now you're free! No more fights, no more strain. You can concentrate on your career."

"Damn it, Liz! That's all I have! My career. I'm a failure at anything else. Anything human."

"Don't be ridiculous."

"It's true. Scott's right. I'm cold."

"That's a guy's favorite line when you don't want to sleep with him."

"But I must be! I'm missing something. I can't sustain any kind of love with anyone. All I can do is act."

"That's a lot more than most people can do. Besides, it's not true. Don't let that moron influence how you think about yourself. You aren't just an actress. You're a warm, lovely woman. Any man would be lucky to have you. But it's difficult for a woman who's successful in her career to have a good relationship with a man. You think I don't know? The higher you get, the more isolated you are. It can be lonely and hard and painful."

Liz's usually vivacious brown eyes were dark and flat, and Jennifer knew that she, too, had experienced the pain of being alone. "Lots of times I've wished that there'd be a man waiting for me when I got home from the office. Somebody I could talk to about my problems with Kelly. Somebody to share the responsibilities and the worries and the money, the fun, the fantastic good luck of it all. Somebody to hold me and tell me I'm pretty and I mean the world to him. But when I get home there's nobody there but Kelly and the housekeeper. The trouble isn't with you; it comes with the territory. You want to be a housewife back in Sweet River, working in some low-paying job, taking care of your husband and kids? You know what she dreams about? Being Jennifer Taylor. You have more than most women will ever have. Take what you can get."

"But is there some law saying I can't have success and love? Why can't I have both?"

Liz shrugged. "Maybe you can. But it's rare. Real rare."

Jennifer dragged through the movie she was filming. She felt guilty for not giving it her best, but these days all she could do was go through the motions. She had thought that when she filed for divorce she would feel better. She did feel a certain amount of relief—life was more pleasant without Scott, even with her nagging sense of failure. But physically she was still a wreck. She was tired all the time; she would go to bed right after supper, and still she hated to get up the next morning. By the end of the day she was often sick to her stomach. She began to worry that she had a disease.

Finally Karen made Jennifer an appointment with a doctor and drove her to his office. He listened to Jennifer's symptoms and checked her heart and lungs, then had his nurse draw blood for tests. Three days later he called her with his news. There was a chuckle in his voice. "Ms.

Taylor, I'm going to recommend that you see a specialist.'' He paused fractionally. "An obstetrician. You're pregnant."

Pregnant! She was pregnant! But she couldn't be. She and Scott were getting a divorce. It would wreak havoc with her career.

But right behind that thought came a sudden, fierce upwelling of joy. A baby. She was going to have a baby. Jennifer realized that that was what she wanted more than anything in the world.

She was able to finish filming before she started to show. After that, she stayed close to the house. She hated going out because there were always photographers around taking her picture. Scott was milking the divorce for all the publicity it was worth, telling reporters that he still loved her and hadn't wanted to lose her. When he learned that she was pregnant, he presented himself as even more the aggrieved husband, deprived of his child. The press had a field day and because Jennifer refused to talk to them, she received the most poison from their pens. In private, among their attorneys, Scott made outrageous demands, asking half of everything Jennifer owned even though they had been married less than a year.

One day, out of the blue, Scott dropped his demands and signed the settlement agreement. Jennifer was astonished. She had no idea that Brett Cameron had invited Scott to lunch at L'Orangerie and had told him how displeased both she and Royal Studios were to find him vilifying the female star of their new hit. Jennifer Taylor, Brett reminded him, was her personal friend. Scott was wise enough to know that there wasn't much that was worth earning Brett Cameron's enmity. Not only would it mean he wouldn't work in one of her pictures again, which would be a great loss in itself, it would probably mean he wouldn't be in any Royal picture. All of Brett's movies had been with Royal, and they would do anything Brett asked in order not to lose the profits her movies brought in. And if Brett spread the word that he was difficult to deal with, many directors and producers would shy away from him.

Scott assured Brett that the divorce would be settled quickly and with a minimum of fuss.

From then on there were no clouds on Jennifer's horizon. For the first time in her entire life Jennifer had nothing to do. It was rather a pleasant feeling, she discovered. She was lazy and sleepy, and it was more than enough for her just to prepare for the baby.

She bought a larger house, with a large bedroom for the nursery and a playroom next to it, plus an extra room for the nurse she would hire for the baby. She redecorated the bedroom and playroom for a baby. She spent hours poring over carpets, shades of paints and sheets of wallpaper, and even more hours watching the workmen put them in. She bought exquisite baby furniture, eyelet coverlets, and padded Mother Goose wall hangings. She bought every baby accessory imaginable and piles of clothes in all shades but pink and blue.

She furnished the playroom with a small indoor slide, toy chests containing all manner of toys, a swing on a stand to rock the baby, and a child-sized table and chairs. She bought stuffed animals, including an almost life-sized tawny lion and a five-feet-tall giraffe. Only the fact that she didn't know whether it would be a boy or a girl kept her from buying more. She had never enjoyed spending money so much in her life.

She bought any book about pregnancy, childbirth and babies and read each one studiously. She took childbirth classes with Karen as her coach, and faithfully followed her doctor's instructions. She forced down milk and vegetables and did her exercises daily.

Jennifer didn't mind the way she looked. She loved it. The larger she grew, the sooner it meant her baby would arrive, and that was the only thing that mattered. She had never been very concerned with her beauty. For much of her life it had been more a hindrance than a help. At best it was a tool, one of the things that got her the roles she wanted. It was a relief not to have to worry about her face and hair and nails, not to feel men's eyes running over her, assessing her, wherever she went.

The baby was born in October, 1981, a baby girl with soft, thin blond hair and big blue eyes. Jennifer named her Krista. It wasn't a hard labor by most standards, a few hours of small, intermittent pains and only two hours of hard pains. She surprised them all by having her so quickly; there wasn't even time for a painkiller or block. They rushed her into the delivery room and soon Krista was there.

"Well, that was quick," her doctor said, winking at her as the nurse bathed the baby in warm water and wrapped her up. He liked Jennifer. She was a wonderful patient and a beautiful woman. He would miss her frequent office visits.

Jennifer laughed. The pain was gone and she was flooded with life and delirious joy. "I'm just a girl from the hills, don't forget."

The nurse laid the baby on Jennifer's chest. She was red all over, even her scalp beneath the fine blond hair, and her face was scrunched up, her eyes closed, as she wailed. Scrawny arms and legs moved wildly, out of control. Jennifer had never seen anything so beautiful. She looked down at her, drinking her in. Jennifer was in love, from the top of her head to her toes completely filled up with love. She had finally found what she had been looking for all her life.

"Jennifer! What am I going to do with you?" Liz stood, hands on hips, gazing down at Jennifer with mixed affection and exasperation. Jennifer lay on the floor on her side, facing Krista, who lay on a blanket, contentedly gurgling and gnawing on a set of plastic keys.

"Nothing," Jennifer responded with a smile, dangling a teething ring in front of Krista. The baby grabbed for it, missed, then caught it. Jennifer laughed and applauded.

Krista was beautiful—chubby and healthy, with pink cheeks and blue eyes and a smile that would melt a rock. Liz's daughter, Kelly, sixteen now, doted on her, and Liz herself loved to hold Krista and play with her. She could understand why Jennifer was crazy about her. But to turn down this part!

"Jennifer, roles like this don't come along everyday."

"Neither does a baby. What if I missed the first time she crawled? Or her first step? It's not worth it. I don't need the money."

"Of course not. And I understand. I can remember when Kelly was that age. Every day was a new discovery. That's why I haven't been bombarding you with offers. You wouldn't believe the number of scripts I've sent back. I knew you wouldn't be interested. But Krista's six months old now. And this is a terrific story!"

"Yes. It is nice." Jennifer had read the screenplay and felt a faint twinge of regret that she wouldn't be playing the female lead. "And I'd like to play opposite Paul Newman."

"What's holding you back?"

"Oh, Liz. It's just not worth it. It would be nice, but—I don't have the desire I used to. It doesn't bother me to think that it won't be me on the screen in that movie. I don't want to take the time away from Krista. She's more important than any role. More important than anything."

Liz sighed and flopped down into a chair. She sat for a moment looking at Jennifer. It was obvious that Jennifer was interested in nothing but the baby. Jennifer was beautiful—Liz doubted that Jennifer could be anything else—but she was no longer the meticulously groomed woman who had captured audiences for ten years. She didn't work on herself. She was ten pounds overweight for the cameras. She wore no makeup, and her nails were colorless and cut short for ease in taking care of the baby. She hadn't had her hair highlighted in months, and she had cut the luxuriant mane off short, saying that it was too much trouble. She wore jeans and a sweatshirt, and there were baby food stains on the shirt.

"Jennifer, I don't understand why you're doing this."

"Doing what?"

"Look at yourself. You're one of the best, most popular actresses in the world, and you're giving away your career with both hands to stay home and take care of a baby."

"I want to be with Krista."

"Take her to the lot with you. She and her nurse can stay in your dressing room; Krista's young enough that she'll be content there. You could see her on breaks and at lunch."

"That's not enough." Jennifer sat up and faced her friend earnestly. "I know it's hard for you to understand. But I don't care about my career anymore. Maybe it will be too late in two or three years if I decide I want to come back. But that will just have to be the price I pay. I've finally found what I've been looking for all these years. It's not a man and it's not a career. It's this baby. She's all I need, all I want. Liz, look at me. I'm happy. Have you ever seen me this happy?"

Reluctantly Liz shook her head.

"That's because I've never been this happy. In my whole life." Except maybe those few months with Matthew in Sweet River, but that was long ago. She no longer thought about that time. "All my life I've been looking for love. Someone to love me, someone for me to love. Daddy didn't love me. Mama did, but she didn't have enough time. She worked so hard. What I was searching for in my career was for people to admire me, audiences to love me. But that wasn't enough, either, so I married Scott. That didn't work. Then I had Krista, and I realized that this was what I needed. I love her, Liz, and she loves me. She makes me feel whole and happy. I love her with everything I have. I don't really care about movies anymore. Krista's all I want."

Liz knew it was true. She felt defeated. Yet she couldn't even wish it were different; that would be too selfish.

Jennifer was blissfully happy for the first time since Liz had known her. Liz had to be glad for her.

Liz leaned over and hugged Jennifer. "I'm glad. And I won't bug you about it anymore." She paused, and her eyes began to twinkle. "But you won't mind if I just show you a script every now and then, when I get something especially good."

Jennifer chuckled. "Of course not. You wouldn't be Liz if you didn't."

Jennifer picked up the baby and walked with Liz to the front door. "Sure you won't stay and eat with us?"

"No. I have to get home. You know me; I'm hardly ever there in time to eat with Kelly. And we've been having so many problems lately..."

"Yeah." Jennifer felt sorry for Liz and her daughter. Kelly, always a quiet, reserved child, had turned into a sullen, rebellious teenager. Jennifer suspected it was the classic case of a Hollywood child, given too much of everything except time and attention. "You can work it out."

"I hope so. We don't seem to be getting anyplace. Sometimes I just don't know what to do with her. I was never good with kids, you know, not like you. I love her; I always have."

"I know you do."

"But I was always working. I never spent enough time with her."

"You did the best you could."

"I suppose. I bought her things after I started making money, at first because I wanted her to have the stuff that I hadn't been able to give her before, and later because I felt guilty. I spoiled her. Now, if she doesn't get everything she wants, she throws a fit."

"But she's a good kid underneath."

"I think so. If only we didn't fight so much! If only I knew what to do. I'm considering sending her to that private school where Lou Kaufmann's daughter goes. Kelly and Cindy are friends."

"You'll come out all right, both you and Kelly. I know it."

"Thanks. I hope you're right." Liz ran a finger down Krista's chubby arm. "They're so much easier when they're this age. Enjoy her."

"I do."

After Liz left Jennifer fed Krista. She was breast-feeding her, and Jennifer loved those peaceful moments with her, Krista tugging hungrily at her breast, pulling life from Jennifer into herself. Krista fell asleep, as she usually did, satisfied and weary from the effort. Jennifer pulled her nipple from the baby's mouth and smiled at the sucking motions Krista made. She wiped away a dot of milk at the corner of Krista's lips. Her heart felt so full, watching Krista sleep, that she thought it might burst. She hadn't been able to explain to Liz how very much Krista meant to her. There was no way to describe it. The baby was all in all to Jennifer. From now on whatever Jennifer did in her life would be done for Krista.

Months passed. Jennifer's life rolled along smoothly. Liz sent her no new projects; she came by only to chat with Jennifer and see the baby. Jennifer's world was the baby. She watched Krista grow and laughed with delight when Krista first crawled. She saw her through the pain of each new tooth. She played peek-a-boo with a blanket and sang songs and read nursery rhymes. Everything small and breakable in the house went up where Krista couldn't reach it, so the baby could roam safely. Jennifer loved to watch her speedy crawl. She was eight months old and a beautiful baby, with huge blue eyes and a skin like strawberries and cream.

One morning Jennifer awakened late. She sat up, puzzled, and looked at the clock radio beside her bed. It was after 9:00. How strange. Krista rarely slept past eight in the morning. Jennifer felt a little clutch of fear, then told herself she was being silly. She was always scared something would happen to Krista, worrying that she would get sick or somehow fall in the pool, even though she'd put a fence around it.

Jennifer walked down the hall to Krista's room. The door stood open and the room was dim, the morning light kept out by a heavy shade beneath the curtains. Krista lay on her stomach in her baby bed, her head turned away. Again Jennifer felt a chill of uneasiness. She tiptoed into the room. Poor thing, she was probably worn out from all that crawling she'd done yesterday.

Jennifer peered over the side of the bed. Krista was sleeping deeply, her mouth slightly open. Jennifer bent closer. She couldn't hear the faint sound of Krista's breathing. That was nothing new; the baby always breathed so softly. She placed her finger in front of Krista's nose to feel the air going out, knowing even as she did it that she would probably wake Krista up and be sorry.

The baby didn't move. Jennifer felt no stir of air against her finger. She went utterly still, her stomach turning to ice. For an instant she couldn't move. Couldn't think. She touched Krista's cheek. Her skin was cold. Frantically, hands shaking, Jennifer lifted Krista from the bed. The baby didn't move. The side of Krista's face that she had been lying on was strangely dark. "Krista!" Jennifer shook her. "Krista!"

Krista lay still and cold in Jennifer's arms. "Krista!"

Jennifer ran from the room, clutching Krista to her chest. She met Karen coming from the other side of the house, where the office was located. "What is it? What's the matter? I heard you—"

"Get the car! Quick. Take me to the hospital."

Karen saw the panic on Jennifer's face and heard it in her voice. She didn't hesitate. She ran back to the office and grabbed her keys, then ran out to her car. Jennifer was already in the car, holding Krista close and rocking her.

"Hurry. Hurry." Jennifer said it again and again as they rushed down out of the hills. Tears streamed down her face and she kept rocking. Karen said nothing, just concentrated on her driving. She'd never driven so fast in her life, and she prayed they wouldn't have a wreck. It seemed so horribly far to Cedars-Sinai. So long.

She screeched to a halt in front of the emergency entrance and Jennifer jumped from the car and ran into the hospital. A nurse had to pry the baby from her arms, and another nurse had to hold Jennifer to keep her from following her child into the examination room. Karen put her arm around Jennifer. She was shaking all over. People were turning to look at them, recognizing Jennifer.

"Do you have someplace private?" Karen asked the nurse. The woman nodded and led them to a small examining room that was not in use.

Karen put Jennifer into a chair and sat down beside her. They waited. Another nurse came in and asked them questions, writing down the answers on a form. Karen answered her. Jennifer seemed unaware of the woman's presence.

A doctor opened the door and came inside. He was middle-aged and balding, and when he spoke the south still clung to his voice. "Ms. Taylor?"

Jennifer rose. There was no color in her face and her eyes seemed twice their usual size. "Yes?" She was shaking so badly she could hardly get the word out.

The doctor came a step closer. "I'm sorry, ma'am. There was nothing we could do. I suspect it was Sudden Infant Death Syndrome. The baby is . . . dead."

For an instant Jennifer stared at him, then a horrible cry broke from her lips. "No! No!" She continued to scream, wordlessly, and Karen thought she had never heard a sound so desolate.

* Chapter 13 *

The bright, sunny day seemed to mock the funeral. Liz stood beside Jennifer, too hot in her black suit. She grasped Jennifer's elbow, and Corey held Jennifer's other arm. The graveside ceremony was over and the crowd was dispersing. An enormous number of people had been there, from Brett Cameron to the assistant grip on Jennifer's last film, from the morbidly curious to well-meaning fans.

Jennifer stared at the tiny white casket, the draping below it carefully concealing the yawning hole of the grave.

"Jennifer." Liz pressed her arm gently. "It's time to go."

Jennifer looked at Liz dully. "I can't leave her."

Corey leaned his head against Jennifer's. "Oh, Jenny." He thought of his own two and what he would do if anything happened to them or Becky. He understood the depth of Jennifer's pain. "I'm sorry, hon. So sorry."

An official from the funeral home approached them, and Liz turned him away with a single hard look. Corey kissed the top of Jennifer's head. "Jenny. We have to go. It's over. It'll never get any easier."

"I can't leave her, Corey."

"I know. But you have to." His arm went around her waist. "I'm here with you." Slowly he turned her and they walked away. Jennifer's head drooped. She felt as if her insides were being torn out and left behind at the grave site. Every step she took pulled her apart. She didn't know why she went, but mindlessly she let Corey propel her toward the white limousine.

The press waited between her and the car. They had been all over the place since Krista died. The brief announcement Jennifer's publicity agent had made outside the hospital had not been enough for them. The reporters had been kept away from the graveside behind a rope, but now they clustered in front of the limo, waiting for Jennifer. Cameras whizzed as they took pictures, and the reporters converged around Jennifer and Corey, swallowing them up.

"Miss Taylor, when did it happen?"

"Do you plan to do benefit work for Sudden Infant Death Syndrome now?"

"Were you the one who found her?"

"Jennifer! Look here!"

Jennifer raised a weak hand as if to ward them off and leaned into her brother. Corey wrapped both arms around her, trying to shield her with his body as they plowed through the crowd. His jaw was set, his eyes blazing with anger, and Liz was sure he would fly at them any moment. Joe Darcy muscled his way through the reporters and, stony-faced and intimidating, opened a path for Jennifer and Corey.

Joe opened the limousine door and they slid inside. Jennifer gave him a tremulous smile. "Thank you, Joe."

He nodded. "I'm sorry." He closed the door, and the limousine pulled away.

The car took them back to Jennifer's house, and Liz followed in her own car with Corey's wife. Jennifer walked into the house without a word and sat down in the den. The others sat and stood awkwardly around the room. No one knew what to say or do. Jennifer was deathly pale, and though she glanced around the room, nothing seemed to register.

The doctor had given her a sedative at the hospital two days before and had kept her sedated since. But Liz couldn't let her say goodbye to her child in a haze of dope, even though it meant she would feel the pain more clearly, and she hadn't given her a pill that morning. Liz wondered if Jennifer was still feeling the effect of the earlier tranquilizers or if she was simply in shock.

Jennifer got up and went over to the glass doors leading to the patio. She looked out at the swimming pool. "Remember how I had the fence built so Krista couldn't get to the pool? I was so scared about that pool, so afraid she'd drown. I was always so careful." Slowly her face began to crumple, the lovely lines shifting and melting, dissolving into agony. "Oh, God! I was always so careful!"

She began to cry in great, wracking sobs. She slid down

to her knees, leaning against the cool glass door, and gave herself up to grief.

Liz hurried to her, her heart wrung by Jennifer's suffering. She knelt beside Jennifer and put her arm around her friend's shoulders. If only she could do something, say something, to ease the pain! But nothing could heal this wound.

"Liz. Liz." Jennifer buried her face in Liz's shoulder and cried. "I've lost everything."

When Corey and his wife returned to Arkansas three days later, Liz began stopping by Jennifer's house every night after she left her office. Karen was with Jennifer during the day, but at night Jennifer was alone. Liz could tell from the dark circles under her eyes that she slept little during those nights. Liz could imagine Jennifer silently roaming the house or sitting, staring, as the hours crept by. It made her shiver to think of it.

Days passed, then weeks, until finally three months had gone by. Jennifer lost weight. Her face was tired and lined with grief, and she looked far older than her twenty-nine years. At first Jennifer was numb, but gradually the numbness wore off, leaving her with a searing pain that filled her mind and body.

One afternoon when Liz came to see Jennifer, Karen pulled Liz into her office and closed the door. "I'm worried about Jennifer."

"So am I. But what can we do? I've suggested that she see a therapist, but she refuses. She doesn't want to talk about it."

"It's too painful for her to talk about. But she's in such misery! I don't know what to do. She refuses to go anywhere, even out for a drive. She just sits in that big rocker in the baby's room all day, holding one of Krista's toys. Or she goes around straightening things, folding the blankets and the baby's clothes, lining up the stuffed toys on her bed. As though she thinks Krista's going to come home!'' Karen shivered. "It's eerie."

"I know. I'm afraid that's what she does all night, too."

Karen nodded. "I'm scared, Liz. I'm afraid she might do something. Hurt herself." She paused and glanced away. "Have a nervous breakdown. I've tried to spend the night here a couple of times, but she tells me to leave."

"I'll see what I can do with her."

Liz left the office and walked through the house to the nursery on the opposite end. Jennifer was there, just as Liz had expected. She looked up. She wore a robe and no shoes. Her face was drawn and pasty, her hair tangled, as if it hadn't been combed. "Hello."

"Hi." Liz tried to smile. She didn't know what to do. "Why don't you come out to the den and we can talk," she asked, infusing brightness into her voice.

Jennifer simply stared at her with dead eyes and shook her head. Liz sat down on the top of a sturdy wooden toy box. "It's not good for you to sit here like this all the time."

Jennifer looked away. Her hand began to smooth the fur of the stuffed kitten she held in her lap.

"Jennifer, please. You need to get out. Why don't we go for a drive?"

"I don't want to."

"This isn't good. You need to talk to someone."

Tears filled Jennifer's eyes. She shook her head. Liz had no idea. Her misery was so huge it was impossible to talk about, so vast it filled her. Filled the world. It was all there was. What was there to say, to tell some shrink? Krista was dead and her life had stopped. Oh, God—if only she hadn't been left behind to endure it.

Liz knelt in front of Jennifer and took her hands. "You know I care about you, don't you?"

"Yes. Of course."

"You know that I want what's best for you."

"Yes."

"Then will you trust me? Will you do what I ask?"

"What?"

"I want you to spend a few days somewhere else."

"A vacation?" Jennifer looked at Liz as if she'd lost her mind.

"No, not a tourist spot. Just someplace soothing and quiet. Away from this house. Why don't you come out to my house?" Liz had moved out to Malibu a couple of years earlier, and she had a small glass-and-wood house on the beach. It was exclusive, private and peaceful. "You could walk on the beach, look at the ocean. Nobody would disturb you."

"Oh, no, Liz, please. I don't want to."

"I know. But sometimes you have to do something you don't want to or things will never get better. Now please, as a favor to me—will you come?"

Jennifer sighed. Liz didn't understand that it would never get better, but there was no point in arguing with her. "All right." Jennifer glanced around the room, and Liz knew she didn't want to leave it.

"Come on. You'll be back in a couple of days." Liz put her hand under Jennifer's elbow and, after a moment's hesitation, Jennifer rose.

Liz walked her to her room and located a small bag, which she packed with the first clothes she found. She pulled a skirt and blouse out of the closet and made Jennifer put them on. Then she brushed Jennifer's hair, appalled by its condition. Jennifer's hair had always been one of her best features, but now it hung limply, none too clean and badly in need of a shaping cut. Liz tossed the brush into the case and optimistically added a makeup bag. She picked up the suitcase and guided Jennifer from the house, afraid that at any moment Jennifer would refuse to leave.

Liz put her in the car and drove to Malibu. Her house was on the beach, nestled at the base of the hill, with a wide wooden deck running across the back and half a flight of steps down to the beach. It was a relatively small house, with three bedrooms, a study, and only one large

living area. The enormous price Liz had paid had been for
the privacy and the ninety feet of beachfront. She loved
the ocean and had wanted to live beside it since she had
moved to LA fourteen years ago. The serenity and calm of
the ocean was the perfect counterpoint to her busy, pres-
sured life.

Liz whipped up a light supper and they ate it out on the
deck. Jennifer picked at the salad, ate a few bites of the
omelet, and pushed aside her plate. Liz frowned. Jennifer
had lost the ten extra pounds she carried after the pregnancy and more. If she didn't begin to eat normally soon, she
would look emaciated. But Liz kept her mouth shut. It had
been enough of a victory getting Jennifer out there.

"I'm glad you decided to visit," Liz said instead,
keeping her voice light and cheerful. "It's lonely out here
now that Kelly's away at school."

"Oh. That's right. She's not here, is she? I'm sorry. I
hadn't noticed."

"Yeah. I finally decided to send her to the school where
Cindy Kaufmann goes. The fall semester started two
weeks ago. So far she seems to like it." Liz pointedly
crossed her fingers. "I hope it continues. I've agonized so
much about what's the best thing to do for her. I feel guilty
about sending her away, but she said she wanted to go. Dr.
Fields thought it might help."

"I'm sure it will."

They had coffee and watched the sun set over the ocean,
scattering fire across the water. It grew darker, and soon
only the foam where the waves broke was visible.

Jennifer glanced up the beach. The next house was
ablaze with lights, and she could see people standing in
little knots on the deck. They must be having a party. The
sight sent a pain through her. She stood up. "I think I'll go
to bed."

"Sure." Liz returned to the house with Jennifer. She
needed to go to bed, too. She had an 8:30 meeting the next
day with an executive from Lorimar.

Jennifer undressed and crawled into bed. Usually she was

wide awake as soon as her head touched the pillow, but tonight she fell asleep, soothed by the faint hiss and roll of the ocean. She dreamed about Krista again; she had been doing so ever since Krista died. Krista was in the car with her. A man walked up and opened the door on the other side and pulled Krista out. Krista cried and held out her arms to Jennifer. Jennifer reached frantically for her, but she couldn't reach her. She couldn't move; something held her in the car. The man walked away with Krista, and Jennifer cried out with pain, reaching, reaching . . .

Jennifer bolted upright in bed. She was bathed in sweat and her eyelashes were wet with tears. A pain racked her chest. She cried, her hands pressed to her face as if they could somehow hold the agony in. It was always worse at night. There was no way to disguise or ignore the awful enormity of her loss. She had nothing in her life now, nothing—except the raw pain of living.

Jennifer got out of bed and walked through the house to the deck. She stood at the railing and gazed out at the ocean. The party next door was still going full swing, but now Jennifer didn't even notice it. She walked down the steps and across the sand to the edge of the ocean. The sand was damp beneath her feet. The ocean mesmerized her. She could feel its thunder through her body.

She stood still, watching it for a long time. Then, without looking back, she walked out into the water.

Sloane Hunter hated the party. He was bored stiff, and as usual Susan was treating him like a piece of meat. He was tired of her and tired of this place. In fact, right now he was tired of his life. It wasn't what he had come to Hollywood for.

Susan saw him standing alone and walked over. She stood so close their bodies almost touched and leaned her head back to look up at him. Her smile was loose and vacant. "There's a party in the back bedroom."

With his little finger Sloane wiped away the smudge of white beneath her left nostril. "There's a party out here."

She giggled. "You know what I mean."

He looked down at her. She was always obnoxious when she got high, which seemed to be most of the time the past few weeks. "Yeah, I know what you mean. Lots of happy dust and group groping. You know I don't go in for that."

Susan pouted. "You're such an old poop. I don't know what I see in you."

But, of course, she did. Even now, when he was being obstinate, just looking at him was enough to bring the hot, familiar dampness between her thighs. He was the sexiest man in the room. He always was, wherever they went, and Susan Ketterman—plain old Susan Ketterman, who hadn't had a date to the Junior-Senior Prom—loved to show him off. She looked better now, of course; a nose job, a boob job, expensive clothes, and long hours behind the red door at Elizabeth Arden could work wonders. But the competition was much fiercer here, and though Susan might not have looks, she knew she had power. That was more important anyway. How much power, how much success she had achieved, showed in the man by her side. Right now she had the best.

Sloane's hair was thick and black, a little long and perfectly styled. His eyes were bright blue beneath heavy lids and a thick fringe of black lashes. His face was handsome, with exactly the right amount of imperfection. His mouth was full and sensual, his voice husky. The suggestion of surliness about him only added to his appeal. Looking at him made any woman think about long, slow, delicious sex.

"Why don't we leave?" he asked now.

It would be fun to return to her bedroom now, Susan thought, but Sloane had been crossing her a lot lately, and she needed to remind him who was in control. "No," she replied flatly. "I don't want to go yet. The party's just getting going."

"It's 1:00."

"You have something you have to get up for?" There was a trace of a sneer in her voice.

His jaw set. "No."

"We'll go home when I'm ready. You may not want to stay and have fun, but I do." She walked away.

Sloane watched her. Anger burned in his gut. Damn but she was difficult to get along with, and he resented having to do it. How in the hell had he gotten into this kind of life, anyway?

Laziness, the answer came mockingly in his head. Sheer laziness and a hunger for the nice things in life. He'd grown up in a lower-middle-class family, never hungry, but always wanting something else, something more. Blessed with good looks and a talent for acting, he had come to Los Angeles when he left high school. Here he had found out that good looks and talent weren't enough—or maybe he didn't have as much talent as he thought. After years of starving without getting anywhere, he realized that he wasn't going to make it. Gradually he gave up acting and drifted into an easier life. A life where his good looks and charm were enough, where he could enjoy the things he'd always wanted.

He wasn't a prostitute, he told himself. He hadn't sunk that low. He never charged or did queers, and one-nighters weren't his thing. He just lived with women, usually older than he and always wealthy, and enjoyed their lifestyle. They bought him things. It wasn't the same as turning tricks.

But lately . . . lately he'd had trouble telling the difference.

Sloane wandered out onto the wide wooden platform. The house was built into the hillside and the deck was on stilts, with stairs down to the beach. He strolled to the edge of the deck and stood looking at the ocean and trying not to think about his life. A woman walked from the next house to the edge of the water, and he watched her idly.

There were other people on the platform, and their chatter bothered him, so he went down the steps to the beach. He walked away from the house toward the ocean.

It was quieter here, peaceful if he ignored the bursts of laughter from the house. He lit a cigarette and glanced down the beach. The woman was still standing at the water, staring out. The moon touched her hair with pale light. She had on a thin garment, and the breeze from the ocean plastered it to her body. She had a lovely figure.

There was something wrong. Something odd. Sloane continued to watch her, not knowing exactly why. She stood that way for minutes, unmoving. Then she walked forward into the ocean, her pace even. The water curled avidly around her legs. She kept walking. The water rose to her waist. She didn't tuck her head down and stretch out in a swim.

A wave of cold ran through Sloane. He realized what she was doing. He ran to the ocean, kicking off his shoes and stripping off his coat jacket as he went. He splashed out into the water, keeping his eyes on her pale face, the only part of her that was visible in the dark ocean. A wave broke over her, and suddenly her head was gone.

He would be too late. Sloane plunged into the water, swimming with fast, sure strokes, angling toward the spot where he had last seen her. He kept his head up, looking, looking . . .

She bobbed to the surface, arms flung up, water-darkened hair plastered to her face. Sloane corrected his direction. His strong arms cut through the water. Kelp tangled around his arms and slithered over his back. He felt the pull of an undertow. He saw a flash of white. She was being carried away from him by the crosscurrent. She didn't struggle. The fact didn't surprise him. Her smooth, unhesitating walk had been a deliberate path to suicide.

The yards between them stretched interminably. Then a wave caught her and tossed her limp body back toward shore, pulling her out of the undercurrent. She was much closer. Only a few more feet. Sloane strained to his limits. He plunged down into the water, eyes open, searching. Her hair wafted toward him, and he grabbed a handful, pulling her up. She was limp. Cupping her chin with one hand, he pulled her against his chest and began a one-armed backstroke toward the beach.

Liz awoke suddenly. She didn't know why, but she felt uneasy. She slipped out of bed and padded across the hall to Jennifer's room. She eased the door open and peeked inside. Jennifer wasn't in her bed. She opened the door wider. Jennifer was nowhere in the room. Frowning, Liz walked down the hall. The door to the guest bathroom stood open; the room lay in darkness. Nor was she in the living room or kitchen. Liz went out onto the deck and looked up and down the beach. Maybe Jennifer had been unable to sleep and had decided to take a walk. The beach was empty as far as she could see. That didn't mean anything; in the dark she couldn't see far; Jennifer could easily have walked out of her range. But her unease increased.

She made a last sweep of the shore, and as she did a movement in the water caught her eye. She leaned forward over the railing, peering out at the water. There was something there, something large and strangely shaped. Her heart began to race.

It splashed through the water and onto the beach, and she realized that it was a man. A man carrying a limp form. "Jennifer!"

Liz raced down the stairs and across the beach toward them.

Sloane laid the woman facedown on the beach and dropped onto his knees beside her. He pressed hard against her back, and water dribbled from her mouth. He pressed again. More water. He felt for the pulse in her neck. It was there. Was she breathing?

He heard a woman's scream. There was someone running toward them, but he didn't look up. He flipped the woman over onto her back and pinched her nose shut. He bent and breathed into her mouth, repeating it again and again.

Liz dropped down beside them. "Jennifer!"

Jennifer coughed, and Sloane turned her to her side. She coughed up more water. She began to breathe.

"Is she okay? Is she all right?"

Sloane sat back on his heels. His hands were trembling, and sweat stood on his forehead. He drew a deep breath. Finally he looked at the woman who had run up to them and dropped down on the other side of the body. She was dressed in a nightgown, and she looked frantic.

He shook his head. "I don't know. She's breathing again."

Sloane looked back down at the woman lying on the beach, and with a start he recognized her. "My God. That's Jennifer Taylor."

Liz nodded, her eyes on Jennifer's face. Jennifer's eyes opened and she stared at Sloane, confused. Her eyes shifted to Liz and remembrance touched them. "Liz. I—I'm sorry."

"Shh. It's all right. Don't try to talk." She turned to Sloane. "Could you help me get her inside?"

"Sure." He pulled Jennifer up to a sitting position and picked her up, one arm under her legs and one behind her back. He carried her into Liz's house, with Liz leading the way, and laid Jennifer down on her bed.

"Shouldn't we take her to a hospital?" he asked doubtfully. She looked so pale and weak lying there.

"No!" Jennifer gasped.

Liz shook her head quickly. "No. She's talking; she must be okay. She couldn't bear the publicity."

She began peeling off Jennifer's wet gown, and Sloane left the room. Liz brought two towels from the bathroom and wrapped them around Jennifer's hair and body.

"I'm so cold," Jennifer whispered. Her teeth were chattering.

Liz pulled up the sheet and bedspread and added an extra blanket from the closet. "I'll fix you a cup of hot coffee. Be back in a minute. I have to thank that man."

She hurried into the living room. He wasn't there, and

at first Liz thought he'd left. Then she saw him standing outside on the deck. She opened the door and joined him. He turned. "I didn't want to ruin your carpet any more than I already had." He glanced down wryly at his soaked clothes.

"Oh! My—I didn't even think. Why don't you take those things off? I'll throw them in the dryer. And I'll fix you a cup of coffee, if you'd like. I'm making Jennifer one."

He shook his head and smiled at her. She was blond, in her thirties and rather attractive, despite the fear and worry in her face. There seemed to be no man around. Sloane knew that under normal circumstances they would be sizing each other up. But there was none of the appraising look in her eyes that was usually there when he met a woman, none of that faint smirk that said she knew what he was. She didn't know him; she wasn't meeting him in his usual milieu. She looked at him frankly, directly. She saw him as a person. As a man who had saved someone's life. There was respect in her eyes, an attitude he seldom saw in anyone's eyes lately. He realized that he liked the look, that he liked her not knowing what he was.

"No. I can't stay. They'll wonder what happened to me." He nodded his head in the direction of the next house. "I just wanted to make sure she was all right."

"She was talking. She seems okay. I don't know how to thank you. You saved her life." She hesitated. "What— what happened?"

"She tried to kill herself," Sloane replied bluntly.

"Oh." Liz sank down onto one of the lawn chairs. "I was afraid that was it. Poor Jennifer." She looked up at Sloane pleadingly. "Could I ask you—would you not—"

"Tell anyone?" Liz nodded. "Of course not."

"Oh, thank you." She reached out and clasped his hand warmly. "Thank you. After all that's happened the publicity would just be too awful." One of the gossip columns yesterday had said that Jennifer had signed herself into a mental hospital. She hated to think what would be written if the press found out about this incident.

"I know. I read about her tragedy. I promise I won't say anything."

"Thank you. Thank you so much."

"I'm glad I was there." Sloane paused. He was strangely reluctant to leave. But there was no reason to stay, and the ocean breeze on his soaked clothes was chilling. "I better get back now."

He shook her hand briefly and trotted down the steps to the beach. Liz watched him go. She hadn't been able to express the full measure of her gratitude. But then, nothing she could have said or done would have been enough for saving Jennifer's life. If he was at a party next door he wouldn't need any money. But if he was in show business she might be able to do him a favor somehow. Then it occurred to her that she didn't know his name. He hadn't said, and she had been too rattled to ask.

She started to call him back, but it was too late. He had disappeared.

Liz sighed and went back inside the house. She needed to make Jennifer a warming cup of coffee. She couldn't do anything about Jennifer's rescuer now, anyway. But tomorrow she'd get in touch with the songwriter who lived next door and find out the man's name. There couldn't be many people who looked like him.

She brought Jennifer a mug of coffee, but when she entered the room, she saw that Jennifer was already asleep. She set the mug down and settled into the only chair in the room. She didn't dare leave Jennifer alone the rest of the night.

Liz slept in snatches, jerking awake whenever her head began to sag forward. She was plagued by restless dreams, reflections of her troubled mind. She awoke when the sun began to seep in around the edges of the curtains. She left Jennifer sleeping and went into the kitchen to make a pot of coffee. She really needed a cup this morning.

After she put coffee and water into the automatic coffee

maker, she sat down at the bar and rested her head on her hands. She felt a hundred years old this morning. What was she going to do about Jennifer?

She could take her home and let Karen keep an eye on her. That would work during the days, but what about the nights? She and Karen couldn't keep shuffling Jennifer back and forth. What Jennifer needed was to be pulled out of this state somehow. A therapist might be able to help her, but the last time Liz had suggested it, Jennifer had rejected the idea out of hand.

She thought of Corey. He was closer to Jennifer than anyone, even though they saw each other only a few weeks every year. If anyone could help her it was he.

Liz dialed information and got his number. He answered on the second ring.

"Hello?"

"Corey?"

"Yeah."

"This is Liz Chandler. Jennifer's agent."

"How are you?"

"Not too good at the moment."

"What's wrong? Is it Jennifer?"

"Yes. I need your help. She tried to commit suicide last night."

There was a long, stunned silence on the other end. Then he said, "I'll catch the first plane out."

Liz sagged with relief. "Good. I'll pick you up. Just call my office and let me know when you'll be in."

She gave him the telephone number of her office and they hung up. Liz poured herself another cup of coffee and took it to her bathroom, where she tried to repair the ravages to her face that last night had brought. Finally, when she was dressed, her face made up and her hair hot-rollered and combed into shape, she still looked as if she hadn't slept all night, but at least she was presentable.

She went into Jennifer's room. Jennifer wasn't there, and Liz's heart leaped in apprehension. She rushed into the living room and found Jennifer sitting cross-legged on the couch, drinking a cup of coffee and gazing out the wide glass windows. She turned as Liz rushed in and offered her a half smile. "Hello."

"Hi." Liz didn't know what to say. "Uh, I'm ready to go to my office. Shall I take you back to your house?"

"It's okay. I won't try it again," Jennifer said softly.

"Thank God." Liz didn't trust her words. Jennifer might feel that way now, but what about the next time the black depression sucked her under?

"But I'd like to go home, anyway. The ocean doesn't soothe me, really. It makes me feel too much."

Liz left Jennifer in Karen's care and drove to her office. She had a grinding headache, and her busy day did nothing to relieve it. To make matters worse, there was a party she had to attend that evening. She would have liked to have begged off, but it was being given by a casting agent who was always quick to find a slight in every word or gesture. Canceling out at the last minute would make the agent furious, and in all likelihood, vindictive. She was too important to offend over nothing more than tiredness and a sick headache. Besides, perhaps it would give Liz a chance to squelch some of the rumors circulating about Jennifer. Work always came first.

Liz picked Corey up at LAX and dropped him off at Jennifer's house, then raced home to change for the party. She should have brought makeup and a dress with her to her office and changed there; that was what she usually did when she was going to a party, rather than make the long trip out to Malibu and back. But that morning she had been too distraught to think of it. She drove back to Bel Air, wearily wondering how long she would have to stay to be polite, and pulled up in front of Susan Ketterman's home.

A red-jacketed parking valet rushed to take Liz's Mercedes. Glancing around at the number of Mercedes there, Liz wondered how he told them apart. There were lights everywhere—luminarios lining the walkway to the front door, spots highlighting various artistic parts of the landscape, floodlights in front and back. Susan Ketterman had never been subtle.

Susan greeted her effusively at the door. She was dripping with gold, as usual. She was also, Liz noticed, already more than a bit high. Liz wondered if she had taken pills or coke or booze. It could be any, or all three. "Liz! Love. Come in. I'm so happy to see you. Tragic, what happened to Jennifer. I know she must be devastated." Susan lowered her voice. "I understand she's fallen completely to pieces."

"It's a hard blow," Liz replied noncommittally. "But you know Jennifer; she'll pull out of it. She has a great deal of strength."

"Of course. But when I heard that you'd had to check her in at that place where Brett's sister goes all the time . . ."

"Susan! That's not true! Not a bit of it. I didn't check Jennifer in anywhere. Why, she's at home right now." Liz' eyes sparkled with anger. Typical Hollywood. Not even a personal tragedy excused a star from the constant bite of gossip.

"I should have known." Susan's tone was disappointed. She pulled out a long cigarette and lighted it. "Lynn Bartek told me, and she always exaggerates. Well—" she made an airy gesture toward the rest of the party. "You know everybody. Bar's in the living room. Enjoy yourself."

"Sure. Bye." Well, Liz thought, she had made her appearance now. She could have a drink, circulate a bit, and do what she could to dispel the rumors about Jennifer, and then she would leave.

She went to the bar in the living room and ordered a gin and tonic. A candy dish full of pills sat at one end of the bar. A man and two women were bent over the coffee table, sniffing up lines of cocaine. Susan Ketterman was always generous with her refreshments.

Liz sipped sparingly at her too-bitter drink and navigat-

ed her way through the party, smiling, waving, chatting
briefly without ever getting caught in a long conversation.
Three people told her they'd heard Jennifer had been
committed to a psychiatric hospital, and two others heard
she'd gone on a prolonged alcoholic binge and was now at
Twin Oaks, near Palm Springs. At least no one had caught
wind of the truth; they'd have a heyday with an attempted
suicide. The young man who had saved Jennifer's life had
obviously kept his mouth shut. Liz had been in Hollywood
long enough to be amazed that he had.

She worked her way into a less crowded room. A man
in Ralph Lauren jeans and a bulky knit white sweater stood
a few feet away with his back to her. He turned, and Liz
saw him full face. She stopped, surprised. It was the man
who had rescued Jennifer.

He recognized her at the same instant and smiled. He
had a gorgeous smile, slow and sexy, with deep dimples on
either side of his mouth. He was even better looking in the
light than he had appeared last night. Thick black hair, just
the slightest bit shaggy. Piercing blue eyes. Tanned skin,
with laugh lines around his eyes.

"Well, hello," he said and came over to her. "How are
you?"

"Fine, thank you. And you?"

"Good. How's your friend?"

Liz shrugged. "Physically she's fine. I want to thank
you for not saying anything about it." It seemed more
amazing now that he hadn't, being here at this party with
all the rumors buzzing around. Last night she had been
grateful to him. Tonight she decided she liked him, as
well.

"No need to thank me. I wouldn't add to her problems." He smiled again. There was a faintly wry, world-
weary quality to his smile that only added to its charm.
"Though I have to admit, I had some fancy explaining to
do when I got back to the party last night dripping wet."

Liz chuckled. "Then I thank you doubly. By the way,
I'm afraid I don't even know your name. I'm Liz Chandler."

She held out her hand and he shook it. His hand was warm and dry; she liked the feel of his skin. "Sloane Hunter."

"It's nice to meet you." There was a pause. Now was the time to slip away from him, as she'd been doing all evening. Hit-and-run social conversation. But she didn't move. Neither did he. "Are you a friend of Susan's?"

His shoulders moved in a faint shrug. "I guess you could say that. Could I freshen your drink?"

"No, thank you. It wasn't very good."

He smiled and took it from her and set it down on a low table, along with his. "Neither was mine. No point in carrying them around."

"You're right." He had a good voice, soothing and rich, but not deep. She wondered if he was an actor. He certainly had the looks for it. "Do you act?"

"I have."

Susan's laugh sounded across the room, and Liz glanced up to see her standing in the doorway. Sloane stiffened, and his eyes flickered to the door and back. Susan spotted Liz and Sloane. Her smile reminded Liz of a tiger. She crossed the room to them, a half-filled glass sloshing in her hand.

"There you are, love." Susan curved her hand around Sloane's arm. Her fingernails were bright pink against his white sweater. She squeezed his arm. "I've been looking for you."

Sloane's smile was rigid and he looked embarrassed. "Well, you found me."

"Yes. I did, didn't I?" Susan looked at Liz. "How are you, Liz? Enjoying yourself?" As she spoke, her hand slid up Sloane's arm and rested on his shoulder. One shocking pink nail lazily scraped his earlobe.

Sloane glanced at Liz and away. He wished Susan Ketterman to hell and gone. He shouldn't have stayed with Liz. He should have known Susan would find them. But he had enjoyed talking to Liz. Now Susan would ruin it.

She would reveal what he was. He hated to think how Liz would look at him then. Just another piece of meat.

"Yes. It's a marvelous party," Liz replied. "You always know how to throw one." She wondered exactly what was going on between these two. Sloane looked less than excited to see Susan, not the way an actor typically greeted one of the most powerful casting agents in town. Yet Susan was obviously interested in him. And she seemed to know him quite well.

"Thank you." Susan polished off the rest of her drink and looked up at Sloane. "Here, sweet, get me another drink." Her hand fanned out over the side of his neck. Her thumbnail slid down his throat, hard enough to leave a white trail.

Sloane took her drink. Color stained his cheeks and he kept his eyes away from Liz. It was then, finally, that Liz realized what he was: a gigolo, Susan's young hired lover. She was disappointed, and at the same time she felt sorry for him. He was obviously embarrassed by the way Susan pawed him. Her other hand was on his chest now.

"All right," he said, and tried to break away. "What do you want?"

"Scotch and water. You know that. Or at least you should. That's part of your job description." Susan swayed against him. "You aren't going to leave without giving me a kiss, are you?"

He glanced at Liz, and she saw the humiliation in his eyes. "For God's sake, Susan, you're drunk."

Liz edged away from them. There was no point in forcing the poor young man to have a witness to the scene. But she couldn't keep from watching, even from several feet away. She noticed that most of the other eyes in the vicinity were on Susan and Sloane, too. Hollywood people seemed to have special antennae for anything with gossip potential.

"What does that matter?" Susan returned, her voice hard. She cupped Sloane's face in her hand, fingernails digging into his skin, and stretched up to kiss him. It was a slow, blatant kiss, and she worked her mouth against his. Sloane didn't pull away from it, but he stood stiffly, not giving anything. When she had finished, Susan released his chin and stepped back. Her fingers had left little red marks on his skin, the only spot of color on his face except for two splotches of angry red high on his cheekbones. His eyes were electric.

"Now, get me my drink like a good boy."

Sloane shoved the glass into her hand. "Get your own goddamn drink."

He whirled and walked away. Susan's face surged with color. "Sloane! Damn it, get back here!"

He walked out of the room, through the hallway, and out the front door. The room was hushed for an instant, then whispers began. Susan looked around her as if to see whether anyone had witnessed the scene. Liz managed to avoid her eye. Susan left the room.

Liz left the party soon afterward. That nasty little scene had been all she could take this evening. She wanted to get back to the tranquility of her beach house. She waited on the porch while the parking attendant brought her car. Rain had begun while she was inside, and the valet escorted her to the car beneath a gold golf umbrella. She tipped him and zipped out of the driveway, lighting a cigarette as she went. Wonderful party, she thought dryly. Just what she needed to pick up her spirits.

Her headlights picked up a man walking. As she got closer, she saw that it was Sloane. She wondered what he was doing. It was hard to get anywhere in LA on foot. When the Bel Air cops saw him, they would probably pick him up.

She passed him and coasted to a stop. In the rearview mirror she saw him hesitate, then trot up to the car. He peered in the passenger window and again he hesitated. Liz pushed the button to roll down his window. "Come on, I'll give you a ride." She grinned. "Promise I won't make a pass at you."

He let out a puffy little breath that passed for amusement

and opened the car door. "I'll get your car all wet," he warned as he slid in.

"It's leather. It can take it." He was soaked through from the rain, his dark hair plastered to his skull. His sweater and jeans were sodden and clinging. Raindrops clustered his thick lashes and rolled down his cheeks. Even wet he was gorgeous.

Sloane stared straight ahead. He didn't want to see what was in Liz's face when she looked at him now.

"Why are you walking?" Liz asked as she started the car forward. "Where's your car?"

"Susan bought it for me." He shrugged, but the gesture turned into a shiver, and Liz reached over to cut off the air conditioning.

"Oh." That surprised her. She would have thought that most men like him would have taken the car with great glee. But then, she couldn't imagine most men like him not using his rescue of Jennifer to his advantage. He hadn't asked her for so much as a favor. He hadn't even told her his name last night.

Sloane stole a sideways look at Liz. There was none of the faintly salacious amusement in her face that he'd expected, no knowing look, no sexual assessment. She glanced at him in the same direct, friendly way.

"Where can I drop you, then?" she asked. "Where do you live?"

He jerked his head in the direction from which they'd come. "Back there."

"I see. I suppose everything you own is back there, then."

"Yeah." He shrugged and looked out the side window. "It's okay. You can drop me off anywhere. Somewhere on Santa Monica or the Strip."

"In the rain?" She could imagine him walking along the Strip with the prostitutes, male and female—and some in between—waiting for someone to pick him up. Her stomach turned at the thought.

"I'll manage." He didn't know how, but it seemed

important not to let her know that. He didn't have even ten bucks in his pocket. The only way he could think of getting a place to sleep for the night was to walk the Strip, but he hated the thought.

"I can't let you do that. That would be a terrible way to repay you after what you did for Jennifer."

His eyes flashed toward her, then back ahead. "I didn't ask you to repay me," he said stiffly.

Her words had offended him, and somehow that made her like him more. "I know you didn't. But that doesn't keep me from wanting to help you in return." She had thought about giving him money for a motel, but doubtless that would offend him, too.

Liz glanced at Sloane. His face was shadowy in the dim light of the car, and he was so intensely male it was almost unnerving to be with him. Yet, as drenched as he was, there was something vulnerable about him, too, something that tugged at her.

"You could spend the night at my place."

* *Chapter 14* *

Sloane glanced at Liz, startled, and his eyes searched her face for a hint of what was behind her offer. Liz felt her face grow hot and was glad it was too dark for him to see her blush. "Don't worry. I'm not trying to pick you up."

"I know." He glanced down at himself ruefully. "I doubt I look too appealing at the moment, anyway."

He looked very appealing, but she wasn't about to say so. "I'd just like to help you out a little."

"Because of what I did for Jennifer Taylor?"

"I guess."

"Or because you feel sorry for me?" He found he didn't much like that thought.

"I don't know. Maybe a little of both." She grinned to lighten the moment. "Maybe it's because I have a heart of gold."

He grinned back. "An agent? Come on. I thought an agent's heart was solid cast iron."

"Bad press," Liz joked back. He had a lot of charm, even in a situation that must have been embarrassing for him. No, not exactly charm, because what he had was less smooth and more sensual than charm. But he had a definite presence. She wondered what he would look like onscreen and whether he really acted or if saying he was an actor was merely a good cover-up for his real vocation.

She wondered about that, too, but she didn't have the nerve to ask. Did he turn tricks or was he a sort of male mistress? Did he do it as a living or as a sideline? He didn't seem quite the type to her, although, God knew, he looked good enough for it. But he seemed more natural, not as slick and polished as the others of his ilk she'd met. Maybe it was because she had first seen him outside his setting. Whatever it was, he was the first guy like that to whom she had been attracted. Liz wished she weren't. She had asked him to her house just to be nice, and being attracted to him tainted her motive. She was not giving him a place to sleep in order to get him into her bed. She was *not*. She wasn't the kind. She had always been contemptuous of the wealthy women in Hollywood who led around their pampered young male companions.

Sloane stared out the window. He wondered what Liz was thinking. What she thought about him. For once it mattered.

When they reached her house Liz led Sloane to the guest bathroom. "Here are a couple of towels. Take off those wet clothes and I'll throw them in the dryer." She smiled. "I always seem to be saying that to you, don't I?"

"Seems like. I'll take the coffee this time, though, if you're going to offer it again."

"Sure." She hesitated, suddenly awkward. "I'm sorry. I don't have a man's bathrobe."

"That's okay. I don't mind wearing a towel if you don't object."

"That's fine. There's a blow dryer in that drawer." She backed out of the door, wondering how a mature, experienced woman like herself could feel so inept, even embarrassed, talking about his wearing a towel. "I'll go make the coffee."

The coffee was ready by the time he came out, one long towel wrapped around his narrow waist and hanging down to his knees, the other draped around his neck. There was nothing soft about him. He was all lean muscle and bone. Black hair covered his chest and ran in a thin line down his stomach, disappearing into the towel. He looked like an ad for men's cologne, Liz thought—or maybe for sex.

"I like your house," he told her, looking around. His lack of clothing appeared to bother him not at all.

"Do you?" It was about half the size of Susan's mansion.

Liz poured their coffee, and they drank it at the kitchen table, she in an elegant black Halston and he in towels. Liz smiled. It was nice to have someone there. Sometimes it was so lonely. She had no close friends other than Jennifer. There were lots of acquaintances in this business but few real friends. The higher she got, the harder it was to trust anyone, to believe an offer of friendship or even companionship. People were always after something. Besides, with the hours she worked, there wasn't time to look for a friend—or a lover. The odds were against closeness, and in the past few years there had been very few men in her life.

In the past it hadn't bothered her. But lately it had, with Kelly gone and Jennifer so ravaged by grief for her child. Love had taken on more importance. Not even love. She didn't ask for that; she wasn't a dreamer. Just simple companionship. Someone to be with, to hold her when she was tired, to sleep with.

Liz glanced at Sloane. She guessed that was what men like him offered to women who were isolated by their own wealth and power—not just sex, but someone to fill the empty spaces in their lives.

Sloane sipped his coffee and looked at Liz. She had a nice, clean profile. Everything about her was nice and clean. She wasn't overblown like so many women were— too much makeup, too weird clothes, too vibrant personalities, too loud voices. She was slender in the way of a woman who was naturally slender, not anorexic or wrung dry by diets and exercise. Her legs were long and attractive, and he watched them when she walked across the kitchen for a refill. He thought about sleeping with her. She didn't expect him to, and somehow that made the idea more appealing. It had been a long time since he had made love for no other reason than that he liked a woman. A long time since a woman had considered him anything but a lay.

But he found that even more he wanted to talk to her. It had been a long time since he'd done that, too—just conversed with a woman without games or sexual innuendoes. Funny. He hadn't even realized the fact until this moment and now he was hungry for conversation, for something normal. Something real.

"Is Ms. Taylor still here?" he asked as she came back with the coffeepot and poured each of them another cup.

"Jennifer? No. I took her home. Her brother came to stay with her." Liz set the pot back and sat down with a sigh. "Poor Jennifer. I don't know what will happen to her if Corey can't help her. I don't know anyone who deserves to be happy more than Jennifer. But she never quite makes it."

"I'm sorry. It must be tough losing a kid."

"Yeah." It was, even when you didn't lose them to death. "My daughter's in a boarding school in Maryland. We can't seem to get along."

"How old is she?"

"Sixteen."

"Nobody gets along with a sixteen-year-old."

Liz smiled faintly. "It's more than that." She began to tell him about Kelly and their relationship through the years, about the things she had wanted for her and the hard work and all the times she'd missed with her daughter. "You can never make up for that kind of thing. You can't recapture it or go back for a second chance. It's just gone. I can't even talk to her anymore."

She stared moodily down into her coffee. Sloane laid his hand over hers on the table and she glanced up, startled. His hand was warm and comforting. Tears started in her eyes and Liz blinked them away. "I'm sorry." She tried a little laugh. "How awful. You've heard nothing but problems from me, haven't you?"

"I don't mind."

"You're a good listener. And you're . . . trustworthy. You didn't say anything about what you did for Jennifer last night. Why not? You could have gotten money for that story from one of the magazines or gossip papers."

He shrugged. "I don't know. I never thought of it."

"Just like you didn't think of the danger when you jumped in and saved her." She turned her hand over and squeezed his hand. "You have kind instincts."

"Maybe I'm just dumb."

"No. You're not dumb." She took a sip of coffee, watching him. "Tell me about yourself."

It wasn't easy at first. He wasn't used to talking about himself. But with her he wanted to, and as he went along it got easier. They stayed up until almost 4:00 talking, smoking and drinking too much coffee. They didn't feel the need for sleep, not just because of the caffeine, but because they were eager and happy.

Finally Liz looked at her watch and knew she had to go to bed. "I have to be in Burbank at 9:30 tomorrow." She rose reluctantly. "Let me show you your room."

He followed her to the room Jennifer had slept in last night. Liz stripped the bed and put clean sheets on it, and he helped her. Liz's heart was pounding. There was something intensely sexual about laying the sheets on the bed with him. The cloth was cool beneath her fingertips. It stretched tightly across the mattress. She straightened the top sheet and smoothed a wrinkle from it. She thought about Sloane's skin against the sheet, dark against the cool pastels. Heat started inside her and she hoped it didn't show on her skin.

She looked up at him, standing on the other side of the bed. His hands were on his hips and he was watching her. His eyes were dark, the blueness almost obscured by the dark pupils. Sloane felt the intimacy of the moment too, and desire curled inside him. He thought about pulling Liz down with him onto the cool, clean sheets and covering her with his body. Pressing into her warmth and softness. Feeling her breasts against his bare chest, the fleshy thrust of her nipples.

He knew he could have her. He could see the hesitant desire on her face. He had only to kiss her and it would flame up.

But he did nothing. Liz had made it clear that she didn't expect him to repay her with his body for the night's refuge. Though right now he wasn't thinking of what he owed her, but only of his desire, he knew she wouldn't believe it. It would color what happened, even for him.

Liz left the room and he watched her go. He pulled off the towel and got into bed. The sheets slid in a cool caress across his skin. He thought of Liz undressing in her room and desire coiled more tightly within him. He wasn't used to delaying sex. But he found that there was something rather pleasurable in the anticipation.

Liz woke up late. She'd forgotten to set the alarm, and the sun was streaming in the window. Groggily she sat up, groping for the clock. Then she remembered Sloane and the sleepiness vanished. She wondered if he were awake, too, if she would see him before she left for work. Not likely. No one who didn't have to go to work would be up after staying awake until four the night before.

She looked at the clock. It was after eight. She'd have to hustle to make her 9:30 appointment. She showered and dressed quickly and was fairly pleased with her reflection when she was through. She didn't look bad for someone who hadn't had enough sleep two nights in a row.

Liz left her bedroom, putting on her watch and earrings as she went down the hall. She might have time for a bite of toast before she left. Coffee would have to wait until the appointment in Burbank.

Delicious smells met her in the living room. Coffee! And bacon. Sloane must be up and cooking breakfast. She crossed the living room to the breakfast room and stopped. The table was set. There were glasses of orange juice and a platter of bacon. Next to the platter was a saucer piled with buttered toast. She looked into the kitchen. Sloane was at the stove, dressed only in jeans, stirring eggs in a skillet. He turned and smiled at her.

"Hi. I hope you like them scrambled."

"I like them any way as long as someone else fixes them. You didn't have to do this."

"I was hungry. I figured you would be, too." He dished up the eggs and set the plates on the table.

Liz sat down across from him. She felt absolutely buoyant, as though she might float up to the ceiling. They ate and talked, and she was careful to say nothing about his leaving. She didn't know exactly what she wanted, but she knew she didn't want him to be gone when she came home that evening. Sloane said nothing about it, either, and she was glad.

Breakfast was so pleasant that she lingered too long and was late. She grabbed her briefcase and ran for the car. The traffic was tough, as it always was, even though she'd missed the worst of it, but today it didn't shred her nerves. Nothing irritated her that day, not even the director who was late for her first appointment or the client who phoned from the police station, asking her to bail him out.

The world was brighter today and far more pleasant. For the first time in months she didn't even worry about Jennifer. It was hard to concentrate on her work, though. Her mind kept slipping back to Sloane and the evening before. She told herself she was acting like a schoolgirl, but that didn't stop her.

She wasn't sure he'd still be there when she got home that evening. He might call a friend to go get him or even set out on foot, as he had from the party last night. He might think she wanted him to leave, since she hadn't asked him to stay. That worried her, and she regretted not specifically telling him he could stay. She started to phone him, but convinced herself that it would be foolish. If he wanted to remain, then he would be there that evening.

She left work early and stopped by Polo on Rodeo Drive to buy him a couple of shirts and a pair of jeans. She told herself that was being foolish, too; he would think she was trying to obligate him, buy him. But he needed new clothes, even if he left that night. His sweater hadn't recovered well from the drenching it had received. Anybody would do the same; it was only kind. Still, she felt the prick of guilt. She suspected that if it meant he would linger at her house she would have purchased a whole rack of shirts.

Liz parked the car in the detached garage and went in the front door. The stereo was on and she was swept with relief. Sloane hadn't gone.

He was coming in the door from the deck, and he smiled when he saw her. "Hi. I thought I heard your car come up."

Excitement ping-ponged around inside her. She had been thinking about him all day, but the reality was far better. Liz walked across the room, clutching the bag from the store in a death grip. She was afraid she was grinning like an idiot. She wished he'd kiss her.

She stopped a little distance away from him and held out the bag. "I—uh, got you a couple a things. You know, something to wear, since that was all you had."

He looked surprised and touched as he took the bag from her. She was glad. She had been afraid her gesture might chill the air between them. "Why, thank you." He pulled out the shirt. "I like it. It's nice." He put one arm around her shoulders and kissed her lightly on the mouth.

She was very aware of the weight of his arm on her shoulders and back. The scent of his skin was all around her. His lips were smooth and warm. It shook her far more than the brief touch warranted.

Sloane stepped back. There was an odd expression on his face. He picked up the bottom of his badly stretched sweater and peeled it off over his head. Liz's mouth went dry. She wanted to moisten her lips, but he was watching her. Still gazing steadily at her, his fingers went to the buttons of the folded shirt she had bought for him. He worked open the first button and the cloth parted. Liz felt it all through her, as if he had undone a button of her dress.

He went to the second button. His fingers were clumsy on it. Liz's breath came faster. Heat began to rise up her throat. She thought she ought to look away, but she didn't want to. Sloane got the button undone and his fingertips slid down the cloth to the next one. She saw that they trembled slightly. Now she couldn't stop her tongue from slipping out to moisten her dry lips. Sloane dropped the shirt.

He stepped over it to her and he grasped her shoulders as though to keep her from leaving. His hands inched across her collarbone and up her neck, hot even through the material of her dress. He slid his fingers into her hair. His thumbs caressed her cheeks. He stared down into her eyes, his body inches from hers. Liz could feel his heat, his strength, the tension in his body. Slowly he bent and kissed her.

The kiss was long and slow and thorough, his mouth hot, his tongue caressing. Desire plunged straight down through Liz and exploded in her abdomen. She arched up into him, closing the slight distance between them and twining her arms around his neck. He made a noise deep in his throat, and his arms went around her tightly, pressing her into him. His body was deliciously hard, his mouth hungry. Liz wanted him desperately, wanted his mouth and hands all over her, wanted him hard and big inside her.

She moved her hips against him and he sucked in his breath. The sound spiraled her desire. Liz had never felt such urgency, such loss of control. It amazed her, but she didn't pause to think about it. It felt too good to spoil.

He pulled away slightly and changed the angle of their kiss. His hands swept down her back and dug into her buttocks, lifting her up into him.

His lips finally left hers and he kissed her cheeks and ears and throat, his mouth moving wildly over her skin. "Liz. Liz." His voice was hoarse.

Her suit jacket impeded him, and with a low curse he released her and unbuttoned it with swift, impatient movements. He pulled the jacket from her and dropped it beside his shirt. Her breasts were soft inside her slip, the nipples dark and visible, pushing against the silk. He circled her nipples with his thumbs, watching them thrust more sharply. His breath was ragged.

Sloane pulled the straps of her slip down over her arms until her breasts were bare. He looked at her. Her skin was lightly tanned, golden down to the demarcation line of her bikini. Most women he'd known the last few years sunbathed topless. He found the contrast in color between her breasts and the rest of her skin exciting. Her nipples were a deep rose, the centers small and pebbled with desire. He covered her breasts with his hands; they were small and exquisitely soft. He caressed her, teasing the nipples to greater hardness, and Liz closed her eyes at the pleasure.

Sloane bent to take one nipple into his mouth. Liz breathed out a little moan and sank her fingers into his hair, digging in at each new pulse of pleasure. His arms were hard around her, holding her up. She thought she would have sunk limply to the floor if not for that.

Liz slid her hands down his neck and across his shoulders and arms, exploring the smooth skin underlaid with muscle. She caressed his chest, and her fingertips wove through the curling hairs to his flat masculine nipples. He sucked in his breath and straightened. His eyes were closed, his face taut and lost in desire. Liz leaned forward and ran her tongue across one nipple. He groaned and caught her hair in his hands, crushing it in his fists.

It had been a long time since a woman had tried to please him. Usually they demanded that he perform, that he caress and kiss and please. How sweet it was to feel the pleasure, the hunger. Desire was huge in him now, sweeping him along.

Sloane unfastened Liz's skirt and they moved apart to undress. They sank to the floor in the midst of their scattered clothes, too eager, too caught up in their desire to seek the comfort of the bed. All that mattered was their wanting.

He covered her, taking his weight on his forearms, and his mouth began a long, slow exploration of her body. His lip-sheathed teeth tugged at her nipples; his tongue slid over them wetly; he burrowed his face in her breasts. He moved lower, his tongue dipping into her navel and trailing down her abdomen. His fingers found the hot, wet center of her desire, and he smiled with satisfaction at the evidence of her eagerness. He caressed her, his fingertips sliding gently over her slick skin, growing ever more demanding, until Liz was arching up against his hand, moaning.

He came into her then, and Liz gasped at the satisfaction of his fullness inside her. He stroked slowly, savoring the tight heat enveloping him and the rushing need within him. He thrust and pulled out almost to the tip, then thrust back in. He was expert at stoking desire, at taking a woman higher and higher without letting her reach the peak until her climax was like an explosion. But tonight he wasn't thinking of that, wasn't trying to impress her. All he wanted was to prolong the joy of their lovemaking, to wring every last moment of pleasure from it. Liz moved her hips under him, urging him on, and then he could hold back no longer. He hurtled forward into a climax so intense it seemed to rob him of his mind and he was aware of nothing but dark, shattering pleasure. Liz cried out, the pleasure crashing through her at the same time.

They collapsed, sweating and gasping for air. Liz wrapped her arms around him tightly. His back was damp beneath her skin. She kissed his shoulder. She knew she would never ask him to leave.

Something woke Corey up. He fumbled for his watch on the nightstand beside the bed and looked at it. It was the middle of the night. He thought about going back to sleep, but with Jenny the way she'd been he knew he'd better check. He got up and opened the door to the hall. It was dark, but a movement at one end of the hall caught his eye. Jennifer was in the baby's room.

He sighed and closed the door. He didn't know what to do. Ever since he had arrived the day before he had felt completely inadequate. When he had walked in the front door, Jennifer had come forward to hug him, but there was none of the exuberant joy he had seen in her face in the past. She had been so thin in his arms it scared him. She was like a wraith, a ghost, all the life drained out of her.

She had tried to kill herself.

She had seemed glad enough to have him there. They had talked, carefully skirting anything relating to Krista. He had persuaded her to go out for a hamburger with him. He didn't say so, but he knew she looked so bad that no one would recognize her. She had listened to him and talked a little and even smiled a few times, but he couldn't shake the feeling that somehow she wasn't really there.

Today it had been much the same. Corey felt useless and frustrated. All his presence here did was keep her from committing suicide right now. But he would have to leave sometime, and then what would happen?

He pulled on a pair of jeans and went down the hall to Krista's room. Jennifer sat in a high-backed rocking chair beside the baby bed, softly rocking. "Jen?"

Her eyes opened. "Hi, Corey."

"It's the middle of the night."

"I know. I couldn't sleep."

"Do you come in here every night?"

She nodded.

"That's not good. You know it's not good."

"Nothing's good anymore."

"Maybe not, but this is worse than not good. It's tearing you up. Sitting here looking at her toys, her clothes. You're keeping the wound open."

"It's the only way I can be close to her." Tears filled Jennifer's eyes. "Oh, Corey! When I think of her in that little casket beneath the ground! I've gone out there and sat beside her grave, but I didn't feel close to her. Here, I do. You know, sometimes at night I wake up and I think I hear her crying. I mean, for just an instant, before I really wake up, I think she's alive and has wakened me by calling for me." She swallowed and looked away. Her voice trembled. "But then I always remember."

"Oh, Jenny." Corey's heart went out to her. He squatted down beside her chair and took one of her hands in his. "I wish I could say something, do something..."

"There's not a thing you can do. It was hard at first to believe she was dead. I'd keep thinking that it was time to feed her; it was time for her bath; I'd wonder why I hadn't heard her." Jennifer gripped his hand so hard his wedding ring dug painfully into his fingers. "But now I realize it. I believe it. She's dead, and I'll never have her again. And—oh, Corey!—that's so hard. I can't live with it. That's why I went into the Pacific. The pain was too much; I just had to get away from it."

Corey cradled her hand against his cheek and she felt a trail of wetness beneath her fingers. He was crying for her, and his tears touched her. In all the years she'd known him, in all the bad times with their father, even at her mother's death, she had never known Corey to cry. "You're crying," she said softly, wonderingly.

She could feel his smile. "Yeah. That's something Becky gave me, the ability to cry. The ability to feel enough to cry. I hurt for you, Jen. I can't say I know how you feel, 'cause I couldn't unless I lost one of the kids. But I know how much my children mean to me. How much Becky means to me. I think it might break me."

"Like it did me."

"It won't break you. It can't."

"It already has."

"No! You're too much of a fighter. Jen, I've known you since you were born. You always fought. You always struggled. You never, ever gave up."

Jennifer sighed and leaned her head back against the rocker. "Maybe you're right. I want to give up. I tried to the other night, but it didn't work."

"Thank God."

"I don't mean because I didn't die. I mean because after I got out there and felt the current pulling me under, I couldn't go with it. I wanted to, but I couldn't. I began to struggle, tried to swim, only the current kept sucking me out and the waves tossed me around. I won't try to kill myself again. It's strange. There isn't anything to live for, but still, somehow, I have to live. I couldn't let go of life."

"You're a survivor."

"I don't want to be! I don't want to have to live. I wish I *could* kill myself. I wish I could fall apart, go so crazy I don't know who I am or what's happened."

"You're not that kind of person."

"But what am I going to do? How can I live? I have nothing, Corey. Nothing."

"That's not true. You have millions of people all over the world who love you. You have friends, the people you work with. Me. Becky and the kids. You have your work."

"Yeah. I have my work." For the first time in months Jennifer felt a faint flicker of interest. A movie—something unconnected with Krista. A warm cocoon of a world, the only place she had ever succeeded or been accepted. Maybe if she had something to do, something she could immerse herself in, a fantasy in which she could lose Jennifer Taylor.

Corey saw the stirring of interest in her face and pressed his point. "It would take you away from this, get you out of your grief. You'd have something to do, so you wouldn't sit here and think all the time."

"Maybe."

"Listen to me. You've gotten through a lot of things. Poverty, our father's rages, Mama's death. Whatever it was that happened with you and that Ferris kid. How did you do it then? You just picked up and kept on going and going until finally it got better. Set yourself something to do each day and get through it. Then get through another one. Until finally you've got a whole string of days and it's not so hard anymore."

Jennifer thought about her mother's death, about how she had wrapped up her grief into a little bundle and stuck it away somewhere inside herself. She had buried it and walked around it. Eventually the pain had gone. She had done it with Matthew, too. Yet how could she do that now? After losing her baby. Her baby!

They sat that way for some time, silently, Corey on the floor beside Jennifer, holding her hand, and finally toward morning she dozed off in the chair.

When she awoke it was light, and Corey was gone. She looked around the room. Krista. Krista. How could she say good-bye? How could she put her away? She stood up and walked over to the tall, narrow white chest. She ran her fingers over the stuffed animals on top and the little lamp that glowed light from colorful balloons. She opened the drawers one by one and straightened the clothes within, taking some of them out and refolding them. Tears streamed silently down her face. She held a pink suit crumpled against her face for a long moment, absorbing the tears. She had loved the way Krista looked when she wore it and she had dressed her in it often. She refolded it and put it back in the drawer, smoothing it out one last time.

She wandered over to the changing table, her eyes traveling over the walls, beautifully papered and adorned with padded hangings—the Man in the Moon, Mother Goose, a rainbow. She touched the pad of the changing table. Disposable diapers were stacked neatly at one end, containers of cotton balls, Q-tips, and wipes at the other. A mobile hung above it to keep the baby occupied while she was being changed. Jennifer ran her hand across the polished back of the rocker and touched the runner of the child's rocker with her foot to make it move. She straightened the stack of books on the nightstand and turned on the Bo-Peep lamp and turned it off.

She went to the baby bed and smoothed out the down comforter. She ran her hand across the yellow blanket that was folded over the side rail. She moved one or two of the stuffed toys at the foot of the bed. She looked down at the comforter. She remembered Krista lying there asleep, lashes dark against her cheeks, her skin all white and rose, her mouth slightly open. She laid her hand on the comforter as though she could touch the sleeping child by doing so. But nothing was there, only cloth. No substance. No child. No life.

Tears rolled down her cheeks, but this time she didn't give way to sobs. Her throat ached from holding them back. She moved away from the bed and walked out the door. She didn't look back; she didn't dare. She closed the door behind her. For a moment she leaned her forehead against the doorjamb, her hand still around the knob. She didn't want to let go.

But at last she straightened and walked away, her hand sliding from the doorknob. She went into her bedroom and sat down on the bed, her fingers clasped tightly together. She swallowed hard.

She picked up the phone and touched the button that would give her Liz's home. Liz answered sleepily. "Hello?"

"Liz? This is Jennifer."

"Jennifer! How are you?" Liz sat up in bed, forgetting to be quiet so as not to awaken Sloane, asleep beside her. Jennifer hadn't called her since the baby died.

"All right. I wanted to know if you have any roles for me."

Liz was stunned. "Of course. Are you kidding? I have stacks of scripts." She tried to recall what was sitting in the file at her office. "Probably one or two decent ones."

"Good. I don't care what it is. I want work, and lots of it."

Los Angeles, June 20, 1987, 9:50 a.m.

Darcy drove Brett out to Liz's home in Malibu. Brett had called Liz's office, and her secretary had told her that Liz had gone home. No one answered their knock at first, but Joe went around back, calling Liz's name, and at last she stepped out of the sliding glass doors.

"Joe! I'm sorry. I thought more reporters were at the door. Come in."

"Brett's out front." Joe trotted up the steps onto the wooden deck. Liz looked awful. Her face was pale and tear-streaked; she looked her age and more. She was taking it harder than Brett. But then, Liz was alone.

Liz opened the front door, Brett came in and they hugged. Liz began to cry. "Oh, damn! I can't stop crying. Everytime I think I'm all cried out it starts all over again."

Joe made a pot of coffee while the two women sat down in front of the television. A game show was on, but after a few minutes the newscaster interrupted with a special report on the airplane crash. There was little news. Liz sighed and took a sip of her coffee.

"I've been thinking," Liz said slowly. "Do you suppose we ought to call him?"

Brett didn't ask who. "I don't know."

"He should know before he hears it on T.V."

"I guess." Brett hesitated. "God, I hate to tell him."

Liz stood up wearily and went to the desk in her bedroom. She pulled out a small address book, looked up a number, and dialed. No one answered. She returned to the living room and took up her vigil before the television set.

Sloane Hunter yawned and ran a hand through his hair. He'd stayed up too late. He always did; he'd had trouble sleeping the past few months. It was the empty bed.

He pulled on a pair of jeans that were lying on a chair and padded down the hall into the kitchen. He opened the refrigerator and stared into it for a moment, wondering whether to fix himself breakfast or lunch. Too late for one, too early for the other. He pulled out the makings of a bologna sandwich.

He switched on the small TV set on the breakfast bar as he put the sandwich together. A game show was on. A woman jumped up and down on the stage, her hands clasped together under her chin. She squealed continuously. Sloane switched channels. There was a news report on the next one. A wilted-looking woman stood in a barren hallway. Sloane paused, his hand on the knob.

"... still unknown whether Jennifer Taylor, the movie star, was in fact on board the fateful flight." His hand fell away from the knob and he stared at the screen. Jennifer! "However, a complete list of the survivors of the crash has been made public, and Miss Taylor's name is not among them."

She began to read a list of the names of the survivors. Sloane stared, then suddenly moved, breaking his trance. "My God!"

He ran into the bedroom, scooped up his car keys from the dresser, and grabbed a shirt and sandals. He rushed out of the apartment.

PART IV

* *Chapter 15* *

Los Angeles, December, 1986

Jennifer took off the headset and put it down with a sigh. She had been looping all afternoon and she was tired. She didn't like looping. There was no creativity or excitement in dubbing in bits of dialogue that had recorded poorly or had too much extraneous noise, watching her mouth to make sure that what she said was in sync with the movement of her lips.

She left the building and cut across the parking lot of the Burbank studio to her car. She was a beautiful woman in her thirties, thinner than she had been when she started out in television, but that didn't detract from her beauty. There were those who maintained that she was even more lovely than she had been in her twenties. Certainly, in the full maturity of her talent, she was more compelling. There was something haunting about her vivid blue eyes that hadn't been there in the past, and it added depth to her delicate face.

"Jennifer!" She heard a man's voice behind her, and

she paused, sighing inwardly. She wanted to go home, not stand around and talk.

She turned and had to smile. It was Ken Rosen, Brett's stepfather. She had met him a few times in the past but hadn't really gotten to know him until recently, when he and Brett approached her about a movie, *Drifter*. Jennifer had immediately told Liz she wanted the part. Ken was directing and Brett was producing it, and Jennifer knew it would have to be good. Over the past few weeks Jennifer had spoken to Ken several times and had found him to be a warm, easygoing man with a wry wit that he rarely used to wound. He had a reputation as one of the best directors in Hollywood and had maintained it for years. Jennifer was eager to work with him, even though they said he worked everyone to death on his films.

"Hi, Ken." She lifted her hand in a wave, and he hurried to join her.

"Jennifer. It's great to see you." They touched cheeks lightly. "How are you?"

"Fine. And you?"

"Well, today . . . I've been better." He shrugged. "But you have days like that, I guess."

They strolled together in the direction of her car. "How are the negotiations coming?" he asked. Liz and Brett's company had been negotiating Jennifer's contract for *Drifter* for weeks.

"Didn't Brett tell you? She and Liz agreed on terms a week and a half ago. I should be getting the contract soon."

"Great. I haven't talked to Brett for a while. I've been in New York auditioning for the past three weeks."

"Still looking for Jace?" Jace was the male protagonist in *Drifter*, the drifter of the title who wound up at her character's farm.

"Yeah." He sighed. "Didn't find him. You'd think with all the actors around we wouldn't have this much trouble finding one."

Jennifer smiled. "What are you going to do?"

Ken shrugged. "Who knows? We're still looking. Brett'll go down to the wire before she'll settle for someone who's not perfect. She wants an unknown. The movie doesn't need a star. Your name alone will attract the crowds."

"*Brett's* name on a picture is enough to bring them in."

"Yeah. There aren't many producers whose names are household words." In the twelve years that Brett had been making movies, her name had become synonymous with a quality, enjoyable movie. "Brett's looking for someone the audiences have never seen before, someone who'll come right off the screen and grab 'em. She thinks he'll have more impact if they don't know him."

"I'm sure she's right."

"She usually is."

They reached Jennifer's royal blue 450 SL, and Ken opened the door for her. "Well, I'll see you at the party."

He was giving a small get-acquainted party for the major members of the cast in a month, right after Brett's much bigger party for the press and all the cast and crew.

Jennifer cast him a teasing grin. "I hope you've found a Jace by then."

"Me too. Believe me."

Jennifer got in her car and backed out of the parking space, giving him a smile and a wave. Ken stood for a moment, watching her car turn out of the lot and disappear down the street. He didn't know Jennifer well. But everytime he'd seen her, in person or on film, he'd known a compelling urge to put his arms around her and comfort her. There was a bittersweet quality to Jennifer Taylor, something in her eyes that was infinitely sad.

He wasn't sure about her in the role of Maggie in *Drifter*. Maggie was a strong, crusty woman, far plainer than Jennifer. It was a real reversal of type for her. But Brett had assured him that Jennifer could do it, and he had learned over the years to rely on Brett's judgment. She was rarely wrong.

Jennifer drove home, undisturbed by the creeping traffic around her. She was thinking about *Drifter*. She, too, wondered if she would be able to handle the role of Maggie. Liz and Brett thought she could. She loved the part. She wanted to do it. But it was the most different role she'd ever played, a woman almost at the opposite pole from herself—not particularly attractive, tough, outspoken. It would require every bit of her skill. The thought both excited and scared her. She hadn't been this eager or this anxious about a movie in years.

Her secretary greeted her at the door when she arrived home. Karen worked long hours, never considering the clock. She usually stayed until Jennifer returned from the set to fill her in on her schedule and the day's phone calls. "Liz phoned. She received the *Drifter* contract and she's set up a signing with Brett on Monday."

"Okay." Jennifer kicked off her shoes and followed Karen into her office, flopping down in a chair by her desk.

"You need some rest," Karen told her. "You don't look well."

"Well, thank you."

"You're working too hard, as usual."

"I like it that way." Work was the only thing she had, and she filled up her days with as much work as possible. She always made sure that she had another movie lined up when she finished one. The cracks and crevices of time in between she stuffed with smaller things, charity appearances, interviews, publicity for a film. She'd worked that way for over four years now.

Karen grimaced. "You should be happy to get this, then." Karen handed her a letter from a charity asking her to appear at a fundraiser. "And a women's press association wants you to speak at their convention."

"Me?" Jennifer looked faintly scared. She hated to give speeches. It was vastly different from saying a writer's lines in front of a camera.

"Don't worry, I turned it down."

"Good."

Karen handed Jennifer a sheaf of papers. "Letters for

you to sign. Here's a script you got in the mail today that looks fairly decent.''

''Okay. I'll add it to my stack upstairs.'' Jennifer took the screenplay and used it as a pad to sign the letters. She hardly glanced at what the letters said or to whom they were addressed. Karen was one of the few people whom she trusted implicitly.

She handed the signed letters back to Karen. Karen reminded her of her schedule tomorrow and finally left for home. Jennifer trailed into the kitchen. It was 7:30. She opened the refrigerator and pulled out the makings for a sandwich. She fixed the sandwich and ate it sitting down at the small table in the breakfast area, where she usually ate.

When she finished, she set her plate and glass in the sink and went into the sunken living room. She glanced through the script Karen had given her, but it didn't hold her interest, and she soon tossed it aside.

The house was silent and dark. It was too big for her, but she couldn't leave it.

Jennifer walked down the hall to the kitchen wing of her U-shaped house, not even glancing back at the dark bedroom wing at the opposite end of the long front hall. She never went into that part of the house anymore. She had moved all her clothes and personal things to the guest bedroom, past the kitchen and rec room. It wasn't as large as the master bedroom nor as plush, but it was nice enough and, just as she couldn't leave the house where Krista had lived, neither could she bear to sleep near her room, to have to walk down the hall past the nursery every time she left her bedroom. The doors to the baby room and playroom were kept closed. Jennifer never went in there. The only person who did was the housekeeper, who cleaned them once a week.

In her bedroom, Jennifer glanced at the stack of scripts on one chair, but decided not to go through them. Instead she opened the closet and sifted through the hangers, looking for a swimsuit. She finally found one and pulled it from the hanger. It was ironic, really, she thought, looking at the long line of expensive clothes for any occasion, once she had been a girl with only three dresses to her name, and now, with all the clothes she had, what she wore no longer mattered to her.

She changed into the swimsuit and went out to the pool. She swam a few laps, then lay back and floated on the gently rocking water, gazing up at the sky. The stars weren't visible tonight. She felt tired. Drained. That was about all she ever felt anymore—exhaustion. Sometimes she had excitement about a role, and she felt what the character she was playing felt. But other than that there was nothing. She was dead inside, had been that way for four years. She no longer cried herself to sleep or knew the searing, tearing pain. She had cut that out of herself long ago. She had worked and ignored it until finally the anguish had eased. She had learned to avoid what caused her pain. She stayed away from children and anything pertaining to them. She refused to do a movie in which there was a child. But if she didn't feel the hurt, neither did she feel joy nor happiness nor love nor even fear. Those things were as dead to her as Krista, all emotions muted. Pale.

Jennifer smiled a little sadly and climbed out of the pool. Sometimes she wished she could feel real emotion again, but it was better, really, this way. It was better.

Sweet River looked much the same. Matthew stepped out of his car and gazed down the street. The First Baptist Church was on the crest of the hill at the edge of downtown. From where he stood he could see the courthouse and, across from it, Byers' Cafe. He thought of that morning long ago when he had offered Jennifer a ride to school, and the memory was so clear, so real, he could almost feel the icy air, even though the day was warm for December. It still brought the old piercing ache to his chest.

After seventeen years he should hardly even remember, let alone feel the hurt. But he guessed you never got over your first love, especially when it ended badly.

Michelle and Laura slid out of the car after him, and he took their hands. Though eighteen months separated the two girls, they were much the same size. Michelle, newly six, was petite, her delicate face beautifully formed. Laura, at four, was as tall as Michelle and weighed almost as much, not chunky, but without any of Michelle's delicacy. She resembled Matthew too much ever to be the beauty Michelle was, but when she smiled you had to love her. Michelle was calm and quiet, very contained, very private. Matthew often wondered what went on in her head. She was closer to her mother—Laura had always been her daddy's girl—yet she showed less trauma from the divorce than Laura. Matthew wasn't sure whether Michelle was more confident of her mother's love than Laura and therefore less frightened by Felicia's leaving or if she was simply better at hiding it.

In front of the church, the driver of the long white funeral limousine got out and opened the back door. Matthew's great-aunt stepped out, followed by Sam and Linda, his second wife. Sam was still slim and good-looking for a man his age. His hair was all white now, but it made him look distinguished rather than old. He was in good shape. He said a young wife kept him young. He'd been married to Linda for sixteen years. Matthew wondered if he had cheated on her as he had with Johnette.

Matthew and the girls followed his father into the church. They sat in the front pew with Gran's sister, Pauline, and Steven Richards and his wife. Matthew's grandmother hadn't left a large family.

A gunmetal gray casket lay at the front of the church, covered by a gigantic spray of pink roses. The choir, seated in the balcony, sang two songs, then the minister went to the pulpit to deliver the eulogy. Afterward a deep-voiced man sang "Nearer, My God, to Thee," his disembodied voice floating down around them from the balcony. Laura raised her face to her father, eyes rounded, and whispered, "Is that God?"

"No." Matthew shook his head and kissed the top of her head to hide his smile. Trust Laura.

When it was over they drove to the cemetery for a brief graveside service, and then it was done. There were people all around, shaking his and Sam's and the others' hands, expressing their sympathy. Matthew knew them all; the population of Sweet River didn't change much, except to grow smaller. Everyone told him how long it had been since he'd visited Sweet River and how much they had missed him.

It had been a long time since he'd visited, over three years, and before that his visits had been just as infrequent and brief. Since he'd left Sweet River seventeen years earlier he hadn't wanted to come back. The memories had always been too painful.

It had taken him years to get over Jennifer. Nothing had ever been the same again. He no longer wanted to see his friends; they were too much a part of his pain. Nor was he really comfortable with his father. Sam had been right about Jennifer; he had won that round. But his father's victory was inextricably tied up in Matthew's mind with his own hurt. Even seeing the town and the places where he and Jennifer had been was painful. It had been much easier to visit his mother in Georgia during school vacations.

Matthew had lost interest in football, too. He had gone to Alabama that first year, as his father had wanted him to, but he had been so unhappy that nothing had mattered to him. He had soon dropped out of the football program. Only his studies were capable of piercing the fog of his misery, particularly his science courses, and by his second year he realized that he wanted to go into medicine. He had transferred to Tulane, then gone on to the University of Texas Medical School. He had done his residency in Dallas, and he had remained there when he finished. His life hadn't followed the route Sam Ferris had mapped out for him.

Matthew drove home from the cemetery, and the girls ran up to change from their dresses into more comfortable jeans and sweaters. Sam came in a few minutes later, Linda and the others with him. Aunt Pauline sat in the living room and stared out the front window. Sam's sister Veronica and Linda disappeared into the kitchen to brew coffee for the people who were sure to drop by the rest of the day. Sam, Matthew and Veronica's husband sat together in the den and looked at one another.

Matthew didn't know what to say to his father. That was the case whenever they saw each other. Matthew wondered what they had once talked about. Football, he guessed— and Sam's plans for Matthew's future.

He picked up the local newspaper from the small end table beside him. It was full of news about school and church groups and whose children were visiting whom and from where. His grandmother's death and funeral took up half the back page. The front page was dominated by a picture of a smiling teenager standing beside his prize-winning Black Angus steer.

Matthew dropped the newspaper onto the table and picked up the Fayetteville paper to flip through it. On the entertainment page there was a quarter-page ad for *Southside*. It was a stylized ad with little blurb; the enticement was in the star's name blazoned across the top: JENNIFER TAYLOR.

Matthew closed the newspaper and stuck it under the first one. It still bothered him a little to see her name. He made it a point not to look at the gossip newspapers at the grocery store checkout counters, which seemed to feature a picture of Jennifer about a third of the time. He hadn't watched her TV show nor had he ever gone to one of her movies. His wife had been a big fan of Jennifer Taylor, but she'd gone to her movies by herself. Matthew knew he was being stupid. It had happened a long time ago, and his life had gone on. He had been married and divorced. He had two children and a successful career. Jennifer Taylor no longer had the power to hurt him. Still, he avoided any mention of her.

She had altered the fabric of his life. Changed him irrevocably. She had made him happier than he had ever been before. She had shown him love; then she had destroyed it. Everything in his life today had been shaped from that moment.

He had spent a year being bitter and staying away from women, then an equal amount of time frantically sleeping with anything in skirts. But those knee-jerk reactions to Jennifer were gone by the time he met Felicia when he was an intern at Baylor. Gone, too, was the desire to date any woman who even faintly resembled Jennifer. When he fell for Felicia, he had been pleased that he was in love with someone so unlike Jennifer.

Felicia was dark-haired and brown-eyed, slender, with lovely long legs and small breasts. Her father was a wealthy man and a deacon in a Baptist church in Texas. She had grown up with all the privileges and morality that Jennifer had not.

But, looking back on it now, he could see that he had married Felicia primarily because she was so much the opposite of Jennifer. He had married her for what she was *not*, not for what she was, and it had been a painful surprise to discover her true nature. Felicia had been emotional, demanding and bitchy, desperate for his affection and horribly jealous. He had been too cool, too calm for her to be happy. He had shared none of the blazing passion she felt for him. Their marriage had been miserable from the start, and over the years it got worse. Felicia indulged in loud, angry scenes and jealous rages. In one vindictive fit she had taken a pair of scissors to his clothes and cut up all his shirts.

There had been no cause for her jealousy. Though his desire for Felicia grew cooler and cooler, he wasn't the type to stray, and, ironically, at the end he discovered that it was Felicia who had been unfaithful to him almost from the beginning. Strangely enough, it hadn't hurt as much as it had when he found out about Jennifer. What had been agonizing was the breakup of the family, the pain his daughters felt when their mother left them. Only because of Michelle and Laura had he remained in the marriage for eight years.

Matthew sighed. It was useless thinking about his failed marriage. Even more useless thinking about Jennifer Taylor. His life was what it was, and he'd found long ago that he couldn't change the past. At least he had Michelle and Laura.

Visitors stopped by the Ferris house the rest of the afternoon, bringing food and offering their condolences to Sam. He was still the wealthiest and most influential man in town, and people were eager for him to know that they were thinking of him.

After supper the doorbell rang again, and Matthew went to answer it. A man about his own age stood on the porch. It took Matthew a moment to recognize him. He was beginning to go bald and had developed a paunch. "Keith!"

"Matt. How are you?"

"Fine. Come in." He stepped aside to let Keith enter. It had been years since he'd seen Keith. For a long time after Keith and Randy told him about Jennifer he had hated them for it. Even when he'd gotten past the anger and pain the old friendship just wasn't there anymore. The few times he had visited Sweet River he had made no effort to see any of the three men who had been his best friends.

Keith went into the den and spoke to Sam. He was a doctor now and he had returned to Sweet River to share a practice with his father. He spoke to Sam with respect, but as an equal. Matthew wondered if Keith now sat at the special table in the cafe with Sam and Judge Holcomb and Dr. Oliver.

Sam motioned to Matthew to join them. "Here, Matt, I won't keep this boy any longer. I'm sure you two would like to catch up on each other. Why don't you take Keith into my study and have a drink?"

"Sure. Sounds good." It seemed important to Sam for some reason that Matthew retain his friendship with the boys he had known in Sweet River. The few times he'd come back to town, Sam had urged him to visit Randy and Keith.

Matthew led Keith into Sam's study. He closed the door, cutting out the sound of the voices in the den, and went to the discreet bar. "What'll you have?"

"Bourbon and water's fine." Keith wandered over to the window and gazed out at the side yard.

Matthew fixed their drinks and handed one to Keith. They each took a sip, then stood awkwardly, not knowing what to say. They had shared a past, yet Matthew didn't know this man. If anything, Keith seemed even more ill-at-ease than Matthew.

"I understand you're in practice here," Matthew said finally.

"Yeah, sure am." Keith seemed relieved at hitting on a topic. "You're in Dallas, aren't you?"

Matthew nodded. "Cardiology."

Medicine gave them something in common, and they managed to get through a few minutes talking about med school and internship and the problems of practice. But that wound down, and they were left with silence again. Keith had finished his drink, and to fill in the awkward pause Matthew poured him another.

They sat down. Keith gave a nervous laugh. "Remember that pass you threw in the Centerville game? Boy, that was the prettiest pass I ever saw."

It took Matthew a minute to recall the play. He smiled slightly and shrugged. "It was mostly luck—and Joe Bob's skill."

"Yeah. Joe Bob wasn't too bright, but he had great hands." There was a pause, and Keith hurried to end it. "He's living in Little Rock now. Did you know that?"

Matthew shook his head.

"Randy's working at the dealership. I run into him now and then." Keith could see Matthew's patent disinterest. He stared down at his drink, watching the cubes bobbing in the pale brown liquid. "Nothing's ever been the same since that day, has it?"

Matthew moved restively. That was the last thing he wanted to talk about. "People change when they get out of school. They grow up. Move away."

"But not as far away as you."

They both knew Keith didn't refer to distance. Matthew glanced at Keith, surprised that he would bring it up. Keith didn't meet his eyes. He focused on the glass in his hands.

"I never dreamed it would break us up like that. None of us are friends anymore, even Randy and me, both living here. We see each other on the street or in a store or something and say, hi, how are you, like business acquaintances."

Did he expect him to feel sorry for them? Matthew wondered. Bitterness rose in him. He said nothing.

"I guess it was because we felt guilty," Keith went on. "Whenever we look at each other it reminds us."

"Keith . . . what point is there in talking about this?"

"I have to!" Keith's head snapped up, and he looked at Matthew. His face was twisted, his eyes bleak. "It's eaten at me ever since. I've felt so guilty, but I was too damned scared to tell you."

Something sharp and cold twisted through Matthew's chest, a feeling of something terribly wrong before it even became a thought. "Tell me what?"

Keith's eyes returned to his drink. His hands were clenched around the glass, his knuckles white. "That we lied."

The room seemed suddenly airless. Matthew couldn't move. He looked at Keith. Throughout his body everything was breaking into a million pieces.

Keith glanced up and back down quickly. He hated the look in Matthew's eyes, as if the world had crumbled into nothingness beneath his feet. He had looked the same way that day seventeen years ago, when Keith had told him that he, too, had slept with Jennifer.

"We lied about Jennifer." Keith's voice was barely above a whisper. "Randy, Joe Bob and I. None of us were ever around her, except with you."

Matthew sat down. He wasn't sure he could stand up any longer. His brain refused to function. He hadn't wanted to believe what Keith had said that day. He wanted to believe this even less. His whole life . . . seventeen years. "Why?"

Keith shook his head. He drew a breath. "Sam asked us over, the three of us, and he told us you were going to quit football, quit 'Bama, for Jennifer. Randy suggested that we all tell you—what we did, and your father agreed. He approved, and I thought, well, surely it must be right."

"Approved, hell! I know Sam Ferris; I'm sure that was what he intended when he called you over."

"We thought you'd gone crazy. We thought Jennifer would ruin your life, that you'd wake up several years down the line and realize it had been a bad mistake, but then it would be too late."

"So you lied to me?" Matthew jumped to his feet, anger surging up in him now. "You destroyed us? You destroyed me! Because you thought I was making a mistake? Jesus! Do you know why I believed you? Because I thought you were my best friend. Because I trusted you even over the girl I loved!"

Keith set his glass down and rose, too. Tears glinted in his eyes. "I know. I've felt like a murderer ever since. I never thought—I never imagined it would hurt you like that. I mean, that it would last so long, do so much damage. I wasn't going to lie to you; I couldn't. But then, when you were so furious with Randy, I thought it would break us up. We'd been friends so long, and when you hit Randy I just couldn't let you hate him. So I lied, too."

Rage filled Matthew. He wanted to hit someone, smash something, get in his car and drive so fast the world blurred, like he had when he was a teenager. Jennifer!

"When you didn't come back to Sweet River for so long, I realized finally what we'd done, how much Jennifer had meant to you. I'm sorry, Matt. I never meant to hurt you like that. I've felt guilty ever since."

Matthew stared at him, his eyes hard and bright, brimming with a fury he could hardly contain. ''Believe me, your guilt isn't enough.''

Matthew thought of the long, dark nights of despair. The pain. The times he'd broken down and cried because he missed Jennifer so, loved her so. Nothing could ever erase the anguish or bring back the joy and love he'd had ripped from him.

''We didn't want to hurt you. We thought you'd get over it in a few weeks, that you were just hot for her and . . . We didn't want her to hurt you. Everybody said she—''

Matthew grabbed Keith by the lapels of his coat. ''Yeah, I know what everybody said! But I was smart enough to believe Jennifer, not them, until I listened to my 'friends.' Goddamn you!'' He wanted to pound Keith with his fists, to throw him against the wall. It was all he could do to unclench his fingers and let go of him. He turned and left the room.

He didn't know what to do. He was throbbing with rage, but too mature now to vent it by driving too fast or hitting something, as he had when he was a youngster. He changed into a sweatsuit and tennis shoes and he ran. He ran until he was exhausted and then ran past that point, until the fury no longer raged through his head and he was left with only a helpless despair.

How different his life would have been, how much happier. He had gotten over her, sure, but it had left him crippled. Empty. He had never been able to feel again as he had felt with Jennifer. And Jennifer—what had he done to her? If he had been in pain, how much more she must have felt. He had believed his friends instead of her. He had rejected her and labeled her trash like everyone else in town. He had trampled on her love. When his love was tested he hadn't been good enough. He had failed and in failing had crushed her, too.

He remembered the pain on her face, the tears filling her eyes, and guilt flooded him. She had tried to tell him, but he wouldn't listen. He wouldn't *believe*.

It was dark when he returned to his father's house. He showered and changed, then put the girls to bed. He went

back downstairs, heading for the front door. His father
stepped out of the den. "Matthew?"

Matthew turned slowly toward him, his face tight and
blank. Sam frowned. "Matt? Is something wrong? Where
are you going?"

"To Fayetteville, to see a movie."

His father looked surprised, but made no comment. "All
right. I'll see you in the morning then."

"Yeah." Matthew paused. "We're leaving tomorrow
morning."

"But I thought you were staying for the weekend."

"I was. But I don't think I can be in the same house
with you for another day."

"What in the hell are you talking about?"

"Keith told me the truth tonight. He told me what you
did to me seventeen years ago. What you did to Jennifer."

Suddenly Sam looked his age and more. "I don't know
what you're talking about."

"The hell you don't. I'm talking about the lies you got
my 'best buddies' to tell me. I'm talking about the way
you set me up. Who in the hell do you think you are to
play with another person's life like that?"

"I was trying to save you from disaster."

"Disaster? You mean disaster like having a miserable
marriage? Disaster like a wife who sleeps with every guy
she meets? Disaster like a divorce and two kids to raise by
myself? Well, thank you, but I found that anyway."

Sam's lips thinned. "That only goes to show that your
second choice was as poor as your first."

"No, it goes to show that I loved the daughter of the
town drunk so much that the deacon's daughter couldn't
make me happy. I loved Jennifer. I've never found anything like that since. Not with my wife and not with casual
affairs, the kind you're so fond of."

"You're being insulting."

"I'm barely scratching the surface."

"I did what I did because I loved you."

"You don't know the meaning of the word. You did it

because you were losing control of me. Because I wasn't doing what you had planned for me. You wanted to bring me back in line." Bitterly he added, "And it worked."

They looked at each other, both stiff and unyielding, the air between them like a wall. "No," Sam said finally. "It didn't work. I lost you."

"Yeah. You did."

The movie had been running for thirty minutes when Matthew reached the theater in Fayetteville. He stepped into the darkened room and stopped abruptly. His heart began to hammer in his chest. Jennifer. Her face filled the screen, lovely and haunting. She was the girl he had known; he saw it in her facial structure, in her creamy skin and brilliant blue eyes. But she was more beautiful now, beautiful in a different way. Mature, sophisticated, in control. She no longer hid her beauty; she used it, reaching out to the audience with its vibrant force. She spoke and her voice was that of a woman, not a girl. But still it was Jennifer.

He thought of the hours they had spent in his car, talking, laughing, kissing. He remembered the way light would jump into her eyes when she was happy or excited, the way her smile melted him. For years he had tried not to think about it, but now the memories flooded in on him, and he could think of nothing but that time. And Jennifer.

He stood, not even trying to find a seat, and watched her, remembering. Tears filled his eyes and rolled unnoticed down his cheeks.

* *Chapter 16* *

The alarm buzzed, jerking Matthew awake, and his hand lashed out to turn it off. He lay there for a moment trying to orient himself. He'd been dreaming, something vague and confused that he couldn't even remember, but it was difficult to move from it into the real world. It was 6:00. Monday. Time to get up. He had a full day of seeing patients ahead of him.

Matthew pulled himself from the bed. It seemed harder to do every morning since Keith had told him about Jennifer. Every night he lay awake in his bed, thinking about her, remembering the time they had been together. The memories he had kept at bay for so long flooded in on him. It was stupid. His love with Jennifer was in the past, and no matter how unfair or senseless it had been, no matter how much he regretted what he'd done, there was nothing that he could do to correct it now. It would be better to forget it.

He shaved quickly and showered, then dressed. Carrying his tie and suit jacket with him, he went down the hall to awaken the girls.

They were asleep in their white twin beds, and he paused for a moment to look at them. Michelle lay curled up into a ball on her side, her dark hair falling across her face. Laura was, as always, sprawled across the bed, arms and legs flung wide and one foot hanging off the side, with Bo-bo, her old ragtag baby blanket, bunched against her side.

He smiled. "Girls. Laura. Michelle."

Michelle's eyes flew open. She was instantly awake, a light sleeper. Laura, on the other hand, was almost impossible to awaken. He had to go over and shake her shoulder before her big blue eyes opened. She looked at him and rolled over, one thumb popping into her mouth and her other hand reaching for the blanket. Michelle slid her arms around him, and he carried her to the bathroom. It would be another ten minutes before Laura would crawl out of bed. She had to adjust to the world every morning by staring into space and sucking on her thumb, Bo-bo comfortingly in her hand.

Michelle brushed her teeth and pulled off Matthew's old

T-shirt that she liked to wear for a nightgown. "I want a braid."

Matthew sighed inwardly and brushed her hair back, carefully dividing it into three sections. He began to weave the sections together, his hands clumsy. He'd gotten to where he could manage a decent ponytail, but his braids always came out too loose or too tight or a little awry.

When he finished, he got out Laura's clothes and pulled her out of the bed. Michelle was able to dress herself, thank God, even tying her tennis shoes. When Felicia left, Michelle had been only four and Laura three, and it had been quite a production each morning getting them both dressed.

He managed to get Laura out of bed and into her clothes. Always the copycat, she wanted a braid too, and got tears in her eyes when he couldn't find another yarn tie the same color as Michelle's to tie at the end of her braid. Exasperated, he searched through the drawers in the girls' room and finally found the other tie wrapped around a Barbie doll's waist.

He trotted down the stairs to the kitchen, the girls following more slowly, Laura trailing the blanket behind her. He wondered how long a kid was supposed to hold onto a blanket. Michelle had never had such a treasured object. And how long should he watch her suck her thumb until he began to worry that she had psychological problems? Or maybe it was Michelle he should worry about. Maybe Laura got rid of all her anxiety by using her thumb and blanket, whereas Michelle held it all in. Well, at least Laura had stopped hiding under the beds and tables everytime he was ready to go somewhere, as she'd done right after Felicia left.

He poured the girls cereal and fixed himself a cup of coffee. Sometimes he tried to make them a full breakfast, with bacon, eggs and toast, but usually he didn't have time.

Both the girls ran up to brush their teeth and spent some

time arguing over the toothbrushes. Matthew glanced at his watch. They were already late. "Come on, you two."

They ran down the stairs where he bundled them up in their coats, and they left the house. Matthew dropped Michelle at her kindergarten a couple of minutes late, then drove Laura to the morning nursery at a Presbyterian church. His housekeeper, who worked from 10:30 to 6:30 everyday, would pick up Laura at 11:00 and also get Michelle in the afternoon.

Laura decided to cling to him when he left her at the nursery, and it took him five minutes to get away. He ran into a traffic jam on Preston, making him even later, and it was almost 9:20 before he reached his office. There were already three patients in the waiting room.

The morning was jammed, and he went straight from one patient to the next, finally finishing about thirty minutes into his lunch hour. His receptionist had gone out for lunch, and she brought him back a hamburger, which he ate in his office while he went through the morning's mail. Most of it was pleas for one charity or another or advertisements. One brochure detailed a tax seminar given on a Caribbean cruise ship, allowing him to write off a vacation on his income tax.

He tossed the brochure in the trash can along with the rest of the mail, but it reminded him of something. He pulled a large envelope from the bottom drawer and laid its contents on the desk before him. It was an invitation to a national cardiologists' convention being held in Los Angeles. He glanced through the list of topics and speakers and the color brochure of the Bonaventure Hotel, headquarters for the convention. The meeting was only two weeks away. Probably the hotel was already filled.

He didn't know why he'd kept the information. He hadn't planned to go. He didn't like conventions. It would mean asking Felicia to take the girls for a few days or arranging for the housekeeper to stay over. Why was he even considering it? But he knew the answer to that. Jennifer. Which was crazy—just because the convention would give him an excuse to go to LA didn't mean he would see Jennifer again. (But he could drive by her house—suddenly he yearned to know where she lived, what it looked like. Maybe he could call her, somehow find out her telephone number.)

No. He was being idiotic. Hell, after all this time, with everything that Jennifer had achieved, she probably wouldn't even remember who he was. If she did, she certainly wouldn't want to talk over old times. Any memories of him would be bad ones.

But reason couldn't stop the compulsion in him, the sudden hunger to go. He had been tired, but now he felt younger, fresher, filled with energy. He wanted to go to LA no matter how silly the notion.

Matthew picked up the papers and went down the hall to the receptionist's desk. "Fill out this registration and send it in for me, would you? And get me a reservation at the Biltmore. You'll have to juggle my appointments to free me up then."

Surprised, his receptionist looked down at the registration form. "You're going to LA?"

"Yeah. I'm going to LA."

Brett Cameron glanced at her watch and grimaced. 5:30. She had to meet Jennifer at Liz's office in an hour, and considering the traffic, she had to start soon. As an inducement to sign another contract with Royal Studios two years earlier, Royal had built her a two-story Victorian frame house on the Royal lot for her office. She had hated to leave her location in Hollywood, but she had outgrown her office there, and it was more practical to be close to the studio. Her office was lovely, and she liked being able to look out her window right onto the busy Royal lot. But it also meant she was stuck out in Burbank and had to allow extra time to get to Liz in Century City.

She sifted through the papers on her desk, selecting

what to put in her briefcase to work on at home that night. Her desk was covered with letters, memos, notes, books, and scripts. So were the credenza, the two elegant oak filing cabinets, and a low set of shelves. Two telephones sat on her desk. One was a large, modernistic thing with several buttons and had the ability to do everything but make coffee; it was the phone for the Dragowynd offices. The other phone was the private line to her office, and only a select few knew the number. The Dragowynd line buzzed, and she pushed down the speaker button and talked while she continued to sort through the papers. Her pace was hectic, but she thrived on it. This was her world.

Brett hung up the phone and almost immediately the private line rang. With a sigh, Brett picked it up, hoping it wasn't her production manager calling with another problem.

"Brett Cameron."

"Brett?" The voice was soft and watery.

"Rosemary."

Her sister began to cry on the other end of the line. Brett repressed another sigh. "What's the problem, Ro?"

"I'm so lonely. I don't like it here."

"I know you don't. But if you'd stay straight you wouldn't have to go back there again and again."

"I knew you'd say that. Everything's always so simple for you."

"Sweetheart, it's not that I'm not sympathetic. I know you're hurting and lonely. But what can I do?"

"You could let me come live with you."

Brett closed her eyes and rested her head on her hand, elbow propped on the desk. She felt immensely weary. "You know that's impossible."

"Why? I'd be good, Brett, I promise. I'm off the drugs now."

"Dr. Collins says you're making good progress. But he assured me that it will be several weeks before you're ready to leave."

"The longer they keep me here the more money they get."

"Rosemary, be reasonable. Twin Oaks has a waiting list as long as my arm. If you left tomorrow morning they'd have your room filled tomorrow afternoon. They don't need you. You need them."

"I don't. I could do okay. I know it. If you'd just let me move in with you . . ."

"No." Frustration knotted in Brett's chest. Why did Rosemary always have to make everything so hard? She knew she couldn't leave the rehabilitation clinic yet. She knew she wouldn't be able to do it alone at Brett's house and that Brett couldn't allow her to try. Yet she put Brett through an emotional grinder anyway.

"You don't want me there. I'd just be in your way."

"No," Brett protested automatically, though it was perfectly true. "But you have to learn to live on your own."

"You think I'm on my own at this place? They do everything but chew my food for me."

"Well, you certainly wouldn't be on your own at my house."

Rosemary's tears started again. "But I miss you. I'm so lonely here. There's nobody here to talk to. They're all nuts except the doctors, and the only thing *they* do is ask a bunch of stupid questions."

Brett thought of her schedule for the rest of the week. She had an enormous amount to do and had planned to work through the weekend, too. She was still looking for an actor to play Jace, and the situation was beginning to seem desperate. If she didn't find him within the next three weeks it would play havoc with her schedule.

But she guessed one day more or less wouldn't hurt. "What if I came up to see you Saturday?"

"That'd be great!" Rosemary's voice sounded like sunshine now, and Brett felt guilty that she begrudged her sister the time when it obviously meant so much to Rosemary. Brett's life was filled with work and excitement, but Rosemary had nothing to do.

The door to her office opened and Joe Darcy walked in.

He looked as he always did—black hair a little too long, a blue bandanna twisted into a headband and wrapped around his head, wearing jeans, boots and a faded Raiders sweatshirt. Not exactly the uniform of a chauffeur. Brett smiled at him. Over the years he had come to be as much friend as chauffeur. There was little about her life that he didn't know. She talked to him about everything from her movies to her ambivalent feelings toward her mother.

Joe held up his wrist and pointed to his watch. She nodded. "Ro . . . I'm sorry, but I have to run. I have an appointment at 6:30. Yeah. See you Saturday. Bye." She hung up on Rosemary's sigh of disappointment.

"That was Rosemary," she explained, closing and snapping shut her briefcase.

"So I gathered." Joe took her briefcase from her and carried it out the door.

"I told her I'd go see her this weekend."

She could tell by the twist of Joe's mouth that he wasn't pleased. "And no doubt stay up working late a few nights to make up for the time you'll lose."

Brett shrugged. "She's lonely."

"She uses you."

Brett sighed. This was an old argument between them and it never varied. She knew that to a large extent Joe was right. But she couldn't get rid of the enormous guilt in her: guilt that she had failed her sister when they were growing up; guilt for choosing the business that Rosemary hated so much; guilt that she had turned out so right, the shining star of the family, while Rosemary had turned out so wrong.

"She's my sister."

"That's right. But you act like she's your daughter. Let Ken and your mother do some caretaking of her for once."

"Ken's in Dallas with the art director working on the location shots."

Joe cast her a sideways glance. He disliked all the people who pulled and tugged on Brett, feeding on her strength, her intelligence, her tremendous ability. Keeping them away from her was one of his main objectives. But he knew he'd never be able to get Brett to stop responding to them. It was her nature. She was responsible and kind. She knew her power, her energy, the abilities she had that others didn't, and she felt a duty to use them for those she cared about—her family, her friends, her employees. He knew he shouldn't complain. If he were to get into trouble he would just have to call Brett and she'd be there for him. That was one reason that he, who'd always been so trouble-prone, did his best to stay away from it now. He would never be another burden to Brett. He loved her too much.

Brett didn't know about his love. He'd always been careful to hide it from her, knowing that it would be another burden to her. She felt nothing that way for him. He was a trusted employee, at best a friend. It would be absurd to think Brett could feel anything more for him. He was just a stray she had helped in her usual way, but she was one of the wealthiest, most powerful and most gifted people in this city. Brett Cameron couldn't love him; he would never hope for that. But she was fond of him, and he knew that if she were aware of his love she would think that she had to be careful of his feelings, had to help him get over it, had to somehow make up for his pain.

And there was pain. Joe wouldn't deny that. It hurt to stand by and watch some studio executive or director or actor put his arm around Brett or kiss her in casual greeting. It hurt to watch her leave the house with a man or drive her to a party and watch her go inside, knowing that half the guys there would try to seduce her, wanting her for what she could do for them, not loving her, as he did, for the sweet clarity of her soul.

Joe had to smile in self-derision at that thought. It wasn't Brett's soul that kept him awake at night, sweating, thinking about her. It wasn't her kindness that sent jealousy slicing through him when some oily opportunist like Sloane Hunter touched her. It wasn't her talent or her brains that made him want to crawl into the backseat with her and cover her with his body, pressing her down into the soft leather.

No. That was the flash of her long legs as she got into the car, the smell of her Joy perfume when she remembered to put it on or the faint, even sweeter smell of her own skin when she forgot. The life and warmth of her hair made him want to sink his hands into it and feel it curl around his fingers. The firm, slender lines of her body inside the boldly printed dresses she liked to wear, the soft mounds of her breasts made him want to back her up against the nearest wall and kiss her senseless.

He wanted her. And he knew he'd never have her, never even be able to express it. It was painful to be around her, to ache for her and know he could never have her, but it was a pain he gladly endured; he wrapped it around himself and held it with a kind of secret joy. For in that way he protected her. In that way he was close to her, and even the pain was somehow sweet because it came from her.

The only way Joe showed his love was in the almost fierce way he took care of Brett. He kept away fans and reporters and whomever she didn't want to see. He guarded her against the wackos who threatened her. He took care of the hundreds of things she didn't have the time for. He was there whenever and wherever she needed him, and he couldn't imagine anything she might ask of him that he wouldn't do for her.

He would have liked to relieve her of all problems, all sorrows. Like Rosemary. He had wished her to hell a hundred times for putting the thin line of worry between Brett's eyes. But he dropped the subject now. He couldn't change Brett, didn't even want to change her, and to continue to express his opinion of Rosemary would hurt her.

They walked to the car in silence. He had brought the car from the lot and parked it directly in front of the building. It was a silver Rolls Royce. Brett had bought it two years before, as much for Joe as for herself. He loved the car, loved to drive it and take care of it, and he kept it in perfect condition. Even though it was ostentatious, Brett felt a little thrill each time she stepped into it. It reminded her of the times King had taken her to the studio with him when she was a child and they had ridden in his long, elegant old black Rolls, with the chauffeur miles in front of them beyond a glass partition, and the rich scent of leather all around.

Joe settled Brett and her briefcase in the back and got in to drive. Brett took out a pad and pen and leaned back against the seat, closing her eyes, to think about an idea that had popped into her mind earlier in the day. She didn't notice the heavy traffic around them. Now and then she opened her eyes to jot a note on the pad in her lap. Joe said nothing to her, just watched the traffic and listened to the radio on low. So deep was Brett in her concentration that it surprised her when they pulled into the parking lot of Liz's building.

"Are we here already?"

Joe grinned. It had been a forty-minute trip.

He parked the car and walked Brett to Liz's office, then returned to the car to wait for her. Joe had made himself her bodyguard as well as chauffeur three years ago when she had gotten a death threat through the mail. Brett had shrugged the note off, saying that it came with the territory, but Joe had taken it seriously. He began accompanying her everywhere except on her infrequent dates, walking with her from the car, staying with her when they were on location—or just about anyplace else except the studio. Brett didn't think it was necessary. Nothing had ever come of that threat or of the two she'd gotten in the years since. But she didn't tell Joe not to come with her. She was used to his being with her, and she found his strong, quiet presence both reassuring and pleasant. Joe was easy to be with. He never asked for anything, never demanded. She could tell him anything, and she knew he would never repeat it. She enjoyed listening to him. What he said was always interesting, unique. He had a way of looking at things that was different from everyone that Brett had ever known, a kind of earthy, practical slant, yet somehow artistic, too. She found herself frequently asking for his opinion or advice. He would tell her exactly what he thought, but he never tried to pressure or persuade her to accept his viewpoint. Most of the time he didn't even talk unless she began the conversation. He was the most silent and inward person Brett had ever known.

He was also the most private. He rarely talked about himself, and as a result Brett knew little about the details of his life. She was often curious about it—whether he had a woman and if so, what she was like; what he did when he wasn't on the job; what his past had been like. But, having grown up in the goldfish bowl that was Hollywood, she had too much respect for privacy to poke into his life. Besides, as little as she knew *about* him, she knew *him* very well, with an instinctive, essential awareness that had little to do with thoughts or facts. Joe would never harm her or allow anyone else to.

She trusted him implicitly. He was one of the few—very few—people about whom she could say that. She wasn't inclined to trust even those she called friends. Ken, probably. Jennifer Taylor. Perhaps Liz, though there was always a faint doubt, because she was, after all, an agent and ambitious. Once her grandfather would have headed the list, but he had damaged her trust when he sold the studio. But above all others, she had faith in Joe Darcy.

The office building was quiet. Most of the tenants had gone home by now; but Liz's office was lighted, and the outer door stood open. The receptionist had gone home an hour and a half earlier, but Liz was still there, glued to the phone, as always. She saw Brett as she came in the outer door and waved at her.

As fresh looking at the end of her busy day as most people were at the beginning, Liz was businesslike in a red Saint John dress, but she seemed softer than she had in the past. Much of the hard edge had worn off Liz the last few years. She was as efficient and sharp and as neat as ever, and she could be cool and cynical. But the brittle quality was no longer there, and the cynicism seemed more an act put on for self-defense than anything real. She moved more slowly, smiled more often. Her hairstyle and her clothes were looser, more casual, less aggressively efficient.

Liz hung up the phone and switched it to mute so they wouldn't be disturbed by any calls. She poured them both drinks from the small bar in the corner of her office and they chatted, winding down from their busy days. The signing was merely a formality and a pleasant one at that, not real business.

Five minutes later Jennifer came flying in the door, apologizing for being late and complaining about the traffic. Jennifer wore no makeup—she never did except when she was filming or attending a party—and she was dressed in plain tan trousers and a simple pale pink blouse. Even so, her beauty was obvious. Yet Brett saw not the beauty, but the lines of tiredness around her mouth and the faint blue stain under Jennifer's eyes. Jennifer worked herself too hard; she had for years.

Brett stood up and hugged her. Jennifer was one of Brett's favorites. She was a favorite of most of the people in the industry. Of course, she had enemies; there were rumors and unkind remarks made about her. One couldn't be important in Hollywood and not have those things. But Jennifer had far fewer enemies than most stars. People liked her. She was a competent professional and easy to work with, not given to tantrums, sulks or excessive ego. She was genuinely kind, and her quiet personality didn't clash with the flashier ones around her. And the trace of sadness in her eyes touched one's heart. Even Joe, the most reserved of men, always had a smile or a hug for Jennifer.

They signed the several copies of the contract quickly, and Liz locked them away in her desk. She poured another round of drinks in celebration. In the middle of the toasts Sloane Hunter walked into the outer office.

He was the epitome of the handsome Hollywood male. He was dressed in a silk Armani suit the color of rich cream, the collar casually turned up, a pastel silk shirt beneath it. His stomach was flat, his arms and shoulders muscular enough to draw the eye, but not enough to spoil the cut of his coat. His thick black hair was perfectly cut, his skin tanned a golden brown, his eyes startlingly blue and ringed with long black lashes. Faint lines fanned out from his eyes and bracketed his mouth, giving his almost perfect face a look of world-weary experience. He looked wealthy, devastatingly masculine, and more than a little bit wicked.

Liz turned and saw him, and a smile broke across her face. "Sloane!"

She set down her drink and went to him, and he met her halfway, taking her into his arms. He kissed her lightly on the lips.

"You act surprised." He smiled down into her face, his intense blue eyes intimate and affectionate. "Did you forget I was going to pick you up?"

"I guess I did." But Liz knew she hadn't. She simply couldn't control the leap of joy inside her whenever she saw Sloane. It had been that way for her for four years.

She was so crazy in love with him it scared her. They had been together ever since the night she'd given him a ride home from Susan Ketterman's party, and it had been the happiest time she could remember. Everyday she grew more and more in love with him. Sometimes she thought of what would happen to her if he left, and it turned her insides to ice. The pain was too awful, the loneliness too unbearable to contemplate. Sloane filled her world with joy. Yet, precisely because of that, she was scared to death that he might leave her. He told her he loved her; he made love to her as if she were the only woman in the world. But she knew what he was, how he had lived before she met him, a man who had given women his body in return for a life of wealth and luxury. Even as she showered him

with gifts, she wondered if he spoke the truth or if he
stayed with her for the things she could give him.

In her doubts and fears she tried to suppress and deny
her love for him. She wasn't aware that the joy on her face
when she saw him always gave her away.

"You're early," Liz said, stepping out of his arms
reluctantly. "I didn't expect you until 7:30."

Sloane shrugged. "My errands didn't take long. Besides, I had an idea. I think the third Brett Cameron movie
starring Jennifer Taylor deserves some kind of celebration,
don't you? Why don't we all go back to our place for
dinner? I'll grill the steaks. What do you say?"

"I think it sounds great," Liz replied promptly.

"Sure. That would be nice." It was fine with Jennifer to
delay going home. There was nothing for her there,
anyway.

They all turned to Brett. She hesitated. She had a lot of
work to do, and she'd intended to get on it tonight, so that
her trip Saturday wouldn't interfere so much with her
business. But it had been a tough day and she was tired.
The thought of an evening relaxing with friends was
appealing. She smiled. "Yes, thank you. I'd like that."

Liz locked up, and they went down to the parking lot
together, talking and laughing, Sloane charming them all.
He had one arm around Liz and his other hand rested
casually on Jennifer's back, but he was careful not to
touch Brett as they stepped outside, for her driver was
there, lounging against the sleek silver Rolls. Once Sloane
had given Brett a good-bye kiss on the cheek in front of
Joe Darcy and Darcy had looked at him as if he'd like to
knife him.

They drove out to the beach house in Malibu in their
separate cars, Liz and Sloane in his Ferrari, Jennifer in her
Mercedes, and Joe driving Brett, as always. Brett sat in
the front seat this time—she was tired of working—and
watched the scenery. Joe drove more circumspectly than
Sloane, and Brett decided to stop and buy some wine for
dinner, so that they arrived at Liz's house after the others.

Joe pulled into the drive and stopped with the engine still running. Brett looked at him. "Don't you want to come in, too? It'll be a while."

He shook his head. "Nah. I'll get a hamburger and come back."

"But it's just friends. Jennifer and Liz." He knew them as well as anyone. He had shared food and conversation with them before.

"I don't want to have to eat with Sloane Hollywood. That faggot."

Brett chuckled at his description of Sloane. "I hardly think *that* is his problem." Joe had some sort of dislike for Sloane, always had, though she wasn't sure why. It never occurred to her that Joe might be jealous of her being around a man that handsome and that at ease in her world.

Brett slid out of the car. Joe watched her walk to the door and drove away when it opened. Brett knew Joe would be waiting outside for her long before she came out. Not for the first time she wondered what he did in those long stretches of time while he waited for her. He always carried a pad of paper with him, and she'd seen him sketching in it from time to time. But he didn't offer to show her anything he drew, and she, respecting his privacy, never asked.

Jennifer opened the door and let her in. Sloane and Liz were in the kitchen preparing the impromptu meal and laughing. It sounded so warm, so nice and intimate that Brett was suddenly lonely.

They joined Liz and Sloane in the kitchen. Sloane had taken off his jacket and was seasoning thick slabs of steak. Liz was scrubbing Irish potatoes and craning to read the directions for microwaving them.

"I always knew you were a gourmet cook," Brett joked, nodding toward the cookbook.

Liz made a face at her. Sloane finished the steaks and made their drinks while Jennifer and Brett threw together a salad. Sloane brought the drinks from the bar and paused dramatically in the kitchen doorway. They looked at him.

He grinned. "This has to be the highest-priced kitchen staff I've ever seen. It's at least a million dollar meal."

Liz rolled her eyes and took her drink from him. "Just grill the steaks."

He gave Brett and Jennifer their drinks and saluted Liz. "Yes, ma'am." He picked up the plate of steaks in one hand and left the kitchen, running his hand down Liz's back in a casual, affectionate gesture.

He went out to the deck to grill the steaks while the women finished up the salad and potatoes, chatting as they worked. They talked about *Drifter* and the movies that various studios had in the cooker. They gossiped about the latest scandals and the most recent breakups, the newest pairings. The movie industry was like a small town, insular and isolated, and everyone knew what everyone else was doing—and those doings were the favorite topic of conversation in any gathering. They didn't leave the coziness of the kitchen when they were finished preparing the food. Liz perched herself up on a counter and Jennifer and Brett leaned against the counter across from her as they sipped their drinks and talked.

Brett was the slightest bit tipsy. Added to the drinks she'd had at Liz's office when they signed, this made three, and she hadn't eaten. She also felt a little sad and wistful. Seeing Liz and Sloane together made her feel that way. She envied the love between them, the closeness. Suddenly, surprising them all, she said, "I'm lonely."

"What?" Liz stared at Brett.

"I'm lonely," Brett repeated. "It just occurred to me. I'm so busy most of the time that I don't notice it. But tonight, watching you and Sloane, I realized how lonely I am."

"There's not a man in this city who wouldn't be happy to fall at your feet," Liz pointed out.

"Yeah, but they all want something from me. You never know whether they mean what they say, or if they want a part or want to sell an idea or make some deal with you. They're always after something."

"Like Scott," Jennifer said softly. She understood Brett's loneliness; the isolation was like being inside a glass showcase, unable to touch or to be touched. It was ironic, because she knew movie people were thought to live glamorous, fun-filled lives. But the reality was rarely like that. They worked from dawn until evening and were usually too tired when they got home to go out or see anyone. They were plagued with doubts whether anyone really liked *them*, the individuals.

"Yeah. Like Scott. I was sorry when you married him. He's a good actor, but he's a user." She paused, then went on. "I was engaged to a guy like him once."

"Really? I never heard that."

"It was a long time ago when I was in college. I'd always known that people were nicer to me because I was King's granddaughter and Ken's stepdaughter. Once a guy even stopped me when I was leaving school and asked me if I would give Ken his manuscript." She smiled at the memory. "King warned me about the people who would try to take advantage of me because of my relationship to him and Ken. I understood that. But for some reason I thought in college it was different, that I had some kind of anonymity there. Cameron wasn't a famous name. And who would know I was King's granddaughter? Of course, I was naive. I was right here in Los Angeles, in the film school at UCLA. Needless to say, a lot of people knew who I was. Anyway, I fell head over heels for this guy. Jeff. We got engaged. I introduced him to King, and Jeff didn't seem at all surprised that King was my grandfather. King didn't like him, and you know King, he checked into him. Surprise. Jeff turned out to be a fortune hunter. He had made a tidy bundle a couple of years before when a movie star paid him off to stay away from his teenage daughter, but he'd blown it and needed more money."

They were silent for a moment. Jennifer reached out and covered Brett's hand. Brett smiled at her. "Thank you. It's okay. It doesn't hurt anymore. But it made me wary. And the relationships I've had since have made me even warier.

It seems like every man I meet wants something from me. And don't grin at me like that, Liz. I don't mean my luscious body."

"I know. It's happened to me, too. You don't know how many actors think they can get me for an agent by slipping into my bed." She shrugged. "It's part of the job."

"Yeah. But I don't like it. You've seen my films; I'm a romantic, remember? I want a man who loves me, not my money or my influence or a role in my next movie."

"Maybe you're asking the impossible," Jennifer put in. "I think being alone is part of the price of success. Being separated from other people."

Brett sighed. "But I'm thirty-five years old and I'm getting tired of being alone."

"I have the answer," Liz volunteered, leaning forward, her hands gripping the edge of the counter.

"What?"

"Pay for your sex and companionship."

Brett's eyebrows went up. "You mean male prostitutes? Gigolos?"

Liz shrugged. "Whatever you want to call it."

"Come on . . . that's not what I want."

"Why not? You get super sex and lots of attention without all the worry about whether he really likes you. He's nice to you, you aren't lonely and it's a clean, commercial transaction."

"Liz! Get serious."

"I am! When you know you're paying him or providing for him or whatever, you aren't deceived. You don't feel used or taken advantage of because you made a bargain. Listen to me, I know. You just said you envied what I had with Sloane."

"Just a second. That's not the same."

"Why not? I pay his way; he lives with me." Liz lit a cigarette, her expression cool and matter-of-fact.

Brett frowned. "It's different. You two love each other. You've been together for four years. Hell, that's longer than most marriages!"

"Don't kid yourself." All the harsh lines and edges were back in Liz's face. "What Sloane and I have is bought sex, pure and simple."

The sliding glass door from the deck opened and Sloane entered. He stopped short at Liz's words.

Liz and Brett were looking at each other, engrossed in their conversation. Only Jennifer saw Sloane come in the house. She stiffened and opened her mouth to tell Liz, but it was too late.

Liz was rolling on, her voice light to cover the fear inside that she was telling the truth. "Sloane doesn't love me. He stays with me because I provide well for him. I stay with him because he's fantastic in bed and he keeps me from being lonely. It's perfect that way. There aren't any of the heartbreaks or entanglements of love."

Sloane turned quickly and slipped back out of the house, shutting the glass door behind him as quietly as he had opened it.

* *Chapter 17* *

Jennifer saw the flash of unmasked hurt on Sloane's face before he turned away. She left the kitchen quietly. The others scarcely noticed her departure, so caught up were they in their conversation. Liz was saying, "Come on, I'll set you up with somebody. I'm sure Sloane knows somebody that . . ." and Brett was protesting, half appalled, half laughing.

Jennifer stepped out onto the deck and shut the door behind her, cutting off the sound of their voices. Sloane stood on the opposite side of the deck, his hands braced against the wooden railing, staring out at the ocean. She remembered the time when she had stood on this porch like that, looking out at the ocean. Sloane had saved her.

"Sloane?"

He turned sharply at the sound of her voice, and Jennifer caught a glimmer of wetness in his eyes. He looked back out at the ocean. He said nothing. Jennifer walked over to stand beside him, and for a moment they simply gazed at the water together.

"She didn't mean it," she said finally.

"Oh, yeah," he replied, his voice flat, "she means it."

"She loves you. Anyone can see, looking at you two, that you're happy."

Jennifer saw his lips quirk up in a brief, unamused grin. "Yeah, we're happy, in our own sick way."

"Sloane . . . she'd had something to drink. And she likes to pretend to be tougher, more cynical than she is. It's a defense against being hurt."

He turned around and crossed his arms over his chest, still not looking at Jennifer. He swallowed, and when he spoke his voice was low and rough with unshed masculine tears. "I know her. I know her defenses. I think she loves me, but she won't admit it. She runs from it. She doesn't believe that I love her."

Jennifer's heart twisted. She liked Sloane. Not only had he saved her life, he'd been a good friend over the years. She hated to see him hurt.

"I do, you know," Sloane went on. "I love Liz very much." He stared down at his crossed arms as he talked, unused to revealing his feelings. "I've loved her for a long, long time. She's scared to accept it, to trust me. I can understand that. She knows what I used to be. And I let her give me stuff—clothes, a car, whatever she thinks I want. I guess I'm weak. I like the things she gives me; I like her wanting to give them to me—it's the only expression of love I ever get from Liz."

He sighed and moved away restlessly. "I don't know what to do to make her believe me. Refuse her presents? Move out and get a job, insist she see me at my crummy place, not here? I've gotten jobs, but hell, I can't make anything near to what she does, and—you know something funny?—Liz doesn't really like it when I have a job. It scares her, like I'm moving away, getting ready to leave. She'll say, 'Why don't you quit? You don't need to work.' So I'll quit. I don't like the jobs. I take the easiest path. But that confirms to her that I'm trading myself for her money. Lately, I don't know why, she's been like she was a minute ago—cruel, insulting. It's almost as if she wants to drive me away or to see how much I'll take.''

"You know what I think? I think that as Liz comes to love you more, to depend on you and need you, she gets more scared that you don't love her. She's afraid you'll leave. Her insults are self-defense, like her cynicism. She's trying to attack first, to keep from being attacked.''

"To push me out before I can leave her?"

"Maybe. Or hoping that if you don't go, it'll prove that you really do love her.''

He looked at Jennifer for the first time, his eyes dark and brooding in the dim light. "I do. But she makes it so damn difficult sometimes!''

"I know." Jennifer put her hand on his arm. It was taut and hard with tension. "And I know you love her. That's one reason I like you. You're one guy who I know isn't going to hit on me because you're always true to Liz.''

He forced a smile. "How damaging to my reputation." Sloane straightened. "Well, I guess I'd better bring those steaks in before they burn.''

He dished the sizzling steaks onto the platter and they went back inside. Liz and Brett were still deep in conversation in the kitchen. They hadn't even noticed the others' absence. They sat down to supper, talking and laughing, joking about their culinary skills. Jennifer was amazed at Sloane's ability to enter into the fun as if nothing was wrong. Looking at him she would never have known that the scene out on the deck had taken place.

When the meal was over they stacked the dishes in the sink and sat down in the living room for a cup of coffee.

Around 10:00 Jennifer stood up, saying she had to go home, that tomorrow was another work day, and Brett immediately followed suit.

"What a wild nightlife you two have," Liz joked.

Liz and Sloane walked with the two women to the door and stood watching them as they walked to their cars. Joe Darcy was standing beside the Rolls, hands in the pockets of his jeans. They heard Brett speak to him, though they couldn't understand the words, and an unaccustomed smile crept across the man's face, softening its hard stolidity.

"Do you suppose the rumors about them are true?" Sloane murmured, watching Brett and Darcy get into the Rolls.

"That he's her lover? I don't know. He seems rather rough for Brett, doesn't he?"

"I don't know. Some women like them rough. He sure as hell doesn't act like a chauffeur."

Disquiet stirred in Liz at Sloane's interest in Brett's love life. Brett was wealthier, more powerful and younger than she. What if Sloane decided he preferred Brett? He would have no trouble capturing her interest; Liz couldn't imagine any woman not falling for him. It was a worry that plagued her often. Would he leave her? Would he find someone he liked better?

That was one reason she pretended that there was nothing more between her and Sloane than an agreeable arrangement. If he left, people wouldn't pity her, wouldn't gossip about how her heart had been broken. It would be a dissolved contract, that's all. She was motivated by pride.

Pride and fear. Liz was thirty-eight years old now, and Sloane was only thirty-one. In two years she'd be forty. Before she met Sloane she hadn't worried about aging, hadn't fretted over the gray hairs or the lines. But now...now she couldn't seem to stop worrying. Sloane must want someone younger. He couldn't love her, no matter what he said. If she let herself believe it, she would be living in a fool's paradise. Pride and fear.

Her insecurity made her bitchy sometimes, she knew.

Made her say things she didn't mean, things she knew hurt Sloane. She always regretted her words as soon as they were out of her mouth, and the anger and hurt she saw in Sloane's face gave her pain, too. She knew it might drive him away from her someday. She knew it was petty and wrong. She told herself to quit it. But the next time the same kind of statement would pop out of her mouth uncontrollably, diminishing him. Diminishing them. Thank God he had been outside with the steaks when she had spouted off to Brett.

Sloane's hand slid down her arm and he pulled her inside, closing the front door. He turned her to face him. His mouth was heavy and sensual, and his eyes were filled with passion—and something else, something she couldn't identify. An intensity, an urgency that was both a little frightening and exciting.

He grasped the lapels of her suit jacket and peeled it down her arms, letting it drop to the floor, and all the while his eyes never left hers. Liz's breath came a little faster in her throat and a familiar, sweet tension played along her nerves. He unfastened the buttons of her blouse, then his hands slid under the edges and shoved it back over her shoulders and down, his hands spread wide on her skin.

He undressed her without a word, without a kiss, and his only caresses were the movements of her clothes over her body. But his eyes made love to her, holding her, burning her, arousing her until she was taut and eager, hungry for his lips. When at last she was naked before him, he stood for a moment looking at her. He reached out a finger to touch her chin and dragged it slowly down her throat and chest.

"I love you," he said, his voice low.

"I love you." For once she couldn't hold back the words.

"And I'm going to make you believe it." He undressed, his eyes still on her face, moving slowly, purposefully, prolonging the tension. With each movement, each shrug and twist and pull as the clothes slipped from him, exposing more of his supple, golden flesh, the excitement grew in Liz until she was thrumming and alive to the slightest touch.

When at last he was naked, he pulled Liz to him and kissed her, and it was as if she had been waiting for it all her life. Heat roared through Liz, taking her, and she clung to Sloane. His mouth was greedy and demanding, and Liz responded with equal fervor. She loved the taste of him on her tongue, the smoothness of his skin beneath her fingers, the slight abrasion of his chest hair against her nipples.

Sloane was hungry and wild, his hands and mouth all over her as if he wanted to know every part of her, to take her inside him. Liz had never known him quite like this, so driven, almost harsh in his desire. He took her there on the floor of the entry, as if he could not wait to reach the more civilized bedroom. Tonight he wasn't civilized. His fingers bit into her skin and his breath came hard and rasping as he thrust himself inside her, driving his aching need home. Liz wrapped her legs around him and welcomed him, as impatient as he.

"I love you," he murmured against her throat, his words almost a groan. "I love you." Then the passion took them, hurling them uncontrollably upward to shatter into a million flashing pieces.

Brett gazed out the side window at the glitter of the city below them as the Rolls climbed into the hills. Joe was silent beside her, leaving her to her thoughts. Tonight she didn't enjoy thinking. She kept returning to what Liz had said. It was absurd, of course. She could never hire a man for sex. It would be too cold, too lifeless. And yet . . .

She was so often lonely these days. There were always people around her, but little real friendship. It spoke volumes about her life, she thought, that her best friend was her chauffeur!

As much as she liked Joe, as easy and pleasant as it was to be around him, that didn't fill the empty space in her life. It didn't make the nights any less lonely or her bed any less vacant.

At first the lack of a love hadn't mattered. When Brett had started out her career had been the most important thing in her life—practically the only thing. She had wanted to create, to make movies, to bring her visions to life. She had wanted to be successful, to prove that she could make it on her own merits, not because her grandfather was Kingsley Gerard. In those days her work had been enough. She hadn't missed the presence of a man in her life and an occasional casual relationship had satisfied her. She had been hurting still from the realization that her fiancé was a fortune hunter, and she hadn't wanted to have any man close to her.

But now it was different. She had proved herself. She had made the movies she'd wanted to and had seen the overwhelming response to them from people all over the world. She still loved movies; she enjoyed the challenge, the pressure, and the excitement. It was part of her, bone, blood and mind. But it was no longer enough.

Brett had been feeling a vague dissatisfaction with her life for months now, a restlessness and longing. She was lonely. She was hungry for companionship—no, more than that, for love and affection. For a man to share her life.

What Liz had suggested wouldn't provide that. It would be only false love, faked affection. It wouldn't be the same. It couldn't. Hired sex was only that: sex. While that was part of what she wanted, it wasn't anywhere near all. Just a man, any man, in her bed wasn't what she needed. After all, she could think of several men who would be happy to provide that, thinking they'd get a role or a favor out of the deal.

Of course, Liz's suggestion would be cleaner, as she had said. It took away the uncertainty, the never-completely-squelched hope that this time, this man would be different. It would remove the constant doubt that could destroy any relationship. If that was truly what Liz and Sloane had, what worked so well for them . . . But no, Brett couldn't believe that. Liz was lying to herself if she believed it. There was love between her and Sloane; it was obvious.

And that was what Brett wanted: real love. She was a romantic, and as absurd as it might seem in the world in which she lived, Brett believed that real love was possible. After all, she had grown up seeing it between her grandparents. There had been a passion and affection between them that had never diminished over the years. As stormy as her mother's relationship with Ken had been, they had truly loved each other. It wasn't impossible, it wasn't just an imaginative outpouring of her mind. It *could* happen, and Brett told herself that she would have to wait, that someday it would happen to her. The problem was when.

Joe stopped in front of the gate to Brett's house and pushed a button on the remote control unit. The high iron gates slid aside and Joe drove through, following the curving asphalt drive to her house. The garage door opened at the flick of another button and they drove in. The door closed automatically behind them and they were inside what Brett sometimes thought of as her fortress.

Joe made it that way. After the death threats a few years ago she had had this house built, and Joe had made sure that the best security system to be bought was installed in it. He had improved on the protection since. The entire grounds could be lit by floodlights, and there were cameras at the gate and front door. A button in Brett's room was connected directly to Joe's lodgings on the bottom floor so that she could call him in an instant if there was an emergency. All the doors and windows were wired. When the system was set, opening any door or window or breaking or even cutting the glass would trigger a deafening alarm and flip on the floodlights, as well as send a message to the Beverly Hills Police. One night last year Brett had gone out for a midnight swim, forgetting to turn off the alarm, and all hell had broken loose as soon as she opened the door.

Joe turned off the system as they stepped inside the house, then reset it. Brett went straight to bed, but Joe walked around the house to check the rooms as he did each night. When that was done he trotted down the side stairs to his rooms. Brett's house was a modern wood-and-glass set of boxes that flowed down the side of the hill. Brett's rooms were on the second story, with a breathtaking view of the city (when the smog lifted), and the formal living areas and guest bedrooms were on the main floor. The bottom floor, built into the ground at the back and open to the view on the other side, was divided in half. One half contained a recreation room, Brett's small projection room, a sauna, and an indoor spa. The back door led to the pool another level down.

The other half of the bottom floor was separated from the rest by a solid wall and could be reached only by a door from the patio or the stairs beside the kitchen. It was Joe's private living quarters, not simply a room, but a suite with a large bedroom and bath, a spacious living area, and even a small kitchen. It was decorated in the same manner as the rest of the house, with plush carpets and elegant woodwork. Joe had never lived in a place as large or as lovely in his life. Brett had built the area with him in mind and, in her usual way, had striven to make it as much like a home and as private as possible. She studiously regarded it as Joe's home and didn't intrude on him there. If she needed him, she called on the intercom; in the two years they'd lived there, she had not once entered his living quarters.

Yet even though she had never been there, Brett was all over the rooms. A bronze sculpture of her head stood on a table in the living room, and there was another stylized, shiny head of her in his bedroom. He had hung a large charcoal sketch of her on one wall of the bedroom, and at least half the sketches in his large portfolio were of Brett. The love he could not reveal came out in his art.

Joe crossed the large living area to his worktable, where a half-finished wax sculpture of a pouncing eagle sat. He ran a finger over the wax feathers, not yet detailed. His art. That was another thing Brett had given him, though she didn't know it.

Years ago he would have laughed at the idea that there was anything of an artist in him. He had always doodled, drawing faces and forms on whatever happened to be near him, and when he was a boy his Mexican grandfather had taught him how to whittle. But he had never conceived of such things as being art. Art was some foreign thing that lived in another world where things were pretty, and people were wealthy, and nobody had to struggle to live.

Then Brett had come along and opened the door to that other world. More than that. She had taken him by the hand and led him inside. Her own talent was so great it awed him; yet it also touched a chord in him. She was of the world of the imagination, and for the first time he saw the reality of that world. She made him long for something, for some way to release what was inside him.

She had gone to the galleries in Santa Fe and Taos, and he had tagged along, and there he had found that something. He saw art in a hundred different forms and it all spoke to him. He bought a pad and pencil and began to sketch. He hated his ineptitude; the pictures he drew never quite expressed what he wanted them to. But he couldn't stop.

After he moved to LA he haunted the museums and galleries during his time off, and always, wherever he was, he drew. He took classes in drawing and in painting with oil and acrylic, but still he felt that he was searching for something else. Then one day, as he stood in a gallery looking at a small statue, aware of an urge to run his hands over it, he remembered the feel of the wood in his hands as a boy. He took a class in modeling clay, and the first time he held the cool clay in his hands he felt as if he had come home.

He took class after class, and every night at his apartment he worked on his pieces. He didn't need much sleep, and he often worked until two or three o'clock in the morning, sometimes even through the night when he was particularly seized by what he was creating. It took him a year to move into metal sculpture, and though he cursed his clumsiness, he knew that it was what he wanted.

It was more than a hobby. It was the only love in his life besides Brett, and he devoted all his spare time and a good deal of his generous salary to it. Every evening after he locked up the house upstairs, he came down here and worked on the wax sculptures that he would eventually turn into bronze.

He sat down now and picked up a small, sharp knife. He worked slowly and patiently, cutting away the wax. But tonight he couldn't seem to get lost in his work as he usually did.

He thought of Brett in her room two floors above him. She was probably undressing for bed now. He wondered if she stood looking out at the lights as she unzipped her skirt and unbuttoned her blouse. The silk blouse would glide across her skin. The thin gold chain would gleam at the base of her bare throat.

Joe's hand tightened around the knife and he looked down at it, surprised, realizing that he had stopped working somewhere along the line. His palms were sweating. Joe set down the knife and wiped his palms across his jeans. He usually didn't let it get to him this way. He wondered why he was doing it tonight.

But he knew why. It had been too dark to sketch most of the time while he waited for Brett, and so he had sat and thought about her. About her skin and the soft curves of her body. About making love to her. About the fact that she was inside the house with Sloane Hunter, who was handsome and slick and wouldn't think twice about using her.

He was jealous and pulsing with desire, and each state aggravated the other until he couldn't think of anything else, do anything else. He wanted her.

He wondered what would happen if he went to her now, if he climbed the stairs to her bedroom. What would she do if he kissed her? He thought of how her lips would taste, of how her mouth would part, of how his tongue would pierce the wet warmth of her mouth.

"Jesus!" Joe jumped to his feet, knocking over the high stool on which he had sat, and began to pace. He crossed his arms tightly across his chest, catching his hands beneath his arms as though to contain himself, and bent his head, watching his boots as they sank into the thick carpet. Why did he do this to himself? Why torture himself with thoughts of making love to Brett when he knew he'd never do it? He wouldn't go to her room, wouldn't pull her into his arms and kiss her. She trusted him, and her trust was a rare and precious thing. The last thing in the world he would do was violate her trust in him or use it to his advantage.

Joe walked back to the table. He righted the stool and forced himself to sit down on it. He sat for a moment, willing himself to relax, then took up the knife again and set to work.

Jennifer couldn't go to sleep when she got home. She swam a few laps in the pool, which usually relaxed her, but tonight it didn't help. Sloane's unhappiness had disturbed her. Jennifer knew that Liz loved Sloane, yet she seemed intent on alienating him. Brett had been troubled, too. For all the laughter and bright conversation, it hadn't been a happy evening.

Jennifer understood Brett's loneliness. She, too, felt separated from most people. And she had learned the hard way that a lover would take advantage of her fame and money. But there was a difference with her. She felt no longing for a man, for love or even companionship. Those things would not ease the desperate loneliness of the past four years. Nothing on earth could do that. All her longings and feelings were dead. If she felt a glass wall between her and the rest of the world it was made as much by the absence of her own emotions as by her fame.

Once she had wanted a man to love her just as Brett did. She had never found him. Now she didn't even want to.

When at last she fell asleep, she dreamed.

Krista was in the pool, floating facedown, arms and legs spread wide. Jennifer was screaming Krista's name and running, running to save her. But she was running in place. Her feet wouldn't go forward. She ran, her heart bursting with terror and frustration, screaming, "No! No!"

"No!" Jennifer sat bolt upright in bed, her eyes flying open and sobs tearing at her throat. She was drenched in sweat. She had jumped out of bed and started toward the pool before she realized that it had been a dream. Krista was not in the pool. Krista was dead.

Still she couldn't keep from going to the glass doors and flipping on the outside lights. The pool was empty. She turned off the lights. She walked through the house to the bedroom wing, turning on the lights as she went. She stopped at Krista's door, her hand on the knob, and stood there. She leaned her forehead against the door. Finally she turned away and walked back down the hall to the den. With the lights blazing all around her she sat and waited out the rest of the night.

* *Chapter 18* *

Matthew browsed through the small gift shop in the lobby of the hotel, stopping for the second time in front of a wire bookrack containing a white pamphlet entitled "Homes of the Stars." He had flown in last evening and had seen the same booklet in a shop at the airport, but he hadn't let himself buy it. This morning he had gone to a couple of lectures, but he hadn't been able to keep his mind on the topics. He had come back to his hotel and wound up here, looking through the books and magazines.

He picked up the booklet and flipped through it to the T section. She probably wouldn't even be in it. But there it was: Jennifer Taylor. Crazy the way his pulse picked up. She lived on Shadow Hill in Beverly Hills. He turned to the map in the back and found the location.

He bought the book and took his rented car out of the parking garage. He drove out to Beverly Hills, passing through Hollywood and the elegant stores along Santa Monica without even a second glance. He found her street and drove up and back down before he located her street number. He stopped across the street. He could see nothing of the house, only a high white wall with a firmly closed gate, so he turned and drove back to Santa Monica Boulevard. What had he expected? he jeered at himself. To see Jennifer standing in her front yard? What good would it have done to have seen her home, anyway? It wouldn't have told him anything about her except that she owned an expensive house.

Matthew drove aimlessly until he spotted a bookstore on Hollywood Boulevard. He turned the corner, parked and went back to the store. There must be some way he could discover her telephone number. Her number was unlisted, but he hoped there would be a book similar to the address one that would list telephone numbers.

It took him twenty minutes to find such a book, a script-writer's handbook that listed the names of producers, directors and actors in the back. Jennifer's name was there and the same address, but for a phone number it gave only the number of her agent. At least that was a start. Matthew bought the book and returned to his hotel.

He called the number and got a secretary who wasn't inclined even to let him talk to the agent. He explained that he wanted to get a message to Jennifer Taylor, and the woman politely took his name and telephone number, saying that she would give Miss Taylor the message. Matthew suspected that she hadn't even written it down.

He sat down to wait.

"Liz? I got another guy wanting Jennifer to call him. Says he used to know her. Shall I give the number to Karen or toss it in the can?"

Liz rolled her eyes. "Did he sound human?"

"Oh, yeah. Very nice and polite. Kind of southern."

"It's a possibility, I guess. Why don't you give it to Karen? What's his name?"

The girl glanced at her note. "Matthew Ferris."

The name sounded familiar to Liz and she frowned, thinking.

"Something the matter?"

"No, I just—oh, jeez. That *is* someone she used to know. Here, give it to me."

Liz took the paper and stared down at it as if it might hold the answer to what she should do. Matthew Ferris. She was certain that was the name of the guy Jennifer had told her about years ago, the boy who had broken Jennifer's heart when she was a teenager in Arkansas. That was the last thing Jennifer needed, to be reminded of a past heartbreak. Jennifer hadn't been the same since Krista died. She was exhausted and overworked, and Liz knew there was a bottomless sorrow beneath the surface, just waiting for Jennifer to break and let it consume her. There was no telling what hearing from Matthew Ferris might do to her.

And yet that was just the thing—she didn't know what it would do to Jennifer. Perhaps it wouldn't hurt her. It could do just the opposite. If it made Jennifer angry, it would be a good release for all the emotions Jennifer kept bottled up inside her. Or she might feel a certain nostalgic pleasure in seeing him after all this time.

Liz turned the paper around and around in her hands. She didn't know what to do. She glanced at her calendar. Jennifer had been on a publicity tour for the past week, but she should have flown in this morning. She was probably at home. Liz sighed, looked at the paper again and picked up the phone.

Jennifer answered her telephone groggily. The publicity tour for her newly released movie had been exhausting, and as soon as she got home that morning she had lain down to take a nap.

"Jennifer?"

"Hi, Liz." Jennifer sat up, brushing back her hair with her hand and trying to clear her head.

"How was the tour?"

"Awful, of course. In the past eight days I've been in New York, Miami, Atlanta, Dallas, Houston, and at least four other cities I can't even remember. I think it would be easier to get run over by a truck."

"Ah, but it wouldn't be as good publicity."

Jennifer chuckled. "Right."

Liz paused. "Jennifer . . . my office got a call today from a man who said he knew you a long time ago. His name's Matthew Ferris."

Jennifer felt as if she were on an elevator that had suddenly risen, leaving her stomach far below. "Matthew Ferris!"

"Yeah. I thought the name was familiar."

"It is."

"Is he the guy you dated in high school?"

"Yeah. Yeah, that's the one." Jennifer's brain began to function. "What did he want? Is he here? Did he call from Arkansas?"

"He's here at the Biltmore. He left the number if you wanted to get in touch with him. You want it?"

"Okay." Automatically Jennifer picked up the pen and pad that sat beside the phone and jotted down the telephone number.

"You going to call him?"

"I don't know," Jennifer replied frankly. "I'll tell you later."

They hung up and Jennifer sat down. She looked at the piece of paper in her hand. Matthew Ferris!

She didn't know what she felt. Shock, maybe. She hadn't dreamed of this happening in years and years, a whole lifetime, it seemed. Why had he called her? What could he want from her?

Feelings were creeping into her now, twisting through her numb surprise—the faint tinge of fear, the bitter aftertaste of a hurt long past, tingling anticipation, a rush of pleasure. Did she want to see him? A part of her said no, the part that felt the fear, that remembered the pain and the humiliation and the aching years it had taken her to get over him.

But that had been so long ago; she was over it now. Jennifer couldn't summon up the deep anger she had harbored against him in the past. She had felt far worse pain since then. She had been a teenager when she had been so hurt by Matthew; she had been brimming with emotions. Now she was immune to them. It couldn't hurt her to see him; she hadn't found anything that had that capacity any longer.

And she was curious. What did he look like? Would she recognize him? Becky had once told her he was married. Was he still? Had he thought about her sometimes? Had he ever realized that he had been wrong? Ever wished he hadn't left her?

She wanted to see him. She had to see him. That overrode whatever pain, whatever fear she might feel.

Jennifer dialed the telephone number. Her fingers were shaking. When the hotel operator answered she couldn't speak. She hung up the phone and stood for a moment, looking down at it. It was stupid to be so scared. She took a deep breath and dialed again. This time when the operator answered she asked for Matthew's room. She heard the phone buzz. The receiver was picked up immediately. "Hello?" It was Matthew's voice.

It went right through her. It was more mature, perhaps a little less accented, but the same. The same. She hadn't heard it in over seventeen years, but she would have recognized it anywhere. She couldn't speak, couldn't even breathe.

"Hello?" he said again, impatience in his voice.

"Matthew?"

On the other end of the line Matthew went still. It was the voice he had heard on the screen, Jenny's voice with the accent stripped away, a little lower, more sophisticated. "Jennifer." He gave a funny little laugh and sat down on the bed. "Jennifer."

The same sort of nervous giggle escaped her, too. "Yes."

"I was afraid you wouldn't call. That you wouldn't even get my message."

"I got it. Liz is very efficient."

"Liz?"

"My agent."

"Oh. Yes." There was an awkward pause. "I'm sorry. I feel like an idiot. I don't know what to say."

"Neither do I." Jennifer was perilously close to laughter or tears, she wasn't sure which. Maybe it was both.

"I'm in Los Angeles at a medical convention."

"I see."

"I wanted to . . . I wondered if I could possibly see you." His heart was hammering in his chest. His hand was clenched around the receiver. *Don't let her say no.* "I'm sure it's an imposition, but—"

"No. No, it's all right. I'd like that."

"Could we have dinner together? Drinks?"

"When?"

"Tonight? Tomorrow? I'm free anytime."

"Tonight would be fine. Say, drinks?" That would be better than dinner. If the situation turned out to be awful, if she regretted meeting him, she could get away sooner.

"Okay." Matthew would have preferred dinner; it would

have meant more time with her. But he wasn't in any position to argue. "When? Shall I pick you up?"

"No, I'll just meet you there. How about 9:00? At the Polo Lounge?" She would have liked to meet him someplace more ordinary, but in a regular restaurant she would probably be recognized and mobbed for autographs. It was better to choose a place frequented by movie people, where no one would be allowed to bother her. "Do you know where that is? The Beverly Hills Hotel."

"That pink place?"

She smiled. "Yeah." God, he sounded good. He sounded like home. Like Matthew.

"Okay. I'll see you there at nine." Matthew paused. He wanted to keep her on the phone, but he couldn't think of what to say. "Well, good-bye then."

"Good-bye." Jennifer hung up the telephone and sat for a moment, staring into space. It was a little hard to believe that this had happened.

She rose and went to her dresser. She opened the bottom drawer of the dresser and pulled out a box that contained a few mementos of her life. Most of them were from years ago, when she was first starting in Hollywood; she never opened the box anymore. Jennifer sifted through the contents and took out a small cardboard box. She opened it. Inside lay a large high school ring. Matthew's ring.

He had refused to take it back when he had broken up with her. Jennifer had never been able to throw it away. She turned the ring in her fingers, looking at it, and she thought about Matthew.

Jennifer spent most of the evening getting ready. She took a long soaking, oiled bath, then tried her hair in a variety of styles. She dithered in front of the closet, trying on first one dress, then another, and discarding them all. The blue taffeta Oscar de la Renta was too dressy, the white Gianfranco Ferre too casual. She didn't want to appear to show off her wealth as if to prove how far she'd come since Sweet River. On the other hand, Matthew would probably expect her to be glamorous, and she did want to look pretty. Admit it, she wanted to knock him off his feet. Finally she settled on a simple black Albert Nippon sheath with spangles at the cuffs and shoulders. It had a matching spangled pillbox hat, which necessitated changing her hairstyle once again, sweeping it up into a tight, flat roll.

When she was dressed and made up, the little hat pinned alluringly on her head, she turned in front of her three-way mirror, carefully inspecting herself. Did she look all right? What would Matthew think? She had been so much younger when he knew her, only fifteen, all fresh and vibrant with youth. She was thirty-three now. Jennifer leaned closer to the mirror, checking for lines around her eyes. Would he think she was beautiful? Sophisticated? Or just older?

She made a face in the mirror and stuck out her tongue, angry at herself for worrying about it. What did it matter what Matthew Ferris thought? So what if she'd gotten older? So had he. Why, he was probably balding and had a paunch, married with three kids and a station wagon in the garage. They would have nothing to say to each other, and she would be counting the minutes until she could gracefully leave.

Jennifer looked at her watch. Almost 9:00. She wondered if he would be on time or late. She would hate to be sitting there, waiting for him when he arrived. She paced around her bedroom for another three minutes before the nerves in her stomach got to her. She picked up her purse and left for the hotel.

Matthew arrived at the Polo Lounge fifteen minutes early, not taking the slightest chance of being late. He was already seated at a table facing the door, waiting, when Jennifer entered the room. He was stunned by her beauty. She was dressed in a simple black dress that didn't cling to her magnificent figure yet left one definitely aware of it. Sequins at the shoulders and cuffs caught the light, and a tiny round hat, also covered in sequins, sat on her head. Her luxuriant hair was hidden under the hat, exposing her face in a way that complemented only real beauty. It complemented Jennifer. She looked glamorous, aloof and lovely.

She was his Jennifer—and not his at all anymore.

The maitre d' spoke to her and she answered. The man led her across the room to Matthew's table, and even in this sophisticated place heads craned to look at her. Matthew stood up almost involuntarily, impelled as much by awe at her beauty as by politeness.

Jennifer had seen Matthew as soon as she stepped into the room, and for a moment she could only stand, frozen, looking at him while her stomach turned flip-flops. He wasn't balding; there was no paunch. She had thought that memory had added gloss to him, that in this town of gorgeous men he would no longer seem handsome. But he was. He was older, his hair a little darker, his face more fleshed out, but, if anything, maturity had made him better looking, added depth to his features.

He didn't seem out of place in this establishment for the well-heeled. His dark suit was silk and well-tailored, and there was a discreet glimmer of gold at his cuffs. But he looked somehow different from the other men there—more real, without the slick patina of Hollywood.

Even knowing that he would be there, it jolted Jennifer to see him. He looked so much the same. So different. Crazily, she wanted to cry. She wanted to run away. She wanted to run to him. There was an old, old ache inside her chest, the stirred-up remnants of emotions that should have died years ago. Longing, anger, sorrow—and overlying it all, a bubbling excitement.

The maitre d' came over to help her, and she let him lead her to Matthew's table. Matthew rose as she approached.

"Hello, Jennifer."

"Matthew." She was surprised she could get the word out. She felt as if she could hardly breathe.

The maitre d' started to pull out her chair for her, but

Matthew came around the table to do it himself. For an instant he was close to her, and she was aware of the bulk of his body, the faint scent of his cologne. Matthew returned to his chair, and for a moment they simply looked at each other.

She was even lovelier close up, Matthew thought. He had forgotten how very blue her eyes were. Her face was thinner, emphasizing its delicate bone structure and her huge eyes.

"I'm glad you came," he said.

Jennifer's smile was quick and a bit nervous. "Thank you. So am I." She shouldn't feel this excited, she thought. After all the years, with all the things she'd done and people she'd met, a high school boyfriend shouldn't cause such an eager rush of emotions inside her.

"Would you like a drink?"

"Yes, thank you. A . . . vodka collins would be fine."

He gave their order to the waiter hovering at their table and turned back to Jennifer. Jennifer looked into Matthew's eyes, then her gaze skittered away. She glanced at his mouth, his hands. She remembered the sweet excitement of his kisses and the sensual movement of his fingers across her skin.

She clenched her fingers tightly around her small purse and forced herself to look into his eyes. They were green, ringed with gold and shadowed by thick brown lashes. She remembered sitting for hours staring into his eyes. She could still feel the pull.

Matthew gazed back at her. She was the girl he had known, yet someone else entirely, and he found both women utterly bewitching. "I'm sorry. I'm staring, I know."

Jennifer shook her head and smiled, a funny shy smile that was so familiar it made his chest hurt. How could he have forgotten that smile? "I am, too. It's been so long."

"Seventeen years." He started to say something more, but the drinks arrived, and he closed his mouth.

They sipped their drinks and searched for something to

say, feeling awkward yet wanting to talk. Finally Jennifer
began, "Becky tells me you're a doctor now."

"Becky?"

"My sister-in-law. Corey's wife. Becky Yates."

"Oh. Yeah, I'm a doctor, a cardiologist. I'm at a
medical convention here."

"Where do you live?"

"Dallas."

"Do you like it?"

"Dallas or being a doctor?"

"Either. Both."

"Yes. I like them both. What about you? You like LA?
Are you happy?"

"Yes, I like LA. I love my career."

He didn't point out that she had sidestepped his question. He wondered what that meant. There was something
sad in her eyes. He wondered what Hollywood had done to
her, what kind of price she'd had to pay to reach success.
"Are you married?"

Jennifer shook her head. "Divorced. And you?"

"The same." He gave her a wry smile and took another
sip of his drink. "Are you working on a movie now?"

"No. I'll be starting another one in a few weeks."

"Really? What's it about?"

She talked about *Drifter* and her part in it, and as she
talked, the awkwardness began to leave her. She told him
about the challenge the part would be for her and the fear
that she wouldn't do it well.

"You shouldn't worry. You're good. I've seen all your
movies, and you're very good." He didn't tell her that he
had checked out every video of her movies that he could
find the past two weeks and had watched them over and
over.

"Thank you. But this one is very different. Sometimes
it's hard for people to accept you in a role they're not used
to."

"You know, it's funny. I never even knew that you
wanted to be an actress."

"I wanted to be one from the first time I saw a movie. But when you . . ." Jennifer shrugged and looked away. "I gave it up for a while."

"Because of me?" he asked softly.

She stared intently at her glass, revolving it slowly on the table. "Yeah. For a while I thought I wanted a different life."

It was time to tell her what he'd come here for. He had been avoiding the subject ever since she sat down, but he couldn't any longer. "You know, I was surprised you were willing to see me."

She smiled faintly. "I was surprised you wanted to see me."

"That's what I came here for. The convention was just a handy excuse."

Jennifer glanced up at him. He was watching her, his eyes intense and rather sad. He reached across the table and laid his hand over hers. His palm was warm and faintly rough. She had an urge to turn her hand over and clasp his, but she didn't. There was a barrier between them, no matter how sweet the past had been for them. A wall of time and pain.

"I was in Sweet River a couple of weeks ago and saw Keith Oliver."

Jennifer dropped her eyes. She felt a funny, sick rush of pain. She tried to pull her hand out from under Matthew's, but he held on tightly.

"He told me something that I—he told me he had lied to me that time. When he told me that you—"

"I remember what he told you." Jennifer's words were clipped, her face icy and remote. There was nothing of the old Jennifer in her now. She was cool, a queen looking at a peasant.

"My father put them up to it, Randy and Keith and Joe Bob. I believed them. I shouldn't have, but I did. I don't have any excuse except that I was young and stupid. What I did to you, the things I said were unforgiveable. I ruined everything that day. I threw away my own life, but worse,

I hurt you. I don't know how you feel about me, if you forgot me or hated me all these years or what. It may not mean anything to you. But I had to apologize for what I did. It was cruel and unreasonable. I'm sorry, Jen. The last thing I should ever have done was hurt you.''

Jennifer hadn't imagined that she could hurt like this again. She knew hurt and grief and a vivid, slashing anger, and suddenly she hated him as fiercely as she had hated him when it happened. Tears welled in her eyes and she pressed her lips together tightly to keep them from quivering. She wanted to yell at him, but she couldn't create a scene in the Polo Lounge. Besides, she knew if she started yelling she would cry, and she refused to cry in front of him. "You bastard!" she said in a tight, low voice and stood up abruptly.

She walked away from him without another word. Matthew tossed some money down on the table and followed her. He wanted to run, but he forced himself to use a more normal pace. He caught up with her just outside the entrance to the hotel, where she stood waiting for her car. He took her elbow. "Jenny, wait."

She gave him a flashing glance full of anger and resentment. "Why?"

"I want to talk to you."

"Well I don't want to talk to you." She looked straight in front of her, ignoring him. But then, as though she couldn't hold it back anymore, she burst out in a low, aching voice, "Why did you have to bring it up? Why couldn't you just leave it alone?"

"I thought you ought to know. I wanted to tell you how sorry I was, how much I regretted what I did."

"Why?" She looked at him again, her eyes bitter. "Did you think I would forgive you? That I would say, 'That's fine. No problem. Hey, people who are in love always cut each other to ribbons'?"

"Yes, of course I want you to forgive me. I wouldn't be human if I didn't. But I don't expect you to. All I wanted was for you to know that I realized what I'd done, that I was sorry. I thought it might help in some way."

"How? All you did is make me remember it, and I don't want to. I don't want to feel that again."

"Couldn't we talk about it? Go someplace where it's more private?"

"Talk about what?"

"I don't know. How you feel. How I feel. What happened."

A parking valet zoomed up in a blue Mercedes sports car and Jennifer hurried over to it. She tipped the attendant, then got into the car without even a backward look toward Matthew and drove away. Matthew stood on the steps, frustration swelling in his chest, and stared after her.

Jennifer jammed her foot down on the accelerator and the car shot forward through the traffic. Her hands were clenched around the wheel. She took the winding roads to her house at a furious pace. She hated him! Hated him with all the force she had felt years ago, hated him for making her feel that way again.

Why did he have to bring it up? Why couldn't he have let well enough alone? She had been doing fine, actually feeling happy—until he decided he had to apologize. Damn it. Damn it!

Jennifer screeched to a halt in front of her gate and jabbed impatiently at the electronic opener. When the gate was barely open enough, she zipped through and raced to the house. She couldn't find the garage door opener, and she was too furious to spend the time looking. She jammed on the brakes, jumped out of the car, and went in the front door, slamming it shut behind her.

Rage churned and bubbled inside her. She felt as if she could spew it out, as if it might at any moment leap out of every pore. She picked up a large glass ashtray from the entry table and threw it onto the hard tile floor. It broke with a satisfying crash.

The action released something inside her, and Jennifer hurled a Lalique bird after it. She charged into the living

room and tossed three ceramic pots into the fireplace. She
threw books and brassware and paperweights, anything she
could get her hands on. She screamed—loud, wordless,
enraged screams.

Finally she sank to the floor on her knees, exhausted,
her rage spent. Her breath came in harsh, loud gasps as if
she'd been running and her muscles quivered. She
contemplated what she had done. The room looked as if it
had been struck by vandals. She imagined her housekeeper's face the next morning when she saw the mess and
Jennifer smiled. She began to chuckle and then to laugh.
Jennifer wished she had done this years ago; in the
aftermath she felt strangely relaxed and at peace.

She pulled herself to her feet and walked to her bedroom. Stepping out of her dress, she left it lying on the
floor. She stretched out across the bed and was instantly
asleep.

Matthew didn't sleep much that night. His mind was on
Jennifer, wondering how he could have said it differently
so she wouldn't have run from him, hurt and angry. The
old desire was there too, eating a hole in him as it always
had. He lay awake thinking about her breasts and eyes and
hair, imagining her taut and quivering, her skin like silk
against him.

He had told himself when he came out here that all he
wanted was to give Jennifer his apology and set things
straight between them. But he couldn't fool himself now.
He knew he had wanted to see if the old spark remained, if
she still turned him inside out. She did. He wanted to
make love to her. He wanted to finally find the satisfaction
he had ached for for so long.

He finally fell asleep close to dawn, but the sleep was
fitful, broken by dreams. He got up around eight and
forced himself to go to a workshop at the Bonaventure. He
reminded himself that he had done what he had come for.
Whatever secret hopes he'd had, there was no reason to
expect anything further from Jennifer.

But he heard hardly anything that was said at the

seminars, and by lunchtime he decided to chuck it and return to his hotel. The red message light was on on his phone when he returned to his room, and he felt a flutter of fear, his mind flying with a parent's anxiety to his girls. He dialed the desk and asked for the message. The desk clerk responded that he was supposed to call Jennifer and gave him a telephone number.

Matthew hung up the phone and stared at it in astonishment. He grinned and reached for the receiver.

Jennifer awakened in a sparkling mood. She felt cleansed, refreshed. She thought of Matthew. Her anger had vanished after the storm the night before. Now she thought that she had been silly to go stalking out on Matthew. After all, he had only apologized. The fact that it had been so many years since the event only made it more amazing that he had done so. She called Matthew's hotel, but he wasn't there. She left a message to call her. She wondered if he would or if she had offended him.

She was restless all morning, unable to concentrate on the script of *Drifter*. When her phone rang she jumped on it. "Hello?"

"Jennifer?"

"Matthew!" A grin spread across her face. "I was afraid you wouldn't call."

"I can't imagine why I wouldn't."

"I thought you might be mad at me."

"I think it was the other way around."

"Yeah, I guess it was. For a while." She paused. "I called to tell you I'm sorry for taking off like that last night. It was rude."

"It's okay. You had every right to be upset."

"It brought everything back to me, and I hated feeling it again. But it wasn't fair to take it out on you."

"Who else would you take it out on? I'm the one who hurt you. I'll regret that all my life."

Tears welled up, and she struggled to hold them back. "Don't. It isn't necessary. I'm not the only one who was hurt."

"No. But I'm the one responsible for the pain both of us felt."

"It was a long time ago, and it's over. There's no point in blaming anyone. I wanted you to know that. I don't blame you, and I don't hate you. For a long time I did, but not anymore. Last night when you apologized it was too much for me. But I got it out of my system and I'm not angry anymore." She paused. "You said you wanted me to forgive you. I do. It wasn't really your fault. Something bad happened to both of us."

Matthew's throat was tight and full. For a moment he couldn't speak. He ran his thumb along the edge of the telephone. He cleared his throat. "Thank you. You're a generous woman. You always were."

"Not so generous. I'm just being honest."

Matthew hesitated. "Jennifer . . ."

"Yes?"

"Would it be possible to see you again?"

Jennifer smiled, flooded with relief. She had been afraid he wouldn't ask. "Yes. Yes, I'd like that very much."

✳ *Chapter 19* ✳

They met at Ma Maison for dinner. This time Jennifer did wear the shimmering blue Oscar de la Renta taffeta with a saucy turned-up tier of ruffles in the back. Her hair hung loose, thick and curling, down to her shoulders. Matthew couldn't keep his eyes off her. He wanted to touch her— her hair, her hand, her cheek. He remembered how he had been when they were dating, constantly on fire for her, aching and hungry. He felt that way again.

Jennifer saw the flicker of desire in Matthew's eyes. She had seen it many times in many men, but it had never stirred her with anyone else. Now it did. She remembered his kisses and his touch. No one else had ever aroused her as Matthew had, and she wondered if it could still be the same with him, if she would feel that hot rush of passion if he kissed her. She had believed that she had lost that heat forever. But now, looking at Matthew's hands as he cut up his meat, watching his mouth as it closed over a bite of food, warmth started in her abdomen. And she wondered . . .

Tonight they talked easily—about LA and Dallas, about his medical practice and moviemaking. They reminisced about Sweet River and the people they had known there and what they were doing now. And they laughed. Jennifer couldn't remember when she had laughed so much. She was giddy and high from the sheer joy of being alive and with Matthew. If she had thought about it Jennifer would have been surprised at her happiness. But tonight she didn't want to think. She just wanted to be, to have, to feel.

They stretched out the meal as long as possible, lingering over after-dinner drinks and coffee, reluctant to part. When finally they were left with no further excuse to stay, Jennifer asked hesitantly, "Would you like to come back to my house? We could have a drink and talk."

He smiled. "I thought you'd never ask."

Matthew followed her in his car. A deep, muted excitement gripped him as the electronic gate to her driveway opened and they slipped inside, the gate closing behind them. It was as if they had been sealed off in some secret world, alone and apart from everything else.

He stopped the car in front of her house and got out. It was a one-story house, cream-colored brick with a slate french roof, beautiful, but it struck him as a trifle cool for Jennifer.

Jennifer parked her car in the garage and walked over to

join him, and they went in the front door. "Would you like to see the house?" Jennifer asked.

"Of course." He wanted to see where she lived, what it looked like. He wondered if he would see her in it.

In some ways he did. It was soft, gentle and lovely, just as she was, all thick carpets and muted walls and graceful furnishings. It was elegant, too, with a sophistication and assurance that his Jenny had never had, but that this Jennifer seemed to. Yet there was something remote about it, almost sterile, as if no one really lived there.

She showed him the master bedroom at one end of the house, past the kitchen. He thought it a strange location for a master bedroom, but he said nothing. He was too busy avoiding looking at the bed. Jennifer led him through the kitchen, dining room and three living areas of various degrees of formality. The taffeta material of her dress rustled as she walked, and her sheer stockings gleamed. Matthew found it hard to keep his mind on what they were doing.

She led him out to the patio and the pool, switching on the underwater lights so that the water glimmered in the deep, enveloping darkness. It seemed both warm and mysterious, and again Matthew felt the tug of a secret excitement in his gut. Jennifer looked at him, her face shadowed in the darkness, and Matthew felt a sudden, fierce rush of desire. He wanted to take her in his arms and kiss her. He wanted to take off his clothes and go into the water with her, to feel it slide around their heated bodies, cool and languorous. He wanted to bury himself within her.

Matthew glanced away to hide the hunger he knew must be in his eyes. Jennifer turned aside. Her heart was pounding like a jackhammer. She had seen the look in Matthew's eyes, had felt the heat and passion emanating from him. He still wanted her. Every fiber in her body responded.

She hadn't experienced anything like it in so long she didn't know what to do. It stunned and frightened her. For an instant she wanted to run, but something stronger made her stay. She gazed at her hands, trying to think of something to say. "Would—uh, would you like a drink?"

"Coffee would be fine." He didn't care about a drink one way or the other, but it offered an excuse to linger.

Matthew followed Jennifer into the house. She started toward the kitchen.

Matthew stopped. "I don't need it immediately," he told her, a little puzzled. "You can show me the rest of the house first."

"What? Oh." Jennifer glanced toward the hall leading to the other wing. "It's only bedrooms."

She flipped on the light and walked briskly down the hall, and turned the corner into the perpendicular corridor. They passed two closed doors, which Jennifer neither opened nor mentioned. Past those doors were another bedroom and, at the end of the hallway, a huge, well-furnished room obviously intended to be the master bedroom. He wondered why she didn't use it. He wondered what was in the closed rooms. But there was something remote and set about Jennifer's face that made him refrain from asking.

They returned to the main part of the house. Jennifer made coffee, and they sat in the living room to drink it, looking out at the lighted pool and yard. Earlier in the evening they had talked freely, rolling from one topic to another, but now they could think of nothing to say. Silence stretched between them and they were again awkward with each other, the former ease gone.

All Matthew could think about was kissing her. He wondered how she would react if he did. He could see nothing in her face to encourage him. She would probably think it was out of line. She had forgiven him, but that didn't mean that she wanted to pick up where they left off. It would be impossible to do that, anyway. There was too much in between, too much distance and sorrow and life lived. They were strangers to each other now. Still, all he could think about was kissing her.

Jennifer wondered if he would kiss her. She had seen that look in his eyes, the one she'd often glimpsed when they were dating, as if he would consume her whole if he could. And she had felt the old answering heat rising in her. She wanted him to kiss her, but she was scared too—scared that the deadness would still be there, that she would respond as poorly as she had with Scott. It would be horrible for Matthew to find her cold, as Scott had, after all these years. After the dreams they'd had.

He must think she was something special, the girl he had loved as a teenager, the love fate had taken away from him. She didn't want him to find out that she wasn't special, that youthful love and time had imbued her with qualities she didn't possess.

The dim light touched Jennifer's features with gold, and she was so beautiful she seemed unreal. Matthew wanted to touch her and didn't dare, and the loss of the past years had never seemed so sharp, so poignant.

"I wish—" He broke off and jumped to his feet, walking over to the wide glass windows. He stood staring out at the shimmer of the pool.

"You wish what?"

"That we could go back. That I could undo the mistakes I made."

Jennifer rose and went to him. "You can't ever do that."

"I know." He turned. She was inches from him. He laid his hand against her cheek. His skin was searing. The feel of it took her breath away.

"Matt . . ."

"What?" His fingers trailed down her cheek and across her lips. They caressed her forehead, her nose, her chin. He couldn't stop himself. He had to touch her.

Jennifer couldn't remember what she had wanted to say. She couldn't think with him touching her. Her eyelids fluttered closed.

Matthew sucked in his breath. Desire stabbed him. "Oh, Jenny." His hands splayed out on either side of her face, holding her tightly. The gentleness was gone. He was taut and urgent now, his skin stretched over his cheekbones, his eyes dark. "I used to lie in bed at night thinking about you, even when I'd just made love to somebody else. I've wanted you for so many years."

Jennifer's hands crept up to his chest. She wanted to tell him not to want her too much, not to give her qualities she didn't possess. But she also wanted him to hold her, and kiss her, to touch her everywhere. She couldn't say anything; she was struck dumb with fear and desire.

He came closer. His head bent. He kissed her.

Jennifer clutched Matthew's suit coat, her fingers digging in, and she trembled under the force of her emotions. He kissed her softly at first, almost wonderingly, rediscovering the sweetness of her mouth. Then his lips turned fierce, digging into hers, his tongue thrusting into her mouth. Passion was humming in him now, pulsing and eager, and he was lost. Lost in the faint spicy scent of her perfume, the incredible softness of her skin, the wealth of her mouth.

His mouth was hot and wet and forceful. It tasted of coffee and of him, that special taste she remembered from long ago. Jennifer wrapped her arms around Matthew and pressed up against him. It was there, all the desire she'd once felt with Matthew and never since, all the eagerness and yearning, the blood racing like liquid fire through her veins. She wanted to laugh and cry and hold onto him forever.

He made a sound, not quite a word yet full of meaning, and pulled his mouth away to kiss her face, her ears, her throat. He couldn't get enough of her, couldn't have her quickly enough. "Jennifer. Jennifer." His voice shook on her name.

She threaded her fingers through his hair, loving the thickness of it, the softness. His lips slid down the tender skin of her throat, nibbling, caressing, tickling, and the sensations pulsed downward, starting an ache between her legs. Her fingertips dug into his scalp.

His lips moved back up and he kissed her mouth again. His lips ground into hers. His tongue explored the jagged ridges of her teeth and tangled with her tongue. His arms loosened around her, and Matthew slid his hands down her back and over the smooth curve of her hips. The material of Jennifer's dress was slick beneath his hands, and it crackled slightly wherever he touched it. The noise sent little flames licking along his nerves. His hand skimmed back up her sides, over the hard lines of her rib cage to the swell of her breasts.

Matthew broke their kiss and looked down into Jennifer's eyes. They were faintly bemused, as though his kisses had stolen part of her reason. The sight stirred him—everything about her stirred him, it seemed. He had wanted her so much for so long. There had been times when they were dating that he had thought he would die from wanting and not having her. And ever since, even after he thought he had gotten rid of his desire, it had been there, smoldering. That was why he had refused to see a Jennifer Taylor movie; he had known inside that seeing her would start that feverish ache for her again.

Now, holding her, kissing her, the passion was raging in him, as feverish and urgent as it had been when he was a boy, but it was a man's hunger now. His need for her was so great it was almost frightening.

He smoothed his forefinger across the line of her eyebrows, over her forehead, then down to the ridges of her cheekbones. Jennifer saw the longing in his eyes, the faint question. She knew Matthew would not push her into anything she didn't want anymore than he had when they were teenagers. For a moment she hesitated, wanting him—on fire for him—yet afraid that he would be disappointed in her, that she would fail him as she had failed her husband, that he would find out that, for all her appearance, deep down she wasn't woman enough to please a man.

Jennifer nodded almost imperceptibly, but Matthew knew what she meant. He swung her up into his arms and carried her into her bedroom. He set her down on her feet, smiling. "I've wanted to do that forever."

He found the zipper of her dress and pulled it down, his hand gliding across the fabric. Jennifer stood gazing into his eyes, her breath uneven. Matthew cupped her face between his hands. With infinite slowness his hands slid along the column of her neck to her collarbone. His fingers spread out and insinuated themselves beneath the material of her dress, and he pushed the garment down over her shoulders and arms. It slithered to her feet. His hands returned to the base of her throat, splaying across her chest.

His hands left her skin, and he undressed her with infinite care. There was an intensity to his face, a concentration, as though his entire being was focused completely on Jennifer. Jennifer felt the faint tremor in his fingers. She saw the unsteady rise and fall of his chest.

When she was naked Matthew simply gazed at her as though he could never get his fill. It was Jennifer who moved this time, reaching up to unknot his tie. She pulled his suit jacket from his shoulders and unbuttoned his shirt. Her hands went under his shirt. His muscles jumped, but he didn't move, only watched her, his eyes dark with passion, his mouth open slightly as if he couldn't get enough air.

Jennifer's hands glided over his back and chest, caressing the flesh she had desired so long ago and had rarely had the courage to touch. He was different, his chest broader, with more hair. His was a man's body now.

Her hands retreated, suddenly shy, but Matthew took them in his and brought them back to his chest, holding them tightly against him. Jennifer could feel the thud of his heart beneath her palm, the uneven movement of his chest. The heat. The wanting. It was too much for her, she thought. *He* was too much for her. But some hope, some longing deep within her wouldn't let her pull away. She wanted—so desperately—to be good enough.

"I wanted you to touch me like this," he whispered.

"All that time. I was hungry to feel your hands on me, to know that you desired me, too."

"I desired you. Always. I was just afraid that you would think—"

"I know." His hands slid up her arms to her shoulders, and he pulled her to him, fitting her body tightly against his. "I know. But all I thought was that you were the most beautiful woman in the world. I still think so."

He kissed her and his hand rose to clench in her hair as if to hold her still beneath his mouth. He kissed her hungrily, desperately, his whole soul in his kiss, trying to erase the years of emptiness that lay between them.

Jennifer clung to him, fingers digging into his back. Her fears fled before the stunning passion he aroused. He filled her mind and heart just as his tongue filled her mouth, and she knew nothing, felt nothing but Matthew. His scent was in her nostrils, spicy with desire. His heat was all around her.

She tugged at his shirt and he moved to let her pull it free without breaking their kiss. Jennifer smoothed her hands across his chest, faintly damp with sweat, and down the muscles of his arms. His flesh quivered beneath her touch. She skimmed her nails down his chest and across the softer flesh of his stomach. He sucked in his breath sharply.

"Oh, Jen."

Her fingers went to his belt, sliding the leather from the buckle and easing out the metal tongue. Her fingers slipped between the waistband of his trousers and his skin, and she felt the roughness of his hair, the indentation of his navel. He buried his face in her hair, and his hands moved restlessly over her hair and neck and shoulders. She fumbled with the clasp of his trousers and he moved quickly to help her.

When his clothes lay on the floor beside hers, he lifted her and laid her down on the bed. Her body was pale against the dark blue cover. He lay down beside her, propped up on his elbow, and inched his hand down her body, caressing her breast, her stomach, her thighs. Jennifer's eyes fluttered closed. The pleasure was almost more than she could bear. She squeezed her legs tightly together, feeling the moisture there.

He covered her breast with his hand and for a long moment he stared down at her breast, full and soft and white beneath his darker hand. He ran a finger across the pinkish brown nipple and it tightened. His finger lingered on the bud of flesh, caressing it to a hard point.

Matthew shifted, moving over her and resting on his elbows so that he could take both her breasts in his hands. He squeezed gently, his thumbs teasing at her nipples. Jennifer arched upward, pressing her breasts against his hands. She was hardly aware of what she was doing, knowing only that she wanted more. He bent and touched his tongue to her nipple.

Jennifer stiffened and let out a funny, shuddery sigh. Matthew circled and lashed the nipple with his tongue, and with each movement heat built in her abdomen, flaring higher and higher. His tongue moved to her other nipple, still teasing, tantalizing. She moved restlessly beneath him until finally her writhings brought him to the brink of his control. Then, at last, Matthew's mouth settled onto her nipple, sucking it into a dark, wet cave of pleasure. His body sank into hers, pushing her down into the bed.

He was hard and heavy against her thigh. His breath shuddered in and out. She wanted him inside her; she ached to feel him piercing her. She thought she could feel no more desire, no more pleasure, yet with each pull of his mouth, each stroke of his tongue, there was more. And more, until she thought she would burst. She dug her fingernails into his back, scoring his flesh, but neither of them noticed.

His mouth left her breasts and trailed over her abdomen, leaving her gasping, and she opened her legs to him, her hands urging him on. He came into her then, hot and hard, pulsing with desire. Jennifer drew in her breath as he filled her, taking away the dreadful emptiness, satisfying the ache—and yet there was still more need, more ache that begged to be eased. He pulled almost out and plunged in again, building the need, the ache, the hunger. Their bodies rubbed together, slick with sweat, as he moved within her. He stared down into her eyes, watching the pleasure and hunger grow there, and what he saw stoked the fire in him. His eyes were dark, his face taut, his lips pulled back in a grimace, caught in a hellish pleasure.

Jennifer moaned, wrapping her legs around him, moving her hips against his. Something was blossoming inside her, huge and urgent, clawing for release. It burst, flooding her with light and heat, and she shuddered, clutching at him. Matthew felt the bite of her nails in his buttocks and the convulsive movement of her body and it vaulted him into his own climax. He surged within her, feeling the life pour from him into her.

They lay beside each other in the dark, Matthew's arm around her, Jennifer's head on his shoulder, the sweat cooling on their bodies. They were drained, exhausted and utterly at peace.

"I've wanted that for so many years, I can't even remember," Matthew murmured, and his hand slid lightly, affectionately down her body to the curve of her hip.

Jennifer smiled. Her fears about her own sexuality had flown that evening. She didn't have to ask to know that she had pleased him, that she hadn't disappointed him. She had felt the hot blood surging through her veins, the explosion of passion within her. No matter what her ex-husband had said, no matter what she had feared about herself, she wasn't cold—or, at least, she wasn't cold with Matthew. She turned her head and kissed his shoulder.

He took a handful of her hair and wrapped it around his hand, bringing it to his mouth to kiss. "I always wanted to bury myself in your hair. It looks like sunshine, and it smells like . . . like you. I used to come home at night after we'd been out together and I could smell your scent on my skin. It drove me crazy. I'd lie there in my bed, thinking about you, dreaming, and smelling that perfume you wore."

He nuzzled her neck. "Different perfume, but you smell just as good." He pulled her over on top of him. "Oh, God, Jenny, when I think of all the time we've missed, all the years we could have had this." His arms tightened around her.

Jennifer kissed his chin and cheeks and nose, finally settling on his lips. "We might not have even stayed together."

"Not the way I felt about you. I hate my father for depriving us of what we could have had."

"Maybe he couldn't have done it if our love had been strong enough."

"Not 'our' love. It was *my* love that failed. I was the one who broke faith." He traced the bones of her face with his forefinger, love and regret mingling in his eyes. "I wasn't as strong as you, and I hurt you terribly. I hate myself for that."

Jennifer smiled and shook her head. Her hair brushed against his chest and arm, and the touch aroused him, even through the bittersweet ache in his chest. "I don't want to hear you talk like that about yourself. You weren't the only one to blame. I could have gone to you, argued with you. I could have seduced you into proving you were wrong. Wouldn't you have gone to bed with me, even then?"

"You know I would. But it wouldn't have been right. You would have had to humble yourself."

"And I wasn't willing to do that. We were teenagers. We were both full of pride and hurt feelings. There's no point in blaming. It happened the way it happened." She kissed the hollow of his throat. "Maybe it was for the best. How would we have turned out if we hadn't broken up? It might have been wonderful. And we might have been another divorce statistic in a few years. We certainly

wouldn't be what we are. We'd have lived in Sweet River.
You wouldn't have been a doctor."

"And you wouldn't have been a movie star."

Yes, but maybe she would have been happier, Jennifer
thought. She didn't say it aloud. "I don't want us regretting," she said. "I just want us to be happy right now."

He smiled lazily. "I think I know just the way to do
that." He rolled over, taking her under him, and kissed
her.

They slept in each other's arms, wakening in the dark
and coming together again, then drifting into sleep. They
awakened late the next morning and spent a lazy day
wrapped up in each other. He made breakfast for them in
her kitchen, barefoot and bare-chested, and Jennifer watched
him, leaning on the breakfast bar, smiling. They didn't
pick up the telephone, turn on the TV or bring in the
newspaper. They were happy, just the two of them together, and they had no need for anything from the outside
world.

Matthew realized with a pang of guilt that he hadn't
even thought about his daughters. He hoped they hadn't
tried to phone him at the hotel. Later that afternoon, when
he went back to the hotel to change, he called Michelle
and Laura, but they were out. He was just as glad. At the
moment his world was Jennifer, and he didn't want anything or anyone intruding on it. He wanted to live right
now, right here, without ties or obligations. He refused
even to think about tomorrow when he would have to fly
back to Dallas.

He returned to Jennifer, and they talked and laughed and
made love, ignoring everything else. Nothing serious,
nothing extraneous entered their conversation; they were
completely absorbed in each other. Liz called once, but
Jennifer told her she would call her back later and hung
up. After that, she turned her phone on mute.

She made their supper: peanut butter and jelly sandwiches.
Matthew teased her about her cooking, and then he kissed
her and they forgot about food. They made love on the

breakfast room table. Jennifer laughed and protested a little, just to prolong the excitement, but she loved his urgency and his passion.

Later they lay in bed, propped up against pillows, with Jennifer resting between Matthew's legs and leaning back against his chest, and watched an old Humphrey Bogart movie on TV. They couldn't remember ever being happier.

Matthew had to leave the next day, though he moved his reservation to the last flight out to Dallas. Their happiness that day was tinged with bittersweet feelings, knowing that in a few hours Matthew would be gone.

He wouldn't let Jennifer go with him to the airport. He didn't want to say good-bye to her in the impersonal surroundings of the huge airport. Instead he said good-bye to her in the bedroom, loving her with a passion haunted by the future.

Afterward Jennifer walked with him to the front door. He laid his hand against her cheek. "I'll call you. Will you—would you come to Dallas sometime?"

She smiled. She had been afraid he would sweep out of her life, leaving her lonelier than ever. "Yes. We'll be on location not far from Dallas in a few months."

"Good. But I can't wait that long." His thumb brushed against her cheekbone. He was as unsure as she about their future. He knew that he wanted her with him, now and always. But he didn't know how he could obtain that—or even whether she wanted it, too. They hadn't discussed what would happen when he left; they hadn't wanted to spoil it. "I'll come back soon. If you want."

"I want."

He kissed her one last time, a deep, searching kiss, and then he was gone. Jennifer closed the door and leaned her head against it. Now, with him gone, all the pain she'd held back came rushing down on her. She was filled with doubts and fears. It was an impossible situation. They couldn't be together in any permanent, real way, living halfway across the country from each other. The past two days had been perfect, like a single sparkling diamond lying against black velvet. Nothing so good, so pure, so perfect could last.

She wondered when, if ever, she would see Matthew again. And would it be the same? And how was she going to bear it?

Her house was horribly empty now without his presence. She was empty, too. She trailed through the house and out to the pool and sat looking at the water. She thought about how short their time had been, how little hope there was for the future, and she cried.

Late that evening the phone rang, and she answered it, welcoming any company. It was Matthew on the other end, and she broke into a smile, her insides trembling.

"Hi," he said, and she could see his smile. "I got lonely without you."

"It's only been five hours."

"I know. But it's too long. I'm making a reservation to come back in two weeks."

Tears clogged her throat. "Oh, Matthew..."

"Do you want me to?"

"Oh, yes. Yes, I want you to."

"This is a hell of a way to get back together."

"I know."

"But we can work it out somehow. I won't let it be any other way."

"I could come to Dallas for a weekend. And maybe we could meet somewhere, like Aspen or Tahoe."

"Yeah." He paused. "Jennifer?"

"Yes?"

"I love you. I don't think I ever stopped."

"Oh, Matthew." She wanted to cry. "I love you, too."

* *Chapter 20* *

Brett pushed back her chair and tossed her pen down on the table in front of her with a sigh. She glanced at her watch. It was after 9:00 and she still wasn't anywhere near finished with her work. Of course, she never was. Things were always hanging, and no day was ever long enough. It was the way the business was. She knew that. The movie industry had been her whole life.

But lately it was getting to her. She was exhausted at night when she went home, yet often she was unable to sleep when she got in bed. She awoke tired, and there were even times when she dreaded getting up and going to work.

Feeling so at odds with her life scared her. She had problems, sure, the main one being unable to find a Jace for *Drifter*, but she had had problems like that before. Usually they were a challenge. Why was she feeling this way?

Brett rose and wandered over to the window to look down on the street in front of her office building. The vast parking lot across the way was deserted, but her silver Rolls sat directly in front of Dragowynd. Joe lounged against the immaculate car, waiting for her. She smiled a little—Joe was always there—but there was something so empty about the scene that tears started in her eyes.

It wasn't enough anymore: the power, the money, the thrill of creating, the fun of outwitting the people and problems in her way. She needed more than the admiration of moviegoers, more than the sycophantic friendship of film people, more than the faithfulness of employees. She needed love.

Brett turned away sharply, annoyed with herself. She was letting the lack of a man ruin her enjoyment in her life and work. Sometimes she wondered if Liz Chandler had been right that night when she'd said a hired lover was the perfect solution. Brett had thought about Liz's words many times since. She wanted love, but she couldn't will it to happen. Nor did she think that she could believe a man in the film world who professed to love her. She had nothing and would have nothing unless she followed Liz's advice.

Brett sat down in a chair. This wasn't the first time she'd considered paying a man to be her companion and lover. But it was so cold, so lacking in anything romantic! She thought about Liz and Sloane. Their arrangement had worked out well for them. She thought about her loneliness, her dissatisfaction with her life. What if she tried and it didn't work out? She wouldn't be any worse off, would she?

She would be nervous, she knew. But that was only natural. In time the nerves would go away.

She stood up and began to pace the room. Why didn't she try it? She was a sophisticated, rational adult. She'd grown up in Hollywood, for heaven's sakes! She ought to be able to accept having sex and companionship without declarations of undying love. It had to be better than the nothing she had now.

Brett flipped through the Rolodex on her desk until she found the number she was looking for, then picked up the receiver and dialed. A woman's voice answered on the other end.

"Liz? This is Brett. Remember the conversation we had that night at your house . . ."

Liz had been cool and efficient, as always. The next morning she had phoned Brett at her office. "His name is Bryan," she said without preamble. "He works for a man whom Sloane says has the best reputation for taste and reliability."

Brett's stomach went cold. She had awakened that morning regretting her impulsive call to Liz the night before. But she couldn't back out now. "All right. Thank you."

"Sure. Listen, he's scheduled to come to your house tonight at 7:30. That's okay, isn't it?"

It wasn't. Brett didn't like the idea of his being in her house. But it would be even worse to meet him at a motel, and she absolutely could not go to his place. It would have to be her house. "That's fine. Better give him the number to punch in at the gate."

She spent the rest of the day stewing, hardly able to get any work done, and she surprised everyone in her office by leaving early.

Perversely, that evening Joe seemed inclined to linger in the house after he brought her home. He made a check of the rooms as he always did, then decided to fix a hinge on the kitchen door. Brett glanced at her watch. The man was supposed to arrive in thirty minutes. She showered and changed into a brightly flowered skirt and a soft blue cashmere sweater. When she returned to the kitchen she found Joe still there, working on the hinge. She gave him a halfhearted smile.

Why did Joe have to choose tonight of all nights to do that? She didn't want him around when the guy came. It would be too embarrassing. Imagine what Joe would think about her!

Brett willed him to finish and leave, but he didn't. She got a glass of water, drank a sip and set it down on the kitchen counter. She didn't really want it; it was just nerves. She watched Joe work, watched the coil and twist of his hand as he worked the screwdriver, the jump of muscles in his arm. She realized she was staring and looked away. Her mouth was dry. She took another sip of water. Was her sweater too soft? she wondered. Did it cling to her breasts? She usually went braless, for her breasts weren't large, but cashmere was so soft . . . She didn't want to look suggestive. She wondered why not. After all, that was what this little transaction was about, wasn't it? An honest arrangement to fulfill a need. Then why did she feel so shy?

The doorbell rang and she jumped.

Joe rose fluidly to his feet and started for the door, and Brett cursed herself for having come inside the kitchen, leaving Joe closer to the door. "That's okay, I'll get it," she said, going after him, but by the time she caught up with Joe, he was already opening the front door.

A young man stood on the doorstep. He was tanned and blond and so handsome he was almost unreal. He was dressed in carefully casual clothes in ice cream colors, his hair artfully windblown. He glanced without interest at Joe. "I'm Bryan Gaines. I'm here to see Brett Cameron."

Joe narrowed his eyes and looked as if he would like to dispute the matter, but he only turned and glanced back at Brett questioningly.

"Yes. It's all right, Joe. I was expecting him."

Joe knew what Bryan was. Brett could see it in his eyes. There was anger there, too, and something else that she couldn't identify—disappointment? Disgust?

Brett's stomach curled and she looked away. She couldn't meet Joe's eyes.

"I'll be downstairs," Joe said shortly and walked past her down the hall.

Bryan came in, closing the front door behind him. "Who was that guy?"

"My driver."

He nodded and glanced around. He flashed her a wide, white grin. "Nice house."

"Thank you. Uh, won't you come in?" Brett gestured vaguely toward the living room. What was one supposed to do in a situation like this?

She sat down on the couch, but Bryan remained on his feet, walking around, looking out the window at the view, now and then snapping his fingers. He laughed. "I never thought I'd meet Brett Cameron."

Brett's smile was stiff. He stopped his explorations and returned to her. He sat down beside her on the couch, half-turned toward her, his knee touching her leg. His eyes were bright and he seemed jumpy. She wondered if he was on something. Probably. It seemed like most people were most of the time.

He touched her cheek, sliding his fingers down it to her jaw. "You're a pretty lady. We're going to have a sweet time tonight."

Did people really talk like this?

He ran his thumb across her lips and stroked his hand down her throat. Brett felt not the slightest twinge of desire.

"Hey, baby, you're too stiff. We gotta loosen you up." He began to knead her shoulders and neck. Brett stiffened even more.

He stopped the movement of his fingers and reached inside his jacket. "Hey, how about a little blow? That'll loosen you up." He unfolded a sheet of paper and began to lay out trails of white powder.

"No. Thank you."

She watched him roll up a dollar bill and sniff up both lines. He wiped away the white powder under his nose and winked at her, then stuffed the plastic bag back inside his jacket. "Got some poppers, too, if you want."

Brett shook her head.

"Bennies?"

Brett stood up. The man was a walking drugstore. What a mistake this had been! Why had she ever thought it would work?

He stood up too, mistaking her intention. "Right." He nuzzled at her neck. It tickled. He took her hand and led her away from the couch. "Where's your bedroom?"

"Upstairs. But Bryan, I don't think . . ."

He put his arm around her. "It's okay. Just relax. You're all knotted up. You gotta relax, give it a chance. I'll help you."

Brett let him lead her up the stairs, thinking perhaps he was right. They'd started off all wrong with Joe being there. She'd been nervous. Maybe if she tried to relax, tried to go along . . .

Once inside her bedroom Bryan took her in his arms and began to kiss her. He kissed her neck, her ears, her cheeks, all the while murmuring to her that she was lovely, beautiful, sexy, that she turned him on, that she was doing fine, just fine. His words were too pat, too false and rehearsed, and they aroused nothing in Brett except the thought that she might use some of his lines in *Drifter*, where they showed one of Jace's former cold sexual relationships with women.

He kissed her lips; his tongue was an intrusion in her mouth. Brett ran over some of his phrases in her mind, trying to remember them, adding them to the dialogue, setting it up in her mind. He unfastened the round buttons down the front of her sweater, and his hand went under it to cup her breasts. Brett felt nothing but violation. He bent to kiss her breasts and Brett stepped back, pulling her sweater together.

"No."

"What?" Bryan stared at her, confused.

"I'm sorry. This isn't working out. I've wasted your time." Oh, God, what kind of story was going to be all over town about her tomorrow? "Naturally, I'll be happy to—"

"Wait. No, wait." He grinned reassuringly. "Give me a chance. You'll see. We've barely gotten started." He put his hands on her shoulders and bent to kiss her mouth again. "Whatever you want," he whispered as his lips moved across her cheek to her ear. "Any way. Anywhere. You want me to say something? Just tell me." His tongue delved into her ear. "Talk dirty? One lady likes me to talk in French."

"I'm not interested in what your clientele likes!" Brett snapped, pushing against his chest. He didn't budge. "Bryan! Stop it."

His arms went around her, lifting her, and he walked her back toward the bed. "A little rough, huh? Is that what you like?" He chuckled throatily. "You want to run and I'll chase? You protest, but I make you do it?" They reached the bed and fell back onto it.

"Bryan!" Brett struggled to get up, but his full weight was on her. He seized her head between his hands and kissed her hard. Brett squirmed, trying to slide out from under him. There was no way to get out of this with any dignity. She managed to twist her face away from him. "You aren't listening!"

"Oh, I hear you, baby, I hear you." He ground his hips into hers. "I've got it now." His mouth slid down to her breasts.

Brett was cold and sick and she was getting scared. "Bryan! Stop it!"

"That's right. That's right, baby. You don't want it, but old bad Bryan's going to make you take it. And, jeez, you're gonna love it." He took her wrists and dragged them up high over her head. He burrowed into her breasts.

"No, stop it!" She felt helpless and suddenly terrified. He was going to rape her, thinking it was some game she was playing!

Joe. Oh, Joe. He was right downstairs in his room, but he would have no idea what was going on. She'd *let* the guy in, after all. There was the button beside her bed that went to Joe's room, but she couldn't reach it. Bryan's grip was tight around her wrists, his body holding her down. His hand plunged up under her skirt and she gritted her teeth, struggling to twist away. "Joe! Joe!"

It was no good. He couldn't hear her. He was two floors down and this was a solid house. Still, she screamed his name. "Joe! Help me!"

Bryan looked down at her, startled. "What the hell?" He clamped his hand over her mouth. Brett bit him, hard, and he pulled back with a yelp, freeing her for an instant. Brett scrambled across the bed and slammed her hand against the button before Bryan caught her. "What the hell are you doing?"

He grabbed her wrists and flung her back onto the bed. His pale blue eyes were wild and frightening. "Are you crazy? What'd you push?" When she didn't answer, he screamed at her, "What did you push?"

There was the thud of boots on the stairs, and before Bryan could turn around Joe burst through the door. He flung himself across the room, tackling Bryan and crashing with him to the floor. He twisted Bryan's arm up high behind his back and pressed down with his weight. With his other hand he shoved Bryan's head down to the floor. "You son of a bitch. What the hell do you think you're doing, touching her? I ought to break your arm. How'd you like that, pretty boy?" Joe jerked Bryan's arm for emphasis, and Bryan groaned.

"No! Please, man, please, I didn't mean nothing."

Brett sat up on the bed. She was shaking all over. "Joe. No, don't hurt him. It's all a mistake. Just give him some money and send him away."

Joe looked at her. Her lips were swollen and red from the man's kisses, and her soft sweater hung open down the front, revealing the creamy swell of her breasts. Desire clawed at his gut, mingling with rage and jealousy. He wanted to kill this jerk for hurting and scaring Brett, and he wanted to kill him just as much for tasting her mouth and touching the skin Joe could not.

Joe glanced back down at the man under him, and for a moment Brett thought he wasn't going to do as she'd asked. Then he rose, pulling Bryan to his feet, and walked him out the door and down the stairs. Brett pulled her knees up to her chest, curling her arms around them and huddling down into her body. She tried to will the trembling to stop, the tears not to come. Oh, God, she'd been so scared!

The front door slammed and she heard Joe's quick footsteps on the stairs again. He came into the room, but Brett kept her head down, too embarrassed to look at him. He paused at the edge of the room. "Are you okay?"

She looked so pitiful all curled up that he wished he had the guy back again. He walked over to the bed. "Did he hurt you?"

Brett shook her head.

"Damn it, Brett! What did you think you were doing? Why in the hell would you get a guy like that? You could have any man in the world. Why bring in a cheap, hustling—"

She raised her head and looked up at him from the shelter of her arms. Tears glimmered in her eyes.

"Oh, baby." When Brett looked like that he couldn't be mad at her, couldn't think, couldn't do what was wise. He reached for her and she flung herself into his arms, crying.

"Oh, Joe, I'm so sorry! It was so stupid! Stupid!"

"It's okay," he murmured, cradling her against his chest, smoothing her hair. "It's okay. We all do dumb things sometimes. I shouldn't have yelled at you."

"It's just that I get so lonely sometimes! I want somebody."

His arms tightened around her involuntarily, and he laid his cheek against her hair. She felt so good in his arms it hurt. Her breasts pressed against his chest, and he thought of the strip of soft white skin he had seen between the gaping sides of her sweater. He had gone crazy downstairs after he left her with Bryan, thinking about what she and her hired lover were doing, jealous and aching with lust all at the same time. But it was nothing to the way desire was pumping through him now, with her slim body tight against his, remembering her kiss-swollen lips and the glimpse of her breasts beneath the soft cashmere.

Joe brushed his lips against her hair, breathing in its scent and luxuriating in its softness. He rubbed his cheek against it. His skin felt on fire. His arms trembled a little around her.

Brett liked it in his arms. Joe's body was hard and powerful, curving around her, holding her secure. She felt safe and warm and pleasantly tingly, and she snuggled into him, rubbing her face against his shirt. She thought she felt the touch of his lips on her hair.

Brett lifted her head to look up at him, and the expression on his face melted everything inside her. He bent his head, pulling her upward with his hard arms, and his mouth met hers. Suddenly all the desire that she had been unable to summon with the professional lover rushed up in her and Brett pressed into Joe, kissing him back wildly.

He made a noise deep in his throat. His lips ground into

hers, his tongue filling her mouth. They kissed as if they could consume one another. He kissed her eyes, her cheeks, her ears, her throat. Licking, biting, sucking, trying to taste all of her, have all of her. His fingers dug into her arms. She sank her fingers into his hair, clutching so hard it hurt, but he loved the pain. He wanted to feel her teeth, her nails.

They fell back against the bed and his weight was across her, but Brett felt no fear this time, only anticipation. She curled one of her legs around his and slid it up and down, liking the feel of his rough jeans against her bare skin.

Joe shifted his weight onto one elbow so that he could look down at her. He pushed the edges of her sweater apart, exposing her breasts. He cupped her breast, grazing the nipple with his thumb. He watched his hand on her breasts, and Brett gazed at his face, stirred by the naked desire she saw there.

Slowly he bent and kissed her throat, trailing down over the tender flesh onto the bony plateau of her chest. The scent of her skin mingled with another, heavier smell. It took a moment for Joe to realize what the scent was. Cologne. Men's cologne. It was her hired lover's smell on her skin. His lips were touching her where the other man's had only minutes before.

Joe stiffened. Brett opened her eyes, surprised and confused. "Joe?"

His eyes were harsh and black with anger. He levered himself up and off the bed. ""Goddamn it! I won't be a substitute for your paid stud!"

He whirled and stalked out of the room. Shakily Brett sat up, staring after him. She was hot and quivering, aching with the loss of his lovemaking, shaken and confused. What in the world had happened!

Liz's voice on the other end of the line was laughing, but firm. "You are going to that party tonight. I insist!"

Jennifer chuckled. "You know I'm not big on parties."

"That is beside the point."

"What is the point?"

"That I haven't heard a thing from you since the day I gave you the phone message from Matthew Ferris—unless, of course, you count the time I called you and you told me to get lost."

"I didn't! I said I'd get back in touch with you."

"Same thing. I haven't noticed you calling."

"I was planning to call you tonight. This morning I have to run down to Royal for costume fittings. I'm already late."

"I'll be at Linda Holloway's party tonight. Which is where you will be, too, because I'm going to kill you if I don't find out what happened!"

"Okay. Okay. I'll be there. But I'm leaving early."

"I'll catch you."

Jennifer hung up the phone and hurried out to her car. She drove to Royal Studios and spent most of the day in Wardrobe, trying on her costumes for *Drifter*. It was one of her least favorite jobs, but today she didn't mind. She was too happy and excited, as bubbly as a teenager in love. In a way she was, she guessed.

She thought about Matthew's phone call last night. They had hung on the phone for at least an hour, saying nothing of significance, simply enjoying the other's voice. He had promised to call again tonight. Jennifer grinned to herself.

Maggie Crenshaw's assistant, adjusting the waist of the thirties-style dress, smiled back at Jennifer. "You seem happy today."

"I am." She missed Matthew. That was the one blot on the day. She wished she could see him tonight. Now. But it wasn't really a sad sort of missing. It was more an anticipation, waiting for his phone call, waiting to see him again. She felt downright giggly, and today the world was a wonderful place. Even attending Linda Holloway's party tonight wouldn't be too bad; in fact, she had some desire to see people and talk. Maybe she'd even wear something stunning.

When she got home she wolfed down the supper her housekeeper had prepared for her and went straight to her closet. She pulled out a long, narrow, shimmering Bill Blass gown in a pale gray-blue. The top was a blouson, leaving one shoulder bare, and flowed into a clinging skirt. It was belted around the hips, making her look impossibly thin and utterly sexy. She bathed and dressed and put her hair up in a loose tumble of curls with wisps escaping to trail down her neck.

Matthew called right before she left, which made her late to the party, but her face was glowing. She had never looked more stunning, and her arrival caused a ripple of whispers all around the house.

The Holloway mansion was enormous, and it was filled with people. Lester Holloway was one of the biggest producers in the city. Every year his wife Linda gave a party to which everyone who counted was invited. Except for a few reclusive souls, everyone who was invited came.

It took Jennifer an hour to find Liz. She was beginning to think she never would, but finally she spotted Sloane, backed up in a corner by a middle-aged woman covered in diamonds. The woman's hand was on his arm, and she was laughing up flirtatiously into his face. Sloane's smile was fixed and polite. When he glanced up and saw Jennifer approaching them, his relief was obvious.

"Jennifer! Liz sent me to find you. She's out by the pool."

Jennifer smiled at the other woman. Sloane detached himself from her and came over to Jennifer, kissing her lightly on the mouth in greeting. "Thank God I saw you," he whispered. "I was going under for the third time."

Jennifer chuckled as they threaded their way through the crowd. "It's your charm. It's lethal. You should learn to tone it down."

"Charm! It was an agony to even be civil to the

woman.'' Sloane grimaced. ''She was telling me how very lonely she is and how very wealthy.''

''Then I imagine she won't have any trouble finding someone else.''

''God, I hope so. And soon.''

''Who is she?''

''Carol something-or-other, the widow of some studio executive.''

''Oh, yes, I've heard of her. Carol Villard. She has a reputation for liking young men.''

''Hell. I'm not even young anymore.''

''Maybe to her you are.''

Sloane spotted Liz. She was deep in conversation with an executive from Paramount and his wife, and Jennifer and Sloane hung back for a moment, waiting for her to finish. Jennifer glanced up at Sloane. She wondered how Liz could ever doubt that he loved her when he looked at her like that.

Liz saw them and smiled. She worked her way out of the conversation and came over to hug Jennifer. ''Jennifer! Love! You look absolutely stunning. I can see that whatever happened, it came out right. I can't remember when I've seen you this happy.''

Jennifer smiled. ''It's been a while.''

''So tell me about it.'' Liz linked her arm through Jennifer's and steered her toward the less-populated rear of the yard. Sloane walked on the other side of Liz, his hand clasped in hers. They sat down at a white wrought-iron table by a small waterfall in the lower yard. ''What happened with Matthew Ferris?''

''I called him and we went out for drinks. He apologized for what had happened, you know, back in Sweet River. It was something his father arranged, and he found out the truth recently. I was angry with him at first, but the next day we went out again and, oh, Liz, it was like it used to be with him!'' Jennifer's eyes were glowing.

Liz grinned. ''You slept with him.''

Jennifer nodded, knowing the color was rising in her face and feeling like an idiot, but too happy to care.

"Well, congratulations!" Liz hugged her. "I'm so happy for you."

Jennifer laughed. "I haven't felt like this in years. Well, since high school. I could jump up and touch the moon."

Liz glanced at Sloane. He was watching them, smiling faintly. He looked unbelievably handsome to her. She had felt that way about him when she first met him. There were still times when she almost exploded with excitement when she saw him. But more often these days it seemed that she felt only fear and insecurity about him. The doubts collected and swelled inside her, dark shadows that tainted her love for him. She wasn't even sure whether the cause of it was Sloane or herself.

They stayed at the table, talking and laughing and catching up on each other. Sloane returned to the house and brought them drinks, and shortly after that Brett Cameron showed up at their table. She wore a brown velvet and gold lace Oscar de la Renta chemise dress, and around her throat was a gold Ilias Lalaounis necklace decorated with clusters of leaves. What she had on was worth thousands of dollars, yet she wore it as casually and carelessly as she wore jeans and tennis shoes. Her hair hung loose and curling, and she wore only the smallest amount of makeup. She looked somehow both exotic and thoroughly natural.

"Hi. I saw Sloane coming this way so I followed him. I thought he'd lead me to you."

"Brett!"

They rose to greet her, and there was a flurry of hugging and kissing before they sat back down again. "I wanted to talk to you, Liz," Brett said, curling her feet up under her.

Jennifer winced. She could imagine what the wrought-iron curlicues on the chair must be doing to the fragile golden lace of Brett's dress. Brett would never think of it.

"Why?" Liz asked, settling down to business.

"I came to beg and plead."

"For what?"

"An actor."

"You still don't have a Jace?" Jennifer asked.

Brett nodded.

"But I've sent you demos of every client I have who could possibly fit."

"I know. But I was hoping you could go back through your files, even look into your old ones. Or maybe you know an agent in New York or Dallas, anywhere, that might have someone. I'm getting desperate."

Liz frowned and took out a cigarette and lighted it, thinking. "Sure. I could call some people in Dallas and New York. I don't know what good it will do, though. Haven't you tried those cities?"

"Of course. I've tried everywhere. I found a couple of men who come close, but they aren't quite what I want. Everyone's too handsome or not good enough looking or too young or too old or they can't act."

"You're looking for a Richard Gere type, right? Dark?"

"Not necessarily. It's not so much his coloring or the way his face is put together. It's a quality. He has to have that sexy something that reaches out and grabs you. Not picture perfect handsome. He has to look right in grubby clothes. He has to be a little rough-and-tumble, as though he's lived a lot. He's a drifter, after all. But he also has a kind of sexuality that just sizzles."

Brett grimaced, trying to think how to describe in words what she saw in her head. "You have to believe that he could come into town and every woman would be dying to have him, dirt and sweat and all. He has that kind of eyes, that kind of face, like all you can think of when you see him is sex. Like Sloane," she said, jabbing a finger at him, pleased that she had found the perfect way to describe him. "He looks like Sloane."

Brett stopped, suddenly aware of what she had said, and she stared at Sloane. He felt as if he were under a microscope.

Brett smiled. "I'll be damned." She looked as though

all the pieces had fallen into place. "Sloane, can you act?"

His eyebrows went up. "You can't be serious." He glanced at Liz. She was watching him as cool and remote as a stranger.

"Of course I'm serious. You know I'm looking for an unknown. Now answer my question. Can you act?"

He shrugged. "Well, sure, I used to act. Half the guys in this town act at some time or other. I did a commercial, and had a small, very forgettable role in a small, very forgettable TV movie. But that's it. It was ages ago, six or seven years probably. I never had enough ambition." He smiled. "Too lazy."

Brett hardly heard his last words. She was thinking that his smile could turn a woman's insides to jelly. "Would you do a screen test for me?"

Emotions flitted across Sloane's face—astonishment, interest, uncertainty—almost too fast to be seen. "I don't know . . ." He looked again at Liz.

She gazed back at him without expression. There was an icy lump in Liz's chest. He would take the test; he'd get the part. He wouldn't need her anymore. He would be gone. She was terrified, and she hated Brett for thinking of it. But there was no way she could let any of that show.

"What do you think?" he asked her.

Liz shrugged. "It's up to you. Do what you want."

It intrigued him. He couldn't deny the ripple of excitement in his stomach. A chance to test for Brett Cameron. Most actors would kill for that opportunity. He'd never completely lost the desire to act. He supposed one never did. He'd just been smart enough to stop beating his head against the wall trying to get in. Now here was a door wide open for him. How could he not try it? How could he resist seeing what he could do, finding out if he had it?

But how could he take the opportunity, either? Liz had gone stiff and cold on him; it was obvious she didn't want him to test for the part. There had been other things she hadn't wanted him to do, other jobs, and he had given them up. That was probably what he ought to do now.

But the other jobs hadn't meant anything to him. They hadn't teased and beckoned him.

"I don't know, Brett," he repeated. "I—"

"Don't answer quickly." Brett put her hand on his arm, her expression earnest. "Just think about it. Will you promise me that? Will you think about it?"

He nodded. "Yeah. I promise."

"Good."

Brett left their group soon afterward, pulled away by a studio executive. Liz flashed Jennifer and Sloane a bright smile.

"Well," she said, "I better go circulate."

They watched her walk away. Jennifer glanced at Sloane. He was frowning. "Don't you want to do the test? Or is it Liz?"

His smile was more a grimace than an expression of amusement. "Sure I want to do the test. Who wouldn't? But it's not that simple."

"I think, deep down, Liz wants you to have what's best for you. She's just scared."

"I know. There's no reason for her to be scared, but she is. I don't want to do anything that would frighten or hurt her. But . . ."

"But you can't live only for her, either," Jennifer finished for him.

Sloane sighed. Jennifer could see the torment in his eyes. She reached across the table and squeezed his hand. He returned the pressure, smiling at her. "Thanks."

She shook her head. "For what? I wish I could do something to help the two of you."

They stayed at the table for a few more minutes, but there was little to say. Jennifer decided to leave, and Sloane walked with her to the front door. He snaked through the crowd, looking for Liz.

He finally found her in the game room. Two men and a woman were playing pool, and there were a couple of people watching. Liz was standing with a young, handsome man whom Sloane pegged immediately as an actor. The man was smiling at Liz, being very charming. They always were to Liz, hoping that she would decide to represent them. Usually Sloane found it amusing. But usually Liz didn't flirt back with them. Tonight she was.

Sloane didn't like the feeling in his gut. Jealousy was something he wasn't accustomed to, and he didn't handle it well. He walked over to Liz and took her arm, his fingers gripping her tightly. He barely glanced at the young man. "Let's go."

Liz looked up at him and he saw the flash of anger in her eyes. "What?"

"Let's leave."

She stared at him, her face set in hard lines. It scared her to death to think that he might make the screen test. The fact that he had the power to upset her so scared her even more. She was angry at him and at herself. After she left their table, she had had two drinks in quick succession and thrown herself into countless conversations, forcing herself to be bright and sparkling. For some reason it seemed important to pretend that she was having a good time, that she wasn't filled with roiling, bitter, frightening emotions. She could almost make herself believe it. Or, at least, she had been able to until Sloane showed up.

"I'm not ready yet," she told him flatly, turning back to the other man.

Sloane pulled her away.

"What in the hell do you think you're doing?" Liz found it a relief to feel this rush of fury instead of that ache, that fear.

Sloane's face was grim. "I'm taking you home before you make a fool of yourself."

"You're what?" She stopped, jerking her arm away from him.

"How much have you had to drink? You were practically salivating over that kid back there! It's time for you to leave."

"Since when do you think you can tell me what to do? You don't have any rights over me, you know."

"Oh, I'm well aware of that. You've pointed it out before. But that doesn't seem to stop *you* from pushing me to do what you want."

"I never tell you what to do!"

"Maybe not in so many words. But you sure as hell have a way of making it clear what's forbidden. Like taking that screen test. Like getting a job. Like any degree of independence."

"Take the goddamn screen test. I don't care," Liz hissed.

They were standing inches apart, their voices low and furious, and it would have been obvious to anyone watching that they were in the midst of an intense personal squabble. But Carol Villard had never been known for her sensitivity, and when she walked in the door and spotted Liz and Sloane, she saw only that the man who had interested her so earlier in the evening was conveniently there in front of her.

"Why, Sloane!" she called, joining them. "How nice to see you again."

Sloane glanced at her. He would have liked to strangle her on the spot. Liz forced a smile. "Hello, Carol. Liz Chandler. We met at Tod Blackman's party a year ago."

"Yes, of course. I'm so happy to meet you again." The older woman cast a dazzling smile at Sloane. "I met you there, too, didn't I? I was sure I'd seen you somewhere before."

"Yes."

"How mean of you to have forgotten," Carol pouted playfully, laying a hand on Sloane's arm.

Sloane ignored both the hand and the look she sent him. "I'm sorry, Ms. Villard—"

"Oh, Carol, please! You'll make me feel ancient." She smiled, but Sloane saw the cool calculation in her eyes as she ran them down his face and chest. She was used to paying for what she got, but she was obviously just as used to getting it.

"Carol." He moved his arm from beneath her hand. "I'm sorry, but Liz and I were about to leave."

"What a terrible man! You can't leave yet. The band's just started." She ran a finger up his arm. "You can't leave without giving me a dance." She cast a look at Liz, who was regarding both of them stonily. "You won't mind if I borrow him for a few minutes, will you?"

"No. Of course I don't mind." Liz looked at Sloane, her eyes icy and remote. "I'll be happy to lend him to you for the whole night."

Carol chuckled. "Why, how nice!"

Sloane stood as if he'd been turned to stone. Then abruptly he turned and strode away.

* *Chapter 21* *

Carol Villard gaped at the doorway through which Sloane had passed, then turned back to Liz. "What in the world?"

Liz began to shake. Dear God, what had she done? She started to go after Sloane, but the actor with whom she'd been flirting earlier intercepted her. "Liz! Hey, I hear the band's started. How about—"

The glare Liz gave him was so fierce he stepped back. She walked around him and left the room. She walked quickly through the house, searching for Sloane. She couldn't find him anywhere, but someone mentioned having seen him leave. Liz hurried out the front door.

A parking valet came toward her. "Car, ma'am?"

Liz looked down the driveway. Sloane's low black Ferrari was still sitting there. He hadn't taken his car—the car she'd given him. She remembered the party years ago at Susan Ketterman's. He hadn't taken his car that time, either. It wasn't surprising that he had done the same thing that he had with Susan. She had treated him with the same humiliating contempt. He must hate her. She hated herself.

"Yes, the black Ferrari there." She pointed. Her voice shook, but she was past caring what anyone thought. She had to find Sloane.

Liz hoped that he had taken a cab. Surely he hadn't set out walking as he had that other time. But who knew what he might do when she had sliced his pride to ribbons?

The parking attendant brought the car and she got in and started down the drive. She drove slowly, alert for any sign of Sloane. Surely this time he wouldn't have set out on foot, though. He would have called a cab. Still, she searched the streets for him. She turned onto Santa Monica Boulevard and cruised up and down it slowly. She did the same thing along Sunset.

Where had he gone? That time when he'd left Susan's he had planned to go to the Strip. But she couldn't picture him doing that now. He wasn't the same man. He was older and smarter. He had cash and credit cards in his pocket and a healthy checking account in a bank. Surely he would have gone to a hotel.

Tossing aside her pride, she drove to the nearest hotels, the Beverly Wilshire, the Beverly Hills Hotel and the Bel Air, and went into each one, asking if he was registered. He was not.

Liz didn't know what to do. He could have gone anywhere. There were thousands of motels in the city. Or he could have gone to a friend's house. She tried to think whose. He had grown away from most of the people he'd known before he met her. His friends were also her friends, and she didn't really think he'd go to any of them. She thought of Brett, but she ignored the idea. Anyway, she couldn't call everyone they knew asking if Sloane were there. They'd know she had lost him and that she was desperate at the thought. Her pride wouldn't go that far.

There was nothing else to do, so she turned toward Malibu. There was a faint hope inside her that Sloane would be there when she arrived, but the house was dark and empty. She walked out to the beach and sat down, careless of her expensive gown, and gazed out at the pounding water. Sloane was gone. She had driven him away. It was no wonder. She had been jealous, biting and cruel to him for months now. The remarkable thing was that it had taken him so long. It didn't matter that she had done it because she was scared to death of losing him. It didn't matter that she regretted what she had said to him more than she ever regretted anything in her life. The result was the same. She had prodded him too far and now he was gone. She was alone.

Sloane took a cab to a downtown hotel and sat up most of the night, smoking and staring out the window. He felt sick inside. He wasn't sure whether it was from hurt or anger. He felt them both.

Perhaps Liz loved him, as he had told himself many times. But she didn't trust him; she didn't believe that he loved her. However much she enjoyed his company, both in bed and out, however much she might love him, she was contemptuous of him, too. He would always be the man she'd bought. Her contempt ate away at his soul.

He was too much in love with her to be only her hired boy. He knew that he had finally reached the point where he had to either give in and be only that to her or leave her altogether.

It wasn't surprising that he didn't have her respect. There wasn't much in him to respect. He had never worked hard for anything, never sweated and struggled, never accomplished anything of any worth. The easiest path had always been the one for him. Once he had had some talent—or at least he'd thought he had—but he hadn't been tough enough to take the pain, rejection, and risk. He had avoided risks, both in work and with Liz.

He watched the sun come up and the traffic begin on the streets below. He shaved and showered, then looked up the number of Dragowynd Productions and dialed it. He was transferred from phone to phone, and finally Brett herself answered.

"Sloane?" There was questioning and a little excitement in her voice.

"I'd like to test if you still want me."

"Are you kidding? I'd love it. Let's see." She paused. "How about eleven?"

"I'll be there."

Liz didn't want to go to work. She had spent most of the night worrying and crying, so that she looked and felt like she'd been through a grinder. But neither did she want to stay home alone with Sloane's phantom presence all around her, so she slapped on some clothes and a little makeup and drove to her office.

The day seemed endless. Everytime the phone rang she froze, hoping, until Carol, her receptionist, said the name of the caller. It was never Sloane.

Late in the afternoon, Carol transferred a call to Liz's line, saying, "It's Brett Cameron."

"Hello, Brett."

"It was fannnntastic!" Brett's voice bounced with excitement.

"What was?" Dread began to gather in Liz's stomach.

"Liz!" Brett exclaimed in mock exasperation. "What do you think? Sloane's test!"

Liz struggled to keep her voice normal. "Then he took it?"

"Of course. This morning. Didn't he tell you?"

"I haven't talked to Sloane today."

Brett chuckled. "He probably wanted to see how he did before he told you. Well, he needn't have worried."

"He was good?" Despite her fears, Liz felt a rush of pleasure. She wanted Sloane to do well, to prove himself, even as she hated what the result would be.

"Yeah. He can act. I pulled Jennifer out of Wardrobe and had her read opposite him, and they play well together. When I looked at the test on the screen—well, he's got charisma and he's gorgeous. He's perfect for the part."

"I'm glad." Tears welled in Liz's eyes.

"So when can we talk terms? Everything's ready to roll in a week."

Liz swallowed. "I don't think I'm the person you ought to talk to about that."

There was a pause on the other end. "What do you mean?"

"I doubt Sloane will want me to be his agent. You better talk to him about it. Didn't he leave a number with you?"

"Yes, I'm sure it's in his file. I didn't even look. I assumed . . ." Brett's voice trailed off. "Liz, what's going on?"

"I haven't seen Sloane since the party last night. We, uh, had a disagreement."

"A disagreement? But, surely—"

"I'm afraid it's permanent."

"Liz! You can't be serious!"

"I am."

"I don't know what to say."

"There's nothing to say."

There was another moment of silence. "I guess I'll look up his number, then."

"Yeah. Good-bye." Liz hung up the phone without even waiting for Brett's good-bye. She sat staring into space. Sloane was lost to her now. Utterly, utterly lost.

* * *

They made a perfect couple: Sloane so handsome and Jennifer so beautiful, both talented and young and exquisitely dressed. They looked good together in the limelight. The picture of a Hollywood pair. That was why Brett insisted that they arrive together at the party for the press to announce the start of *Drifter*. Brett had carefully let it leak that the male lead of the movie would be a mystery man, new and sexy and destined for stardom, so that the reporters were eager to see him. Then she made sure that Jennifer and Sloane came in later than anyone else, hand in hand. The reporters swamped them.

Brett, Jennifer and Sloane were surrounded the whole evening, unable to break away even to sample some of the delicious food that Brett had had catered by Chasen's. They were lucky to be able to catch a glass of champagne as the waiters circled by. They talked until they were hoarse. Brett was her usual easy self with the press, fielding questions, bringing laughter even as she turned aside a subject. Jennifer, usually shy with reporters, sparkled tonight. She was glowing, and the press grinned to themselves, attributing her sparkle to love and already linking her with her future co-star.

Sloane was a natural. All he had to do to impress anyone was stand there and look sexy, but he was smooth as well. He chatted with the reporters as though there were nothing he would rather spend an evening doing. But Jennifer saw him unobtrusively glance around the room every few minutes, and she knew he was searching for Liz. She wasn't there.

Jennifer and Sloane left early, Brett's idea again. She liked to leave the press wanting more. Jennifer drove Sloane to the small apartment he had taken the week before and he invited her up for a drink.

His apartment was comfortable and pleasantly furnished, but it was a far cry from what he had been accustomed to and less than he could afford, given the money he was receiving for *Drifter*. But Sloane didn't intend to blow his money. One movie didn't guarantee his future; he knew he had been chosen not for his acting skills but because physically he was right for the part. There might be other roles coming his way and there might not. If there weren't, he knew he couldn't return to his old way of surviving. So he saved his money and lived simply. He found that he no longer cared so much about possessions, anyway.

Sloane mixed each of them a drink, gave Jennifer hers, and sat down across from her. "Tonight I need this," he said, holding up the glass. "What a zoo."

Jennifer smiled. "Isn't it? Brett knows how to woo the press. They love her."

He nodded. Jennifer glanced around. "I guess you miss the beach?"

"Yeah, I miss it. I miss a lot of things."

Jennifer looked at him with sympathetic eyes. "I'm sorry. How have you been doing?"

"Okay. I've been so busy getting this place and a car and everything, not to mention spending half my time in Wardrobe and the rest trying to learn my part, that I haven't had much time to feel sorry for myself. It's been hectic."

"I'm sure it is. At least Brett's arranged the filming so you won't have to start for two weeks." First they would be shooting scenes between herself and the actress who played her sister, in order to give Sloane a little more time.

"Yeah. And it's not a hard part. I know this guy real well."

"You think he's like you?"

Sloane smiled faintly. "Enough that I don't have to worry about his motivation. He's rougher, gets in trouble more than I did, but he always slides through life, too. Using people."

Jennifer frowned. "You think you used Liz?"

He shrugged. "Probably. In a way."

"But you loved her, too."

"Yeah. I loved her."

"I don't want to pry. So tell me if you don't want to talk about it, but it's awful watching you two hurt like this.

Liz looks like she hasn't slept in a week. Yesterday she didn't even go to her office."

Sloane glanced at her sharply. "Is she sick?"

"Not physically." She paused. "Sloane, isn't there any chance the two of you could get back together? I don't know what happened, and I don't really want to know, but couldn't you somehow resolve it?"

He stood up abruptly, shaking his head. "No. I'm nothing in her eyes. She doesn't want a relationship with a full and contributing partner. Liz just wants a supporting cast."

"Oh no, I'm sure you're wrong."

"Am I? She kicked me in the teeth, Jennifer. She treated me like dirt. And you know why? Because Brett asked me to test for this part. Liz didn't want me to grow, to do anything. She's afraid of losing control of me. If I went back to her I'd have to give up myself. I can't do that. Not now. Not anymore. We're over."

The party two nights later at Ken Rosen's was entirely different. There were no press members, publicists or studio executives—only Ken, Brett, and the principal members of the cast. It was a casual, intimate evening of drinks and food at Ken's home. Brett's gala had been for show. Ken's party was for the actors to get to know one another and him.

There was no need for Jennifer and Sloane to come together in order to create a stir. Sloane arrived alone, and Jennifer walked in a few minutes later on Matthew Ferris' arm.

It had been two weeks since Jennifer and Matthew had seen each other. He had flown into LAX that afternoon. Jennifer had donned a short, dark wig, sunglasses and a baggy sweatshirt and jeans and had met him at the airport. For an instant he hadn't recognized her. Then he had lifted her off the ground and kissed her until they both were breathless.

They had driven straight home, holding hands and looking at each other and grinning like a couple of teenagers. When they reached the house they had headed straight for the bed and hadn't left it until they had to dress for the party. Jennifer hadn't wanted to go to the party; she would have liked to keep Matthew all to herself. But she couldn't insult the director of her next movie before they even got started. Besides, she had an equally strong urge to show Matthew off to everyone.

He was worth showing off. The most handsome man there, she thought, more real and rugged than Sloane. Her face shone with love. Jennifer introduced Matthew around, proud of him and of the way he greeted everyone with interest, yet without awe.

Jennifer put the young actress who would play her sister at ease. Matthew discussed horses with Dan Keebe, the ex-stunt man who had the role of the town sheriff, and tried to get a smile out of Dan's wife, who was obviously both thrilled and terrified at dining with such celebrities. But even though they made an effort to be part of the group, it was obvious that they were in a world apart, bound up in each other to the exclusion of all else. Their hands were constantly entwined, and when they were separated physically the eyes of each still sought out the other.

To no one's surprise they were the first to leave the party. They drove around in the hills, looking at the lights of the city and enjoying being alone.

"I wonder what percentage of our time together has been spent in a car," Matthew joked.

Jennifer smiled. "A lot, I guess." She curled her hand around his. "I still enjoy it."

Matthew raised her hand to his lips. "Me, too."

They drove out of the city, sharing a need to get away from the structure of their lives. They took the coastal highway, sometimes talking, sometimes silent, and happy to be either. They stopped at a motel on the beach in Santa Barbara. It was a simpler place than either one of them was used to staying in, but they didn't care. They wanted only to be together, away from the rest of the world.

They walked along the beach, wrapped up against the chill ocean breeze. Neither wanted to sleep, for it would mean losing time with the other, but at last they returned to the room and went to sleep curled together.

They slept until almost noon the next day. The only clothes they had were the elegant evening attire they had worn the night before, so after a breakfast bought at the drive-up window of a fast-food restaurant, Matthew went into a store and bought jeans, sweatshirts, and sneakers for them both. Jennifer stuffed her hair up under a ball cap and put on sunglasses to give herself some anonymity. They walked on the beach and ate pizza in their room and even went to a movie, Jennifer keeping her cap pulled low and her eyes on her feet. She felt wonderfully normal and madly in love.

They returned to the motel room late that night, and Matthew peeled an orange he had bought at a nearby convenience store and fed it to Jennifer slice by slice. They removed their clothes and made love on the too-soft double bed. Matthew's hands smelled of oranges, and his mouth tasted like heaven. Afterward they lay beside each other, hands linked, talking softly in the dark.

Jennifer told him about her disastrous marriage to Scott and, smiling, added, "I don't know why I married him, except that when I first saw him he reminded me of you."

Matthew kissed her shoulder. "I went to the opposite extreme. I married someone as unlike you as possible. I should have realized I couldn't have loved anyone that different from you."

"How long were you married?"

"Seven years."

"I was married less than two years."

"Some of us are slow." He shrugged. "It took a couple of years to admit what a mistake I'd made, but by that time she was pregnant with Michelle. I couldn't leave her then."

Jennifer froze. "Michelle?"

"Yeah. My oldest daughter. Haven't I told you about them?"

"No." Jennifer could barely get the word out. Her heart was pounding, racing. A child! Matthew had a child!

"God, I must seem like a terrible father. I don't know, I guess I've been so wrapped up in us that I haven't even thought about them. I have two girls, Michelle and Laura. Michelle is six, and Laura's four. They're beautiful."

Krista would have been five. They would have been almost the same size.

Matthew got out of bed and switched on the light. He dug in his trousers and brought out his wallet. "Here. I'll show you their picture."

He handed her a photograph of two girls, both brown-haired and smiling. Jennifer stared down at the picture. They were, in fact, beautiful. Her hand trembled and she handed the photo back to him quickly.

"They're lovely."

"Thanks. I think so. Michelle looks more like her mother; Laura's like me."

He stuck the photograph back into his wallet and switched off the light. Jennifer was grateful for the enveloping darkness. She was sure her shock must show on her face. Matthew had children—daughters! She couldn't face that.

Matthew reached out and pulled her into his arms. He went to sleep, as they did every night, with his arms around her. As soon as Jennifer felt the loosening of his arms and the change in his breathing that meant he was asleep, she rolled away to the other side of the bed.

She stared into the darkness. She had never even considered the possibility of Matthew having children. In her heart he was still the boy she had known years ago, and it had seemed natural that he have no family.

What was she going to do? She felt torn apart. She couldn't give him up, not when she had found such happiness again. But there was no way that she could be around his children. Why, she refused to even be in a movie with a child actor!

Jennifer slipped out of bed and dressed. She stuck the room key in her pocket and eased out of the door, careful not to awaken Matthew. She walked along the beach. The rhythmic rush of the waves soothed her, and she began to think more clearly.

Matthew had two children. That was the place to start. It was a fact, and there was no way she could wiggle out of it. She could not bear to be with them, that was another fact. But nothing said she had to be around them.

Jennifer sat down on the sand. It was damp and cold, but she didn't notice it. She watched the white spume as the waves broke and rolled in. The children lived half a country away. Why was she so worried about seeing them?

She realized then how much she had come to think of herself and Matthew as a permanent couple. Though she had never consciously had the thought, deep inside her she must have hoped that they would somehow, someday be together. She had been dreaming, however subtly, of marriage.

That had been foolish, of course, and she was angry with herself for harboring such hopes, even subconsciously. She had learned long ago that there was no chance for her of a happily ever after. That had died with Krista. Jennifer felt a rush of guilt for even thinking about a sweet future with Krista in her grave.

Well, there was no possibility of that now. She couldn't marry Matthew or even live with him. She would have to release that dream.

But she couldn't give him up completely. There was no reason to, as long as they kept their relationship long-distance. They could continue to talk on the phone and see each other occasionally on weekends. It wasn't completely satisfactory, of course, and Jennifer knew that such a relationship wouldn't last for any length of time. Eventually it would crumble under the weight of its own unwieldiness. But for now she could be happy. She could be loved.

If she had to meet the girls when she visited him in Dallas—well, it would be only a brief incident, perhaps dinner or a children's movie. After all, the girls would live with their mother; they wouldn't be at Matthew's house all the time. She could handle meeting them, even spending a little time with them. Surely she could—if it meant not giving up Matthew.

Jennifer stood and walked back to the motel. She entered their room quietly. Matthew was on his side, sound asleep. She stripped off her clothes and slid into bed beside him. Her skin was cold and damp. Jennifer snuggled up against Matthew's back and let his heat warm her chilled body.

* *Chapter 22* *

For the first time since Brett had known Joe Darcy, she was uncomfortable around him. The morning after he left her bedroom so abruptly, he had been waiting at the car to drive her to work, as always. But this time the unexpectedly sweet smile didn't cross his rough face when he saw her. His eyes didn't even meet hers. He opened the door for her as politely and remotely as any chauffeur, saying nothing. Brett's stomach squeezed inside her. She didn't know what to do or say, how to act.

The way Joe kissed her had left her breathless and melting. After he left she had almost cried in frustration. Her desire had stunned her. She had never really thought of Joe in that way. Oh, she had noticed his bare skin and the hard muscles beneath it when she had seen him with his shirt off, washing the car. She had been aware of the harsh, essential masculinity of his dark face. She had wondered whether he had a girlfriend. But she had never imagined him kissing her or cupping her breast in his palm, never dreamed how good it would feel. She had never thought of him in her bed.

Now she couldn't seem to think of anything else.

As he drove her to work and back each day Brett found herself unable to concentrate on her work, watching Joe instead. She noticed the way his thick black hair lay upon his neck. She studied the curve of his cheek and jaw, the shape of his mouth, the texture of his skin, the lines fanning out from the corners of his eyes and cutting deep around his mouth. She looked at him as if she'd never seen him before. And in a way she hadn't, not with eyes that desired him.

It was a constant amazement how good he looked to her.

There was a deep, secret pleasure in watching him. She liked seeing his hands on the steering wheel, the faint movement of muscles in his powerful arms and chest as he drove. Every morning when he left her at the office she stood inside, watching him return to the car, loving the smooth, careless way he walked, the tight, thin jeans stretched over his legs. The sight of him never failed to stir a hot, dark yearning inside her.

Over a week went by. Joe gave no indication that anything had happened between them except for his retreat into a remote stiffness. Brett tried to act equally indifferent despite the emotions bubbling within her.

One Sunday morning Brett was at home working in her study, as she usually did on the weekends. She went into the kitchen to pour herself another cup of coffee. She glanced out the window and saw Joe in the driveway, tinkering with the engine of the Rolls. She found herself standing, the forgotten cup of coffee cooling in her hand as she watched him. She would never have believed that seeing him working on a car could have sent such deep visceral excitement through her. But there was something intensely sexual about the way he slid beneath the engine. All of him was hidden under the car except his legs. He had on his usual jeans, thinned and softened by wear until they molded to his legs, and motorcycle boots. He lay with one leg straight out, the other bent at the knee. A wide leather belt ran around the waist of his jeans, fastened with a heavy oval metal buckle. He was primitively, essentially male, and Brett responded to that maleness.

He moved out from under the car and stood up to bend over the engine. A line of sweat ran down the back of his white cotton undershirt. His legs were stretched taut against the blue jeans. There was a streak of black on the denim where he had wiped off his hand. He turned a wrench, and the muscles of his arm bulged with the effort. After a few more turns he finished twisting off the bolt with his hands. They were sure and swift and skillful in their movements. Light. Knowledgeable. Brett remembered his hands upon her breasts. His fingers were stained with dirt and grease. She thought of them on her, marking her clothes. Marking her body.

Brett turned away and set down the coffee cup with a clatter on the counter. Her body surged with heat. How could just looking at Joe have such an effect on her? She couldn't remember any other man who had. She wondered what he would do if she went outside and put her arms around him, if she kissed him. That was the question that had been bothering her ever since the night he kissed her. How did Joe feel about her? Did he want her?

He had seemed to that night. His mouth had been hungry; his skin had seared her. But then he had stopped and left her. Nothing had been the same since. Their old relationship was gone, exploded by the impact of his kisses. But Joe didn't seem to want any new relationship with her. He would hardly talk to her or look at her; he did his job and nothing more. He had looked disgusted and angry when he had left her after their brief burst of passion. She wondered if she had earned his contempt by bringing Bryan into the house. Certainly she had felt contempt for herself afterward. Why wouldn't Joe?

She missed him. She missed their old friendship. The ache of her desire had been mixed up with the ache of losing his companionship. She wanted Joe, and she wanted just as much not to lose him as a friend. But these days it seemed as though she would get none of her wishes.

Brett went back to her study and tried to work, but her mind wouldn't stick to anything. There were countless things she needed to do, but none of them appealed. After an hour of fruitless endeavors, she left her desk and returned to the kitchen for another cup of coffee. She looked out the window. Joe was no longer working in the driveway.

She poured a cup. She wondered where Joe was. Probably down in his room. Brett had never been there. She wondered what it looked like. She wondered what he did there, how he occupied his time.

It was strange how little she knew about Joe after all these years. He knew everything about her. But he was a very private man and she had respected that. She had never pried or questioned or even set foot in his territory. She had been careful to make that part of the house Joe's alone.

In the past it had never been a particular effort to stay away from his rooms, but now curiosity teased Brett. She wondered what he would do if she went down there. Would he be offended? She tried to think of a reason for showing up at his door, but subterfuge wasn't like her. She had always been straightforward with Joe.

Brett sighed. That was the problem between them right now. There was no more straightforwardness between them. Everything was all at angles, all silences and sideways glances, as though they had suddenly become strangers. She couldn't let it happen; she felt the loss too severely. Even if it meant subduing her suddenly awakened desire for him.

She had to talk to Joe about it. She would ask him

straight out, as she always had with Joe. She would find out why he had left her that night and why he shied away from her now. Then she would change whatever it was that was wrong. Because she wasn't about to give up Joe's friendship, not for anything.

Brett took the circular metal staircase down to his apartment. Her stomach was as jumpy with nerves as it had been when she was a twenty-two-year-old girl going to a meeting with a producer. She knocked on the door. It seemed to take Joe forever to open it.

He had obviously just showered. His hair was damp and his feet were bare. He wore a clean pair of jeans and no shirt. "Brett." He glanced at her, then quickly away in that manner he had developed recently.

"Joe. Could I come in? I want to talk to you."

"Sure." He stepped back for her to enter the room and closed the door after her.

Brett came to a dead stop. She hadn't expected this. The simple, angular furniture, yes; she had known Joe would have something like this. And the sand painting, the Navajo rug, the print of a Georgia O'Keefe oil—she knew him well enough not to be surprised by those. But the vibrant colors surprised her—the blazing orange and the fierce red mingling with the tans and beiges. But most astounding were the metal sculptures all over the room and the sturdy wooden worktable near the windows, on which sat a pouncing eagle, carved in great detail in wax.

For a long moment Brett simply looked. Then she turned to him with something close to accusation. "You made these, didn't you?"

Joe nodded and leaned back against the closed door, crossing his arms over his chest. He had envisioned Brett in this room millions of times. He didn't know what to do now that she was really here.

Ever since the night that he'd wound up stretched out on top of Brett on the bed, kissing her, he had been on fire. He couldn't see her, couldn't even think of her without itching to take her in his arms. It was worse now, knowing exactly how her mouth tasted, exactly how her soft body yielded under his. Those few moments had released the wild desires he'd kept carefully under control before. He had been like a caged animal suddenly set free, and if the smell of the other man's cologne on Brett's skin hadn't slapped him in the face he would have gone straight on to the one thing he wanted most in the world. He would have taken Brett without any thought for her or what she wanted.

He hadn't known how to act with her since then. He didn't know what she thought of him or how she felt about what had happened between them in her bedroom. She had been willing. She had responded to him when he kissed her, but Joe couldn't forget that she had come fresh from another man's kisses. Probably it had been the pretty boy who'd gotten her stirred up, not him. Even if for that brief moment Brett had desired him, it couldn't be what she would want in the general scheme of things.

Brett Cameron wasn't the kind to sleep with her chauffeur. Afterward she must have been horrified by letting him kiss her. He had ruined the easy rapport between them. Brett was uncomfortable around him now. God knew he was uncomfortable around her, knowing that his passion simmered just below the surface and wondering whether his control might break again.

Brett walked from sculpture to sculpture, her face filled with wonder. "Joe, they're marvelous!"

Joe released the breath he had been holding. Usually other people's opinions didn't bother him. But Brett's mattered. He had been rigid with the hope that she would like what he had done and with the need to hide his pain if she did not. "Thank you."

She stopped in front of a bronze bust of an Indian with a feathered headdress and feather-and-bone breastplate. Instinctively her hand went out to it, then she jerked it back guiltily.

"That's okay. Touch it. It won't hurt."

She gave him the smile of a child allowed to play in the

mud and reached out her hand to the cool metal. Her
fingers ran gently down the statue. Joe could almost feel
the caress on his own skin. "I love it," she said. "Can I
buy it?"

"It's yours if you want it."

She glanced at him, surprised. "No, I couldn't . . ."

"Take it."

Brett turned back to the sculpture. Something about it
pulled at her. The Indian didn't look like Joe, yet somehow
it reminded her of him. She touched the rough hair. She
wanted it too much to refuse it. "All right. Thank you."

"You're welcome." He couldn't tell her that her being
there, touching it and wanting his work was worth more
than any amount of money.

She turned to him, putting her hands on her hips and
assuming an aggrieved air. "Why didn't you tell me you
did this?"

He shrugged. "I don't know. It never seemed important,
I guess."

"Not important! It's beautiful. I knew you had some
sort of hobby. I've seen you drawing sketches, but I had
no idea. No wonder you have such a good eye for form
and design! You faker."

Brett wandered over to his worktable. "How do you do
it?"

"I use the lost wax method." He walked up beside her
and explained how he sculpted his ideas in wax, making
molds from the wax and the finished metal pieces from the
molds.

Brett listened intently, caught up as she always was in
any form of artistic expression. She asked intelligent
questions, he expounded, and they talked together more
easily than they had in two weeks.

"Joe, you're good. Why don't you show your work?"

"I do. A friend of mine—the one whose foundry I use
to make my stuff—has taken some of my pieces to art fairs
with his own."

"Oh, Joe!" Brett snapped, exasperated. "I mean really show them—at a gallery, not a sidewalk art show."

"There's no reason."

"What do you mean?" She was fired up, her expressive face intent and alive. "What good is art unless someone sees it? Look, I have a friend who owns part of an art gallery, and—"

"No. People see my work. I don't have to be in some fancy gallery for that. I don't need the money, and I don't need the hassle. There's no way I'm going to an opening to sip champagne and listen to people criticize my work."

"So don't go. Be reclusive. It'll add a nice touch of mystery, probably make your stuff sell even better."

Joe's smile was indulgent, his eyes warm, but he continued to shake his head.

Brett laughed. She knew better than to keep running up against a brick wall. She would figure out another angle and come at him from it later. "Artists!"

"What are you talking about? You're an artist, too."

"Part artist, part businesswoman. You obviously haven't acquired the business part."

She continued to stroll around the room examining every piece close-up. Joe watched her, smiling. He knew Brett. She hadn't given up; she never did. Before long she'd come at him again. He could feel the anticipation rising in him. He liked watching her maneuver. She was like water around a rock.

Brett stopped in front of a bronze sculpture of a woman's head and exclaimed in soft surprise. "Why, that's me!" She turned to Joe. "Isn't it?"

"Yeah. It's you."

She gazed at the sculpture. She smiled. "I'm flattered. You make me look so strong."

"You are."

"Me?" She chuckled. "No. You're the one who's strong. I'm the one who was brought up in the lap of luxury, remember?"

"You think you don't have to be strong to come out of
that the way you did?"

Brett looked a little amazed. "Maybe you're right."

She ran her thumb thoughtfully across the face's forehead. "How could I have not known about this? That you
did all this? Have I been that self-centered and insensitive?"

"Of course not. Why should you have known? I never
said anything about it."

Brett turned to face him, and Joe thought he saw the
glimmer of tears in her eyes. "Why didn't you?"

Involuntarily he came closer. "Brett . . ."

"Why didn't you?" she repeated. "I've told you everything about me, about what I did. You've never revealed
anything of yourself. I'm realizing that I don't really know
you at all. Don't you trust me?"

"Of course I trust you. That's not it at all. I just don't
talk much about myself. You wouldn't be interested."

"I don't know; I've always been intrigued by myster-
ies." Joe made a face and turned away. Brett dropped the
subject. "Were you working on that eagle before I came
here?"

"Yeah."

"Could I watch? I mean, if it wouldn't bother you I'd
like to see what you do."

"Okay." It would bother him all right. He wouldn't be
able to keep his mind off her, knowing that she was right
beside him. He would keep thinking about how she looked,
how she smelled, how her skin had felt beneath his
fingertips. He would be lucky if his hand didn't shake too
much to work. But he couldn't deny himself her presence.
He had done that too much lately, until he was starving for
her—starving just to hear her voice, to see her, to know
she was with him. And in some primitive way he wanted
to perform for her, to let her see his skill, like a caveman
bringing home the meat.

Joe sat down on the stool at the high worktable and
began to work on the detail of the feathers. It was familiar
work, soothing, and his nervousness eased. He didn't

forget that Brett was there—he couldn't possibly—but she was perfectly still and quiet, and he was able to concentrate, feeling only a pleasant sense of companionship from her presence.

Brett enjoyed watching him. The sun coming through the windows washed his dark skin with gold. She watched the play of muscles in his bare back and arms as he worked. She looked at his shoulder blades, padded with muscle, at his narrow waist, at the hollow between the muscles where his spine was. She knew an urge to kiss each bony outcropping of his backbone, to let her hands slide over his shoulders and arms.

Brett moved away, suddenly too jittery to stand still. Joe continued to work. Brett wandered around the living room. Joe needed more space down here, she thought. Perhaps they should knock out part of the wall and give him some of the rest of the bottom floor for a studio. The projection room wouldn't do, of course; there were no windows. But the game room would be fine.

There was a sculpture in the hallway to Joe's bedroom that Brett hadn't seen, and she drew nearer to look at it. She glanced into his bedroom, unable to resist the impulse. A sculpture of silvery metal caught her eye. She moved inside the bedroom, pulled by its unique beauty.

It was the head of a woman, stylistic rather than realistic. The chin was tilted up slightly, and the hair streamed back from the face as if windblown. She bent over the head to look more closely. She recognized the eyes, the forehead, the shape of the nose, even if it wasn't exactly representational. It was herself. But better. Full of strength, character and vision. Beautiful.

Brett ran her hand over the face and back along the windswept hair. It was only a face; the back of the head was cut away. Curiously she leaned around and looked into the back. It wasn't blank, unfinished metal. Rather it was another sculpture growing out of the other side of the face, a riot of vines, leaves and flowers. She realized that it was the inside of herself, again more lovely than she would ever be.

Joe loved her.

The sculpture screamed it in every beautifully detailed inch. She looked around the room. There was a watercolor of her on one wall and a charcoal sketch on another. She thought of the bronze sculpture in the other room. Joe loved her. Why else had he done so many renderings of her? And why else would they have been so full of caring?

Why had she never seen it?

Brett sat down heavily on the bed. It seemed crazy, yet it must be true. Now a lot of things made sense—Joe's overprotectiveness of her, the way he was always there when she needed him, the fact that there seemed to be no woman of importance in his life, the anger and dislike he'd displayed that evening when Bryan rang the doorbell.

Brett smiled. She felt suddenly giggly. Joe had been jealous. He had kissed her because he loved her and had torn away from her because he was jealous of Bryan kissing her only minutes earlier. It even explained, in some strange way, why things had been so awkward between them since. That night had unleashed something that Joe had kept hidden from her for years.

At first Brett wondered why he had kept it hidden, why he disliked it being out in the open now. But then she thought about his pride. She remembered his contempt for Sloane Hunter. He wouldn't want to be labeled as Brett Cameron's kept man. And no doubt he believed that he wasn't good enough for her, that she couldn't love him in return.

Brett considered the idea. She knew she felt passion for him, and liking. But could she come to love him?

She smiled. She was already halfway there.

Brett walked back into the living room. Joe was absorbed in his sculpting. She leaned against the wall for a moment, looking at him, enjoying the sight of him, the anticipation.

She crossed the room softly and came up behind him. She kissed the back of his neck. Joe's hand froze. Lightly

Brett laid her hands on his shoulders. She kissed each vertebra, moving slowly down the length of his back. Joe dropped his knife onto the table beside the wax bird. Brett ran her hands around him from the back, caressing his chest. Her fingertips found his nipples. Joe gripped the edge of the table tightly.

"What do you think you're doing?" Each word was torn from him.

Brett chuckled and her breath brushed his back. "Isn't that obvious?"

"Brett . . ."

"Joe . . ." She copied his intonation. Her forefingers circled his nipples. She nipped at his back and he jerked involuntarily.

"Jesus." The word sounded part prayer, part curse.

Brett explored his ribs and stomach with her hands while she trailed kisses across his shoulders. "I want you." Her hands slid down to the waistband of his jeans.

"Brett."

"I want you to make love to me."

"Brett." Joe turned, his hands reaching for her. He pulled her between his legs so that she was flush against his body. His arousal would have been obvious even if she hadn't already seen it in the fullness of his mouth and the heaviness of his eyelids. He squeezed his legs together, imprisoning her.

Brett slid her arms around his neck, smiling into his eyes. "Well? Aren't you even going to kiss me?"

"Oh, yeah. I'm going to kiss you." She had never heard his voice like this, low and hoarse and throbbing with passion. "I'm going to kiss you."

His mouth hovered over hers. He stared into her eyes. Brett gazed back steadily. She was open, trusting and beautiful. He loved her more than he had ever loved anything, more than he had dreamed he could love anyone. Once, in a movie set in the Middle Ages, he had heard a knight tell a queen that he was her man. It was a phrase that went far beyond sexuality, denoting a depth of love and loyalty that made her the single thing in the world that he adhered to. In that way Joe was Brett's man. She was everything to him. He knew her as well as he knew himself, and he loved her more.

And she was offering herself to him. She wanted him, and that knowledge made his own need explode inside him. It was everything he could have dreamed, everything he wanted and knew he couldn't have. The rush of passion he experienced was instantaneous and shattering. He had to go slowly because he had to make it good for her, yet he ached to pull Brett to the floor and take her right here, right now. It was torture not to, but it was a torture he loved.

Brett moved within the prison of his legs, rubbing against him, and he sucked in his breath. He brushed his mouth against hers. His tongue traced the outline of her lips. Brett trembled; her hands dug into his arms. His mouth settled on hers, gentle and coaxing. His tongue slipped into her mouth. He tasted and explored. He would consume her by degrees.

His hands slid into the thick mass of her hair. It was silky and soft. The tendrils curled and separated around his fingers, the hairs clinging to the roughened skin of his fingertips. It stirred him to have her hair envelop his tough, thick hands, capturing and softening them.

He bunched her hair in his hands and his mouth deepened on hers. Brett pressed up into him, flattening herself against his chest. He was like a rock, solid and unmoving. She knew that she could throw herself against him and he wouldn't even sway. His superior strength and toughness both reassured and excited her. All the power she possessed was nothing against his primitive strength. The influence she wielded held no fear for him. He could not be coerced, just as he would never seek any advantage over her.

Joe slid off the stool without ending the kiss, his body scraping down hers. His hands moved over her back to her buttocks, and he lifted her up into him. Brett clung to him, dizzy, giddy and wild. Joe was her only security and the source of her pleasure.

"Love me," she whispered. "Love me."

A tremor ran through him at her words, and it gratified Brett in a primitively feminine way. She could shake his strength.

Joe lifted her higher and buried his face in her breasts. She stroked his shoulders and back. His skin was burning. There was a faint film of sweat over it. She curled her head down over his and kissed his hair. Her fingers dug into the pads of his muscles.

Joe groaned and released her slowly, so that she slid down his body. His breath rasped in his throat. He stepped back. His eyes were black and so bright they seared her. He began to unbutton her blouse. Brett could hardly breathe. His blunt fingers brushed against her breasts as they moved down the row of buttons. When he was done, he grasped both sides of the shirt and slowly peeled it back and off her shoulders. Below it she wore a midnight blue silk and lace teddy. The garment cupped her breasts, the dark circles of her nipples evident through the flimsy material. He sucked in his lower lip, his teeth digging into it.

He hooked his thumbs in the spaghetti straps and eased them down Brett's arms, inch by inch revealing her breasts. She was beautiful. He spread his hands out on her collarbone and dragged them slowly down her chest until they touched her breasts. He watched the movement of his hands. His mouth was open slightly; his fingers trembled.

Joe cupped one breast in both his hands. His skin was dark against her flesh. He bent and softly kissed the top of her breast. His mouth trailed down to her nipple. It tightened at his touch. His tongue circled the nipple; he pulled it into his mouth. Brett thrust her hands into his hair. She wanted to move, to push her body against his, but the pleasure of his mouth was too wonderful to interrupt. She clenched her fingers in his hair, but the slight pain only heightened Joe's passion and his mouth tugged more forcibly. The sensation shot straight to her hot, moist center.

His mouth moved to her other breast. One hand slid down her stomach and in between her legs. He pressed hard against her, and she squeezed her legs around his hand. His hand moved rhythmically, rubbing her jeans against her. Moisture flooded her. "Joe!" she gasped. "Oh, Joe, please."

He raised his head. His face was flushed, his eyes wild and black. He pulled the rest of her clothes from her. He couldn't wait any longer. His hands went to the waistband of his jeans to unfasten them, but Brett stopped him, smiling a secret, feminine smile. He let his hands fall to his side and stood watching her. Her fingers slid beneath the waistband, her polished nails slick against his skin. She popped open the snap. Her eyes remained on his face, watching his reaction. She moved the zipper downward slowly, still smiling, and her sexual teasing sent his desire soaring. He wanted to make her hurry. He wanted to slam into her, hard, fast and conquering. But he wanted even more to feel her hands on him and to revel in her seduction.

She slid the jeans down his legs and he stepped out of them. Brett gazed at his naked body—his smoothly muscled thighs, his hard, tight buttocks, his powerful flow of chest, abdomen, and legs. He was far from perfect. He was, perhaps, too muscular for pure beauty. There were scars here and there upon his flesh, and his nose had been broken. He was rough. But he was supremely male. And he was hers.

Brett ran her finger over a scar that crossed his ribs. His skin jumped beneath her touch. "What happened?"

"Knife."

"And here?" She followed a long scar on his thigh.

She heard his quickly indrawn breath. "Barbed wire."

"I hate it that anything hurt you."

He shook his head, dismissing any former pain. Brett looked up at his face and smiled, skimming her hands down his chest and stomach to his thighs. The pleasure was so great it hurt him. Joe took her hands and raised them to his mouth, kissing each one in turn. "You'll make me explode if you keep this up."

"I want to."

He smiled. "Later." He pulled her to the floor. He wanted to make love with her here, amidst his work, his only other love. He spread out her blouse beneath her to protect her skin from the abrasion of the carpet. Brett noticed the gesture. He was always her protector. It was a pleasant sensation for one used to taking care of everyone else.

She kissed the palm of his hand as he had kissed hers and he closed his eyes. Her tender gesture nearly unmanned him.

Joe opened his eyes and looked at her. Softly he touched her face. "I'm not worth your time."

"No. You're worth all of it, and far more than that."

He knew it wasn't true, but she was kind and generous, as always. He would take the heaven she offered; he'd wanted her too much for too long not to.

He leaned over her, supporting his weight on his forearms. He kissed her eyes, forehead, cheeks, and chin, coming at last to her mouth. His kiss was deep and slow, and it fired Brett's blood. She ran her hands over him, exploring his tough body, enticing and urging him. Finally his mouth left hers and he kissed her all over. His breathing was labored and the heavy sound stirred her.

His hand caressed her stomach and legs. His mouth loved her breasts. Brett moaned and twisted. His fingers slid to the soft folds of her femininity, finding the heat and the moisture of her desire. He made a noise in his throat and the suction of his mouth on her nipple was suddenly hard and demanding. Brett dug her fingers into his back and moved her legs apart, wordlessly pleading.

He came into her hard, without finesse. It was the way she wanted him. He filled her, satisfied and possessed her. His movements were strong and primal, deep thrusts that shook her to the core. She moved with him, staring up into his face. His eyes were closed, his face contorted with the almost unbearable pleasure of building passion.

The pressure rose in Brett, too, crying for release. For a moment she held back, savoring the sensation, them tumbled over into the dark, mindless chasm. She tightened around Joe, pulling him into her, and he exploded into his own climax.

He collapsed against her and they lay twined together, their bodies slick with sweat, weary and drained and completely at peace.

* *Chapter 23* *

Drifter seemed charmed. Filming began and progressed almost without a hitch. Jennifer hadn't enjoyed making a movie so much in years. There was all the patience, care and efficiency that characterized a Brett Cameron production. The other actors were professional, Sloane the only one without experience. But he had talent and he worked hard. Sloane was eager to learn. He listened to Ken and the other actors and was always willing to try something again. There were times when he looked exhausted or sad, but he was able to banish such emotions in front of the camera. Ken Rosen was adept at pulling what he wanted out of Sloane and Jennifer in such a way that they hardly realized what was happening. There were times when Jennifer saw the dailies that she was amazed at what she had done.

But it wasn't just Ken or the production team or Sloane and the actors that made Jennifer's performance unusually good. There was a fundamental difference inside herself.

She was in love; she was happy. Suddenly she was full of creativity and depth. For the past few years she had poured whatever emotions she had into her films, existing herself in an almost numb state. The constant succession of roles had drained her, taking from her again and again with nothing added. Now she was brimming with emotions, with more than enough for her role. Her love for Matthew had replenished her.

She missed him, of course, and there were times when she was struck by sadness when she thought of the impossibility of their being together permanently. And sometimes at night, as she lay in bed, she would know a gnawing, formless guilt. But she was able to push away such feelings most of the time. She could ignore the existence of his children, the time they were apart, and the distance between them, and feel only the bubbling happiness of being in love with Matthew.

Rarely did a day pass without one of them calling the other, and they talked for long minutes on the phone. They met two weekends in Aspen, where they did little skiing, preferring to spend most of their time together in front of the fireplace in the house Jennifer had rented. Matthew flew out to LA twice, and they met another time in Phoenix.

Every moment Jennifer spent with Matthew, each time she talked to him on the phone, she fell more deeply in love with him. He was the boy she had loved, but now he had new depth and maturity, was both a familiar lover and an enticing stranger. She was so blissfully happy that Wardrobe and Makeup had quite a job keeping her vibrant looks toned down for the plain part.

Jennifer wasn't the only woman in love on the set of *Drifter*. It was obvious that the same sort of drastic change had occurred in Brett's life as well; she was suddenly softer, slower, glowing. Nor did it take a great deal of detective work to discover who was responsible for the change in Brett. There was never any overt sign of affection between her and Joe Darcy, but their eyes went frequently to each other, always with a special warmth, and when they spoke to each other one could almost see the heat between them, the careful restraint from touching. Once, in the early evening after the day's shooting was over, as Jennifer drove past the Dragowynd building, she saw Joe and Brett walking to their car. His arm was around her shoulders, his head close to hers. He opened the door for Brett and she slid inside, but as she did so, she turned and grasped the front of his shirt, pulling him into the back seat with her. He went, smiling.

There were rumors about them all over the place, though no one had the nerve to ask Brett outright. Jennifer thought that if she were to ask Brett, she would answer openly. It was Joe who was the more guarded of the two, who was careful not to touch Brett or kiss her in public.

Jennifer was happy for Brett. Like everyone in love, she wanted to see others in the same situation. As pleased as she was for Brett, she was equally unhappy over Liz. Everytime Jennifer saw Liz she looked thinner and more unhappy. Her trim suits now hung loosely upon her and she was not as carefully groomed. Jennifer had heard rumors that Liz's business was suffering, that she often stayed home instead of going to work and that her enormous drive, so essential to an agent, was gone.

It saddened Jennifer to see her that way. She often called Liz and they had supper together. Late in April, shortly before the cast and crew were to go on location in Texas, Jennifer met Liz at La Scala. Liz was made up and wore one of her favorite Oscar de la Renta suits, but nothing could mask the tight lines around her mouth or the consuming misery in her eyes.

Impulsively Jennifer squeezed her hand. "Oh, Liz . . ."

Liz smiled with a false brightness. "How are you, dear? Shall we order some wine?"

"If you want." It was obvious that Liz wanted to keep the conversation on an impersonal plane, and Jennifer complied. "Tell me what's going on. You know I never hear any of the gossip."

"You're around the biggest gossip item all the time."

"You mean Brett?"

"And her chauffeur. They're all over the scandal sheets. Everyone's thrilled; Brett's always been so perfect, it's one of the few things they've ever gotten on her."

"Brett seems happy. I think Joe's good for her."

"I'm glad." Liz gave the first spontaneous grin Jennifer had seen on her in weeks. "Although I've often wondered whether he actually talks or not. What do you think?"

Jennifer chuckled. "On occasion."

"Sloane dislikes him." Liz's smile faltered, and she struggled to recapture it. Her voice turned brittle. "I think Joe offended Sloane's sartorial sense."

"Liz, why haven't you called Sloane or gone to see him?"

Liz shrugged. "I don't know where he is."

"His number's in the book."

"He doesn't want to see me."

"How do you know?"

"Jennifer, please, it's obvious. He has a new life; I have no place in it."

"He's not happy."

"I think you're seeing things that aren't there." Liz looked at her bleakly. "Why would he be unhappy without me? I'm sure he has plenty of money. He's making a movie with Brett Cameron. He'll do well."

"I'm talking about personally, not business-wise."

"He doesn't need me in any way. I'm sure he hates me. I deserve it; I hurt him badly. He'll never forgive me for what I said."

"Why don't you give him a chance?"

"No. I couldn't—it would be more than I could bear to see the revulsion on his face again."

"I've seen him talk about you, and there was no revulsion on his face then. He still loves you."

"He hasn't spoken to me. He didn't pick up his clothes. I'm sure he's happy to be free of me. It couldn't have been pleasant having to pretend affection and desire."

Jennifer grimaced. "Why do you insist on attributing the worst possible motives to him? He lived with you for four years; I never heard even a whisper of gossip that he was unfaithful to you. There are lots of other women in this town who would have loved to have him, who could have given him more things than you. He loved you."

Tears formed in Liz's eyes and she glanced down to hide them.

"I'm sorry." Jennifer sighed. "I didn't mean to hurt you. It's just—I've been with Sloane a lot making this movie. I know he cares for you. He's unhappy. But he's as scared to come to you as you are to go to him. You hurt him deeply, Liz. I think you'll have to make the first move." She paused. Liz said nothing. "Look. Why don't you drop by the set one day?"

Liz shook her head. "No. I couldn't."

Jennifer sighed. She thought that if Sloane and Liz were thrown together they might realize how much the other had been hurt, too. They might see how stubborn and foolish they were being.

"No!" Liz thought of going to the set, of seeing Sloane. She had been tempted to do it many times. He was always on her mind; she couldn't sleep at night for missing him. The need to see him was a raw, constant ache within her. But she couldn't crawl to him—and wasn't that how he would interpret her visit to the set? She knew her heart would be in her eyes. Besides, seeing him would only increase her pain and longing. "Please, could we talk about something else now?"

"Of course." Jennifer couldn't bear to see the pain on Liz's face any longer. They began to talk about the business, and the subject of Sloane Hunter was not brought up again.

Liz had no intention of dropping by the set of *Drifter* as Jennifer had suggested. But two days later, after a meeting with a producer in one of the offices at Royal Studios, she found herself asking where *Drifter* was being shot, then walking over to Studio D. She went inside the cavernous sound stage. Technicians were setting up the lighting on the *Drifter* set, and a minor actress and Sloane's stand-in were in position so that the lights could be adjusted to them. Everyone else was sitting around, waiting. Jennifer was not there. Ken was talking to the cinematographer, and Ken's AD was smoking and pacing. Brett was working on a file of papers. Someone from Makeup fussed over Sloane, who was leaning back in a chair, his eyes closed. He wore boots, skintight denim trousers and a faded blue plaid shirt.

Liz looked at him. She couldn't get enough of looking at him. It had been so long.

The lighting crew finished and everyone began to move. Quietly Liz went closer. Sloane stretched in a way that was achingly familiar, twisting his body first to one side then the other as he pulled out the muscles of his arms. As he twisted in Liz's direction he saw her. His arms slid back to his sides and he looked at her.

Liz stared back at him. She wanted to cry.

Brett spotted her too, and called, "Liz! I didn't know you were here. Come over here where you can see better."

Liz shook her head, forcing a smile. "It's okay. I can see fine from here. I just dropped in for a minute."

Ken called Sloane's name. Sloane pulled his eyes away from Liz and walked to the set to join Diana Fuller, the young actress who would play the scene with him. He could feel Liz watching him. It had jolted him to see Liz. It had brought back the pain and humiliation of their parting all over again. But, at the same time he had wanted to take her in his arms; she looked so pale and fragile, without her usual slick sophistication. He yearned for her. He was tired of the empty nights. He wanted to go to her and kiss her into taking him back, to feel the victory of her body yielding to him. But he couldn't return to that life, either. Somehow, in the course of a few months, he'd changed too much.

Briefly Ken set up the scene, though both the actors already understood it. It took place early in the movie before Jace met Olivia, the character Jennifer played, and it was there to show the way he had used women before he arrived at Olivia's farm. It was a cold, calculated seduction. Sloane would rather Liz see any scene but that one. She would think it was just like him.

He felt hurt and angry and lonely, just as he did everytime he thought about Liz. She hadn't called him, hadn't tried in any way to get in touch with him. This was the first time she had even visited the set. She didn't seem to miss him or need him at all.

Sloane glanced over at Liz again. He couldn't read the expression on her face. He wondered if she had found another lover, if she had taken some well-paid young man into their bed. The thought made him want to dig his hands into her shoulders and shake her until she cried. Until she admitted she still wanted him.

Did she still want him? Or had some other man satisfied her? He didn't think so. No other man knew her inside out as he did. No other man knew exactly how to kiss her, how to touch her, how to bring her higher and higher until she was writhing, on fire for him to take her. Jealousy and anger consumed him. Suddenly he wanted Liz to see this scene. He wanted to play it to her so that she would know what she was missing, so that she, too, would feel the bite of jealousy. So that she would want him back.

Ken Rosen finished speaking, and automatically Sloane took his position behind Diana. They faced the camera.

Before the cameras rolled Sloane looked straight at Liz, his gaze angry and hot and direct. Then he looked back down at Diana. Ken called for quiet, and everything settled down.

"Roll."

"Action."

"You're an awfully pretty lady," Sloane said, his voice

slow and lazy, just a little husky. He ran a forefinger across Diana's shoulder and down her arm.

Liz felt his touch as if it had been her own flesh he stroked. She shivered.

"Am I?" the woman countered faintly, nerves and excitement showing on her face.

"Oh, yeah." Sloane's hand came back up, fingers spread out now, and moved up her neck. Her head tilted away from him, and he bent to kiss the side of her face. Lightly his lips brushed her cheek, then her neck. He twisted her long hair around his hand, lifting it to kiss the back of her neck.

Liz swallowed. She remembered the feel of his lips on the sensitive skin of her neck and she was flooded again with the same raw passion that Sloane had always evoked in her.

The air was thick with sexuality. Liz couldn't look away. She felt every touch of Sloane's hands and lips, every movement of his body. He turned the actress around to face him. She moved limply, mesmerized by him. So was everyone else. The crew watched, unstirring, hardly breathing. Tension built, and then, at last, Sloane kissed her on the mouth. The kiss was deep and long, building in heat and intensity. He kissed her again and again. Liz felt the kisses all through her, as if he were kissing her. She was filled with such longing and pain and jealousy she wanted to scream. Sloane pulled back and looked down at the girl.

"I live just down the street," she said shakily. Liz didn't know how she could remember her line—or even talk.

He smiled slowly. "Then what are we waiting for?"

His arm went around her shoulders and they walked off. No one said a word. An electric silence hung over the set. Then Ken seemed to come to himself. "Cut."

Someone let out a nervous laugh and one of the cameramen said, "Whew!"

They all began to chuckle. "Hey, Sloane," Ken teased. "I said a *cold* seduction. That one'll scorch the screen."

There was more laughter. Sloane turned and looked for Liz. She was gone. The burst of anger and jealousy that had propelled him through the scene fled, and he was empty and sick inside. He managed a weak smile. "Sorry."

"Let's try it again, with a little more calculation and coolness, please."

"Sure." They moved back into their places. Sloane knew he wouldn't have to work to project coldness this time. That was all he had now.

The cast and crew of *Drifter* flew to Texas the next week to begin filming on location. The house and barn settings were shot on a farm in eastern Texas, and the town sequences were done in a small town nearby. The movie people stayed in a motel in Tyler, about twenty miles from each location and a little less than two hours from Dallas.

They had expected to suffer from the heat, but the area was experiencing a mild May. Sloane didn't sweat enough for a movie set in the summer, so periodically the makeup people sprayed his bare chest and back with an oily spray to simulate sweat. Rather than the heat, the problem was rain. Almost half their scheduled days were lost to rain, and three weeks of location shooting stretched into five. Bored and restless, the actors and technicians were stuck in their motel rooms, talking, reading and playing endless rounds of cards.

Only Jennifer was not upset by the weather and the long location time. She and Matthew spent the first weekend in her room in Tyler and the second weekend in San Antonio. Then Matthew took a week of vacation and stayed with her on location. They shot only two days that week, so that Jennifer and Matthew were able to spend most of the time alone together.

On Sunday afternoon before he left for Dallas, Matthew turned to Jennifer with a serious air. "Jennifer..."

His attitude frightened Jennifer. Something bad was coming. "Yes?"

"I don't—I'm probably going to make a mess of this." He stared down at his hands, his handsome face contorting into a frown. "I want to know if you would consider marrying me."

"What?" Why hadn't she realized this was coming? She must have been blind—no, just stubbornly ignoring it. It was different from what she had feared, but equally bad.

Matthew smiled. "Surely it can't be that big a surprise. It seems like what we've been leading up to."

"I guess it is at that." Jennifer sat down heavily. "I don't know what to say."

"How about yes? It's nice and succinct."

"But, how? I mean, we live halfway across the country from each other."

"We can work that out. You could live in Dallas. It's possible. I've heard of other actors who don't live in LA. They live in New York or someplace. Another country, even."

"There are some."

"That's what I mean. You'd have to go back there to film, and you'd go on location. I realize that. But it would be better than the situation we have now. We could be together a lot more."

Jennifer knew that Matthew's idea was feasible. She wouldn't be right in the heart of the industry, but she was well-established; it wouldn't hurt her career. She couldn't make as many movies, of course, but that was okay. Before Matthew, she had desperately needed to fill every tiny crack in her life, but she no longer had that need. She didn't have to race around trying to do so much that she wouldn't feel the loneliness and the pain. With Matthew there was no loneliness, and the pain was far, far in the background.

Longing rushed over her. She wanted to marry him. She wanted to be with him for the rest of her life. In her most

hopeful dreams she couldn't have asked for anything better
than living with Matthew, warm and secure in his love.

But he had two little girls.

She had managed to push his daughters out of her mind
most of the time. It had been relatively easy because she
had never met them. She and Matthew had spent all their
precious time alone together.

"I don't know." Tears filled her eyes.

Matthew took her hands. "Sweetheart, if you like Los
Angeles that much we can live there. I could relocate. I
hate to because it would be hard on Michelle and Laura,
but if that's what it takes . . ."

"No. It's not that. I could live in Dallas."

A smile began to spread across Matthew's face. "Then
you're saying yes? You'll marry me?"

"No. I didn't say that. I don't know."

"Then what's the problem?" His face grew serious
again and he released her hands. "You don't want to be
with me?"

"Oh, no! I love you! I love you more than anything. I
want to be with you."

"Then what is it?"

She couldn't tell him that it was his daughters. She had
never told him about Krista. She didn't talk about Krista to
anyone. It was something she kept locked up inside herself, the unbearable pain sealed away. But even if she told
him about Krista's death she wasn't sure he would understand her feelings. She didn't know if anyone could unless
his own child had died. Just the sight of a child filled her
with such pain and anger and guilt, such jealousy and
longing that she couldn't bear it. How could she possibly
sit down to breakfast across the table from two of them?
How could she go to McDonald's with them or watch
them play? When her own child, her own sweet Krista was
cold and buried beneath the ground!

Jennifer turned away from Matthew. "It's just that—I
need some time to think. You shocked me."

Matthew frowned, his eyes warm but puzzled. What

would he do if she turned him down? Jennifer wondered. He might not want to see her again. Even if he did it would be the beginning of the end. A proposal was a turning point. They couldn't go back to what had been before, only away from it in one direction or the other. They might continue to see each other for a while, but Matthew would feel the hurt of rejection, and she would regret not being able to marry him. Eventually their love affair would die. The thought of going back to that empty life she had known before chilled her. She couldn't! It would be far worse now, having experienced these months of happiness.

And she *wanted* to marry him. Why couldn't she have this one thing in her life? Why couldn't she at last find the love she had always wanted and never been given?

The children, after all, lived with their mother. Though Matthew had never talked about it, he must see them only on the weekends, perhaps not even that often. Surely she could stand being around them for a short time like that. They would want to do things with Matthew alone, and she could find things to do herself so that she wouldn't have to be around them all the time when they were there. Couldn't she manage to live with it?

"What about your children?"

"Is that what you're worried about?" Matthew's face went slack with relief. "Oh, honey, that won't be a problem. I swear. They're sweet kids; you'll like them. Hell, Laura's been bugging me about when I'm going to marry you. She wants another mommy, she tells me. I guess one isn't enough. They like your picture; they think you're pretty." He smiled boyishly. "My girls have good taste."

"I'm sure they're very nice. It's not that."

"Look. This is settled really easily. Just spend next weekend in Dallas and you can meet Michelle and Laura. You'll find out how well you all will get along. Will you do it?"

Jennifer hesitated for a moment. She felt as if she were stepping into fire. "Yes. I'll do it."

Matthew pulled her to him, smiling down into her face. "Do you love me?"

"Yes."

"Will you marry me?"

"I want to."

"Will you?" He gave her a quick, hard kiss. "Come on, give me the right answer or I'll keep this up until you do."

Jennifer tilted her head, considering. "Hmm. That might be rather nice."

He kissed her again, more lingeringly. "Will you?"

"I think I need a little more convincing."

"I can take care of that."

He kissed her. His tongue went deep into her mouth and wound around hers caressingly. Jennifer leaned into him, her hands clutching his shirt to draw him closer, if that was possible. Their bodies were molded together all the way down, the familiar curves fitting together as they always did, as though there were no other home for them. They kissed and touched, lost in the wonder that was always there between them. Haphazardly they took off their clothes and dropped them between kisses and caresses, making their way with lazy purpose toward the bed.

They lay down upon the bed and for a long moment Matthew simply looked down at her. His eyes were warm and heavy with passion. "Sometimes," he murmured, "I still can't believe I have you. You're like a dream." His long fingers drifted over the curves of her face. She was as beautiful as porcelain. When he had been a teenager he had accepted her beauty as his due. But now he was mature enough to know how very rare she was and how very lucky he was to have her love.

"I'm not a dream," she replied, smiling, and drew his head down.

They kissed with all the leisure of a couple recently and frequently satisfied. The fire burned in them, but they were deep, banked and well known. They no longer had to rush to find them.

His hand roamed her body and delved between her legs, his fingers seeking out the soft, damp folds of her femininity. His thumb caressed her mound of Venus and slipped down through the silky curls to the parting of her lips and the small, fleshy button between them. Jennifer made a noise and moved involuntarily, and her own hands went down to curl around him. Matthew froze, loving the feel of her soft hand upon him and unwilling to disturb it by the slightest movement.

Jennifer stroked and caressed him until any thought of leisure had been stripped from his mind and he was all heat and pounding desire. His mouth moved down her, following the path of his hands. He lifted her buttocks, his fingers digging in as his mouth feasted greedily upon her. Passion spiraled in Jennifer, carrying her up and out past the realm of sanity. She dug her heels in the bed, her legs trembling with the force of her building desire, and moaned his name, begging him for release. She clenched her legs and he could feel her shake as she reached her peak.

Then, with a soft, satisfied noise she relaxed on the bed. But Matthew had no intention of leaving her with only that, and his mouth began to work upon her again, his hands moving to cup her breasts and tease her nipples into diamond hardness. Again he built the force of her passion. He slid into her, filling her with his hard, satiny heat; and she closed around him. They moved together in a slow rhythm. His body was slick with sweat, his forearms clenched in restraint as he stoked their desire into an almost unbearable heat. At last they exploded together, for an instant wild and free, a single, soaring flame.

They lay together, exhausted and tingling, in the afterglow of passion, touching each other lightly and murmuring simple, age-old words of love. At last Matthew pulled himself away and dressed and left for Dallas, kissing Jennifer good-bye lingeringly. He forgot that Jennifer had

never answered his question of whether or not she would
marry him.

Joe drove toward Palm Springs, one hand curled around
Brett's on the seat between them. He glanced over at her.
Her head was back against the seat, her eyes closed. He
wasn't sure whether she was sleeping, but he knew she
was bone weary. She had spent the morning working; then
they had driven to Twin Oaks, the clinic just west of Palm
Springs where her sister was staying. Though he hadn't
been in the room, he could tell by Brett's face when she
came out that it had been a trying session with Rosemary.
There were times when Joe hated Rosemary for the trouble
she caused Brett, for the countless occasions Brett put
aside her own tiredness, her own plans, her own needs, to
give of herself to her younger sister.

He stroked his thumb down the back of her hand and
lifted her hand to his mouth to kiss it. Brett opened her
eyes and turned them toward him, smiling. He grinned
back, his heart bounding up wildly as it did so often these
days.

He loved her. He loved making love with her. It was a
joy he had never thought he would know to wake up
beside her in the morning. He was with Brett almost
constantly now. He couldn't stay away. Though he still
worked in his apartment downstairs, he lived upstairs with
Brett and slept with her in her aerie atop the house.
Whenever she went to a party she insisted that he go with
her, and though he hated parties, he went, proud of her
hand in his and of the way she boldly faced the gossip.

His work suffered, but he didn't care about that. What
bothered him was the tremendous guilt he felt. He wasn't
good enough for Brett, not nearly good enough. Her love
affair with him had made her vulnerable to the vicious
gossip and backbiting that abounded in Hollywood. He
was afraid it would hurt her career. He was afraid it

lessened her in others' eyes. He was afraid she would regret it someday. But he didn't have the courage or nobility to leave as long as she wanted him to stay.

"We're almost there," Joe said quietly.

Brett sat up, looking around her. They had turned off the highway onto the narrow road leading to Kingsley Gerard's Palm Springs estate. He had moved there shortly after he sold Royal Studios, selling the grandiose mansion in Bel Air to an affluent Arab. The house in Palm Springs had been his and Lora's weekend retreat. It was not nearly as large as their home in LA, but no one could call it small—except Kingsley—and it sprawled over the hillside, commanding a panoramic view of the valley below.

They parked in the four-car garage. It looked sadly empty now with only Kingsley's black Rolls Royce inside. Brett could remember when it had held her grandfather's Jaguar, Lora's Cadillac and a spare car for their guests' use, as well as the stately limousine.

A maid opened the door and directed them to the den, where Kingsley was sitting in front of the windows, looking out at the valley. It was purplish dusk outside, and lights were beginning to come on over the city.

Brett paused for a moment, pushing down the tearful emotion that rose in her throat. King looked old and frail. A gold-topped cane rested against his chair arm. He had grown so old the past few years! Sometimes she didn't think she could bear it. Surreptitiously Joe squeezed her hand, and Brett flashed him a smile of thanks for his support.

"Granddad?" She stepped into the room and King swiveled his head around.

"Brett! I didn't expect you today!" It was an effort for him to rise, but he did so, grasping the sides of his chair and thrusting himself out of it. He wavered for a moment, then took hold. He picked up his cane and started forward, but Brett was already at his side, reaching out to hug him.

"I wasn't planning to come, but I went to visit Rosemary, so I thought I'd run over and see you."

"Good." He patted her back. Both his hand and his voice were weaker than she remembered. He looked over her shoulder at Joe. "Hello, Darcy. Glad you're here. I've been wanting to beat somebody at a game of poker."

Joe smiled. He liked the old man. When he had first met King Joe had been overawed by him, but over the years he had come to know and like him. King loved poker, all kinds of card games really, and he had been delighted when Joe started playing with him. However fragile he was becoming, his mind was still alert enough for ten men. Joe thought he enjoyed the chance to talk as much as the card game itself. King asked him questions while they played, mostly about Brett, but also about LA and the film industry. Joe, sensing the love and loneliness behind the questions, was always happy to talk.

Joe shook King's hand, then carried in their luggage and placed it in the two rooms where they had stayed in the past. He didn't want to disturb Brett's grandfather by sleeping with her in his house. He sat in his room, sketching until it was time for supper, to give Brett and King a chance to talk.

Brett scooted a low hassock over next to her grandfather's chair and sat beside him, holding his hand. They looked out at the valley. "It's beautiful, isn't it?"

"Lora always liked the view. She'd sit out on the terrace at night and look at it for hours. I still do it. Force of habit, I guess. I never could see what was so special about it."

Brett smiled. "You like to think you're an old curmudgeon."

He chuckled. "Lora phrased it differently."

That made Brett chuckle, too. King gave her a considering look. "You seem very happy."

"I am. Everything's going wonderfully right now."

"I'm glad."

She squeezed his hand. "You were always my best friend. Did you know that?"

"I never thought about it. You were my heir, the person I loved most in the world besides Lora."

Tears stung Brett's eyes and it was hard to keep her voice even, but seeing how frail he looked tonight, she knew she had to say it. "I was angry with you when you sold the studio."

His bushy white eyebrows soared. "I'd never have known."

"Don't be sarcastic." She tapped him lightly on the arm. "I'm trying to be serious."

He smiled. "Okay. Be serious."

"There's been some distance between us because of that. Because I was hurt."

"I've felt it. I never meant to hurt you, sweetheart."

"I know. But I wanted you to know that I've realized you were right. I was in a meeting with the CEO at Royal the other day. I looked at him and I thought, that's the job I wanted, what I wanted Granddad to give me. I was so glad that you hadn't. It was my dream, but it wasn't what I was suited for. It wouldn't have made me happy."

King patted her arm. His eyes looked suspiciously wet for a moment. "Thank you. I'm glad."

"Me, too."

Brett rested her head against Kingsley's arm and they sat together in companionable silence.

That evening after supper, King and Joe sat down to a game of draw poker at the small table in the den. Brett was in the room with them, reading, but after a few minutes she rose, stretched and went out to sit on the terrace. Joe watched her go, as he always watched her wherever she went. He didn't notice King's quick, shrewd look in his direction.

Joe returned his attention to his cards. King had just raised him, and he had nothing in his hand. He never knew with King; the man was a champion bluffer and he enjoyed the risk of it. Joe tossed in his cards. "I fold."

King grinned and raked in his chips. "Right now is when I'd like a cigar."

"Your doctor outlaw them?"

"Sure. But that never stopped me. The damn things just don't taste good anymore. That's the worst thing about getting old. You lose all your enjoyment of the vices you can still participate in."

Joe smiled. King was one of the few people who could make him do so. He stacked the cards together and began to shuffle.

"Brett's different this time," King commented. "Softer. Happier. You finally sleeping with her?"

Joe's head shot up. "What?"

King chuckled. "Don't look so amazed. I'm not dead yet. I can see." Joe continued to stare at him. "I've known for years that you were in love with her."

Joe looked away. "I didn't know it was so obvious."

"It was to me. You forget that I made my fortune playing on people's emotions." He paused. "Well?"

"Yeah," Joe admitted, staring at the cards in his hands. "I love her. Who could help it?"

"You didn't answer my original question. Are you sleeping with her?"

Joe met King's eyes, bracing himself for the old man's anger. "Yes."

To his amazement, King smiled broadly. "Thought so."

"That's all you're going to say?"

"What else should I say?" He chuckled. "You think I'm going to play the stern father routine? Hell, Brett's her own woman; she can do whatever she wants. I have no say in it. And if I did have any say, well, I'm happy for both of you."

"You're happy?"

"Shouldn't I be?"

"No!" King gave him an odd look. "You couldn't want Brett living with me."

"Why not? She seems very happy doing it."

"It's all wrong. *I'm* wrong for her. Anybody could see that." Joe flung himself out of his chair and began to pace, his hands jammed into his pockets. "I feel so goddamn guilty about it! I know she deserves better than me, but I don't have the courage to walk away.''

King's head craned around and he snapped, ''Would you sit down? You're making me dizzy charging around like that!''

Joe returned to his chair and flopped down in it, scowling at the floor.

''All right. Now, would you like to tell me why you're wrong for her?''

''There's no way I'm not! I'm her driver, for Christ's sake! They're all talking about her now; I've given the gossips an opportunity to tear her apart. They say she's sleeping with her chauffeur, as if that's what she really pays me for.''

''Is that all?'' King snorted. ''Hell, the gossips had Lora and me divorced or having affairs practically every other week. Brett's used to that kind of stuff. She knows how to handle it. She's too powerful, too good at what she does for it to hurt her career.''

''I don't like them thinking that way about her!''

''Then marry her.''

''Are you crazy?''

''You'd be her husband then, not her chauffeur.''

''She couldn't marry somebody like me. Look at her!'' Joe gestured to where Brett stood on the terrace, looking down at the valley below. ''She's wealthy and powerful, one of the most respected people in Hollywood. She has more talent, creativity and worth than ten other people!''

''That's true.''

''Well, she needs a man worthy of her! Someone like herself, a man who fits in her world. Not somebody like me.''

''What's wrong with you?''

''Well, I'm an ex-con to begin with. I don't have anything. I'm just some poor jerk who was lucky enough to have Brett pick him up off the street and take him in. I don't have any education. I don't know how to act with those fancy people she hangs around with.''

"Tell me something." King leaned forward intently, fixing Joe with the hard, bright stare that had once intimidated half the movie industry. "Can someone else protect her better than you can?"

"No."

"Can someone else love her more than you?"

"No."

"Listen to her more? Treat her better? Be more loyal to her?"

Joe glared back at him, insulted. "Of course not."

"Well, those are the things she needs, not wealth and power. She's got enough of those for both of you. The kind of person you're talking about would clash with her. I know; I've clashed with her myself lots of times. They'd always be in competition. Nor does she need some slick joker who'll fit in with the movie crowd. That kind of guy's a dime a dozen. They can't give her what she wants. What she needs. *You're* the man she needs. Brett lives in a crazy world. I know it; I lived in it, too. She needs stability. She needs a man who's solid, who's dependable, who will always be there for her. You understand Brett. You know her. You love her. She can trust you. Do you have any idea how rare a commodity that is for someone in Brett's position? Everybody wants something from her; she can never be sure whether they like her or are just trying to get somewhere through her. But she knows that you tell her the truth. I've heard her say that the one person she trusts absolutely is you. And, most importantly, you're the man she loves."

Joe glanced at him sharply. "How do you know that?"

"I know my granddaughter. I've seen the change in her since the last time she was here. She has a glow, a certain look in her eye. She's happy. Just look at her. There's your proof that you're right for her. Have you ever seen her looking this relaxed and happy?"

Joe looked out the window at Brett, then turned away. "Will you excuse me? I think I need to be by myself."

He turned and walked out of the room without waiting

for the other man's answer. He went to the bedroom he'd assigned himself and lay down, staring sightlessly up at the ceiling. He thought about Brett and about what the old man had said. He knew in his gut that Kingsley was right. The only reason he hadn't seen it before was simply because of his own blind belief that he wasn't worth much.

God knew he wasn't the kind of person Brett was. But then, who was? Brett cared for him, and that meant he couldn't be bad. He had changed since Brett found him. He wasn't the same man who had gone to prison, who had stolen Brett's car. He had something now. He was something now.

And he was what Brett needed. He could see that now that King had said it. She didn't need a man like herself, sizzling with ideas and constantly racing to and fro. She needed a rock, an anchor in her life. She needed his unqualified, undemanding love. Joy began to swell timidly, hopefully within him. Could it be that he wouldn't have to feel guilt anymore? That he could relax and enjoy his love for her?

His bedroom door opened quietly and Brett came in. She was smiling, her hair tousled from the evening breeze. Joe's heart began to pound in his chest. He'd never seen anything as beautiful as she was at that moment.

"What are you doing in this bedroom by yourself? Were you scared Granddad would find out you're sleeping with me?" she teased.

"I was, a little."

"I should have warned you—King Gerard is not exactly a moralist."

"I realize that now." Joe swung off the bed and onto his feet.

"Think you could switch rooms?" Brett came to him and slid her hands up his chest to his neck. Her thumbs traced the cords of his throat. Her touch sent hot fire through him as it always did.

"Maybe." Joe's hands went to her waist. He looked

down into her eyes, anticipating what lay before him. But he had to know something first. "Brett..."

"Yes?" She looked puzzled at his serious tone.

"Do you love me?"

Brett burst into a grin. "Of course I do!"

He pulled her against him tightly, burying his face in her hair. "Oh, God, Brett, I love you. I love you."

* *Chapter 24* *

They finished filming late on Friday, and Jennifer drove to Matthew's house in north Dallas, finding it with the aid of a map Matthew had scribbled on the motel stationery. It was a large house with a narrow lawn, and it was made of tan brick and glass in a contemporary style. When Matthew answered the door he swept her inside and kissed her until she was breathless.

"The girls are at their mother's. I thought we should have one night alone."

Jennifer was relieved. Anxiety had been building inside her all the way to Dallas until she was as tight as a stretched wire.

They went into the kitchen. Matthew had fixed her a meal, but Jennifer was tired and not very hungry, so she only nibbled at the food as she looked around. A small pair of roller skates stood by the back door, one tipped over on its side. There was a white plastic cup adorned with a picture of Mickey Mouse and the name "Laura" on the counter by the sink, waiting to be washed. Her heart squeezed inside her chest. What was she doing here? Could she really be thinking of enduring this the rest of her life?

Jennifer was glad Matthew didn't suggest that he show her the rest of the house. She didn't want to see the rooms where his daughters stayed when they visited him.

They talked, but Matthew could see how tired Jennifer was, and soon he led her upstairs to his bedroom. They undressed and crawled into bed and made love with a sort of gentle laziness unlike the usual heat with which they came together. Afterward they lay in bed, propped up on pillows, Matthew's arm around her, and watched the late news on the television set. Jennifer smiled, drowsy and content, thinking how domestic they were; and before the news was over she was asleep.

The next morning Matthew left Jennifer at the house to get dressed and made up leisurely while he went to pick up the girls at his ex-wife's apartment. Jennifer was grateful for the time alone to steel herself mentally to face the girls. When she was dressed she went downstairs to make coffee. She looked through the cabinets for the coffee and cups. It almost undid her to open a cabinet and find a mug full of crayons sitting in front of the dishes. She shut the door immediately, then forced herself to open it again and take out a coffee mug.

She made coffee and drank two cups. Her stomach wasn't up to eating anything. She was tight inside, wound up like an old-fashioned clock, and with every minute that passed her nervousness increased. How could she possibly do this?

Jennifer heard the garage door open outside and she rose to her feet, her hands clenching at her sides. The door from the garage into the utility room opened and a small figure bounced through the utility room into the kitchen. She stopped and gazed at Jennifer, a shy smile on her face. She looked to be about four years old, with a rounded, sturdy body and a chubby-cheeked face. Her hair was shoulder-length and light brown, disordered by the wind, and her eyes were greenish. Behind her, more slowly, came another girl. She stopped beside her sister. Her hair was darker and her eyes were brown. She was slightly taller than the other child, but thinner. Her slender body and small, triangular face gave her a delicate look that was entirely missing in the other one. Her expression was solemn.

Matthew walked in after them, beaming. "Jennifer, this is Laura." He put his hand on the head of the plumper child. "She's four. And this is Michelle. She's six." He tousled Michelle's hair. "Girls, this is Jennifer Taylor."

"How old is she?" Laura inquired curiously.

Matthew laughed, and even Jennifer had to relax into a smile at the innocent question.

"It's not polite to—" Matthew began.

Jennifer cut him off, saying, "Thirty-four this month. It's only fair to know, isn't it, since he told me your ages?"

Laura nodded, glad that Jennifer could see the logic of her question. "You're pretty."

Again Jennifer smiled. "Thank you. So are you. Both of you."

It was true. They were beautiful children. Just seeing them filled her with a fierce, painful longing. Jennifer wanted to turn and run away, yet she wanted to stay, too. She wanted to look at them. She felt almost hungry to look at them.

Jennifer squatted down to their level. "I see you brought your bear with you."

Laura nodded. "He's Grumpy Bear." She pointed to the stuffed animal's tummy. "See? He's got a raincloud."

"I see. He's very nice."

"I know." Laura wrapped her arms tightly around the bear. "Daddy bought him for me."

"I have a Barbie," Michelle put in. She had been standing watching Jennifer a little warily.

"Do you? I had one when I was a kid." It had been Karen Richards' doll. Jennifer's mother had cleaned house for the Richards family, and when Karen tired of her doll, Mrs. Richards had given it to Jennifer. The doll's hair had been discolored, and she'd had only one set of clothes, but Jennifer had treasured it.

"Really?" Michelle looked amazed. "I didn't know they made them back then."

Matthew made a pained expression and Jennifer laughed.

"I promised the girls I'd take them to the park. Are you game?"

"Sure."

Jennifer hadn't expected Matt's daughters to warm up to her so quickly. Laura insisted on sitting next to Jennifer in the car. While she played, she kept calling for Jenny to watch her do something. Even Michelle, more reserved than the effervescent Laura, slipped her hand into Jennifer's as they walked back to the car.

Jennifer wanted to cry at the feel of the small hand in hers. The girls were so pretty, so sweet, so little and trusting and defenseless. Jennifer was almost physically sick from the huge, clashing emotions the children aroused in her. She liked them. She couldn't help but like them. And when Michelle put her hand in hers or Laura gave her a hard, spontaneous hug, Jennifer wanted to fold them to her chest and squeeze them, never let them go. And yet . . .

And yet she was also swamped with past grief and torn with guilt. She wanted to laugh and cry, to hold them and push them away from her all at the same time. She didn't know how to deal with the tangled feelings, and she was glad that she would be with Michelle and Laura only one more day. After they were gone, maybe she'd be able to sort out her feelings.

They spent a quiet afternoon at Matthew's house, and later the four of them, laughing, cooked supper together. They watched a children's video, and afterward the girls went to bed, insisting that Jennifer read them a story. She read with great expression and used funny voices for the different characters, but each word was like a blow to her heart. She had bought a bookcase full of books when Krista was born, dreaming of the time when she would read her bedtime stories, and she had read them to Krista despite the fact that the baby had been too young to understand. But Krista had loved to hear her mother's voice, and Jennifer could remember how she would listen, suddenly crowing with delight and clapping her hands.

Jennifer finished the story and rose. Laura held out her arms. "Good night kiss, please."

Jennifer's throat was raw and swollen with tears. She mustered a smile and bent to kiss Laura. The little girl's arms went around her neck and Laura hugged her. Laura smelled good, with the distinctive scent of a freshly washed child. Jennifer kissed her on the cheek and hugged her back. It was all she could do not to cry. She hugged and kissed Michelle, too. Matthew stood in the doorway, watching the bedtime ritual with a smile on his face.

Matthew came over to kiss the girls good night. Jennifer almost ran from the room. She went down the stairs and out the back door to the patio. She had to have some air. Being with the girls had opened the floodgates to her memories of Krista. She kept thinking of her all day, seeing her, remembering the precious things she had done. Telling the girls good night had been the worst of all. She couldn't bear it. The pain was too great. Was this what it would be like if she married Matthew? Would seeing his daughters always make her remember Krista and feel the anguish all over again? She had done so well at keeping the pain at bay, at burying the memories and the feelings deep inside. She couldn't open herself up to that again! Yet how could she not marry Matthew? That would be just another path to pain.

"Nice night, huh?" Matthew stepped out onto the patio behind her.

Jennifer bit her lips and tried to keep the panic out of her voice. "Yes, it is."

Matthew took her hand, and they sat down on the patio lounge chairs. Jennifer leaned back, her hand still in Matthew's, and closed her eyes, willing the hurt and the memories to recede.

"You're good with Laura and Michelle," Matthew said.

"You sound surprised."

"I am, a little. I've never imagined you with kids. I guess you look so glamorous that it's hard to think of you playing with a child. But you did it beautifully."

"Thank you. They're nice children. It isn't hard to get along with them."

Matthew smiled. "That's not always the case, believe me. They have their moments. There were times right after the divorce when I didn't know what to do with Laura. She had this trick where she'd hide whenever I got ready to go somewhere. I'd have to track her down and pull her out from under the bed or out of the closet or wherever."

"The poor thing."

"Yeah. She seemed to take Felicia's leaving harder than Michelle did. She'd always been a daddy's girl, so you'd think it wouldn't have been as bad for her. But she must have felt guilty, thought she'd driven Felicia away because she didn't love her enough or something. Or maybe it was that she was scared of losing me, too, so she tried to keep me from leaving her for any reason."

His words chilled Jennifer. "Your wife left you?"

He glanced at her, puzzled. "Yeah. I've told you."

"But I mean—she left the girls with you?"

"Yes. I have custody of Laura and Michelle. I'm sorry. Didn't I tell you?"

"No. No, you didn't." Jennifer sat up and swung her legs off the lounger. She thought she might be sick. "Then they live here all the time?"

"Sure. Except when they go to visit Felicia. At first she rarely wanted to see them, but during the past few months she's been much better about taking them for the weekend." He stopped and looked at Jennifer. "Jennifer? What's the matter?"

Jennifer stood up, pulling her hand from his. Her mind was blank with panic. She couldn't think; she just knew she had to run. "I—I've got to go."

"What?" Matthew rose and grasped her shoulders. "What are you talking about? Jennifer! What's wrong?"

"Please. Just let me go."

"No. Not till you tell me what's going on."

"Please. I feel sick."

"Then come inside." His hand went to her forehead. "Tell me what's the matter. I am a doctor, you know."

"No!" She pulled away. "It's not that kind of sick. Oh, Matthew, please!" Her voice broke and tears spilled out of her eyes. "I can't talk about it, not right now. I have to get away. I want to go back to the motel. I—oh, Matthew, I can't marry you! I can't!"

He went rigid. "What are you talking about? What do you mean?"

"I can't marry you."

"Why not?"

She shook her head, struggling with her tears.

"Is it something to do with the girls? When I said—is it because they live with me?"

Jennifer nodded, brushing at the tears staining her face. "Yes. Now, let me go."

He looked shocked. His hands fell away, and Jennifer stepped back from him. "But you were so good with them. They liked you, and you got along."

"They're sweet. Anybody would get along with them. Most women would love to have the chance to be their mother."

"Why wouldn't you?" He stood very still, watching her.

Jennifer began to cry harder, her words coming out in choked spurts. "I can't be a mother. I can't—love them. My baby—my baby died."

"Oh, Jennifer . . ." Matthew pulled her stiff body into his arms, cradling her head against his shoulder. "Sweetheart. I didn't know. I never heard. Why didn't you tell me?"

Jennifer clenched his shirt in her hands, holding on yet still keeping herself closed up. She cried, trying desperately to stop. "She wasn't a year old. She died—she died in her crib." Jennifer's body shook with the force of her tears.

Matthew smoothed his hand down her hair and back. He kissed the top of her head. "I'm sorry, so sorry."

He held her, comforting her with his calm voice and the strength of his arms, but her body remained stiff.

Jennifer finally brought her sobs under control and let go of Matthew's shirt, pulling away from him. He didn't want to, but he opened his arms and let her go. He felt sorry for Jennifer and confused and a little hurt. "Why didn't you tell me?" She had closed off the most important part of her life to him as though she didn't trust him enough.

Jennifer shrugged and turned her face away, not wanting him to see the ravages of her tears. "It was a long time ago. And I—never talk about it to anyone. I can't. It's very hard. At first—at first I wanted to die." She clamped down on her lower lip with her teeth to stop the tears that were springing anew in her eyes. She cleared her throat. "But I made it through. I closed the door on it. I don't think about it or talk about it. And I don't go near children."

"Oh, love." Matthew put his hands on her shoulders, feeling helpless. He laid his cheek against her hair. "But I don't understand. I would think that, having lost a child, you would want to have children to love."

Jennifer jerked away from him. "How can you say that? No one—no one!—can replace my baby. Not ever!" She was furious. In that moment she hated him. "I loved Krista with all my heart, and when she died, I died inside, too!"

"I didn't mean that Laura or Michelle could replace her. I just thought that a child would give you someone to love and—"

"I don't have any love to give! Don't you understand that? Children are just painful reminders of what I lost! When I see one I'm jealous. I think, why is she alive and not my baby? I feel the horror and misery again, just like I did when Krista died. I can't live with that. It's too much.''

Matthew looked at her and his face twisted with pain. "What can I do? I love you. But I can't give up my children. Are you asking me to choose between you and them?''

"No. I'd never do that. But I can't live with them. I can't marry you.''

"No. Don't say that." His voice was filled with desperation. "I couldn't bear to lose you again.''

"Oh, Matt, I don't want it either!" Tears seeped from her eyes and trickled down her face.

"Then don't say you won't marry me. Try it for another day. Or go back to Tyler and we'll try again next weekend. Maybe if you got used to it . . .''

"I can't! It tears me apart!''

"You're tearing me apart!''

Jennifer shoved her hands into her hair as if to hold her skull together. Tears gushed from her eyes. Matthew started toward her, but she held up her hands as if to ward him off and he stopped. "No. Please, don't. I have to go now.''

"At least think about it. Promise me you'll think about it. Don't just break it off like this.''

Jennifer looked at Matthew. His face was lined, his eyes dark with pain, and the knowledge that she was hurting him increased her own anguish. "I promise." She paused, then whispered, "I love you.''

Matthew swallowed. "I love you, too. You know how much I love you.''

Jennifer nodded. "I have to go now.''

She went into the house and washed the tears from her face, but her eyes were still red and puffy and her skin pasty. Matthew walked her out to her car. She couldn't bring herself to look at him. She felt as if she were drowning in her own misery.

Matthew put her bag into the trunk. He put his hands on her arms. She wouldn't look up at him. He bent and kissed her forehead. "Please come back to me. I swear we'll work it out somehow."

Jennifer broke away and got into the car. She drove off. Matthew watched her leave, the ache in his chest swelling. He wanted to go after her and force her to return to the house. He couldn't lose her again. He couldn't!

Matthew called the motel several times the next week, but Jennifer didn't answer the phone when she was in her room and tore up the messages he left for her while she was filming. She couldn't bring herself to talk to him yet. She was always on the verge of tears.

Fortunately the outdoor scenes they were shooting that week didn't require much depth or intensity from her. She saw Sloane glance at her worriedly several times and look as though he was about to speak, but Jennifer always turned away or began to talk to someone else. She didn't want to talk about it. Sympathy would make her fall apart completely.

As it was she was barely making it through each day. She was soaked in misery. She missed Matthew with a constant ache. Even though she and Matthew had been apart much of the time that winter and spring, she had known she would see him again soon. There had been anticipation and the buoying knowledge of their love for each other. Now there was nothing to look forward to, nothing to hold her up.

When Friday came Jennifer stayed at the motel. She decided that she would write Matthew a letter explaining that she couldn't marry him. She didn't have the courage to tell him face-to-face. She couldn't bear to see the hurt and anger and betrayal in his eyes.

She found that writing the letter wasn't much easier. She was struggling with her third effort when someone knocked at her door. She went to answer it, thinking it was one of the other cast members who had stayed behind. But when she opened the door it was Matthew who stood outside.

"Matthew." Her heart began to pound. He looked so good! She wanted to throw herself into his arms and kiss him.

"Yeah." He looked at her. Jennifer had lost much of her vibrancy the past week. She could never be anything but beautiful, of course, but she seemed weary, her looks dulled. He felt the same way inside. "Can I come in or are you going to lock me out?"

"No. Of course not." Jennifer stepped back to let him in and closed the door. She wanted to run, but she couldn't. She braced herself for the confrontation.

Matthew turned toward her. His face was set and stern, but she could see the pain in his eyes. "I've called you all week."

"I know." Jennifer looked away. Why did things always have to be so hard? So unhappy?

"Why didn't you answer? Why didn't you call me back?"

"I couldn't. I couldn't talk to you."

"Why not? Because you're not going to marry me? You want to run off without having to see me again?"

"I'm sorry. I was writing you a letter. It was too painful for me."

"What in the hell do you think it is for me?"

Jennifer crossed her arms across her chest and swallowed the raw emotions welling in her throat. "I know. I'm sorry. You don't know how sorry."

"I don't want sorry. I want *you*." He came toward her, and Jennifer backed away. "That's why I drove down here. I'm not going to lose you again."

Jennifer's chin came up. "You didn't *lose* me the first time. You *threw* me away."

"And I've paid for it ever since. I'm tired of paying, Jennifer."

"So am I."

"Then come home with me. Let us have another chance."

"I can't. I can't marry you."

"Then don't. We'll go on like before. I don't like seeing you so little, but, Jesus, it's better than nothing!"

"You can't go back, Matthew. It wouldn't be the same, no matter how hard we tried. You'd always know that I wouldn't marry you. I'd know how much I wanted to and how I'd failed you. It would eat at us. You come to a point where you either have to go forward or lose it. You can't just stay in the same place. It wouldn't work."

"Then marry me."

"I can't!"

"You won't!"

"You think I don't want to?"

"I think you're scared to. You're scared to face up to life, scared to give yourself a chance to live. So you remain in your old sorrow, refusing to come out. Refusing to be happy."

"You're right, I'm scared! I'm scared of the pain! You don't know what it's like. Krista was all I had, all I'd ever had. She loved me, and I was so happy. So content. When she died . . ." Jennifer stiffened, fighting her tears. "It was unbearable. I can't live with that pain again. Please, Matt, I can't." She began to cry; she couldn't hold it back. She huddled in her arms. Matthew started toward her, but she made a sharp gesture, motioning him away.

"Damn it!" he exploded. "Why won't you let me near you? Why won't you let me comfort you?"

"Nothing could!"

"Oh, yes. Something could. The girls could. I could. I think that's what you're really afraid of. It's not the pain of remembering your child everytime you look at Michelle and Laura. You're afraid of being happy. You're scared to give yourself to someone again, to love me and the girls. What is it, Jen? Is it guilt because you're happy even though your daughter's dead? Or are you punishing yourself for her death by refusing to be happy? You told me the other day that nothing could replace your daughter, but I think that's what frightens you—that you will come to love my Michelle and Laura and that they will replace Krista in your life. You're holding onto your grief. You're denying yourself a life so that you can hold onto your daughter.''

"You're wrong!"

"No. You're the one who's wrong. You won't lose Krista just because you let yourself be happy. You can love someone else, even another child, without losing your memories of Krista, your love for her. She'll always be inside you no matter what.''

"No. That's not it at all.''

"Isn't it? I've been thinking since the other night when you left me. I've put a few things together. Those rooms that you never open up in your house, those were Krista's, weren't they?''

Jennifer nodded, the tears flowing so hard she couldn't speak. She wanted to double up with the pain and drop to the floor; she wasn't sure what kept her up.

"They're a shrine to her, aren't they? Everything exactly as it was when she died?''

"I couldn't!'' Jennifer's voice came out raw and grating. "I couldn't put her away.''

"You have to! Those rooms aren't her. The clothes, the toys, the furniture—none of that is her!''

"It's all I have of her!'' she shrieked.

"It's not. You have her in your head and heart. You're holding on, Jennifer, and it's bad for you. You need a life of your own. You have to accept her death and go on.''

"I have gone on.''

"Not with a real life. Your daughter's death haunts you. You aren't whole or happy or free.''

"Damn you!'' Jennifer covered her face with her hands and broke down into sobs. Once again Matthew came toward her, his hands stretched out to her, but she moved backward quickly. "No! Don't touch me! Leave me alone. Please. Please. Get out and leave me alone.''

Matthew stopped. His hands clenched and he pressed his lips together until they were bloodless, visibly struggling for calm. "All right. If that's what you want, I will—this time. But I'm not giving up, Jennifer. I'll never give up on making us happy again."

He turned and walked out. Jennifer heard the click of the door as it closed after him and she slid to the floor, giving way to a storm of tears.

Jennifer managed to struggle through the last two weeks in Texas. On Monday Brett arrived on location. She and Joe Darcy walked into the motel restaurant where everyone was eating breakfast. His arm was around Brett's waist. Everyone stared at them in surprise, then burst into a babel of greetings. Brett laughed and waved her hands for quiet.

"Just a second! Before anything else, I have an announcement to make." She glanced at Joe, smiling. "Joe and I got married last week."

There was pure silence for a moment, then Ken Rosen chuckled and went over to hug her. "Well, it's about time!"

"Congratulations!" Jennifer hugged Joe and Brett, sincerely happy for them. But she also felt envy and regret, and when she glanced at Sloane, she saw the same emotions mirrored in his eyes. Joe and Brett's joy was a reminder of just how much she and Sloane had lost.

As always when Brett was on the set, things picked up. She generated enthusiasm and efficiency even when she wasn't the one directing. The filming that day went well, but Jennifer found it exhausting. When the shooting was done for the day everyone was invited to a dinner celebrating Brett's and Joe's marriage. Jennifer begged off. She was too tired, and she didn't think she could bear to watch Brett's face all evening, glowing with love.

As the others drove away she went back into the motor home that served as her dressing room on location. She glanced through the small refrigerator for something to eat, but nothing appealed to her, and she wound up just having a diet soft drink. There was a tap on the door. It swung open and Sloane stuck his head inside. "So you couldn't take anymore love and marriage, either, huh?"

Jennifer smiled at him, shaking her head. "It wasn't that."

"Sure." He flopped down on the small couch. "Just like I didn't go because I preferred a salami sandwich from the fridge, not because watching them reminds me how long it's been since I've seen Liz. How I'm never going to be with her again."

"Don't say that."

"It's the truth."

"You and Liz will get back together, I just know it. Why don't you call her?"

He shook his head. "I've told you. There's no chance for us. She doesn't believe that I love her. I don't think she wants to be with me again. I haven't heard from her since we split up."

"It's just pride. She's scared to be the one to call. She's afraid you'll reject her."

"You think she's got the corner on pride and fear?"

"Of course not. But pride and fear aren't going to make you any happier than they do her."

"Sometimes I think I'd give this up—the money, the work, everything—if it would bring Liz back. But even if I did it would never work. She would always distrust me."

"And you wouldn't be happy."

"No. I wouldn't be happy." A self-derisive grin touched his lips. "I'm so happy now."

"It'll work out. I really believe that. It has to."

"Like yours has worked out?"

Jennifer glanced up at him sharply. "What do you mean?"

"Come on, sweetheart. You think you've been hiding it? All of a sudden the doctor from Dallas isn't hanging around every weekend, you look like the sky fell in on you, and you think people aren't going to notice?"

Jennifer shrugged and looked away. "Well, you're right, of course. It's over."

"What happened?"

She shook her head. "Let's not talk about it, okay?"

"You know something? You are one closed-up person."

"So I've heard." She sighed. "I don't know how to be any other way. I've always kept things inside myself."

"Except when you're acting."

"Yeah. Except then."

"Is that why you split up? Because of your career?"

Jennifer shook her head. "No. We could handle that, I think. I'm a little tired these days. I wouldn't have minded a rest—you know, make a film every once in a while, when I found one that was too good to pass up."

"So what's the problem?"

"You're persistent, aren't you?" Jennifer paused. "The problem is his kids."

"Little monsters?"

"No. Actually they're very sweet. Loving and pretty and—"

"Oh. I see."

"Do you?"

"Yeah, I think so. If they'd been monsters they wouldn't have made you sad for Krista."

"No, they wouldn't." Jennifer paused. "Do you think I'm wrong, Sloane? Do you think I hold onto my grief, that I'm scared to let go and be happy?"

He shrugged. "I don't presume to tell anybody what's right or wrong. I just wish you could be happy. I'd like you to try whatever would do that."

"Thank you. You're very sweet."

"Now." He put on a cheerful smile. "I just happen to have a deck of cards in my trailer. What say we spend a wild evening playing gin?"

Jennifer made herself match his smile. "Sure."

Location filming ended in another week and the cast and crew returned to LA. It was almost the end of May.

Jennifer hadn't heard anything from Matthew. She wasn't sure whether he had given up on her or was simply biding his time. She didn't want him to continue his pursuit; she didn't want to face another confrontation like the last one. But somehow it hurt to think that he might have decided to let her go.

Her house in Beverly Hills had never seemed so empty before, so filled with loneliness, except right after Krista died. She thought about selling it and moving into a smaller place. There had been so much sadness there. But happiness, too. She thought of the first night Matthew had been there, how they had stood by the pool and talked, how later they had made love. She remembered making breakfast in the kitchen the next day, the two of them laughing like kids. She remembered Krista learning to crawl on the den floor, her diapered rear end chugging back and forth, revving up as if for a race.

No! She wouldn't think about that. She never thought about those memories; it was too painful. That was how she had gotten through the years without Krista. Her love for Matthew, his children, the sorrow—something—brought back those emotions, those memories. She had to stop it.

She sought to bury herself in her work, as she had always done. There were a few more scenes to be shot at the studio for *Drifter*, one that had been rewritten and one that Brett had added, but those were soon over. She'd have to do publicity work for the movie she had shot before *Drifter*, but that wouldn't be out for another two months. So Jennifer scrambled to find something to occupy her time. She read scripts, searching for a new story to do—soon. She had two interviews and photographic sessions with magazines. She filmed a commercial that she had signed to do months ago. There was a charity dinner in New York June twentieth. She hadn't planned to attend it, but now she decided she would. That would take care of a whole weekend. She had known it would hurt to end it with Matthew, but she had never dreamed how bitter and agonizing it would be.

Thursday evening before she flew to New York she had dinner with Liz. Liz looked bad, too thin and not as careful of her appearance. Though she was too professional to neglect her clients, it was obvious that her zest for the business had greatly diminished. She had few questions about *Drifter* except to ask how Sloane had done. Jennifer knew how much Liz missed him, how much she loved him, and it angered and frustrated her that Liz would make no effort to get him back.

"Why won't you call him and tell him you're sorry?"

"He doesn't want to hear from me."

"You're scared," Jennifer retorted. "Just too scared to take the risk of being in love. You'd rather hide from it and suffer."

Liz stared coolly into Jennifer's eyes. "Aren't you doing the same thing?"

She couldn't answer. All the way home she thought about Liz's question. Matthew had said she was avoiding risk too. Of course she was scared. She had been hurt too much by love not to be. But it was more than fear. Some things were too painful to bear. Being around Matthew's children was one of those things. They would make her remember, and she couldn't stand to remember. She couldn't face it. There it was, fear again.

She hadn't thought of herself as a coward. She had always taken what life dished out and fought on, and she had labeled that courage. But now, thinking back on it, she realized how much fear had dominated her life. Fear of her father's drunken rages, of what people thought about her, of all the dark, roiling emotions inside her. She had always felt too much, too hard, and the depth of her anger and pain had frightened her. She realized in surprise that her sweeping, uncontrollable emotions had reminded her of her father and his wild, drunken lack of control.

Jennifer sat down on the first chair she could find, feeling as if the breath had been knocked out of her. Why had she never thought of that before? But the answer was easy. Because she ran from self-examination just as she ran

from everything else. She thought of the emotions she had
suppressed all these years, letting them come out only in
her acting—and in her love. That was the thing. Acting
was controllable; love was not. Love could consume her,
as it had with Krista and with Matthew. Each time bitter
pain had been the result. How could she stand to face the
pain again?

But what did she have now except pain? What had she
had since Krista's death except pain? She hadn't avoided
it, really, only tamped it down. It had festered and seeped
through her entire life, destroying any happiness. Any
chance at happiness.

Matthew had pierced that web of misery, had come in
and awakened her to life again. Yet she was throwing him
away.

Jennifer ran a hand through her hair. She noticed that it
was trembling. She was trembling all over. She sensed that
she was on the verge of something, and she was scared
and excited and sick all at once.

She thought of what Matthew had said to her, that she
was holding onto her grief out of fear that she would lose
Krista entirely. Fear.

Jennifer rose and walked to the bedroom wing. Her
heart pounded in her chest; her hands were icy. She
stopped at the closed door. Krista's room. Her hand went
to the knob and fell away. She swallowed. She couldn't go
in.

She lifted her hand again and turned the knob. She
opened the door and stepped inside, turning on the light
switch. The Little Bo-Peep lamp came on. Jennifer closed
the door behind her and walked slowly into the room.
There was Krista's bed, the fluffy down cover still on it, a
blanket folded over the side rail. The short white chest; the
changing table, a stack of disposable diapers lying atop it.
The rocker.

Memories flooded in on her. She remembered Krista
standing in her bed, holding onto the railing and bouncing
vigorously, her face beaming. She remembered the blond

flyaway hair and the little dimpled fingers. The huge blue eyes and soft white skin, the clean baby smell of her.

Jennifer quivered inside with pain. She wanted to shut the memories out, but this time she would not allow herself to. She let the memories in. She remembered Krista laughing, crying, playing with her toys, reaching out to grasp a fistful of Jennifer's hair. She remembered the smile—oh, that smile! It had always melted her heart.

Jennifer began to cry, tears streaming from her silently. She took the blanket from the side of the bed and smoothed her hands over it, and the tears came harder. Old, dead tears, long denied, came rushing up from deep within her, and she began to sob. She clutched the blanket to her chest and wept with every fiber of her being, sliding to the floor and lying crumpled in a ball while the tears took her.

She felt it all again: the anguish, the loss, the unbearable ache. She cried until she thought she could cry no more, then continued to cry. Finally the tears dwindled and stopped. Jennifer lay on the floor, exhausted, staring. Slowly she sat up. She pushed herself up off the floor and stood. Her head ached, her eyes were swollen and burning, and her chest and stomach hurt from the sobs. Yet somehow she felt better. She felt . . . released.

Jennifer went to the kitchen pantry and pulled out a box of large plastic garbage bags. She climbed up into the small attic and took down several boxes. She carried everything back down the hall to Krista's room. Carefully, methodically, she began to pull open each drawer and take out the little clothes within. She stacked them in the black plastic bags, and when she was done with the clothes she started on the toys. She even stripped the bed and packed the sheets, cover, and blanket away. When she was through she put the sacks in the boxes, sealed the boxes tightly and marked Krista's name on them in ink.

She had thought there were no tears left in her, but as she worked they poured down her face. Now and then she paused to wipe them away or blow her nose, but she didn't stop working until there was nothing left in the room but

the bare furniture. She carried the boxes out into the hall.
She would have the maid put them up in the attic.

Jennifer looked back into the room a last time. "Good-
bye, Krissy," she whispered. "Mommy loves you."

She turned and walked away, leaving the door open
behind her.

Los Angeles, June 20, 1987, 11:05 A.M.

*The doorbell buzzed repeatedly. Liz sighed and glanced at
Brett. "Probably another reporter."*

*Reporters had been phoning almost continuously since
the news about Jennifer came out, and four enterprising
ones had come to Liz's beach house and rung the doorbell.*

Joe went to answer the door. "I'll check."

*Brett watched him go, unconsciously twisting the wed-
ding band on her third finger. Thank God for Joe. She
didn't know what she would have done without him. He
had been indispensable to her for years, but now he filled
her emotional needs as well. He had been strong and
comforting all morning, giving her his love unstintingly.*

*Joe looked out the security peephole in the door. Sloane
Hunter filled the small viewing area. Joe opened the door
and Sloane slipped through. Joe slammed the door shut
behind Sloane in the face of one of the reporters. He
locked the door and turned to speak to Sloane, but he was
already in the living room, going to Liz.*

*Brett turned her head, expecting Joe, and saw Sloane.
Her eyes widened. Liz swiveled around at Brett's expression. She froze. "Sloane."*

*"Liz." He paused. Then suddenly the two of them
moved at the same time, Liz springing up from her seat on
the couch and Sloane covering the last few feet to her in
quick strides. He pulled her into his arms and she wrapped*

her arms around him, burying her face in his chest.

"Oh, Sloane." She began to cry. He smoothed his hand across her hair and down her back while his other arm held her tightly, comfortingly against him.

"It's okay. It's okay. I'm here."

Joe and Brett glanced at each other and went into the kitchen to give Liz and Sloane privacy. There was no question of walking out to the beach, as they would have liked to have done. There were reporters there, too.

For a long while Liz could do nothing but cry and hold onto Sloane as to a lifeline, but finally her tears subsided and she stepped back. He eased her down onto the couch and sat beside her, handing her a handkerchief to wipe away her tears.

"I'm sorry. I—"

"Don't apologize. You think I don't know what you're going through?"

"Poor Jennifer. Oh, God, I wish we'd hear something! They say she's not among the survivors."

"I know. I heard on the TV. I just turned it on a little while ago. I came over as soon as I heard."

"Why? Why did you come?"

Sloane looked stunned. "Why! Because I knew how you would feel. I love you. I had to be here for you." He hesitated and glanced away. "If I was wrong, if you'd rather I'd leave . . ."

"No! Oh, no!" Liz threw her arms around him desperately, the tears starting again in her eyes. "I just can't believe—"

"That I love you?"

She nodded. "Now that you're successful, that you don't need me."

"Who said I didn't need you?" He grasped her chin and made her look at him. "I need you all the time. Not your money, but you—your love, your body, your mind. How can I stop needing that? It was never for the money, Liz. I stayed with you for you, not for the things you gave me. I've loved you from the start. You were the one who didn't love me enough to risk committing yourself."

Liz stared, not quite able to absorb it all. Sloane was back, telling her that he loved her even though he was making lots of money, even though his future was unbelievably bright. Jennifer had been right. Sloane loved her, and Liz had been too scared to take the chance. She thought of Jennifer giving up the man she loved because of her fears and then dying, robbed of life and happiness.

"Oh, Sloane." Liz's voice shook. "I love you. And I want to take the risk. If you're willing to give me another chance."

"I'd give you a million," Sloane said fiercely and pulled her to him.

They clung, kissing long and deeply, unaware that the program on the television suddenly stopped and a live report from the airport came on. But Joe and Brett heard it and hurried back into the room.

"We have just received a manifest from Trans Continental Airlines of the passengers and crew who were on board Flight 145 at the time of the crash. The name of Jennifer Taylor, the television and screen actress believed to have been on the flight, did not appear on the manifest. Apparently, although there was a ticket purchased in the name of Miss Taylor, she was in fact not on Flight 145."

That announcement brought Liz and Sloane out of their absorption. They stared at each other, then turned to Joe and Brett, hope dawning in their eyes.

* *Chapter 25* *

Los Angeles, June 20, 1987, 6:30 A.M.

A sleek black limousine pulled to a stop in front of the airport terminal and a chauffeur jumped out. He took a suitcase from the trunk, then came around to open the door for his passenger. Jennifer Taylor stepped out and walked into the building.

There wasn't a long line in front of the ticket counter, but the chauffeur bypassed it. Jennifer was soon ensconced in a private VIP room to await her flight.

She opened her purse to get change for the telephone and saw the Trans Con ticket for the flight she had planned to take to New York that morning. She should have left the ticket on Karen's desk so that Karen could cancel it. She also should have left Karen a note, but she had been in such a rush to pack and catch this flight that she had forgotten. She would call Karen after she got to Matthew's house. There would be ample time for her secretary to let the charity banquet officials know that she would not be attending after all.

Jennifer pulled out a quarter and her telephone card and went to the pay phone to place a call. It was already 8:30 in Texas, but she caught Matthew before he left the house. He answered the phone, his voice short and impatient.

"Matthew?"

There was a moment of stunned silence. "Jennifer?"

"Yes. I called to tell you that I'll be arriving at DFW about 12:00 your time." She gave him the name of the airline and number of her flight.

"Jennifer, are you telling me that you're—"

"Yes, I am." She smiled. "I most certainly am. I love you, Matt. Will you be there to pick me up?"

"If I have to crawl."

She laughed. "I have to go. They're calling the flight."

"I love you. Good-bye."

"Bye." Jennifer hung up the phone, her face glowing. She left the room and walked down the hall to the plane that would carry her back to Matthew.

SENSATIONAL ROMANCES

☐ **AUTUMNFIRE** by Emily Carmichael
(D34-717, $3.95, U.S.A.)
(D34-718, $4.95, Canada)
Autumnfire, an Irish American beauty who was
raised by Indians, is captured by handsome
cowboy Jason Sinclair who rouses her heart and
stirs her desire.

☐ **GOLDEN LADY** by Shirl Henke
(D30-165, $3.95, U.S.A.)
(D30-166, $4.95, Canada)
Amanda's past was one filled with burning
shame. Now she wonders whether she dares to
risk losing the one man who claims her heart by
revealing the dark secrets she's kept hidden.

☐ **THE BAYOU FOX** by Helene Sinclair
(D30-219, $3.95, U.S.A.)
(D30-220, $4.95, Canada)
Bethany vows revenge on the gambler she
believes cheated her father of all he owned. But
when she plans a daring deception to beat the
man at his own game, she finds herself losing
her heart to him instead.

**Warner Books P.O. Box 690
New York, NY 10019**

Please send me the books I have checked. I enclose a check or money
order (not cash), plus 75¢ per order and 75¢ per copy to cover postage
and handling.* (Allow 4 weeks for delivery.)

___Please send me your free mail order catalog. (If ordering only the
catalog, include a large self-addressed, stamped envelope.)

Name_____

Address_____

City_____State_____Zip_____

*New York and California residents add applicable sales tax.   307